REIGN of IRON

Spring couldn't fight five. If they'd had the decency to run at her from several hundred paces across an empty field, and she'd had a bow and some arrows, then she'd have taken out the lot of them, no bother, but she'd left her bow on Frogshold and they were right next to her. All she had was Dug's hammer, which she had trouble lifting, let alone wielding. One of them would have been unassailable. Five . . . Clever words would be needed to save her here.

REIGN
of
IRON

Age of Iron: Book Three

Angus Watson

www.orbitbooks.net

ORBIT

First published in Great Britain in 2015 by Orbit

1 3 5 7 9 10 8 6 4 2

A CIP catalogue record for this book is available from the British Library.

ISBN 978-0-356-50260-1

Typeset in Apollo MT by Palimpsest Book Production Limited,
Falkirk, Stirlingshire
Printed and bound in Great Britain by CPI Group (UK) Ltd,
Croydon CR0 4YY

Papers used by Orbit are from well-managed forests
and other responsible sources.

MIX
Paper from
responsible sources
FSC
www.fsc.org   FSC® C104740

Orbit
An imprint of
Little, Brown Book Group
Carmelite House
50 Victoria Embankment
London EC4Y 0DZ

An Hachette UK Company
www.hachette.co.uk

www.orbitbooks.net

For David, Penny, Camilla and Christo

Prologue: The Aegean Sea, 85 BC

As shipwrecks went, it was undramatic. Arguing over whether the basking shark a hundred yards to starboard was larger than the basking shark that they'd seen earlier, the two lookouts failed to spot a granite megalith, relic of a town drowned by the sea many years before, which brooded a couple of hands' breadth beneath the sparkling surface. The cargo vessel rolled up on a gentle wave, crunched down onto the rock, scraped along horribly for a few heartbeats, then sailed on. A hundred paces later, the deck was sloping unnaturally and the captain shouted the order to lower the sail. Water lapped over the starboard gunwale, curses and pleas rang out from the cargo below deck and the ship tilted more worryingly. There was an island ever nearby, but waves exploded all along its cliff-fringed coastline.

Still young Titus Pontius Felix didn't understand that anything was particularly amiss. The cargo was always yelling and, according to stories that a string of nannies had told him, ships sank in storms. Today was sunny, so he was sure that everything was all right and the grown-ups would swiftly resolve the problem. Only when he heard a voice below shout in broken Latin: "*Chains take off! Bel-cursed stinkenshits! Sinken we! Sinken! We are sinken!*" did the six-year-old who'd grow up to be King Zadar's and Julius Caesar's druid grasp what was going on.

"Crew and passengers to the tenders!" shouted the Iberian captain, fists on hips, red-bearded face split by a foul-toothed grin. "She's going down like a Roman boy on his tutor!"

Felix didn't know what he meant but he did not like the man's tone. Surely a shipwreck was a time for seriousness? His father clearly agreed. "It is *not* going down!" he shouted, short arms flapping as he struggled to keep his feet on the slanting deck. "We *cannot* be sinking. Do you have *any* concept of the cargo's value?"

"I do. I can give you an exact price for your wares," said the Iberian. He was almost twice Felix's father's height. "Considering the current market, our situation and the condition of the goods, the entire cargo comes to the princely sum of . . . precisely fuck-all. Nobody buys drowned slaves."

"We're not sinking. You cannot sink. All my money is in that hold. My whole life! You will get us to a beach or a port or . . . please!"

The captain laughed. "Poseidon and his arse own these waves and today he floated one of his mighty shits in our direction. It happens. The boat's going down. We could free your cargo, but they are many, they are desperate and there's no room for them in the tenders. Best for everyone if they remain chained." The captain raised his already loud voice to be heard above the screams from below deck. "Buck up, man, you'll make more money! Life is always more valuable than cargo."

Felix's father raved until he was purple, then went with the others. Felix followed him to the side of the ship and watched him climb down into the tender. Because of the ship's list it was even further down to the water than normal, and the little swell-swayed boat was banging hard against the ship's exposed, slippery-looking underside. Felix couldn't see how he would get down there and was frightened. The captain noticed his plight and climbed back up to help him.

As they rowed away, his father looked very ill. "All my money," he said, staring at the sinking ship, tears dripping off his chin. The others found this very amusing and Felix hated them for it.

Shortly afterwards, they found a break in the cliffs. Once they'd pulled the boats up a bright beach fringed by shattered white rock and gnarled, scrubby trees, a few dozen terrifying men and women strolled from cover and laid into the crew with blades and clubs, slaughtering the lot of them apart from Felix, his father, two women and the captain. These latter three seemed to be friends of the attackers. All of them turned to look at the Romans.

"Don't kill me! Take the boy!" Felix's father's wailed, cowering behind his son. A man whose face was mostly moustache pulled Felix away and held him tight while others cut off his father's toga and sandals. Laughing all the while, they jostled the newly naked Roman towards a flint-eyed, bronze-skinned woman with long, black hair. She peeled off her own clothes, then charged. Felix's father tried to run but she caught him, tripped him and leapt onto him, all to the cheers of the pirates. His dad clawed at her pinning legs and pummelled her torso with little fists. She held him firm, ignored his attacks, punched his face until his nose was pulped and he was moaning and useless, then strangled him until he juddered like a caught fish and was still.

Felix followed the pirates back to their port. He didn't know what else to do. They ignored him but let him eat their food. He found a place to sleep in a tent with four other children who didn't seem to mind him being there, but who didn't talk to him either.

He spent the days wandering the island on his own, killing insects, lizards and any other animals that he could catch. The killing made him feel good.

One day he climbed down a low cliff to a small beach on the east of the island and found a string of large rock pools. He smashed some limpets to lure crabs from the safety of their mini caves, then set to investigating how many legs they could lose before becoming unable to walk. He was so

engrossed in his studies that he didn't notice the small
wooden boat with a white sail until it had bobbed nearly
all the way to shore. He stood to watch as its bow wedged
into sand and wavelets slapped its stern.

Little Felix couldn't see anyone in it, so he left his crabs
and ambled over to find what the mysterious vessel might
contain. It contained a dead woman. He screamed.

He recovered and wondered if his delimbed crabs would
like human flesh. He put one on her chest, another on her
face. Her head moved. She wasn't dead! She caught the face
crab in her mouth and bit through its shell. Felix felt rather
than heard a whoosh! and something very odd flowed out of
the woman, washing over him like water, but it wasn't water.
It made him tingle but it wasn't hot or cold. He'd never felt
anything like it before, yet the sensation was familiar.

The woman groaned, sat, plucked the other crab from
her chest and dashed it against the side of the boat. That
seemed to energise her. She stood, flicked dried seagull shit
off her salt-whitened black robe, jumped out of the boat
and looked at him. She was very old — as old as his dad
had been — with curly black and silver hair, black eyes,
full, salt-cracked lips and a nose like a misshapen pear. She
raised a hand as if to strike him, then smiled and lowered
her arm.

"Thank you, little man," she'd said, although she was not
much taller than him. "Are your parents nearby?"

He didn't know what to say.

She peered at him and he felt uncomfortable, then she
said: "No parents? No matter, mothers and fathers never
helped anyone much. Just tell me everything you know
about this place and *please* don't tell me we're on an island."

"We *are* on an island."

"Oh cat's piss," she said and Felix giggled. "Tell me what
you know about the island then. How big is it? Who else
is on it? Why are you here?"

Felix told her everything. He asked her where she'd come from, but she told him only that her name was Thaya and asked if he knew anywhere safe from the pirates where she might rest and recover. He said he'd found a secret cave under a waterfall on the south of the island, near the ruined Cyclops temple. She asked him to lead her to it and he did.

She gave him a funny look when she saw the pile of small animal corpses on a rock a little way into the cave, but didn't say anything.

He didn't tell anybody else about Thaya, not because it was a secret but because he never spoke to anyone else. The next day he took her food, and the next and the next, until he noticed that she hadn't eaten any of it. He carried on visiting her, though. He didn't have anything else to do and he liked being away from the others.

One day, she taught him how to use magic.

She showed him how to squash a frog and use his mind to direct its ebbing life power to kill a bird. A few days later she showed him how to reach inside a wild pig, crush its heart and use the force created to send another pig into a killing frenzy.

After a month or so, Thaya asked Felix to bring two children to her. He did, enticing them with the promise of cakes at the cave.

All four of them walked back to the pirates' port. The pirates gathered and approached. Thaya reached into the chest of one child, and squeezed. The pirates attacked one another. Soon they were all dead apart from the red-bearded Iberian captain. He staggered towards them, bleeding from several wounds, cudgel in one hand, still grinning as he had when his ship had sunk. Felix did not need asking twice when Thaya offered him the remaining child. He plunged his hand into the girl's chest and squeezed, his little fingers popping through the delicate walls of her heart. He felt her life energy flow up his arm. He twisted it in his mind, pushed it out into his other arm and flung it at the captain. The grin melted from the red-bearded face. He fell, dead, and it was Felix's turn to smile.

Thaya said that she was very tired, so he should gather supplies for a boat journey while she slept. Felix waited until she was snoring, found a large rock, lifted it as high as he could and dropped it on her head. He used the rush of her life power to explode a dozen or so wheeling seagulls, then loaded up a boat himself and set off over the sea.

As he sailed away, he chewed on Thaya's heart, which he'd cut from her chest with the Iberian captain's cutlass. It was disgusting – gristly and tough – but a little voice inside told him that eating it was the right thing to do.

Part One

Britain and Gaul
56 and 55 BC

Chapter 1

The water from the great wave receded. Spring walked down Frogshold hill. Her knees jarred on the steep slope but she didn't notice. People were shouting at her but she hardly heard them. She was aware of Lowa's voice telling everyone to leave her be. Somewhere deep down she was grateful, but over the top of that a dull but overwhelming rage exploded into her mind. It was all Lowa's fault! If only they'd never met Lowa! She and Dug might have been travelling together and getting into adventures, but, no, all because of Lowa, Spring had had to kill the only person, bar her mother, she'd ever loved. He'd looked after her and done a million things for her without ever asking for anything. She'd never done anything in return, then she'd killed him.

She found Dug's hammer leaning against a pile of stones that might once have been a storage hut, its head half buried. She pulled it free with a schlock of wet mud, slung it over her shoulder and walked away. She didn't look for his body because there were no bodies. All had been washed out to sea as the wave retreated, she guessed, to be a feast for the fish and the birds. She hardly noticed the rain, drizzle at first but then a downpour like the tears of a million mourners, washing the mud from the hammer's head and the broken land.

At first she walked along the coast, but the devastation that she'd caused with the flood was too harrowing – the few

people left alive rummaging through wreckage and wailing
multiple bereavements – so she headed inland. She walked
all day, all night, all the next day and on. She ate nothing,
drank nothing and did not sleep. She'd killed so many that
she deserved no comfort. The only thing she saw was her
arrow piercing Dug's forehead. The only thing she could
hear was the scream of tens of thousands of men and women
crushed by the giant wave. She didn't feel the blisters form,
pop and bleed on her feet. She didn't feel the handle of the
hammer wear through the material of her smock and the
skin on her shoulder.

After several nights – she neither knew nor cared how
many – she emerged from a wood onto a grassy hillside
at dawn and collapsed on the dew-soaked grass to die.
Sensing someone was there, she looked up. Her father
King Zadar was looming over her, shaking his head, a
twist of disapproval on his usually dispassionate face. He
opened his mouth to mock her but was silenced by dogs'
barking. Sadist and Pig Fucker, the dogs that Dug had
inherited by killing Zadar's champion, Tadman, bounded
up, tongues lolling. They champed their ghostly jaws into
the increasingly spectral Zadar until he disappeared. Tyrant
dispatched, the dogs looked at her stupid-eyed, saliva
drooling in cords, tails wagging. Sadist scurried forward
to lick her.

"Back, Sadist, leave her. That one does not like the licking,"
said someone in an accent from the far north of Britain. Dug
Sealskinner strode up behind his dogs. Spring's arrow was
still protruding from his forehead, its feathers quivering as
he walked.

"You're alive!" Spring's tiredness and sorrow evaporated.
Her energy flooded back for an instant, then all flowed out
again as she realised what Dug's appearance must mean.

"So I'm dead, too?"

"Nope."

"So you're talking to me from the Otherworld because I'm *about* to die?"

"No, no, nothing like that. I'm just in your mind, nowhere else. You're really talking to yourself."

"I see. But I'll see you soon, when I die?"

"I'd rather you stayed alive."

"Why? I killed you. I don't deserve to live."

"Probably true, but someone needs to look after the dogs."

Pig Fucker barked, Sadist stared vacantly. Spring nearly smiled.

"If I have to look after them I'm going to change their names."

"No. We've discussed this. You cannot change a dog's name. I don't know why Tadman gave them those names, but he did and that's that."

"You're dead. Why should I do what you say?"

"Because you did this, you wee badger's bollock." Dug turned to show the sharp end of the arrow protruding from the back of his head.

"I'm sorry! But it was all Lowa's fault."

Dug sighed. Were his eyes bigger and browner now that he was dead, she wondered? "No, Spring," he said, shaking his head, "it was not Lowa's fault. By bringing those armies together so you could finish them off by killing me she saved us all. Well, *you* all anyway."

"If we'd never met her you'd be alive."

"Maybe, but a lot of other good and helpless people would be dead and a lot of shitty people would be busy ravaging the land and killing the rest of them. You must not blame her. As you know very well, because I'm just part of your mind talking to you."

"Bollocks to that. If you are part of my mind you're a stupid part. It was all Lowa's fault."

"Fine. I'm not going to convince you, but you could at

least help me out with the dogs? You did put an arrow through my head and my wee dogs are all alone."

Spring sighed. "All right. But there's nothing 'wee' about those dogs, and I don't want you rolling the 'you put an arrow through my head' dice every time you want your own way."

"You assume you're going to see me again?"

"You said you were in my head."

"Aye?"

"So I'll see you again when I want to."

"Not if you die now, and you're not far off it. You should've died of thirst sometime yesterday or the day before, and the hunger's not good for you either. So hurry up and get something to drink then something to eat very soon, or the dogs'll be alone. There's a stream in the woods at the bottom of this hill. Head for that."

"Sure, just magic me to the bank and I'll drink. Or how about a mug of beer right here?"

"Magic you? No no no. Do you not get what you did?"

"What do you mean?"

Dug shook his head. "And you're meant to be the bright one. Your magic came from me, and you killed me. I'm not blaming you, you had to do it to produce power enough to collapse a great big fuck-off island and create a wave that Leeban or any sea god would have bragged about for centuries. But I'm gone now and that's it for you, magic-wise. No more, ever. You'll have to walk to the stream, like everyone else would, without complaining."

The idea of walking almost made Spring pass out. "I don't think I can walk."

"Then you'll have to slither. You can do it!" Dug winked and disappeared.

Spring opened her eyes. The sun's rays stabbed into her brain. When her vision had swum into a cloudy semblance of normality, the woods were a long way away. She was buggered if she was going to slither down the hill. She had dignity. She would crawl.

She pushed up onto her hands and set off.

With the rational part of her mind begging her to give up, collapse and die, she crawled down the slope, hands and knees sliding on the slick grass. When she reached the trees, darkness bloomed. She thought for a confused moment that night had come, then realised that it was her vision failing. Consciousness teetered. Her hands slid away, her arms buckled, she face-planted into the grass and closed her eyes. The relief was amazing. A quick rest couldn't hurt, could it? So what if she died? The dogs would understand and surely they were big enough to look after themselves? They were certainly ugly enough . . .

"Wake up, Spring!" shouted a northern voice, startling her.

Come on, she told herself. She tried to push up into a crawl, but could not. So, she thought, I'll be slithering after all.

Digging elbows and feet into soft soil, she pushed herself under the shade of the branches and on through leaf litter and twigs. She managed to lift her head and saw a blackbird watching her from a log, head cocked. She opened her mouth to tell him to piss off or help her, not just perch there, but her throat was too dry and she only rasped at him quietly.

Finally, the shallow gully of the stream.

She tumbled down the bank, floppy as a boneless squirrel, and squelched face first into the water. Mud filled her mouth and clogged her nose.

Oh, she thought. How apt. The girl who killed thousands with a giant wave was going to drown in a shallow stream. But she managed to twist her head so her face was only half submerged. She lapped cold, delicious, muddy water. Soon she had the strength to slide the rest of her body down into the stream, kneel, and drink water from her cupped hands.

A good while later she managed to stand. Shivering with
cold and shuddering with effort, she staggered to a black-
berry bush.

Two days later the young archer crested the rise and walked
down the track to Dug's farm, his hammer over her left
shoulder, its shaft wrapped with moss and cloth to prevent
further chafing. Her right shoulder was coated in a poultice
to soothe the hammer's earlier rubbage.

Dug's sheep ran to the fence, bleating accusingly, but
there was no sign of the dogs. She'd expected the huge,
idiotic animals to come bouncing up the track barking a
happy welcome as usual, but Pigsy and Sadie were nowhere
to be seen. Perhaps someone from the nearby village had
taken them in?

She turned the corner into Dug's yard. Dug's yard . . .
She staggered under the weight of the grief, then straightened. She could indulge her grief later. Right now she had
things to do. There were dogs to be found, chickens to be
fed, honey to be collected, sheep to be reassured and—

"Ahem!" someone fake-coughed behind her.

There were five men, clad in British-style smocks and
tartan trousers which didn't quite fit, as if they'd borrowed
or stolen them. Two of the smocks were holed and blood-
stained: evidence, Spring guessed, of what had happened
to their previous owners. The men's hair was cut short in
the Roman way, which wasn't unusual since plenty of Britons
those days aped Roman styles. Each carried a short, double-
edged legionary's sword on his belt, which was more unusual
but not unheard of. People liked to copy the Romans. But
everything about this lot *looked* foreign – their skin, their
eyes, the way they stood, the set of their mouths – and
Spring was pretty much certain that they were, in fact,
Roman. Now what, by all the bristly badgers' arses in the
world, would five Romans be doing at Dug's hut?

They were a tough-looking lot, apart from the man in the centre, who looked extraordinary, right up with the druid Maggot in the gang of weirdest-looking weirdos that Spring had ever seen. He was toweringly tall and bulky, but with a tiny ball of a head. Black, pinprick eyes stared out of his tanned, wrinkled face. Despite his preposterous appearance, he had the expression of a man who took himself very seriously. His hair, suspiciously jet for someone his age, was greased and wrenched back from his leather-look forehead into a pert little ponytail.

She looked around. Pigsy and Sadie were nowhere. Even the chickens that usually scratched about in the yard despite Dug's efforts to teach them to scratch about elsewhere had buggered off. There was no way she'd get through the door or any of the windows before they were on her, and they were blocking the mouth of the yard. She was caught, with no help on hand.

She couldn't fight five. If they'd had the decency to run at her from several hundred paces across an empty field, and she'd had a bow and some arrows, then she'd have taken out the lot of them, no bother, but she'd left her bow on Frogshold and they were right next to her. All she had was Dug's hammer, which she had trouble lifting, let alone wielding. One of them would have been unassailable. Five . . . Clever words would be needed to save her here.

"First of all, I'd like you all to know," she said, smiling and thinking that they probably wouldn't be able to understand British, "that you look a bunch of prize pricks. I'd heard that Romans were ugly, but if I had pigs that looked like you I'd paint faces on their arses on market day and make them walk backwards into town."

Four of them looked blank, but the big one's eyes narrowed even further. He raised his sword.

"And the second thing," added Spring quickly, "is that I surrender, totally. If you're here to rob, go for it. Rob away.

If it's slaves you're after, I will be a *brilliant* slave – compliant, happy and diligent, I promise. If you want to rob *and* take me as a slave, go for your lives. I will not stand in your way. I'm sure clever Romans like you know that you'll get *much* more for me if I'm unharmed."

The tall, fat one smiled a nasty smile. The ball of fear that had been growing in Spring's stomach bobbed up into her throat.

"We're not here to rob you, or to take you," he said in Gaulish, which was pretty much the same as British, with an accent that sounded like a man holding his nose and trying to sound tough at the same time.

"Well, that's marvellous," said Spring. "In that case, perhaps I can get you some food, then you can help me look for the dogs and—"

"We're here to kill you," interrupted the large man.

Spring swallowed. "I see. Why?"

"That, I do not know," said the man, "but we have been well paid, and we will get more when we present your corpse. Much more."

"Where do you have to present my corpse?" Spring tightened her grip on the hammer. Dug could have beaten ten men like this with the weapon. *Help me, Dug?* she pleaded silently. There was no reply.

"We will take it to Gaul."

"Who wants it?"

"Honestly, I do not know. Someone rich and important because only the powerful use middle men and only the rich can afford me."

"My body's going to be in a much better condition if you leave it alive until we get to Gaul," Spring tried. "I promise to keep it well fed and make sure it doesn't get knocked about too much."

The large man chuckled. "Believe me, I'd like to keep you alive a little longer. You are funny, and you remind me of

two of my daughters. But if we kill you here, it greatly
reduces your chance of escape."

"Yes, I see your point . . ." Spring's mind raced. She
pulled the hammer from her shoulder. By Toutatis' thun-
derbolts, it was heavy. "We're going to have to fight, aren't
we? I should warn you, however, that I'm very good with
this. I suggest you retreat. I swear I'll never tell anyone you
were here or that you chickened out. Your secret will be
safe with me."

The leader smiled and gestured to the two men on his
right. They raised their swords and came at her.

Chapter 2

Ragnall Sheeplord arrived at the command tent, thankfully freed from the unpleasant Decimus Junius Brutus Albinus' occupation by the return of Julius Caesar. Unsmiling, black-clad praetorians ushered him in. Caesar acknowledged him with an only just perceptible widening of his eyes. The newly Roman ex-Briton knew it was a signal to wait.

Caesar seemed bizarrely unmoved by the loss of almost his entire invasion fleet to the great wave. He'd simply ordered Gaulish shipwrights and slaves to build another, bigger navy, claimed that he hadn't intended to sail to Britain until next year anyway, and sent his legions off to scour north-west Gaul, capturing and enslaving any of the Veneti tribe who'd survived the sea battle – men, women and children and killing any that resisted.

Ragnall stood to one side of the cavernous tent and listened as the general dictated the official version of the sea battle and subsequent events to his diarists. There had been no drop in the wind and no great wave. In Caesar's version, Brutus had used superior strategy and hooked rigging-cutters to defeat the Gauls' sailing boats. After the battle, he told them, he'd had the rebellious Veneti leaders killed to show the price of rebellion, and enslaved the rest.

As usual, Caesar's intention was more to do with maintaining the support of Rome than reporting the truth. The notion had troubled Ragnall initially, but now he was convinced that spreading Roman civilisation throughout the world was the worthiest and greatest goal. If that required lying to the people back home who didn't understand war, and employing means in that war that might seem extreme, even brutal – and maybe even the services of dark magic – so be it. You couldn't make a loaf without pounding wheat.

Finished with his diaries, the commander announced that he was off to check the outlying watches and beckoned Ragnall to follow him.

"Tell Caesar again," said Caesar as they swept from the tent, "about your father."

Semi-jogging to keep up with Caesar's long-legged gait up the slight hill, Ragnall recounted how he'd found his father, Kris Sheeplord, king of Boddingham, and his entire family and tribe murdered by King Zadar of Maidun. He began to say how it had affected him, changed him from a boy into the kind of man who could understand the general's goals better then most, but Caesar cut him short.

"So you are king of Boddingham?"

"Uh—"

"Rule of the Boddingham tribe is hereditary, passing along the male line?"

"Well, male or fem—"

"And you are Sheeplord's last surviving offspring?"

"Yes . . ."

"So you are the rightful king of Boddingham. And the man who ruled the tribe that killed your people and took your land, this King Zadar, has been succeeded by a Queen Lowa?"

"Not succeeded as such. She killed him, but she didn't want to be queen. However, the people—"

"Answer the question, Ragnall. Is Lowa ruler of the Maidun tribe?"

"Yes." Maidun wasn't strictly a tribe. Like Armorica, it was an agglomeration of several towns, villages and tribes, but Ragnall knew that Caesar wasn't in a details mood. There were times when he would have been – sometimes the minutiae intrigued him most of all. Ragnall had decided a while back that the way to get on with Caesar was to read his mood and adapt accordingly. That, and agree with everything he said.

"And it is this Queen Lowa, you say, who sent these three Britons to aid the rebel Gauls...what were their names?"

"Atlas Agrippa, Carden Nancarrow and Chamanca . . . I don't know her full name. Just Chamanca, I think." There was no point telling Caesar that two of them weren't actually from Britain.

"So Maidun, the tribe that killed your family and illegally took your lands, also sent forces to Gaul, unprovoked, to attack Rome and her Gaulish allies. Combine those two points, Ragnall, and you have a strong case to petition Rome for help in returning your lands to you." Caesar stopped by a tall tree, looked up at the observation platform high in its denuded branches, scanned the land around, nodded, then set off again. "After your vital help with our Gaulish victories, I should think Rome will feel duty bound to come to Boddingham's aid. Yes, you are the deposed British king who embraced Rome, killed the German oppressor Ariovistus. You saved many Roman lives by employing your wits and using the enemy's own trap against him in the battle against the Nervee. Moreover, the gods certainly wish to see Queen Lowa pay for her crimes. They have allowed her a period of success and impunity so that she will feel the reversal of her fortunes all the more keenly. Added to this, of course, is the fact that many of the rebellious Gaulish leaders have fled to Britain—"

"Have they?"

"I have reason to believe that they have, and we have already seen British soldiers fighting with the Gauls. How many more will come? Avenging attacks on Romans, preventing further incursions into our territory and restoring Britain's rightful king – who is a friend to the Romans – will play well in Rome with the Senate, Tribunate and people. Thank you, Ragnall. Leave Caesar now, but remain nearby. Caesar will return to Rome soon and you will accompany him."

Ragnall watched Caesar zoom off and smiled. Back to Rome, hopefully for a long while. After spending the previous winter in dangerous and dirty Gaul, a return to the place he felt most at home and happiest would be very, very welcome.

He walked back to the camp. Caesar had been right; Ragnall couldn't believe he'd never thought of it before. He'd always assumed that when Zadar had destroyed Boddingham, he'd destroyed his father's right to rule and Ragnall's right to inherit that rule. But of course he hadn't. He'd stolen the land for Maidun and Maidun should have given it back when Zadar was killed. Lowa, in other words, should have given Boddingham to him. Why hadn't he realised it before? Perhaps that was why she'd sent him off to Rome, to keep him from claiming his rightful land? In fact, Lowa had no right to be queen of anything. She had no royal blood, she was just a common soldier. So when Zadar died, Ragnall himself had been the best candidate to take over the kingship of not just Boddingham but Maidun, too! Lowa might be common, but she was a canny one . . .

No matter, he thought. It would all be resolved. She'd be knocked off her perch within hours of the Romans landing in Britain, and Ragnall would be king of Boddingham, and, if he played his dice right, a lot more.

Chapter 3

The leftmost Roman came at Spring, swinging his sword at her neck.

She screamed and held one hand in front of her face, at the same time letting the hammer's head fall to the ground, so that the sharpened end of its handle was pointing upwards. The Roman paused, enjoying her terror, laughed and swung again. Spring ducked, thrust the wooden handle point into his gut, wrenched it out and swung the hammerhead upwards. It crunched into his jaw, shattering bone and teeth. He fell. Using the weight of the hammer's trajectory but twisting her wrists to alter its path, she powered the lumpen metal head down onto the head of the next legionary. As he collapsed she diverted the hammer's arc into a backhanded swing. The leader was fast and his sword was already slashing down at her, but the hammer knocked it from his hand and slammed into his face, and he too was down.

The hammer didn't seem so heavy, Spring thought, when it was swing or die.

The two remaining Romans stared at her, goggle-eyed. One of them dropped his sword. He made to pick it up. Spring took a step forward, hefting the hammer. He gave up on the sword, turned and ran.

"Just you and me now," Spring said to the remaining Roman, feinting at him with the hammer. It really was very heavy. She was going to have to put it down any moment.

He looked about at his fallen mates.

"How did you move so fast?" he said.

"Come at me and I'll show you," Spring winked, letting the hammer head drop to the ground, trying to make it look like it wasn't because she couldn't hold it up any more. It seemed for a heartbeat like the legionary was about to attack her dropped guard and she'd be screwed, but he glanced at his felled captain, changed his mind and ran too, following his surviving friend along the track that led to the cliff top.

"You'd be better off fleeing the other way," Spring yelled after him, "that path—"

She was interrupted by barking. Sadie and Pigsy streaked from cover and pounded after the men.

She sat down on Dug's criss-crossed log-cutting stump. Life, she thought, was odd. Sitting here, at Dug's house, on the scores made by Dug's log-chopping, next to three dead Romans, she should have been as miserable as a person could be. Instead, she felt content. What she'd just done with the hammer had been extraordinary. It hadn't been magic, at least it didn't feel like her old magic; it was more like she'd inherited the skill from someone else, and that someone else had to be Dug. She'd never met anyone else who used a hammer. So part of him was still alive in her, and that made her happy. She looked at the dead Romans and was saddened anew. So much death! All of these people – the armies to the west and the Romans – had come at her and hers with murder on their minds, so they deserved what they got . . . but why couldn't they just stay at home and enjoy watching the world go by? Building useful things, looking after animals, creating thriving villages, walking in woods, hunting boar and listening to the birds – all these things and a million more were immeasurably preferable to fighting and killing.

She walked into the house, wondering what she was going to do with the bodies. She put the hammer down and went into the room that Dug kept for her. She stopped in the doorway. Before he'd headed to his final battle, Dug had

put a new tartan blanket on her bed and used that potter's
wheel she was sure he'd never use to make a bowl for the
shelf under her window, then filled it with dried flowers.
She looked from blanket to bowl and back again. She thought
about Dug choosing which flowers she'd like most, picking
them and laying them out to dry. Her face collapsed, her
shoulders fell and she stood, sobbing.

Lowa blinked back tears. She'd walked into her hut, realised
it still smelled of Dug, and that had set her off. Pregnancy,
she told herself, was making her prone to childish emotions.
It was making her vomit a lot, too, which was at least as
irksome. And her breasts were swollen and sore. At least
their inflation had a milky purpose, but why the vomit?
Could feeling sick most of the time and being sick regularly
really help with the development of a baby? And the spots,
backache and constant, debilitating weariness – did all these
have some secret baby-enhancing function? Whichever god
had designed women and baby production, thought Lowa,
he'd hadn't like women much.

   She shook her head. She'd only just arrived back at Maidun
Castle, but she needed to head straight out again to tour
Maidun's lands and visit her allies. The wave hadn't been
nearly so high on Britain's south coast as it had on the west,
and the water had retreated before rising so people had had
warning to get themselves and their livestock away from
the sea. However, crops had been spoiled and huts ruined,
so they needed help. Inland stores would have to be assessed
and shared with coastal regions.

   She also needed to rebuild the army. She'd lost three-
quarters of her infantry to Eroo and the Fassites, so she
needed to recruit more and train them in time for the Roman
invasion which was massing across the eastern sea in
Armorica. It was an impossible task. The men and women
she'd lost had had years of training. Those remaining would

struggle to quell a tavern brawl, let alone take on an army that had conquered the multitudinous Warrior tribes of Gaul in only two years. But she had to try.

Heading out, Lowa spotted Spring's bow propped by the door. She'd brought it back from Frogshold. She hadn't seen Spring since the day of the great wave, but she guessed — she hoped — that she'd be at Dug's farm. She was young and she'd killed tens of thousands of people, so chances were that that was messing with her mind a little — or even a lot. Lowa would have been fine with it — all of those fuckers had had it coming — but Spring was more sensitive. Everyone in Maidun was talking about the Spring Tide, the terrifyingly powerful wave that had wiped out the Dumnonian, Eroo, Fassite and Murkan armies in one go. The gossips all swore that the girl had caused it by killing Dug, so it was probably best that Spring stayed at the farm for a while to avoid all the attention.

Lowa resolved to send someone over with her bow right away to show the girl that she was thinking of her and didn't blame her for Dug's death, then to head out that way herself as soon as she got a chance. Much as she'd liked to have gone that very moment to console her friend — her surrogate daughter, really — she simply couldn't. She was queen and she had people to feed and house and an army to rebuild.

The merchant ship bumped alongside the quay at last. Chamanca saw that the wave had struck in Britain, too, at least as hard as it had in Gaul. The stone quay had survived, as had some of the boats, but the town itself had been gouged from the earth. The seafront had been testament to the success of slave trading under Zadar's reign, lined with a row of towering, ornate wooden buildings and a gigantic wooden carving of the sea god Leeban, all of which screamed "Look how prosperous we are!" And all of which was now

gone. A few stone warehouses and a few disused iron slave
pens survived, although the roofs were destroyed on the
former and one had a large boat sticking out of it. The
coasters had begun to rebuild their town around these more
doughty buildings. So far it was a tumbledown collection
of lean-to shelters with the odd leather sail stretched between
them. The coin had stopped flowing when Lowa had banned
slavery, so it was unlikely that the town would ever look
as well-heeled as it once had. Probably a good thing, thought
the Iberian. She had no sympathy for slaves – fools who
found themselves enslaved deserved everything they got
– but displaying the proceeds from selling fellow humans
like cocks showing feathers was Fenn-cursed vulgar.

"Captain? Captain Jervers?" shouted a nearby crewman.
"Where's the captain?"

"I think he's in his cabin!" shouted another.

Chamanca took that as her cue to vault the ship's rail and
melt away. It wouldn't take them long to find Jervers. He
was in his cabin, unconscious, missing several teeth and a
couple of pints of blood. She'd gone in there once she'd
sighted the port to give him coin for her passage, but the
fat fool had tried to demand more, and come at her with a
cutlass when she'd refused. Chamanca had been glad for it.
She'd been hungry.

She didn't bother looking for a horse. It was a bright,
fresh-aired, late summer's day, she was full of energy from
her feed and the walk to Maidun after the day and night
at sea appealed.

On the way out of town a boy tagged along with her for
a while. He was a verbose little fellow, determined to tell
her all about the battle of Frogshold and the Spring Tide
that had destroyed the evil armies and saved Maidun.

"Spring Tide?" asked Chamanca.

"That's what they're calling the giant wave. A great magician named Spring made it."

She listened to the boy's tale then gave him a coin to bugger off. She wanted to be alone with her thoughts as she walked the final few miles to Maidun. She was torn. She was not looking forward to reporting Carden Nancarrow's death. He'd been popular, and with reason. He was a good man and he'd died so that she might escape. His mother, the blacksmith Elann, would be deeply upset, even though she was sure not to show it. Chamanca had killed her other son Weylin – on Zadar's orders, so it wasn't her fault – but she was empathetic enough to see that a mother might blame her for both his and Carden's deaths. The wrong-headed wrath of a bereaved mother usually wouldn't have fazed Chamanca one jot, but there was something about Elann. She hardly ever spoke, showed emotion even more rarely, yet she made the finest weapons and other iron works that the Iberian had ever seen. And there was more, a quiet power emanating from the woman like warmth from one of her forges.

So she wasn't looking forward to talking to her. On the other hand, she'd found herself missing Atlas Agrippa more and more. It had been just her and Carden on the most recent trip to Gaul and initially she'd been glad to be in charge, free from the African's boringly pragmatic command. But she'd found herself wishing that he'd been there. Not for help against the Romans – she was quite capable of fighting those little men on her own – but . . . well, she wasn't sure what it was. She just missed him being there.

Chapter 4

The birth was apparently a quick one, but it hadn't seemed that way to Lowa. Most women she'd spoken to had warned her that childbirth was no fun, but a few had claimed that it was inspiringly natural and that the pain was life-affirming. She'd hoped the latter few had been right, but now she knew they'd been either lying or deluded. There had been nothing good about pushing the little bastard out of her splitting vagina and the only thing that it had affirmed was that she did not like being in agony. It hadn't been as bad as the torture when she'd been a captive of Pomax the Murkan, but it hadn't been far off.

Not as bad, but still seriously irksome, was that she'd been through it all in front of Maggot. There was nobody she would have preferred to help her through the birth, but now that he'd seen her at her worst, her most abuse-screamingly bestial, she wasn't sure that she'd ever be able to look him squarely in the eye again.

The baby on her chest shifted, and for a dreadful moment she thought he was going to wake up and yowl, but mercifully he didn't.

"All happy?" said Maggot, ducking into the warm, well-lit hut. It was freezing outsize, but Maggot was still clad only in his habitual tartan trousers, leather waistcoat and enough jewellery to sink a small merchant ship.

Lowa thought for a moment. No, she wasn't happy. She was sore and she felt no great affection for the tiny human tucked up in blankets on her chest. That was something

else the life-affirming lot had told her – that she'd be immediately overwhelmed with all-encompassing love for her
child. Well, maybe *they* weren't lying about that, maybe
they had immediately fallen for their babies, but the only
emotion she felt was frustration that she was cooped up in
her hut when she could have been out training the army.

"I cannot remember being more cheery," she replied.

Maggot winked. "You did well. Squeezed him out good
and quick with minimum fuss. I've seen a lot of babies and
he's a beauty, too. Any idea what you'll call him?"

"I have a name in mind," she said.

Chapter 5

Ragnall walked through the crowds on the Sacred Road, gawping up at temples and the painted statues looking down at him from their roofs. There was a bounce in his step. "Nobody in Rome looks up any more, and they're all missing out," someone had said to him at Clodia Metelli's house a few nights before, so now he looked up whenever he remembered, and he was glad for it. There was a great deal more ornamentation on the buildings than he'd realised, stretching up to the highest roofs, and that ornamentation was amazing. The more basic sculpture on the least showy building was more impressive than any artwork he'd seen in Britain. The most ornate and humungous designs – crowd scenes of gods and men and mythical animals all entwined – made him stop and blink and forget to breathe.

Rome filled him with happiness. He'd lived in Britain for his first twenty years, but this city was his natural home. The moment he arrived it felt like his soul was lowering itself into the warmest bath and sighing with pleasure. It felt right, it *was* right. The sooner the rest of the world learnt Roman ways, the better for everyone. There were bound to be people who'd say that they didn't want to live like the Romans, but they were the sort of thick, older people who didn't like any change. "Shall I take that half-decayed squirrel off your face for you?" you might say to one of them. "No, thanks very much, I like things just the way they are," they'd reply.

He scooted around a woman with a hairstyle like a

precarious pile of powdered peacocks and jinked his way through a crowd of fashionably bearded young men, effortfully casual togas roped with loose belts in emulation of their hero Caesar. Ever since the city had been flooded with loot and been granted a twenty-day holiday in celebration of his successes in Gaul, Julius Caesar's name was on everybody's lips and his distinctive belt style was on all the young men's hips.

"Oi, Ragnall! *Wan-kar!*" The good-natured insult was hurled by a knot of legionaries who Ragnall knew from Gaul, men who'd been shipped into town by Caesar to help ensure that his cronies Pompey and Crassus won that year's consular election. The soldiers would vote for the candidates themselves and anybody else who didn't could be sure of a beating.

Their attention pleased Ragnall. Out in the field of Gaul, soldiers wouldn't bother to shout a greeting at a clerk like him. Back home, however, campaign camaraderie bubbled out like water from squeezed sponges and men were the best of mates simply because they'd once marched to the same place at the same time.

"You're looking insufferably cheerful. I'd say *denarius for your thoughts* if I didn't disdain clichés," said a mellifluous voice behind him. Ragnall turned. It was Marcus Tullius Cicero, known to all as plain Cicero. Ragnall had met him with Drustan on the night that Drustan had been killed. Cicero had been one of the two ruling consuls a few years before, he was Rome's leading lawyer and was often cited as the most intelligent man in the empire. Since Ragnall had met him he'd been exiled, called home, then fallen out and back in again with Caesar. Ragnall knew all this because they often talked about Cicero in Clodia's house, where Ragnall had been welcomed back with opened arms (opened everything, in fact). Clodia was somewhat in awe of Cicero, despite the fact that, or perhaps because, Cicero had unsuccessfully persecuted her brother Clodius for incest with her. It was Clodius who'd had Cicero exiled, as revenge.

"I'm happy to be back in Rome," said Ragnall.

"I understand. I was driven almost to suicide during my forced sojourn to Greece, although that says more about Greece than it does about Rome." Cicero spoke loudly, so that passers-by might hear, and he smiled a "Haven't I just said a clever thing?" smile. Ragnall wasn't sure whether to laugh or nod, so he did both. "However, I'm surprised to find you enjoying Rome quite so much," Cicero continued, in a less public voice. "But then again you are a contrarian, are you not, Ragnall?"

Ragnall was both flattered and unnerved that such a famous character should not only remember him after only one meeting years before, but also deign to have an opinion about him. "I don't think I'm a contrarian . . .?" he offered. He wasn't sure what the great man meant.

"You were a barbarian, now you're a Roman. Your new master is the man who murdered your old one, the druid Drustan. I'd say there were few more contrary."

"Caesar did not murder Drustan. It was Felix. And besides," Ragnall looked around. None of the pedestrians filing past seemed interested in their chat and the soldiers were long gone, "he wasn't entirely wrong to suspect that we were spies." It was more perhaps than he should have said, but he did not like Caesar to be called into question.

Cicero smiled and swallowed, his Bel's apple ascending and falling like a mouse in a sausage skin in his long, scrawny throat. "I see you are under Caesar's spell," he said. "No matter, most are. I don't expect you to heed these words, Ragnall, but you should realise what's happened to you. You and many young men like you have been whipped up in the new hero's wake like autumn leaves behind a galloping chariot. Perhaps, before you fall back onto the hard road, you should fly away?"

A few years before, maybe even the year before, Ragnall would have nodded obsequiously, but he wasn't going to accept this nonsense, not even from a man of Cicero's standing. Perhaps war had toughened him? Whatever it was, he shook his head and said: "Caesar is the greatest man in the world and I am proud to serve him, as you should be."

Cicero smiled warmly. "Well said, young man, well said! Why don't you walk with me for a while and tell me what's next on the campaign for you and the great leader?"

Ragnall was confused by the elder statesman's mercurial standpoint, but he didn't want to miss an opportunity to boast about Caesar's achievements, nor to be seen in the company of such an eminent figure.

As they passed the blackened remains of a freshly burnt shanty swarming with destitute wretches picking about for anything valuable or edible, Ragnall began: "Gaul is all but conquered. Everybody said that it was last year, but it wasn't. It would have been impossible to conquer it in a year. It should have been impossible to conquer it in two, but Caesar did it. The last tribe to hold out, the Armoricans, are beaten, and the tribes to the north of them – the Menapii – are more or less vanquished. We haven't actually beaten them in the field, but most of them fled. They might still cause trouble, but it's unlikely to be anything significant. If they do manage to muster a decent force, Caesar will triumph as he always has against much greater foes."

"That is what has happened already," said Cicero, jinking to avoid a gaggle of senators wearing red leather sandals and togas with broad purple stripes, "but tell me, what will be the next conquest for the great general?"

"Britain," said Ragnall. "As soon as the ships are rebuilt, I mean built, the army will cross the eastern sea and bring the wonderful gifts of Roman life to Britain."

"And will you have a role in the new Britain?"

Ragnall looked around, then back at Cicero. The man was

almost as tall as him, which was unusual for an Italian. "I am going to be king."

The orator's eyes widened. "King? That's marvellous. I'm sure you'll be an effective and just ruler. But do tell, why you?"

They walked on through the afternoon crowds. Ragnall told Cicero his life story, then found himself telling the former consul everything that people in Rome weren't meant to know – about the great wave, about Felix's rumoured dark legion, about Caesar's necessary massacres and tortures of the Gauls. It couldn't matter, Ragnall told himself. Cicero was such a decent man and, even if he'd sounded a little negative initially, surely he'd been playing Hades' advocate? Of course he was on Caesar's side. How could he not be?

It was early evening when they came upon a gladiator battle, set up in a broad street as part of the holiday festivities. Two fighters were squaring up at the bottom of a wide set of marble steps crammed with spectators. One gladiator was dressed in the leather and metal armour of a legionary, including helmet, and armed with the standard short sword. He was little fellow, wiry with lean muscle, maybe thirty-five years old. The other was much larger and younger, but enormously fat, even for a Roman civilian, with a round, shining stomach and pendulous, hairless breasts. He was mocked up as a German Warrior, wearing the fur groin cloth and armed with a wooden club. Ragnall had seen more than his fair share of German soldiers and they'd got the outfit spot on, but he'd never seen one armed with a club. He guessed it was artistic licence on the part of the fight's organisers to accentuate the Germans' barbarism, which was fair enough. Ragnall had never met a more barbarian shower than King Ariovistus and his bone-headed tribes.

Cicero asked a man who he knew about the combatants. They heard that the Roman was a real legionary, fighting for money. The young fat one was a minor aristocrat who'd crawled onto the wrong man's wife at an orgy. Ragnall would have bet everything he owned on the legionary, but nobody would take the wager because all agreed it was going to be more of an execution than a battle. Ragnall thought it was pretty distasteful, and guessed that Cicero did too but, without saying anything, they not only stayed to watch, but climbed up a few steps to get a better view.

The fight began. The soldier was infinitely quicker and fitter and his blade was wickedly sharp. He could have finished the faux German in seconds, but he played to the crowd, cutting slices into legs, arms and torso that made the spectators wince and the aristocrat yell, all the while ducking and sidestepping the flabby youth's increasingly clumsy club swipes. The younger man bellowed and swore, then cried. The legionary gave him plenty of time and space to stare with disbelief at the depth of the cuts on his limbs and body, then nipped in and carved into his flesh again. With the fat young man woozy from blood loss, heaving and panting, the soldier dropped his sword, darted around his opponent and leapt onto his back. The youth staggered, trying to throw his limpet-like mount and prying uselessly at muscle-hard limbs with weakened fingers. The legionary pretended to ride him as if he were a horse, then thrust his index fingers into the young man's eyes and gouged them out. Many of the spectators loved this, whooping as they clapped. The legionary jumped from his fat, blinded mount, removed his helmet, raised his arms and turned to bask in the citizens' adoration. Behind him, the young man staggered, bleeding from empty eye sockets and a hundred cuts, lifted his club and flailed blindly with the last of his strength. The sweet spot of the club met the legionary's head with a cracking thud.

Both men fell and lay still.

There was a pregnant pause of gaping disbelief, then many of the crowd howled with laughter. Ragnall and Cicero did not.

"I hope that's not an omen," said Ragnall.

"I shouldn't think so," said Cicero, "but it's a useful lesson. Never underestimate your opponent, even when they seem beaten. Now, I must be going." He gripped Ragnall by the shoulder. "I don't expect you to heed my words, but I'm going to tell you anyway. Caesar has been a great benefit to you, but following others should not be a lifelong pursuit. One day, Ragnall, you should have the courage to remember who you are and pursue your own goals."

"Right."

Cicero smiled sadly. "Few have the courage to be their own person, but it is a noble goal."

Chapter 6

Far from Rome, deep in the Roman-controlled western Alps, the druid Titus Pontius Felix sat on his bed in the well-insulated longhouse that he'd made his winter quarters. He'd had his pleasure with a dark-skinned slave and she'd left, whimpering but grateful to be alive. It was funny, Felix mused, that people always seemed grateful when you stopped being cruel to them rather than angry that you'd been cruel in the first place, assuming they were alive enough to display gratitude.

Muffled sounds of his legion training outside penetrated the log walls. His Celermen and Maximen needed several hours of exercise a day and they didn't seem to mind the bone-piercing cold of the mountains. Felix did, but he was cosy in the longhouse with furs and a large fire built from the wood of smashed grain stores and the corpses of the valley's former inhabitants. There were gigantic baskets on either side of the fire, one full of wood, one full of bodies, both filled from larger piles outside. Semi-frozen bodies burnt marvellously well once they got going, radiating rosy heat and a wonderful smell. He wondered why more people didn't use corpses as fuel. Bodies were easier to come by than trees in Gaul those days. It was possibly a waste to burn so much meat, Felix conceded, but he and his legion had herds of livestock which the mountain tribe didn't need now, he didn't like the taste of human flesh, and besides, there was a pile of dead the height of Pompey's theatre, nicely preserved in the sub-zero temperature. If any of his troops wanted to eat human flesh, there was plenty to go round.

Despite the warmth, the little Roman was unhappy. He'd recently ejaculated, which always put him in a black mood, but that wasn't the underlying reason. There were two larger, more important things sullying his humour.

First off, he was pissed off to be billeted up here in the mountains for the winter. His dark legion had killed so many in the Alps over the previous winter that Caesar had insisted that Felix stay with them this year to control them. He was, after all, the only one who could tell them what to do. It would have been a reasonable request if you gave a shit about the lives of a few thousand Gauls and Helvetians, but he didn't and he knew that Caesar didn't either. The general was more worried that the legion would become common knowledge in Rome if it killed too many people. Felix thought the opposite was true, since dead people didn't spread rumours, but one didn't argue with Caesar.

The second, more irksome thing was that he'd have had Spring's body by now if his assassination squad had succeeded, so he had to assume that she was still alive. Jupiter's cock, it was annoying. He hadn't told Caesar the details, but he had told him that there was a powerful druid in Britain whose magic could be used to conquer the world. It was at least part of the reason for charging up through Gaul to invade Britain. But Felix didn't want to wait. He wanted to kill Spring, specifically to eat her heart, to inherit her magic and become unstoppable.

He'd taken Thaya's magic by eating her heart all those years ago. He'd known it was the right thing to do in the same way, he guessed, that birds knew how to fly and which berries to eat.

He might send more assassins at Spring immediately after the winter, but probably he'd have to wait until they invaded Britain. Most annoying. He had little desire to go back to the island, although the notion of having his revenge on Lowa was rather delicious. He'd had a good thing going with Zadar until she and Spring had spoiled it all. He cursed himself. If he'd only worked out that Zadar's daughter was the super-druid they'd all been waiting for, he could have eaten her heart years before and never needed Zadar or Caesar. He smiled to himself. Yes, he needed Caesar now, but once he got his hands on Spring's corpse, he wouldn't need anybody else ever again.

A pop from the fire startled him, but it was just something bursting in one of the burning bodies. He returned to his fantasising, picturing himself marching on Rome at the head of fifty dark legions of Maximen and Celermen, killing, torturing, enslaving – doing whatever he wanted. He'd build a palace in the centre of Rome that would make every other building look like a British hut. He'd send out armies to conquer the world. He would go with them and kill someone from every tribe on earth. He'd build thousand-pace-tall statues of himself in every town and port. He'd live forever, king of the world, ruler of all, worshipped as a god. Egypt! He'd take Egypt! Those arrogant crocodile worshippers would queue up to lick his feet. He'd build a pyramid that would make Khufu's great mausoleum look like an anthill next to a mountain. And Greece! The things he could to do to the beautiful, haughty young men of Greece . . .

So for now he'd put up with his shitty billet in the Alps. He'd bide his time. Once he had Spring in his hands, everything would be his and he would never be unhappy again.

Chapter 7

At the end of each British winter, Chamanca was always surprised by the day that came along and proved that the world could be warm again. It was the morning of that day – high-skied and clear with a sun that actually managed to warm her skin – when she, Atlas and Spring boarded the merchant ship to Gaul. The captain, a squat Dumnonian woman, commanded them to give their packs to the crew to be stowed, then chivvied them to a place by the port rail where they'd be out of the way.

"I know they all say that I made the wave," said Spring as they leant on the rail, "but I didn't. Do you mind if we don't talk about it?"

"Sure," said Atlas Agrippa.

"Why not?" asked Chamanca.

"Because—" Spring was cut off by the captain's shouts as she ordered her crew through the processes of leaving the quay and setting sail. The complex commands were unnecessary if the crew knew what they were doing, thought Chamanca, and by the look on the crew's faces they agreed with her.

The Iberian had no desire to talk about the wave but she didn't like to be told what to do by anyone, let alone a fifteen-year-old girl. She wasn't sure about Spring. Lowa had insisted she'd be useful as a replacement for Carden Nancarrow in their mission to destabilise the Roman army, so she'd sent Chamanca to Dug's farm to find her. The girl had refused to come back to Maidun, mumbling something about not wanting to see Lowa, but had been happy enough to meet them at the port. Other people might have questioned her further about avoiding Lowa, but Chamanca neither liked to pry into others' business (because she didn't like other people prying into hers), nor did she really give a crap for the girl's motives.

The child was certainly brighter than the previous member of their trio but, much as she'd liked him and was sorry that he'd died saving her on Karnac Bay, Chamanca had met dogs brighter than Carden. Atlas and Chamanca had all the brains they'd ever need between them. The question was, would Spring be so loyal, dependable and, above all, as useful in a fight as Carden?

The girl was perhaps a quarter of Carden's weight, if that. She was a head taller than Chamanca, but much narrower from neck to toe; Atlas could have put his hands around her delicate waist. By the way she moved, she was strong-limbed under her loose shirt and long skirt, but how would she fare against one campaign-hardened legionary, let alone a group of them? She carried the same type of longbow as Lowa, as well as Dug's hammer, but Chamanca was sure she wouldn't be able to use either of them effectively. There was the magic, of course, which had beaten Chamanca in a fight when Spring had channelled it through Lowa, but the girl claimed that her magic powers had died with Dug and the wave. So why exactly was she coming?

Chamanca reckoned Lowa wanted her out of Britain. Many had lost friends or family to the wave, so Spring was a likely target for revenge attacks. The Iberian had seen it when she'd been young herself – a group of twats could easily whip themselves into a vengeful, murderous communal rage, even if their target had only drunk a little blood . . . That might be the case, but it was still no reason to send Spring on their dangerous mission. The last thing they needed was a tagalong. One weak link would get them all killed.

She did like the girl – she was amusing and quite beautiful – but the Iberian liked herself more. If it looked like she was going to get them all killed, Chamanca would kill her first. No, in fact she wouldn't kill her. She would break her leg and pay a village or a farm to look after her until she healed. Was she getting soft in her old age, she mused? Maybe that's why she was having these bizarre feelings of affection – of attraction! – for sensible, boring, dependable, old, handsome, muscular, mighty Atlas . . .

"I'd just rather you didn't mention the wave," Spring said when the palaver of setting sail was over and the boat was creaking its tubby way out to sea. Her voice was a strange mix. Mostly it was a melodious and refined British accent like Zadar's, but she pronounced some sounds in the German way like Lowa and others in Dug's strange northern accent. It was rather a pleasant effect, Chamanca thought.

"Don't worry, Spring, we won't talk about the wave, will we, Chamanca?" Atlas spoke quietly, his Kushite bass even lower than normal.

"What wave?" asked Chamanca.

Atlas nodded. "Remember, when we get to Gaul we will not do or say anything to draw attention to ourselves. Not to begin with, at least."

Chamanca thought that simply being a massive African Warrior carrying an axe that could chop an ox in two would draw plenty of attention, and that the Gauls would be certain to notice the most attractive and well-dressed women they'd ever seen, but she held her tongue. The nondescript girl would go unnoticed, at least.

"Why don't you tell me all you found and did in Gaul?" asked Spring. "It would probably be best if I know as much as possible. About the Romans, too?"

"Sure thing," said Atlas. "The first thing to understand about the Romans and the Gaulish is that they are not

Britons . . ." and on he droned, as the boat slipped through the night.

The next day, after some badgering from Spring, Chamanca found herself filling in the gaps that Atlas had left, especially about the most recent expedition when it had been just her and Carden. It helped pass the time as the boat bobbed on, and the girl proved to be a pleasingly perceptive audience.

They arrived at a small beach shortly after sunset two days later. Walfdan, the elderly Fenn-Nodens druid from the Gaulish town of Sea View, was waiting. So he'd escaped the Roman purges, Chamanca was glad to see. Most druids were idiots, but she liked this one. He welcomed them effusively and offered food and rest after their long journey. They were grateful for the food but Atlas insisted that they were ready to move on and would eat on the hoof – not literally, since they'd be walking to begin with, to limit chances of detection. As they climbed the steep dunes that back-dropped the beach, Chamanca glanced at Spring for signs of shirking or fatigue, but the girl looked sprightly.

As they paced quietly through the night, inland and eastward, Atlas explained to Walfdan that Lowa's army was all but destroyed so they needed to delay the Roman invasion until she could muster and prepare a new one.

Walfdan already knew about the situation in Britain from merchants and had a reply ready. "Gaul is finished," he said. "The land is united for once, but unfortunately it is united in a mood of beaten, dejected submission. Tribes all over Gaul, vastly more numerous than the invader, with much greater resources than the Bel-cursed Romans, have capitulated with little more than a whimper. Some of them did not even whimper. A little backbone and cooperation would have seen us triumph, but most Gauls have behaved like self-interested cowards. I've lived a long time and hitherto been proud to call myself a Gaul. Now I am ashamed."

Atlas said a few consoling things about the Romans' military training and the Gaulish tribes' lack of cohesion, but Chamanca stayed quiet. She agreed with Walfdan. Ducklings with their beaks removed would have given ravening wolves more of a challenge than most of Gaul had offered the Romans. Walfdan's own tribe, the Fenn-Nodens, had almost all died in the struggle against the invaders so at least, she thought, he had that rock of pride to cling to.

Atlas finished by telling Walfdan that the Britons sang the praises of the Fenn-Nodens and toasted their valour, then asked, "So what can we do?"

"My plan is to go helmet in hands to the Germans to see if they can help. A vast German army has crossed the Renos river. They are the best chance of defeating the Romans, or at least delaying their invasion of Britain."

"Your information is a year old," Atlas said. "Caesar massacred a huge host of Germans under Harry the Fister last year."

"These are different Germans – two tribes from further east, the Ootipeats and the Tengoterry. They were all set to wage glorious war and conquer Harry the Fister's territory in Germany and Gaul, but they arrived and found nobody to fight apart from the old, the young and the few blind Warriors who had survived the Romans' torture. Now they have a gigantic army which they've never used. I do not think it will be hard to persuade them to march against our common foe. I suspect that Caesar knows this, and is already on his way north to meet them."

Atlas grunted his assent. It did seem like the best option; the only option in fact. They walked on, Atlas and Chamanca leading, Walfdan and the girl behind.

A short time later they were surprised by a Roman patrol. Chamanca cursed herself for not hearing or sensing them, but when the cheating bastards hid in woodland, downwind in the dark, there wasn't much you could do. As soon as legionary silhouettes appeared on the road ahead she reached for her weapons, but Atlas put a hand on her arm. He was right, they couldn't fight. Dozens of Romans emerged from the trees all around them, many holding aloft previously concealed torches which shone off their weapons and armour.

They held their hands up in submission as the legionaries parted to let through a centurion. He was possibly the tallest man Chamanca had ever seen; certainly the tallest Roman. He had a cheery face and the stoop of a man who had banged his head on many doorframes.

"So!" he said in broken Gaulish. "What do you?"

"These two are a merchant and his daughter," said Atlas in Latin, pointing at Walfdan and Spring. "We are their guards, escorting them back to Soyzonix land."

The centurion laughed and replied in Latin. "Can I buy something then?"

"We have no wares."

"Exactly!" he chuckled, shaking his head. "Of all the terrible excuses! You really should have carried a cauldron and a ladle or two if you'd wanted me to believe that you're merchants. You don't even have a donkey! Oh, it's too much. You are morons. Men, take—"

"We sold all our wares to the Romans at Karnac," said Walfdan.

"Including your donkey?"

"We sold our cart and two oxen. As you know, you are building a fleet so demand there is high and they are selling nothing. It is what we merchants call a sellers' market. Only my daughter's protestations stopped me from selling our clothes and having us walk home naked."

"Hmmm, well that's a tiny bit more plausible." The centurion rubbed his chin and Chamanca thought that they might get away with it. "But it's still pretty thin. I'll send you back to the garrison and—"

"You will send us nowhere," said Spring, in faultless Latin. Everyone turned to look at her, Chamanca more surprised than the Romans.

"You're very astute," she continued, "although any fool could see through my guard's idiot tale. We are not merchants."

"Well, you're a cocky one," said the centurion. "And I knew you weren't merchants. You can explain exactly who you are back at—"

"You will let us pass now, unmolested, or you will regret it," said Spring. "I am Persomanima, daughter of Queen Galba of the Soyzonix. This is my adviser and these are indeed my guards. We have been in Karnac, in secret talks with your commander there. Now, tell me your name so that I can tell him how helpful you've been, letting us pass. I'll tell my mother, too, and perhaps she'll pass it on to Caesar, who is, after all, a great friend of hers."

"I see!" said the Roman. "Well, if you've been in secret talks with the commander at Karnac then you'll know his name."

"This is your last warning," said Spring. "Let us through now, or your family will rue your decision for generations to come."

"The commander's name first."

"Let us pass."

"It's a simple thing. Perhaps your talks were secret, but the name of the commander is not. If you can tell me that, I will let you go. Unless your talks were so secret that he didn't tell you his name?" The centurion chuckled and beckoned his men to seize them.

"All right, if I must accede to your insolence – the commander at Karnac is Decimus Junius Brutus Albinus."

"Oh!" The centurion held up a hand to stop the legionaries, looking surprised and suddenly nervous. "Very well. Be on your way."

They legionaries parted and they walked on.

"Well done, Spring," said Atlas a little while later.

"Indeed," said Walfdan. "Where did you learn Latin?"

"Maidun Castle, from a Roman girl. My father took her from a merchant he killed, and told her to teach me Latin."

"I am glad he did. You saved us all then."

"She taught me how to write it, too. We were friends."

"What happened to her?"

"She wanted to go back to her mother in Rome, so I tried to help her escape. But we were very young and we mucked it up and we were caught. Zadar gave the Roman girl to Felix and he killed her."

"Oh."

"I left Maidun shortly after that."

Chamanca stayed quiet. She was a little impressed. She'd mentioned the name of the Roman commander only once when telling Spring about her time with the Fenn-Nodens. Moreover, she was reminded that a privileged childhood did not necessarily mean an easy one.

As the sky morphed gently from rich, star-studded blue to delicate pink, Walfdan told them about the Ootipeats and the Tengoterry in his careful, measured way. Spring listened with about a quarter of her mind. The rest of it watched out for more Romans and investigated the sights, smells and sounds of the new land. This was the first time she'd left Britain. She expected Gaul to be completely different – purple clouds, black trees, orange grass perhaps – but it was almost exactly the same. Same smells, same trees, same birds. The only odd thing she'd seen – bar the Roman patrol – were some small, rotund, overly fluffy hares. She'd thought they must be leverets, but they were very fat for baby hares and you never saw those in groups.

"They're rabbits," said Dug, ambling along next to her, apparently unseen by the others, arrow still sticking from his head.

"Rabbits?"

"The small fat hares. They're animals called rabbits. We don't have them in Britain. They're reasonable eating — nothing compared to boar, mind you — but they ruin crops, so nobody's brought them over the Channel."

"Are you a ghost now then?"

"No, just in your mind still."

"I see, hang on. Walfdan!"

The druid stopped his description of the excellent Tengoterry cavalry mid-sentence. "Yes, child?"

"Are those animals with long ears back there called rabbits?"

"Yes."

"Different from hares?"

"Yes."

"Can they swim?"

"Spring, that's enough," said Chamanca. "Don't interrupt again unless we're under attack."

"OK!" said Spring, then, silently to Dug, "I've got you, you big cheat. You are a ghost! I didn't know those were rabbits, and you did, so you can't be part of my mind. Ha! What's it like being a ghost? Tell me about it! What happens when you die?"

"I'm not a ghost. I am in your head. Look a little deeper and you'll remember that your mother told you about rabbits when you were a wee girl."

It was possible, Spring conceded. Her mother had told her a lot of things.

"And, anyway, if I was a ghost I wouldn't be walking around with this stupid arrow sticking out of my face."

"I suppose not . . ."

"How about you get rid of it?"

"All right," said Spring, and the arrow was gone.

"See, part of your imagination. Nothing more!"

"That proves nothing. You could have done that. And another thing—"

But Dug had disappeared. Spring tried to conjure him back but he remained stubbornly invisible – proof, if proof had been needed, which it wasn't – that it was Dug, the real Dug, happy and thriving in the Otherworld and not just a figment of her mind. Her steps sprightlier, Spring returned to investigating the passing countryside for further Gaulish aberrations like rabbits and gangs of gullible Romans.

The following day they commandeered horses and rode on across Gaul. Spring saw no new animals, which was a disappointment. She saw more rabbits and was increasingly charmed by their sniffing and hopping, but they were hardly the man-eating lizards or birds the size of cows that she'd been hoping for, and she didn't see Dug again. Atlas and Chamanca were fairly rotten company, all wrapped up in each other and hardly talking to her at all.

The Gaulish people were even less impressive than the animals. It was like they were all sulking. Atlas told her that they were ashamed at letting the Romans beat them so easily. Chamanca said they'd always been miserable.

Finally, they arrived in eastern Gaul. The vast camps of the newly invading German army were easy to find. Chamanca had said that Germans wore nothing but tiny fur pants, so Spring had been looking forward to seeing them, but disappointingly there were no hairy tackle-pouches to be seen. These Germans dressed, looked and sounded much like Britons, with some differences. They were, on average, taller and blonder; Spring saw a couple who looked like Lowa, which made her growl. Many wore ornate armour, there was more fur than you'd have seen in the Maidun army (draped over shoulders and wrapped round legs, not cupping genitals as she'd been led to expect) and more people were on horseback. They didn't seem to have any chariots. It was quite unnerving, she thought, this same but different world. When things were completely different, like in the merchants' town of Bladonfort compared to Maidun's army camp, for example, it was fun and exciting. When things were just a bit different from the norm, as they were here, it disquieted her. It was like she'd woken up one morning in a fake world, which the gods had built to trick her but got a few details wrong.

They rode through the slightly odd masses of Germans to the temporary court of Senlack and Brostona of the Ootipeats and Tengoterry tribes. Senlack had been king of the Ootipeats and Brostona queen of the Tengoterry, Walfdan told them. Each had murdered their spouses and united both themselves and their tribes.

Queen Brostona rose from the double throne and greeted the Britons. She did not look like a husband killer. She looked to be in her twenties with a big, even-toothed smile, light tan, high cheekbones, shiningly clean blonde hair and a sleeveless cream dress embroidered with a pattern of blue and red-petalled flowers. The dress's material was taut over firm little breasts and a narrow waist, but then exploded out over a disproportionately large bottom half. It looked as if a person as slim as Spring had been chopped in two and stuck onto the arse and legs of Danu, the marvellously fat earth goddess. Brostona's bare arms were slender like a young woman's but she *waddled*. Spring thought initially that she had a wooden framework under her skirts to flounce them up like that, but, no, further subtle investigation confirmed that it was all bottom and limbs under there. It was hard not to stare.

Senlack, watching from his chair, seemed older, from what Spring could see of him. His hair was a spongy black ball of curls and his beard separated into two curly balls with little rat's tail ends. His long, knobbly nose stuck out of this mass of hair like, Spring couldn't help but think, the penis of a wild-pubed monster. At the top of his cock-nose, shadowed beneath his fringe, she could just make out two black eyes peering out. She smiled at them.

Walfdan congratulated Senlack and Brostona on their ascension as rulers, then said that he, Atlas, Chamanca and Spring were from the Fenn-Nodens tribe, come to help the Ootipeats and Tengoterry to wage war on the Romans. They had witnessed and studied Roman methods, he said, so would be invaluable advisers.

"Well," said Brostona brightly, in an accent that sounded like a bard doing a parody of Lowa's voice, "thanks so much for coming all this way, with such good intentions, however . . ."

She raised a small pipe to her mouth and blew out a piercing note. A moment later there were twenty spear tips levelled at Spring and the others. More men and women rushed in, slings twirling.

They were caught.

"The thing is," Brostona continued, in the same chirpy tone, "we don't intend to fight the Romans, you see? We're going to tell them that the land west of our new territory is theirs, and our new territory is ours. We won't interfere if they leave us alone. Lovely plan, don't you think? Both empires gain a long, peaceful border. And since you're Fenn-Nodens and therefore enemies of the Romans, we'll be handing you over to them."

Spring felt Chamanca tense beside her, as if about to leap and bite Brostona's throat out. Atlas held out a hand, shook his head and the Iberian relaxed.

"The Romans will lie to you," he said. "They will accept your treaty, then strengthen their position in Gaul. When they are ready, they will cross the Rhenus and they will crush you. You must strike now, before they are too powerful and while you have your army gathered."

"NO!" Brostona screamed and Spring finally saw evidence of the person who had murdered her husband so she could have more subjects. "They're boring me now. Take them away. TAKE THEM AWAY!"

Chapter 8

The miles-long army train was marching through green mountains, next to a bright river boisterous with snow-melt, when a rider came galloping from the north. He brought news that more than four hundred thousand men, women and children from the German Usipete and Tencteri tribes had crossed the Rhenus river. Caesar nodded as if he been told that his chef had run out of pork so it would be beef for supper, called in the centurions and rearranged the marching order and direction.

Shortly after dawn and half a moon later, Ragnall was on horseback next to a curve of the Rhenus, part of Caesar's retinue awaiting the king and queen of the Usipetes and Tencteri, who were late. The Romans chatted patiently. They weren't unduly worried, since barbarians were always late. The valley here was perhaps two hundred paces across and thickly wooded. Ragnall had heard Titus Labienus, Caesar's deputy, warn of possible ambush, but the engineers had cut down the nearest fifty yards of trees on their side of the river and the praetorians had swept the woodland beyond that and claimed all was clear. Ragnall looked across at the trees on the other side of the river, where they hadn't swept. Nothing stirred, but those eastern woods brooded with menace. Perhaps it was a hangover from the stories about monsters in the German forests from the liars in Vesontio, but he was certain he could feel evil eyes staring at him from the darkness.

They said in Rome that no Roman had ever crossed the
Rhenus. It wasn't true: Rome's traders and explorers had
been everywhere, but it was a convenient mistruth that
both excited Ragnall and filled him with fear for what was
on the other side. He'd also heard in Rome that no Roman
had ever been to Britain, and that Britain was populated by
mustachioed cannibals who painted themselves blue, shaved
their bodies and drank nothing but milk. The Romans'
notions of the rest of the world were usually wilder than
the reality.

The Germans came into sight and Caesar kicked his horse
a few paces ahead, beyond Titus Labienus and the praetorians. They were meeting the leaders of an unknown tribe
who could easily be assassins, but Caesar rode forward, head
high. Although much of Caesar's reputation for bravery came
from exaggerated reports, he was genuinely courageous.
Ragnall was proud, and worried. He gripped the pommel
of his sword.

Various other legates, including Felix, were behind
Labienus and next to Ragnall, with two dozen of Caesar's
black-leather and iron-armoured praetorian guards fanning
out on their mounts to either side.

The German queen and king approached, followed by a
disorderly guard of perhaps a dozen. It looked, thought
Ragnall with some relief, like Caesar was safe. It would have
been hard to find a less likely looking pair of assassins. The
king was a skinny man with shaggy black hair wrenched
into what looked like three balls of hairy wool. The queen,
by far the more impressive-looking of the two, was riding
an aurochs – one of the giant oxen common in the German
forests.

"Greetings, noble Caesar!" said the queen. "I am Queen
Brostona of the Tengoterry and this is Senlack of the
Ootipeats!" She swept a majestic hand to indicate her hirsute

companion. Her voice was loud and haughtily enthusiastic. German accent aside, it reminded Ragnall of his mother.

Caesar gestured to the praetorians. They charged the Usipete and Tencteri guard. It was over in moments. The German soldiers were all unseated and dying, not a praetorian was harmed. The Romans closed in on the regal pair.

King Senlack flicked his reins. His horse gave a high-pitched snort, whipped round and sprang as if stung by a wasp. The king ducked one praetorian's sword swipe, parried two more with his curved blade and then he was off down the road, horse galloping as if it was fleeing from the Underworld, the king's big hair bouncing in rhythm with its stride. A knot of Romans set off in pursuit, but the Usipete's horse was faster and he was away.

Brostona watched from her seat on the aurochs until Senlack had disappeared over a rise, then turned back to Caesar, still smiling as confidently as a queen whose entire guard hadn't just been slaughtered. "Don't worry, Caesar, he won't come back with the army. They do only what I tell them. Now perhaps we can talk terms? If you look in that man's satchel," she pointed to a man on the ground who was scrabbling weakly at his slashed, blood-pulsing throat, "you'll find a map that shows my plans."

Caesar turned to his deputy. "Labienus, this woman amuses me. Have her disarmed and brought to my tent this evening."

"I am not armed, and I look forward to seeing you as a peer in the evening. We will discuss terms. I have a plan that will surely . . ." She tailed off because Caesar had turned his horse from her and begun to talk to Labienus. Ragnall saw knuckles whiten on the hand holding her aurochs' reins. She was angrier about the general snubbing her than the death of her entire retinue.

"Keep the praetorians here to hold the road," Caesar continued to Labienus. "I'll send up a cohort of the Tenth as well to cover the country around. No Roman is to go any further north than this point. Any Germans who attempts to come south of it will be killed."

Labienus nodded agreement, but glanced at Felix, tightening his cheeks and pursing his lips as if he'd put something unpleasant in his mouth. Ragnall wondered what was going on.

Chapter 9

Little Dug lay on Lowa's lap, wrapped in cotton and wool, breathing softly and staring into her eyes. He was a pretty little thing – thank Kornonos, since she'd seen some grotesque babies in her time – and she definitely felt some affection for him. But love? No. Why should she? Shitting, crying and sleeping, his sole activities thus far, were not endearing. Everyone said that being a mother would change the way she thought about everything forever, but she hadn't expected it to and it hadn't. She had a child and that was that. She liked him, but if he was taken away right then and she never saw him again? She'd live. She'd lost people before.

Perhaps other mothers saw more of their babies, and that's why they fell for them. Lowa had hardly seen Dug since his birth because she spent most daylight moments and many of the nights training her army. She was in charge of the cavalry, Mal looked after the scorpion crews, Atlas was head of the infantry and Chamanca commanded the heavy and light chariots, but with those latter two in Gaul and Lowa as overarching chief, she spent as much time with the other sections as her own.

It was hard work. They were slowly learning new methods, and gradually mastering new weapons and equipment, but so many had been killed in the battle with the Eroo and their Fassites that their real problem was numbers. The coming Roman army was likely to be a good deal larger than hers, not to mention vastly more experienced, with years more training and, apparently, supported by a legion of unspecified but powerful demons.

As well as preparing to defend against an invincible foe, she had to continue to manage resources to avoid the famine that might have followed the Spring Tide – and might still– and she had to ensure her army and its ancillary support was fed, sheltered, fuelled, stopped from running wild, that its shit was taken away, outbreaks of disease contained, squabbles stifled before they could escalate . . . She'd put people in charge of all these tasks, but found herself having to intervene again and again. With a few exceptions, her commanders simply did not give nearly as much of a fuck about getting everything right as she did.

The only thing that she'd done since she'd been queen that could be considered selfish was learning to swim. Escaping from Zadar years before, she'd almost been caught because she couldn't swim. She never wanted to be in that situation again, so on a succession of calm evenings she rode south to the sea alone, waded into the frigid water and worked out how to float and paddle about. She hadn't expected it to be difficult – as she'd told herself all those years ago, many children could swim and children were idiots – and it hadn't been.

With running a conglomeration of tribes and invasion preparation taking up every heartbeat of her time, she reckoned Danu might forgive her if she didn't go all weak in the limbs and gushy about her son.

People told her, all the time, that the boy looked exactly like his father, Dug. Yes, maybe there was some Dug in his eyes, but it was no big surprise that a baby looked like his father and not something to coo about like a brain-damaged hen. On the other hand, in her rare moments when she wasn't obsessing about her army and she had enough energy left after the long day not to be cynical, it did please her that little Dug looked like big Dug. It was fitting that the line of the man who had died to save them all might be continued. But the cooers and gushers implied that this baby had *replaced* Dug. That was wrong. Very wrong. Dug Sealskinner had been the love of her life and nobody would ever replace him.

"Run a finger across his mouth and he'll smile," said Keelin Orton, who was standing and watching her. Her tone was brisk. She was brisk about everything, but she clearly adored the little boy. She didn't wince when he was sick on her, and wiped the weird green shit from his little pink arse as if she were mopping spilled water.

The queen had been surprised when Keelin had turned up on the day of Dug's birth and asked to wet-nurse the child. She hadn't seen Keelin since the day she'd killed her lover, King Zadar, and shortly before she'd broken the girl's jaw with a stool when escaping Barton. However, if Keelin wasn't going to hold that that against her, then Lowa didn't need to remember that Keelin had been sleeping with the man who'd murdered her sister and tried to kill her.

Moreover, Keelin seemed to have grown from a pouting sex chattel into a sensible young woman, and her breasts were even bigger now that they were making milk. Dug would get enough sustenance, and Lowa was pretty sure there was no truth in the jokes that any baby nursed by Keelin would become a wide-mouthed adult. Discreet enquiries revealed that Keelin's own daughter had died shortly before little Dug had been born and that the child's father had been killed fighting the Eroo, so Lowa was glad to give the girl a baby to mother and something to distract her from her grief.

The queen brushed the tip of her finger along tiny lips. The baby flapped a hand weakly and his little face puckered into a smile. Lowa was surprised to find her smile twitching to life, the first time for a good while. The boy wasn't entirely unappealing. She ran a finger along his cheek. So smooth.

It was amazing, she thought, that she had Dug and somehow combined to produce this beautiful little bugger.

"He likes it as well when you—"

Lowa held up a hand to interrupt her. "I'm sorry, Keelin. I have to go." Lowa held him out to his nanny.

"Oh, stay a moment longer, Lowa. Dug loves seeing his mum and—"

"Keelin. If his *mum* doesn't get the army organised, he'll have no eyes to see anything with because the Romans will gouge them out. And I hate to think what they'll do to you. I am sorry, but I must go."

"All right."

"And it's Queen Lowa."

"Sorry, *Queen* Lowa," Keelin muttered as she bounded from the hut.

Chapter 10

They'd been there for three days, attached to a thick chain running through iron ankle bracelets, and she was bored bored bored. Atlas and Walfdan were kindly enough, although patronising, but Chamanca clearly thought that Spring was no more than a foolish little girl and a hindrance, despite the fact that they'd all be prisoners of the Romans if it wasn't for her and it wasn't her fault at all that they were now prisoners of the Germans. The Iberian barely listened while she spoke, and never asked her opinion as she made plans with Atlas and Walfdan. Dug had always treated Spring as an equal but it had taken a while before Lowa had, so she guessed it was the same deal again. What was it Dug had told her – "People judge you by what you do, not by what you say you're going to do'? Unless you say you're going to make love to a pig or something like that, she thought, then they'll judge you, but he did have a point. She hadn't done much yet – talking them out of trouble hadn't been that big a deal if she was honest – so she'd just have to do a few more things to make Chamanca like her. The strange thing was that she found herself much keener to please Chamanca than the two men who were much kinder to her. What, she wondered, was that about?

It didn't look like the Iberian had that much time for Walfdan either. She'd asked him to use druid magic to break their chains but he'd said that his magic was of a more subtle variety. This had not impressed Chamanca at all. It hadn't impressed Spring much either. If she'd still had her magic,

she'd have at least tried to free them. She suspected that
Walfdan was one of the many charlatan druids that Lowa
so often cursed.

Chamanca did, however, seem very keen on Atlas. They
often sat with their limbs touching, and they slept right
next to each other. Spring hadn't heard that they were a
couple, however she had been away from Maidun for a
while. But they didn't seem like a couple, not quite. They
were more like two children who fancied each other but
didn't know what to do about it.

They were chained in the open air, on a foot-high wooden
platform at the edge of a square area clear of tents. Tall
posts at each corner of their dais held up a leather canopy
which kept the sun off for most of the day and would have
kept them dry if there'd been any rain. Spring was pleased
and a little surprised that her captors had been so thoughtful.
Chamanca had spat when she'd seen the awning and said,
"That's Germans for you, so fucking sensible." The clearing
seemed to be the central meeting point, but it was impossible
to tell how central it was in relation to the rest of the camp
because she couldn't see any further than the tents that
surrounded it and she'd been blindfolded when they'd
brought them in.

Spring expected the Ootipeats and Tengoterry to jeer and
throw rotten food at them, as people would have done in
Britain, but either the looks on Atlas' and Chamanca's faces
stopped that from happening, or the Germans were simply
more decent that the Britons. Despite the four armoured
guards glowering at them silently from a safe distance, plenty
of passers stopped to chat. After she'd heard the life stories
of ten boring old farts while dodging repeated requests to
tell her own, Spring began to think that a few decaying
apples in the face would be vastly preferable to the intrusive
politeness of her captors.

So, unwillingly, Spring learnt a lot about the Germans.

The Ootipeats and Tengoterry weren't so much an invading army as an evading one, driven from their own lands by an even larger force of yet another German tribe called the Suby. The numerically superior Suby drank nothing but milk and ate only meat. As a result they were all sturdy giants with no sense of humour, unbeatable in battle.

"And they never discipline their children," one thin-lipped, effusive gossip enthusiast told her.

"That doesn't sound so bad," Spring managed to say as the woman paused for breath,

"Oh no, you have to bollock children regularly and beat them every now and then or they become selfish little shits and grow up into arrogant arseholes. That's what's happened to the Suby. They're huge, never hung over and they take violent offence at the smallest thing. They're *dreadful*."

Spring also learnt from the loquacious woman that Senlack hadn't killed his queen, who'd been a beautiful and stylish young woman. Brostona had done for her, as well as her own husband, then insisted that Senlack marry her. Senlack had just gone with it. He was that sort of guy. He was also mute. Spring actually found that titbit interesting. She'd put his quietness down to Brostona being overbearing, but, no, Senlack had never spoken. It was generally assumed that he was so lazy he simply couldn't be bothered. Spring asked a few people how such a lackadaisical man had managed to become king. He just had, they told her.

Spring was half listening to yet another explanation of Ootipeat or Tengoterry history with personal side stories and wishing that the entirety of both tribes were mutes, when she heard distant shouts and screams.

"Shhhh!" she said to the bore. He looked offended but paused his droning.

"Quiet!" she said to the others.

"You be quiet," said Chamanca, but she did shut up and listen for a while, then said, "What is it?"

"The Germans are under attack, from the east," said Spring.

"Nonsense. I cannot hear . . . oh . . . actually . . ."

"Unchain us," Atlas said to the leader of the guards, a small man in new-looking leathers with black, neatly combed hair and a patch of square moustache trimmed to sit under his nose like a tar spill from his nostrils.

"No. Maybe," said the guard leader, looking about as if he'd just been told that there was a semi-concealed bear somewhere in the square. "Wait until I have assessed the threat. Follow me!" he cried to the other guards and ran off in the direction of the fighting. The others followed.

The noise of the battle approached rapidly, growing louder. It was a strange sort of battle sound. Usually you heard shouting, the clanging of iron on iron, the thumping of iron on wood and some screaming. This one was almost all screaming. There was a sound of metal on metal, but it didn't sound like swords striking other swords or shields, more like cartloads of iron tools being pulled at speed across rough ground. The strangest thing about the noise was that Spring was sure that she'd heard it before . . . What was it? It was frustrating that they couldn't see past the high tents that surrounded them.

Chamanca and Atlas strained at the chains, to no avail. They looked about for someone to help, but everyone had either fled or run to join the fighting.

"There's something wrong with this attack," said Chamanca.

"Indeed," said Atlas. "It's coming far too quickly and there's too much screaming. And what, by Sobek, is that other noise? It sounds like Tadman running in giant's armour when he fought Dug."

"Yes. That's it!" said Spring, the relief of remembering massively outweighed by what it might mean. "But more than one of him – many more."

Atlas nodded.

Thinking that an army of armoured Tadmans might at any moment burst into the clearing made Spring feel sick and light-headed. It was becoming increasingly important that they get free of these chains. She looked for something that Atlas or Chamanca might have missed, but saw nothing.

A German tribesman sprinted into the square and carried on through, throwing his sword aside without checking his stride. Chamanca called to him but he didn't respond. More German soldiers ran headlong into the clearing and out the other side, then more and more, until dozens were streaming through. Atlas managed to grab a passing woman.

"What's happening?"

Her eyes were huge, the pupils flying around and bouncing off the sides. "Let me go, let me go!"

Atlas slapped her. "What is happening?"

"Devils! Gods! I saw Makka himself! Killing everyone! Everyone! Please, please let me go!"

"You will undo our chains."

"I will, I will, I promise, the moment you let me go."

Atlas let her go. She ran. Atlas shook his head, then put the chain over his shoulder and heaved like the hero from a bard's tale. The muscles in his arms pulsed, his jerkin stretched across his huge back, his tartan trousers strained to contain his bulging thighs. But the chain held.

Many of the Germans streaming through the clearing now were bloodied. Some stumbled and regained their footing, some fell and stayed down. The screaming came ever closer. Something caught Spring's eye. It was a person, flying through the air over the tents from the west. He landed with a cracking thud. Two more, a woman and a child, followed in similar trajectories. The woman landed hard, lifted her head and stared at Spring as if she were Bel himself, then collapsed.

"What *is* it? What's coming?" someone said and Spring realised it had been her. Her voice had been strangely squeaky. She was terrified, she realised, properly afraid with a chance of shitting herself. She'd charged at Dumnonians and been charged at by Murkans in her time and it had been scary, but nothing compared to this. Not knowing what was coming but knowing it was something awful was much more frightening. So much for proving herself to Chamanca by her deeds. She tried to breathe calmly. She wanted to cry.

Chamanca and Atlas continued to work at the chains. Walfdan stood between Spring and the approaching menace. The screams and metallic clangs grew ever louder. More Germans flew screaming up into the air, some astonishingly high. Whatever it was would be in the clearing at any moment.

A horse galloped into the square, its rider's black curly hair bouncing like an inflated bladder on the end of a stick – King Senlack. He leapt off and slapped his horse on the rump. It sped away. The king of the Ootipeats unsheathed his sword and charged their platform. Spring held up her hands, ready to defend herself as best she could.

Senlack chopped through the rope holding up the leather awning. One corner fell and the king ran to another.

"Crowd in and lie down!" shouted Walfdan. "He means to hide us!"

They threw themselves into a pile and pulled the canopy down onto themselves as Senlack cut it free. Spring's head ended up on Chamanca's bare midriff, her cheek pressed against the cool, firm skin. She felt a hand grip her hair and thought the Iberian was going to pull her off, but the hand gripped her in tighter, holding her still.

Spring lay in the dark and listened. The stampede in the square grew louder and the screaming intensified. They heard pleas for mercy, thumps, whacks, cracks that could have been bones snapping and squelching rips that could have been flesh tearing, all overlaid by the clanking of iron. The noise crescendoed. It sounded like the war of the gods had started in the square, apart from one odd noise. Was that *giggling* she could hear? She strained her ears, but something landed on their hiding place and Walfdan made an oofing sound.

Spring expected a giant iron-clad hand to rip away their covering any moment. Something crashed down on her own leg and she gasped. Chamanca gripped her hair harder and lifted a thigh against her mouth to silence her. More objects thumped down onto their covering. One landed on Chamanca but she didn't flinch. Spring held her breath and pressed her cheek into the Iberian's stomach, trying to squeeze out the terror, waited to be pierced by a sword, or crushed . . .

The noises of the killing abated, then became muffled. The killers were gone from the square. The groans of the dying remained. Spring heard one of her fellow hiders crawling out from under the tarpaulin. Chamanca dropped her leg and released her grip, but Spring stayed put. She was in no hurry to see what was out there. She heard chains jangling, and felt hers slip away from her anklet.

The tarpaulin was pulled back and there stood Senlack.

By the time Spring was on her feet, Atlas and Chamanca were already among the dead, hunting for weapons. The dead . . . there were hundreds of them, butchered. The lumps that had fallen on their hiding place were limbs, ripped torsos and heads. Blood pooled in shining red puddles, unable to sink into the already blood-saturated ground. All of the bodies were Germans. Whatever had killed them in the clearing – given the numbers it must have been an army, not a single beast – had done for hundreds of them without loss.

Spring thought she'd better find something to fight with herself but felt a hand on her shoulder – the mute king Senlack. He shook his woolly head, gestured for her to follow him, then pointed at the others.

"Atlas, Chamanca, Walfdan – he wants us to follow," she said.

Atlas and Chamanca shrugged at each other and nodded. They were the finest Warriors that Spring had seen, with the exception of Dug and Lowa, of course, but Spring thought they looked happy for an excuse not to follow whatever murderous force was sweeping through the German camp, and she didn't blame them.

"You thinking what I'm thinking?" Chamanca said to Atlas.

"Felix's legion?"

"Without a doubt. I want to see them. I want to kill them."

"Not here. Come on."

Senlack led them to an opulently decorated tent, where they found Atlas' axe, Chamanca's ball-mace and blade and Spring's bow, quiver and hammer.

Happier now that they were reunited with their weapons, they followed Senlack north, towards the Renos river. Throughout the camp, the carnage was extraordinary. At times the ground was so thick with bodies that they had to step on them. There were survivors, too. People emerged from tents and from under carts, mouths agape. Senlack gestured for them all to follow.

"Where are we heading?" Chamanca asked a woman jogging along with a toddler in her arms.

"To the bridge," she replied, "back across the Renos, and hope that the devils cannot follow us."

"I will run no more," Chamanca said to Atlas. She'd never been part of a fleeing crowd before and she did not like trotting along in the panicked ranks like a terrified sheep, not one bit. "This legion of Felix's might kill Germans with little bother, but have they fought an Iberian? I think not."

She looked about. On second thoughts this was not a

good place to make a stand. There were in a narrow avenue between tents, surrounded by refugees. She strained her ears. Possibly she was mistaken but...

"Spring," she said, "can you hear what's happening?"

The girl cocked her head. "Sounds like they're coming back towards us."

Chamanca nodded. That's what she'd thought, too. She guessed they'd reached the other side of the camp and were retracing their steps to kill those they'd missed on the first pass. The screams were fewer now and more isolated, which supported her theory.

"As soon as there is room to fight," Chamanca said, "I will stop fleeing."

"We'll see," said Atlas.

They burst out of the camp and on to an expansive riverside meadow. It was short-grassed and busy with small brown sheep. A track across the centre of the meadow led to a thin wooden bridge. There was a trickle of Germans pounding across it. Given the size of the camp, the number escaping was pitiful.

"Right," said Chamanca, "I will fight here. Atlas, Walfdan and Spring, cross the bridge and prepare to break it down in case I cannot kill them all."

"I'll stand with you," said Atlas, "but let's get closer to the bridge. These . . . things are fast. I want to see how they move before they're on us. It may be that retreat is our best option."

"Fine. I'll pander to your African cowardice." She was secretly a little relieved. She wasn't worried for herself, but she'd rather Atlas didn't throw his life away unnecessarily.

They chose a place fifty paces from the bridge. Atlas stood on one side of Chamanca, Senlack on the other. Spring and Walfdan headed for the bridge and safety. Chamanca was not surprised. Spring was a child and would be ineffectual, so it was sensible for her to live to fight another day, Chamanca would have done the same in her position. Walfdan's retreat, on the other hand, was shameful. Now she knew how he'd survived the Roman's purge of the Fenn-Nodens — by fleeing!

Chamanca was keen to see the monsters. She wasn't frightened. Wounds that would have done for others had never killed her. She'd often wondered if she was immortal, but had decided that if she was injured badly enough — her head removed, for example — then she would die. Perhaps she'd find out today? It would be interesting to know.

She looked at Atlas. He was hefting his axe and breathing like an angry ox.

"If they prove too much," she said, "I'll try to hold them while you get across the river and break the bridge. I don't trust the child and the old man."

Atlas turned and grinned whitely. "We'll be all right. But if we need to run, you run first. And you, Senlack."

Senlack nodded and hoicked a thumb over his shoulder, as if to say that he'd be out of there the moment it started looking bad, thanks very much.

The trickle of Germans coming from the tents petered out then stopped. One last man appeared, fell and lay still.

The first of Felix's dark legion appeared.

Chamanca looked at Atlas. He raised an eyebrow. She looked back.

Walking from the edge of the camp were four smallish, slender men. They were clad entirely in leather, including hoods and face coverings. The only gaps in their outfits were eye slits. Each held a slim, slightly curved, single-edged sword. As they neared, Chamanca saw that their blades were bloodied and their leathers shone with gore.

She knew that you couldn't necessarily judge a fighter by appearance — she herself looked more like a beautiful princess than a Warrior, for example — so she should have been cautious. But she had the idea that the four of them were smiling under their masks, mocking her. So she charged.

The foremost stepped to meet her. She swooped her ball-mace in a graceful, duckable curve at his head, then lashed with her blade at the last moment for the gut shot. For the first time ever, the move failed. The Leatherman sidestepped with viper speed. He grabbed her sword hand and pulled her past him, tripping her and slicing at the back of her leg as she went down. She was so surprised at his pace that she almost forgot to block, swishing her blade round as she fell, just in time to bang his sword off target, then back for the disembowelling blow. He leapt like a deer so that her blade found only air, but she'd gained the space to land on her hands and spring over into a fighting stance.

Her opponent stepped away but she saw his eyes flicker to something behind her. She dropped into a crouch as a sword parted the air where her neck had been an instant earlier, and swung her ball-mace back in a knee-crusher. That missed, too. By Fenn, they were *fast*!

But not as fast as she was. They couldn't be. Chamanca charged back at the first Leatherman, blade whirling. He dodged. She'd expected the dodge and had already compensated by swinging her ball-mace. He dodged that, too – she hadn't expected that. A fist hit her jaw like a hurled boulder. She was stunned. He darted behind her and pinned her arms in an unshakeable grip.

The second Leatherman came back at her, sword stabbing at her exposed midriff. She stamped and kicked, but dancing feet avoided her heels. She was caught, about to take a sword in the guts. She could see the smile in the swordsman's eyes. He pressed the tip of his weapon into her stomach. Skin punctured and she felt the blade cleave muscle.

An arrow nicked her ear and sliced through the stabbing swordsman's eye slit. The grip on her arms loosened for an eyeblink and Chamanca managed to wrench her arms free, slap a hand back, grab the man's bollocks through leather, fall and twist . . . and he went limp, too, an arrow in his heart.

She stood. Twenty paces away, Senlack was dying, his stomach sliced open. Atlas was wrenching his axe from a Leatherman's corpse. The other assailant was lying nearby, an arrow through his head. She looked towards the bridge. There was Spring, new arrow nocked, ready for anything else that emerged from the tent city. Chamanca herself had killed none, Atlas had killed one and the girl had done for three. Walfdan was nowhere to be seen.

"Come on," said Atlas, "let's go." He set off for the bridge at a run.

Chamanca caught up with him. "I do not run!"

"Without Spring's bow I would have died just then. You, too, by the looks of things."

"So?"

"We fought only four. How many more are to come? From the noise in the square, many. And I don't think those little leather-clad men are the worst of it either." He glanced down at her bleeding stomach. "And you're hurt. We go now. Can you walk?"

"Of course I can walk. I can run."

Spring scanned the edge of the tents, arrow ready, as the two British Warriors ran towards her and the bridge. There were more Germans fleeing the camp, some of whom were wearing leathers. She nearly let fly at a couple of them before realising at the last moment that they weren't the enemy.

The enemy . . . had been extraordinary. She'd held back initially, since killing the attackers after the others had claimed them would have been like shooting someone else's bird on a game shoot and she knew that Chamanca in particular would not have been impressed. By the time she realised they were in trouble, it had been too late to save Senlack. She'd tried, but his attacker had dodged her first two arrows – while parrying Senlack's attack – then sliced the Ootipeat king's stomach open before she'd managed to hit him. Atlas had beaten one, but not easily, and Chamanca, facing two, had been losing when Spring intervened. How many troops like this did the Romans have? How could Lowa's depleted army hope to hold against them? And would Chamanca be angry about Spring shooting her attackers before she'd had a chance to kill them?

"Come on!" Atlas said as he and the Iberian ran by. "And well done." The clanging of iron on iron was so loud that it sounded like a crowd of giants in iron armour were running towards them through the camp. She was very happy to join the retreat.

"Thank you," said Chamanca as they ran.

"Don't mention it," said Spring.

"Wasn't planning to again," said the Iberian, but she turned and flashed a genuine, pointy-toothed grin that gave Spring a warm rush despite the circumstances.

They bounded up the steps onto the bridge. It was a thin, wooden affair, supported on stone columns. The river below was brown and churning, fizzing white around the bridge supports. It was not a waterway you'd want to swim across.

On the other side was Walfdan, holding a flaming torch and standing next to a barrel of oil. Spring turned to look at the line of tents and her breath caught in her throat. An iron-encased giant ran into sight among the crowds of refugees. He picked up a German by the leg and threw her forty paces into the air. He grabbed another and did the same, then another and another. A couple of dozen more iron giants appeared. They had blades attached to their wrists and shins, and swords the length of hut posts. They set to killing. She saw one throw a German to another, who whacked the flying man with his wrist blade, slicing him in two in a spray of guts and blood. Another picked up a man, pulled his arm off, then beat him about the head with his own limb. They all killed in different ways with one uniting theme – they enjoyed it. They were playing.

"Wait until the Romans are on the bridge, then burn it," said Atlas.

Spring opened her mouth to disagree – there were a lot of Germans on the other side of the Renos still – but he was right. It they didn't burn the bridge those who'd made it across would die as well. She tried a few arrows on the giants but her missiles bounced off thick armour. More of the Leathermen appeared and she tried to hit them, but they moved so quickly that it was impossible at that distance. She'd just as likely hit one of the Germans. Not that that would matter really, since they were all going to die anyway.

A couple of iron giants gave up killing for a moment to sprint for the bridge.

"Now," said Atlas.

"No," said Walfdan. Spring saw that he was right. The armoured men didn't intend to cross the bridge; they were there to stop any more Germans reaching safety. A company of Ootipeats and Tengoterry mustered and tried to fight their way past the Romans. They died.

"There will be no more coming. Light it," said Atlas.

Walfdan leant forward, but the long blast of a horn rang out from the other side of the river, the thundering of hooves filled the air and he stayed his hand.

Stretching the entire width of the riverside meadow, galloping hard from the west, were the German cavalry, hundreds of them, hooting and shouting battle calls, blaring trumpets, holding coloured, rippling pennants aloft. All along the leading edge long spears were lifted then lowered. A horse-powered surge of spiked death thundered towards the Roman monsters.

"The Tengoterry cavalry!" shouted Walfdan, fire in his voice. "The finest cavalry in the world. The Roman creatures will not last long."

They certainly did look good, thought Chamanca, but why were they fading? Oh, there we go, she was passing out. That punch to the head must have been harder than she'd realised. She took a step towards Atlas. He saw what was happening and took her in his arms. She collapsed into his embrace, the world swirled around her, narrowed into a point, then disappeared.

Chapter 11

"I'm sorry, Lowa. I've thought about it and I've changed my mind. My men and women will stay here."

Jocanta Fairtresses, chief of the Haxmite tribe, looked far from sorry. She batted long eyelashes and smiled her increasingly irritating smile, the one that said, "I'm *so* beautiful, *aren't* I?" Annoyingly, she probably was quite good-looking. She was a head taller than Lowa with a willowy bearing and the bright, slanted, appealing eyes of a fox cub. She was wearing a simple, long white dress, no more than a white sheet wrapped around her chest really, which showed off her lightly tanned, clear skin. The "Fairtresses" nickname was aggravatingly apt, too. Gleaming golden locks cascaded down either side of her elfishly beautiful face and bounced off her bare shoulders like weightless, gold-spun curtains. Lowa suspected that she kept her court and her flower-decorated throne outside her longhouse purely so that her hair would glow in the sun.

"You promised two hundred and fifty, armed and armoured."

"A perk of being chief is that one is allowed to change one's mind. Is it not very simple? Would you like me to explain again?" She smiled her smile once more, picked a flower from her wicker throne, sniffed it, crushed it and tossed it away.

Lowa clenched her fists. "The Romans threaten us all, Jocanta. Every other tribe has given or pledged men, women and supplies to fight them."

"Oh, I know that, but why should I help? You seem to have it covered. You've got lovely hair, by the way."

"I do have it covered. But you know that my army was reduced to a tenth of its strength when we fought—"

"I heard. It sounded simply awful – but also very much your problem, not mine."

"The Romans—"

"Threaten us all, blah blah blah. I understand. I even believe you. But you're going to try to fight them off with or without my two hundred and fifty, aren't you? If you beat them, hooray for you, we're all safe, let's have a feast. If you don't, the Romans will look favourably on the tribes that didn't resist them. Like us. So go away, beat the Romans or don't beat the Romans. Whatever happens, I win, without risking the lives of two hundred and fifty soldiers and the wrath of their kin."

"If everyone thought like that, the land would be—"

"I'm not everyone." The chief stepped forward, so that she was a couple of hands' breadth from Lowa. The Maidun queen had the annoying choice of looking at Jocanta's chest or tilting her head to look in her eyes. She chose the latter. Stepping back did not occur to her.

Jocanta looked down for a long pause, then said: "Now, would you rather walk out of my town or be carried out?" Her guards closed in behind her.

Mal put a hand on Lowa's arm and she checked herself. She'd been reaching for her blade, but he was right. She could have killed Fairtresses before the guards reacted, but she and Mal would never have made it out of Haxam to the Two Hundred, who were waiting in the woods nearby. Since Grummog had captured her she'd been careful not to enter unknown territory without an appropriate guard, but Queen Jocanta had been so effusively welcoming and accommodating when they'd visited half a moon before that she'd thought she was just popping in to collect the promised quota before heading on her way, two hundred and fifty recruits stronger.

"Jocanta, I implore you, for your own sake, not to renege on your pledge."

"For my own sake? Are you threatening me in my own hillfort? That would not be clever. Perhaps you'd like to discuss the matter with our champion, Yilgarn Craton, Warrior and slayer of a hundred?"

A dark-eyed, big-nosed man in a thick, sleeveless leather jerkin and a plain iron helmet stepped forward from the other guards. He stood square and jutted his bony chin at the Maidunites. He was absurdly stocky – not much taller than Lowa, but about three times as wide. Black hair sprouted from his helmet and down his back. He tossed his axe from hand to hand, stretching his arms out to show the size of his biceps. They were enormous, wildly disproportionate to his height, bigger even than Atlas'. He was wearing the wild boar necklace of a Warrior – someone who'd killed more than ten in a single battle. Lowa had one, too – she'd fulfilled the Warrior quota many times over in many battles – but she never wore it because she preferred to be underestimated.

She quashed the impulse to challenge Yilgarn Craton in exchange for the troops. She'd been training with the blade like a woman obsessed recently and was almost back to her pre-childbirth ability. So she could have taken on three oafs like Craton quite happily but, given that Jocanta had already gone back on her word, she seemed unlikely to honour any pledges made on the outcome of a duel. No: if she fought Yilgarn and won, her chances of leaving the Haxmite hillfort alive were around zero. Even without a fight, odds on escape wasn't much higher than zero. Surely Jocanta knew that Lowa would not let her get away with this; that her safest option by far would have been to have her slingers kill Lowa and Mal as they walked away?

"All right, Jocanta, I understand," said Lowa. "Your desire to protect your people is admirable. I urge you to reconsider, but I cannot make you. If you change your mind, your troops will be welcome at Maidun. I didn't intend to threaten you, merely to stress the point that the Romans will be trouble for everyone if they invade successfully. I shall try to ensure that they do not."

"Very well," said Jocanta. "Good luck against those nasty invaders!"

"O noble and beautiful Jocanta, let me fight her." The head guard Yilgarn took a step forward and knelt with his head down, his axe out in front of him, shaft in his hands and its double-bladed head on the ground.

"No, no, no, get back, Yilgarn!" Jocanta laughed. "Who will defend us from the Romans if you kill Lowa? No, she must go. Goodbye, Queen Lowa!"

Lowa pulled up the corners of her mouth in an attempt at a smile, turned and walked away through the town of Haxam, Mal at her side.

"Town" was something of a misnomer. Haxam was really a sprawling village on a bulge of land, surrounded by a single ditch and a low, palisaded bank. The palisade was leaning in many places, a sign that its posts had been dug too shallow, not packed in well enough or both. There clearly hadn't been any raiding here for a long time. Spaced around the wall were towers built of bone and interlaced with flowers to honour Branwin, the goddess of love and beauty. The bones were human – nothing sinister, Lowa guessed – just the dead of the tribe left to be picked clean by birds at the top of the ever-growing towers.

The Haxmites stopped their smithing, shearing, bartering or chatting to watch the Maidunites pass. Most of them nodded cheery greetings. Many of the women had over-styled hair in emulation of Jocanta Fairtresses, but Lowa didn't despise them for it. She'd noticed that a lot of women, and men in fact, in Maidun had started wearing outfits similar to the iron-heeled riding boots, leather trousers and white cotton shirt that she herself wore pretty much every day. People copied rulers. It wasn't a big deal and didn't make them bad people. It made them idiots and sheep, but not bad people.

Despite the Haxmites' ostensible congeniality, Lowa expected them to pull blades and attack at any moment. Surely Jocanta knew that she couldn't break a promise and expect nothing to happen? In case she didn't, and somehow they were allowed to go free, Lowa made careful note of the layout of huts and tracks as they walked along, both her and Mal trying to look cheery and unthreatening. There was no need to share her fears; Mal knew the danger they were in.

They reached the gate. It was overelaborate, twice the height of the surrounding palisade, with slinger towers at each side. Three slingers stood atop each tower, all looking at her and Mal, leather thongs loaded. A dozen spear holders stood between them and the gate.

Here we go, thought Lowa. She was ready. As soon as the stones flew, she'd leap in among the spears and see how many she could take down before one managed to stick her. She considered fleeing. After all she'd been through, she thought, she did not want to die at Jocanta's hands. She reckoned she'd be able to outrun the gate guard and vault the palisade, but she doubted that Mal would be able to, and she couldn't leave him. He was a skilled fighter. Perhaps the strength of both their swords might . . .

The spear holders parted and the gates swung open.

They walked out and onto a track that curved across a field dotted with sheep to a forest. After a hundred paces they saw Adler waving from the trees, where she was waiting with the Two Hundred. Lowa was overall head of her five-hundred-strong cavalry, but she had made Adler captain of the elite squad and had so far been impressed by the woman's refreshingly humourless dedication to the task.

Lowa turned. There were no archers rushing out to shoot them, no riders galloping out to spear them. "Well. They let us go. I would not have done that."

"No," said Mal. "So what are we going to do now?"

Lowa looked into his dark, questioning eyes shining from his tanned and increasingly wrinkled face. The spark of happiness had been replaced by a melancholy gleam of constant sorrow since his wife, Nita, had been killed in the battle before the great wave. Dug's death had left Lowa angry. Nita's death had left Mal sad.

"It's a tricky one. In theory, we should wait until nightfall, then set fire to Haxam and kill every Haxmite man, woman and child that comes running out."

"Is that necessary?"

"If we ride away without the promised troops, every other tribe will hear of it and none of them will give us soldiers. On the other hand, if we make an example of the Haxmites, it should make recruitment easier elsewhere and give us all the more chance of beating the Romans. So, for the sake of the future of every generation of every tribe in Britain, we should do to them what Zadar did to Cowton and Barton. Nobody messed with him after that."

"Apart from you. Surely we don't need to kill them all? Certainly not the children. I agree we need to do something, but surely there's something else?"

"Yeah, don't worry, I don't want to kill them either and there is something else. It's a bit more risky for us – actually, a lot more risky – but it means, with some luck, that we won't have to kill any adults, let alone their kids. Don't worry, Mal, I'm not Zadar."

"Don't become him."

"I'm not planning to."

After a quick check back over her shoulder that there
were no cavalry streaming out of Haxam to chop them down,
Lowa outlined her plan.

Chapter 12

Spring held her breath as the cavalry charged the demons. The drumming of German hooves shook the very air, its thundering rhythm speeding up as they approached the armoured giants. The Leathermen had spotted the attack and fallen behind their iron-clad allies.

"This is going to be interesting," said Chamanca.

"Surely not," Walfdan shook his head. "It will be a massacre! Surely nothing can stand for a moment against a charge like that. Watch, watch, my friends, and remember. Few have been or will ever be lucky enough to see such a thing."

Thirty paces away, in precise unison, the cavalrymen and -women howled a shiveringly rousing battle cry and lowered their spears. The horses, already galloping as fast as Spring thought horses could gallop, sped up.

They struck.

Spears splintered. Not a single Ironman fell. Several grabbed German horses by their necks and hurled them in the air, riders and all. Beasts and people flew up, then tumbled and landed behind the Ironmen, shy of the Leathermen, who dashed about and chopped their swords into struggling people and animals.

As the Leathermen hacked the fallen Germans into chunks of meat, the heavier Roman demons went to work with their arm blades, leg blades and swords on the remainder of the cavalry, butchering horses and men.

"Spring?" said Atlas. He was standing next to her, still

holding Chamanca around the waist even though she'd been unconscious only for a moment and looked fine now.

"Yes?"

"While they're distracted?" He nodded at her bow.

It was a good point. Spring plucked an arrow from her quiver, nocked it, drew, aimed and loosed. Her target, a Leatherman who was holding a German rider by the shoulder with one hand and twisting his sword in his stomach with the other, looked up at the last moment. An arm flashed and he *caught* the arrow. He smiled and hurled it back. Spring stepped to the side. The arrow whizzed by and thwocked into the ground behind them. If she hadn't moved, it would have hit her.

"They didn't do that before," she said.

"I suspect," said Walfdan, "that their power comes from killing, as with much druid magic. The more they kill, the faster, stronger and more skilled they become. It is horrific."

"So you'd better burn their route to us." Atlas nodded at the bridge. He was *still* holding Chamanca. She had one palm flat on his chest and the other hand on his big bicep. Spring had seen Lowa and Dug stand like that.

"Yes, good point." Walfdan held a torch to the pitch-soaked wood and flames raced along the bridge. And not a moment too soon. Already the famous Tengoterry cavalry were no more and the Roman demons were looking for something else to kill.

Chapter 13

With a leg up from Mal, Lowa vaulted the palisade. She landed in the shadow of one of Branwin's bone towers and held her crouch. All was quiet. As intended, she'd crossed the fence into the town's industrial area. Halfway between sunset and sunrise, there wasn't a sound from the blacksmith huts, retting pool or wheel yard.

Movement caught her eye. Danu's tits, she thought to herself. Never congratulate yourself too early. A hundred paces away along the wall, a perimeter patrol – a man and a hunting dog – were walking quietly towards her.

They'd discussed this possibility and planned for it. Lowa had said it was regretful, but if a guard had to die, so be it. But Mal had come up with another idea, which seemed even more stupid now that Lowa was about to try it.

She slipped one of the arrows he'd prepared from her quiver and nocked it, feeling foolish and shaking her head. She could only draw three-quarters because tied behind the arrowhead was the freshly butchered rib of a pig.

She shot the meaty arrow into a palisade post next to the guard. The dog yipped once then leapt at the rib, trying to wrench it out of the fence while the patrolman tried to pull him away.

Lowa tiptoe ran to them. The guard turned at the last moment and Lowa cracked him across the temple with her bow staff. He collapsed. She took the tailbone of a calf from her pouch, gave it to the dog then gagged and bound the Haxmite. She crouched for twenty heartbeats next to the guzzling dog, stroking it. Well, it had worked. If Lowa hadn't believed that the gods were human inventions for teaching morals to children, keeping the masses in line and giving succour to the dying, she would have thanked them.

There was no sign of other guards, so Lowa left the happily gnawing hound, jogged back to where she'd leapt the palisade and coughed twice. Some splintering wrenches and a couple of snaps, and three poles were dislodged while Lowa kept guard, arrow ready. No more Haxmites came and Mal, Adler and four more of the Two Hundred crept in.

Lowa led them through the sleeping fort to Jocanta's longhouse. Mal had thought it wouldn't be guarded at night; Lowa had been sure it would be. She was right. Torches burnt either side of the entranceway, lighting up Jocanta's floral throne and shining dully on the iron helmet of her champion, Yilgarn Craton. He stood peering out into the darkness, war axe in one hand.

He was big, thought Lowa, but not bright. Any useful guard would have been in the shadow, looking out into the light. Lowa waited and watched until she was sure that Yilgarn was the only sentry then gestured to the others to stay put, handed her bow to Mal and strode towards him.

"What the—?" said Yilgarn, but Lowa put her finger to her lips, unsheathed her blade then beckoned him to approach. He smiled and came. She dropped her sword onto the grass, put her right hand behind her back and tucked her fingers into the waistband of her leather trousers.

Yilgarn's brow knitted, his lips pursed, but then he seemed to understand that she intended to take him on unarmed and one-handed. He grinned and nodded. "If that's what you want . . ." he said. He danced on his toes, hair bouncing from shoulder to shoulder, flashed the axe around in a series of complicated arcs, then charged.

Lowa leant back. A decapitation blow swished through empty air and Yilgarn stumbled. He regained his footing and lifted his axe high. Lowa darted in and drove the straightened fingers of her left hand into his armpit. The Haxmite champion's eyes flew open and he dropped the axe onto his helmet with a clang. His right arm fell to his side, useless. One hand still behind her back, Lowa chopped his windpipe with the edge of her left, then balled her fist and jabbed him on the nose, one, two, three times. He flailed at her with his remaining good arm. She grabbed it, used his momentum to bring it across his body, leapt, and powered her knee into the dead arm spot between bicep and tricep.

He stood, both arms useless, blinking at her in pain, disbelief and rage, trying to cry out, but unable to make a sound through his damaged throat.

She jabbed him twice more with her left. He staggered, blinking as she wound up a mighty uppercut then powered a fist into his jaw. He went down, out cold.

Rubbing her sore left hand, Lowa walked into the candle-lit longhouse and found Jocanta Fairtresses on a large, fur-covered bed with an older woman and a younger man. All were naked, all were asleep.

Adler and the Warriors from the Two Hundred bound and gagged them before they were fully awake. They tied the chief's friends to the bed and the chief herself to a chair. She struggled and glared hatred.

Lowa gripped her by her lovely locks and rested the sword blade on her throat. "Jocanta, you promised me two hundred and fifty men and women, armed and armoured. Tomorrow we leave. If three hundred – yes, three hundred – good Haxmite men and women have not reported to me at Maidun by the next full moon, fully equipped, then I will return, burn your fort and slaughter your tribe – man, woman, child and sheep. Nod if you understand and agree."

Jocanta nodded. "Good. And because I don't want you to think I'm all kindness . . ."

Lowa pulled the hank of hair tight and sliced through its roots with her sword. She repeated the manoeuvre until there was a carpet of golden hair on the floor and only a scrub of short, uneven stubble on Jocanta Fairtresses' outraged head.

Chapter 14

Felix stood in the meadow. Only pillars of stone remained of the bridge, jutting from the heaving, muddy water like charred bones. The river was five hundred paces from bank to bank, fully in spate with logs and whole trees bobbing along briskly on filthy mountain snowmelt. They would not be swimming across.

Standing next to him, half his height again, was Gub, leader of the Maximen. Felix had originally called them Herculeses and Nymphs, but Caesar has said he disliked such fey Greek appellations, and renamed the giants Maximen and the speedy ones Celermen. Felix thought those names were exceedingly boring, but he didn't care enough to argue. He hadn't argued with Caesar yet and, if he did, it would be about something that mattered. "Pick your battles" was one of the very few things he remembered his father telling him.

"Yus, Suh, four Celerman kill, all by same. Big dark man, sexy woman and archer woman," said the Maximan, finally, in answer to Felix's question about who'd killed the four Celermen.

"How can you know who killed them? If you were there, why didn't you kill their killers?"

"Duh?"

"Oh, for Jupiter's sake," said Felix, stamping his little feet. The magic that had increased his Maximen's size, strength and speed had unfortunately decreased their intellect. Felix guessed that the growth of their skulls had squashed their brains. The thicker the bone, the thicker the man, it seemed.

"Jupiter's?" said the Maximan, the deep flesh on his meaty brow coalescing in confusion.

"Forget Jupiter. This dark man – in what way was he dark?"

"Guh?"

"Dark man. Dark clothes, dark hair or dark skin?"

"Dark clothes."

"Ah."

"And dark hair. Dark skin, too."

"I see. And did the sexy woman have a mace and a sword?"

"Little mace. Little knife."

"And the archer, was she a blonde-haired woman?"

"She had hair."

"Blonde?"

"Guh?"

"Never mind. Where did they go, these three?"

Gub looked over to where the bridge had been, his face a picture of gormlessness. "Don't know. Was different before." He looked back to Felix. The druid swore he could see through Gub's dark eyes right to the back of his skull.

"OK. Now get back to the others."

"Guh?"

"Back. Home! Find Kelter and send him to me."

"Guh?"

"Send. Kelter. The. Celerman. To. Me."

"Gub."

The Maximan waddled away, back to the nest or whatever one wanted to call the sordid filth holes that the giants had dug themselves amid the corpses and dereliction of the Ootipeat and Tengoterry camp. The Maximen were little more than the basest animals, until they started killing, when they became beautiful, marvellous acrobats. The

Celermen also killed wonderfully well, but if anything their intelligence had been increased by their metamorphosis. It was odd, because Felix applied the same dark magic process to produce both Celermen and Maximen. He never knew which he was going to get until it was done. Usually he got a corpse. Sometimes he produced one of his mutants. So far he had forty Celermen and twenty Maximen. Caesar had banned him from making any more, and so he wouldn't for now. It was another battle he wasn't going to pick, not yet.

Initially he'd found the Celermen better company. You could have a conversation with a Celerman. But now he preferred the Maximen. Felix had never much enjoyed conversation and the big ones were easier to control.

He looked across the river. So, Chamanca and Atlas were still around. It was a shame his troops hadn't caught them. Caesar would have rewarded him well for killing them after all the trouble they'd caused. By the skill it would have taken to shoot three Celermen, the archer surely had to be Lowa. That was interesting. He'd assumed that Chamanca and Atlas were working as mercenaries with the Gauls and the Germans, but if Lowa was with them it seemed like they were indeed a British effort to hamper the Roman advance. Lowa would have been a good kill, too . . . No matter, he thought, all three would be dead soon enough.

"Pondering your successes?"

Felix span round. It was Kelter, chief Celerman.

"Hello, boss," he said, his accent thick Sicilian. "What's next?" He'd stripped to the waist and removed his hood. Kelter had been a beautiful man once, with prime skin, high cheekbones, thick, dark hair and a lean, muscled body. Unfortunately, the magic that gave the Celermen speed also caused their hair to wither and fall out, and blazing red pustules constantly surfaced all over their heads, each blooming, yellowing and erupting in a few hours. The pus-spouting spots were why Felix made them wear hoods.

From the neck down, they were hairless but unblemished, their torsos and limbs not far from perfect in the druid's eyes.

"Next," said Felix, letting his eyes stray over Kelter's pectoral and abdominal muscles then pretending that he'd looked down because he'd seen something interesting on the ground, "we rebuild the bridge, cross it and kill everything we find: man, woman, child, dog, cat, bird – everything. The Germans will learn that Gaul is Roman territory. They will never cross the Rhenus again. When we've killed all we can find, we cross back and destroy our bridge."

"There are many injured Germans in the camp," smiled Kelter. "We can use their energy to build this bridge."

"Good, yes. Have the Maximen gather building materials from the smashed camp – large stones, long planks of wood, rope and pottery – and bring them here."

"Pottery?"

"To be ground and mixed with limestone for cement that will set underwater. I'll have engineers deliver the limestone and requisite tools and show you how to make it. Have the other Celermen corral the German survivors, and appoint three in rotation to guard them from the Maximen. Keep four hundred Germans alive to power the bridge building. The rest you can kill. Got it?"

"I have it."

"Set it in motion then, quickly."

Chapter 15

Ragnall walked through the thriving industry of an itinerant Roman army making camp, glad that he was spared the donkey work of digging ditches and pitching tents every night. The centurions and legionaries did all that. Ragnall was officially a legate now, one of Caesar's inner circle, upgraded from clerk. Nobody had told him what his new role was, but it seemed that he was expected to follow the army, hang around the other legates, keep quiet and simply be a British king in waiting. So he spent his waking hours marvelling at Roman efficiency and watching the scenery change as they marched across the land. It was enough to keep him busy.

Now he'd been summoned to Caesar's tent, however, and was worried that he might be called upon to do something dangerous like going on another envoy mission. Surely Caesar wasn't going to send him to Britain? Carden and Atlas had seen him acting as Roman envoy to King Ariovistus. If he went back to Maidun, who knew what they'd do to him?

As usual, Caesar was dictating his diary when Ragnall arrived: "So Caesar pursued the treacherous Germans to the Rhenus where he found that the bulk of their army had escaped by boat. His advisers suggested that he and his army cross in the same manner. However, travelling by boat is beneath Caesar's dignity, so he ordered that a bridge be built. In ten days, Roman engineers and legionaries built a strong bridge across the Rhenus, forty feet wide and fifteen hundred feet long. Caesar crossed and spent eighteen days ravaging the land to discourage further German incursion . . ."

Caesar continued. Ragnall only half listened, but his ears pricked up when Caesar began describing some of the creatures that they'd found on the other side of the Rhenus. The men, he said, had reported seeing unicorns, and elk with no knees that ran along straight-legged and rested by leaning on trees. These latter creatures, the general said, his men had captured by half sawing through trees so that they broke when the elk leant on them.

These made-up tales of bizarre creatures perplexed Ragnall for a while, then he realised what the general was doing. If the rumour of a monstrous legion was the only tall story that the chattering citizens of Rome heard then they might give it some credence. If the tale of monsters was just one more unbelievable story in the fountain of nonsense spouting from fantasist legionaries in Gaul, nobody would believe it for a moment.

When he'd finished making up animals and creating the most Rome-palatable tale of the Usipetes' and Tencteri's destruction, Caesar sent his scribes away and turned to Ragnall.

"Stay for wine, king of the Britons. Tell Caesar more about your land."

The slaves poured two goblets and Caesar shooed them away, ordering them to leave the amphora. Ragnall and the general sat in collapsible chairs facing each other across a small table, in front of the screens painted with pictures of the battle of Aquae Sextiae, in which Caesar's uncle Marius had killed a hundred thousand barbarians – far fewer than Caesar's own campaign had killed over the previous two years.

Ragnall told him about the Island of Angels, Drustan, his adventures on the floating island, his love affair with Lowa, the death of Zadar and more. All the while Caesar kept refilling Ragnall's goblet, but never his own. Ragnall, excited to be alone with the great leader and to be telling his own story, drank heartily.

Halfway through the fifth or possibly the sixth goblet, Ragnall found himself saying: "So these rumours about Felix's dark legion . . . they're true, right? They attacked the Germans?"

Caesar regarded the younger man without blinking. His dark, sparkling eyes seemed to look through Ragnall's and into his mind and the young man shifted uncomfortably, even half drunk as he was. Finally the general said:

"Felix does command something like a legion, and, yes, it did rout the Usipete and Tencteri forces. Caesar has judged that its existence should be kept a secret from Rome, and, as far as possible, the rest of the army. So you will tell nobody about it, and discuss it with nobody, even if you think that they also know about it."

"Right," said Ragnall, thinking that was that, and reckoning it unwise to probe further, but Caesar continued.

"The legion has only two companies, each smaller than a century but larger than a contubernium. One is made of large, powerful men whom we call the Maximen. The other is comprised of men who are blessed with the speed of Mercury – the Celermen. With their combined talents, despite their meagre number, they could defeat any army on earth – including any Roman one."

"Where are they from?"

Caesar sat back, stretched out his legs, made a pyramid of his fingers and looked down his bony nose as if deciding whether to say more. Torchlight glinted in the remainder of the general's silver hair and shone off his freshly shaven shins. Finally, he leant forward. "The short answer, Ragnall, is that Caesar does not know. Neither does Felix understand the mechanisms that have created his little army. The longer answer is that when Crassus defeated Spartacus, he gave

Felix a multitude of captured rebel slaves. Most of these, six thousand men, Felix had Crassus crucify in a line that stretched shore to shore across Italy. Felix used the *energy* – for want of a better word – released by the death of these men to bring about a metamorphosis in some of the remaining captives. Almost all of them died in the process, but a few became larger and stronger. A few more became quicker. Now, they both still feed from death. Killing gives them their power."

"How . . .?"

"Only the gods know."

"And you have no worries about—"

"Of course there must be concern about their utilisation. It is done sparingly, only to save Roman life."

"And when they can operate secretly, out of sight of anyone who might get word of them back to Rome?"

Caesar breathed in sharply through his nose and Ragnall thought he had gone too far, but the general said: "Caesar has sent them into battle three times. Once to obliterate Ariovistus' cavalry when it threatened to starve his army. Once to clear the Nervee ambush from the forest. And once. Before Caesar leads the legions to Britain, he needs to neutralise the German threat to his Gaulish territories. Caesar could use his legions to achieve this, but it would take a year, perhaps two, and he needs to be in Britain this year. After today's battle with the Usipetes and Tencteri, and the harrying of the Germans which Felix's legion will now carry out, Caesar need fear no interference from the east."

"What did Felix's legion do? What will they do?"

"Do not trouble with the means, only the outcome. Now, return to your tent and sleep. Tomorrow the army will head west, towards your throne."

Ragnall felt a rush of excitement – he was going to be a king! He nodded, stood, and thanked the general for the wine. He left the headquarters and walked away between the rows of tents, step jaunty and arms swinging. He looked about, assessing his new allies – his new tribesmen.

A British army camp would have been full of men and woman drinking, shouting stories at each other, dancing and otherwise preparing for the long day ahead in the most idiotic way possible. The Roman camp, in anticipation of the morrow's march, was silent, other than for the odd whinnies from horses and snorts from snorers.

The Roman way was *so much* better and Britain would benefit from it to an immeasurable degree. And if Caesar used Felix's dark magic troops to conquer Britain? If this unstoppable host was unleashed against Lowa and her army . . .? Well, that was all the better. Fewer Romans would be killed, as Caesar had pointed out, and surely Britain would capitulate and surrender the moment they saw what the dark legion could do, so fewer Britons would be killed as well?

Chapter 16

Lowa rode back over the rise and there was Maidun Castle, shining like a white beacon fire from a sea of mud. They'd managed to keep grass from growing on the walls while she was away, which was a good sign. Hopefully everything else would be in similarly good order.

Riding next to her was Mal Fletcher, then came the Two Hundred followed by three thousand men and women, mostly on foot. After two moons travelling around Britain, Lowa had hoped for at least twice the amount of infantry recruits. She now had around ten thousand foot soldiers in total. According to Atlas and the others' previous reconnaissance, the Romans could send double that, possibly more. She had a much smaller number of chariots and cavalry as well as the infantry, but the Romans would have cavalry, too, and in a full-force, pitched battle on open ground – the kind the Romans would strive to make her fight and she might not be able to avoid – infantry numbers would be the most important factor. Unless Felix's dark legion slaughtered all the Britons before they so much as clashed swords with a legionary, that was, as it had done to the Nervee in the woods. She wished she had more information. Knowing next to nothing, as she did, she couldn't plan counter-measures, other than encouraging and bullying her soldiers until they became tough and skilled enough to fight anything. That, and hope that reports of the demons were exaggerated.

Monsters aside, Rome's legions were professional soldiers, rigorously trained for years, with several seasons of battle experience. A great deal of Lowa's force were pressed farmers, craftsmen and layabouts, many of whom were more likely to trip over and spear themselves to death than kill an enemy. Still, they had to try.

She left Mal and others to billet the new recruits – there were plenty of spare tents after the previous year's battle at Frogshold – and headed up to the castle, the eyrie and little Dug. She hadn't expected to miss her son while she was on the road, and she'd been right; she hadn't much. When she'd left, he'd been screaming, snotty and shit-smelling and she'd been glad to hand him over to Keelin. On the road she had sometimes found herself picturing his small face smiling or sleeping, or imagining his tiny fingers encircling one of her own, but most of the time she'd been too exhausted by the time she went to bed for such imaginative frivolities, and too busy during the day to consider anything but immediate business.

The Haxmites had been the most obstructive, but, by Bel, what a bunch of whingers the rulers of the British tribes had proven to be. You'd have thought the threat of a conquering horde coming to kill or enslave them all was reason enough to give as many people as possible for her army, but, no, she'd heard tales of how palisades needed rebuilding, religious rituals needed to be observed, ponds needed draining – countless excuses not to send every single adult south and learn the skills they'd need to fight the invaders. It had taken her every ounce of patience and persuasion to garner even the meagre, inadequate number that she had.

Keelin was waiting inside the main gate, baby on one arm. The child saw his mother, stuck his whole fist in his mouth and ducked his head into Keelin's capacious chest.

"Hello, Keelin, hello, Dug," said Lowa, wondering if babies were meant to be able to fit their fists in their mouths.

Dug waggled a saliva-dripping hand at her, said, "Ba! Ba! Ba!" and smiled. The change since she'd last seen him was startling. He was enormous. His comically round head was nearly as large as Keelin's. He'd been more or less bald and eyebrow-free when she left, but now a thick fuzz of blond-brown hair had overrun his scalp and pale arcs heralded the growth of eyebrows. He raised one of these proto-brows at her quizzically, just as his father had done. Six moons old. He didn't look like a baby any more, he looked like a little boy – a big-eyed, clear-skinned little Dug. Lowa felt her breath catch and tears press.

"Do you want to hold him?"

Lowa nodded and Keelin held him out. The fat little boy's face purpled instantly, his arms flailed and he screamed as if his legs were being torn from his body. The queen retracted her hands. Keelin hugged him into her bosom.

"It's because he's late for his sleep," she said, in the pause while Dug was sucking in breath to scream again. "I was just putting him down" – Dug wailed and Keelin paused – "when I saw you coming. I'll take him back now. He'll be better after his morning nap."

She walked away, clutching Dug. The baby quietened, looked over Keelin's shoulder with tear-filled eyes, saw Lowa and began to wail again. Lowa watched them go.

"He looks a lot like Dug," said Atlas. Lowa snapped round. Atlas and Chamanca nodded greetings. She'd been so focused on her baby that she hadn't seen them.

"Send a shout, alert the tribes," said Lowa, "a baby looks like his father."

"Don't worry about him crying like that when he saw you," said Chamanca. "Babies do that with new people. He was the same with us yesterday."

"When did you get back?" said Lowa, thinking *I am not a new person.*

"Yesterday."

"Where's Spring?" Lowa suddenly feared the worst.

"Dug's farm," said Chamanca. "She said there were dogs to check and chickens to feed, but really she blames you for Dug's death and seeks to avoid you."

"She told you this?"

"No, but I could tell."

"OK, thanks for letting me know . . . And have you stopped Caesar's armies? Should I send all my new recruits home?"

"Not just yet," said Chamanca. "We have some shit news, some really shit news, and some even shittier news."

"I see. You'd better come back to the eyrie and tell me all."

The day was fine so they sat on the grassy expanse outside her hut. Atlas and Chamanca took turns to tell her about the Ironmen and the Leathermen. They were sitting so that their knees touched, and Lowa had noticed immediately that there was a change in them. Before, they'd both been about the most individual people Lowa had met; now they moved and acted like a couple, each constantly aware of the other. So they'd got it on, she thought, stifling a sting of jealousy that Dug had died and Atlas had survived.

They told her about being captured, the German massacre, their escape, the inefficacy of the famous Tengoterry cavalry against the demons, then the astonishing rate at which the Roman super-soldiers had built a bridge forty paces across and five hundred long. Lowa asked why they hadn't harried the crossing's construction.

"We did," said Chamanca. "Spring shot at them. It had no effect on the big ones. The little ones dodged her arrows – they are faster even than me – then they found a couple of boats and some shields, at which point we decided it was best to . . ."

"Live so we could report back," filled in Atlas.

"Yes. We were lucky to make it home," said Chamanca. "Without Spring's bow the big black one and I would have been killed. She took down three Leathermen. Atlas and I killed one between us."

"Or, put another way," said Atlas, "Chamanca killed none and I killed one."

Chamanca scowled, Atlas smiled and Lowa felt a surprising flush of pride for Spring's prowess and the endless hours of longbow training that the two of them had endured. She resolved to head to Dug's farm at the first possible opportunity and sort out Spring's silliness. The girl was crazy to blame her for Dug's death when she would have done anything to prevent it.

"And after that?" she asked, dragging herself back into the role of a queen planning a war.

"Sensibly, the Germans put as many miles as they could between themselves and the Rhenus," said Atlas. "They had a plan to make a stand a few hundred miles east, but we don't know if Felix's monsters pursued them that far because we travelled west and crossed back over the river. There we found the Roman army mobilising, about to head this way. So we came home to warn you. We had some setbacks and two or three minor adventures, but nothing relevant to report. Most of Gaul is cowed and surrendered to the foe—"

"But some north-western tribes are still holding out against the invaders," Chamanca interrupted, "running from the marshes, poking the Romans and running back into the marshes. It is not a gallant way of fighting, but it is effective, and it means that the Romans will be able to send fewer troops over here than they planned."

"Although," continued Atlas, "it will not delay the enemy for long, and I wouldn't be surprised if some Gaulish tribes actually joined the Roman invasion. Of course, most importantly of all, the number of legionaries or any ancillary forces becomes irrelevant when we consider Felix's monsters. I cannot see a way to defeat them. To avoid our own extinction, I suggest we cede this land to the invader and relocate west to Eroo, south to Africa or perhaps further west, across the great sea."

Lowa nodded, but discarded his council. There would be no retreat.

"How many Romans will cross the Channel – standard humans, not demons?"

"Impossible to tell how many he'll bring across. Maybe two legions, maybe four," said Atlas.

"So maybe twenty thousand legionaries." Lowa sucked air over her teeth.

"Plus slingers, archers and cavalry."

"Yes."

"And of course you cannot ignore the demons. Retreat is an option that should not be dismissed."

It already had been, but Lowa didn't want to argue further.

"I will consider our moves."

She sent for Mal, Adler, Elann Nancarrow the weaponsmith and Maggot the druid.

While they were waiting, Keelin appeared with Dug, fresh from his nap. When he spotted his mother, the baby screamed like a happy seagull then chirruped merrily, all the while wiggling his fingers towards her and kicking his legs. She took him from Keelin and he cackled throatily as if this development was the funniest, most all-consumingly joyous thing that could possibly have happened.

"He does that finger waggling thing when he sees horses and running water, which are his favourite things," said Keelin, "but I've never seen him react like that to a person."

"I'm flattered," said Lowa, holding the cheery boy at arm's length. He was shaking with chuckles, his big, shining brown eyes staring into hers. Keelin had dressed him in a hooded cotton suit but his limbs stuck out, bracelet and anklet-like fat folds where podgy arms and legs met hands and feet.

She played with the baby until Elann and Maggot arrived. She found that he had one of two reactions to everything. Anything that he could reach was jammed into his mouth and anything out of his reach was hilarious. At one point he grabbed her by the ear and clamped his lips around her nose, which was a little disgusting, but she found herself laughing along with him and even Chamanca chuckled. The baby's unfettered happiness was infectious and she couldn't remember the last time she'd laughed so freely, or in fact if she ever had. She wondered from where the child had inherited his cheeriness. Certainly not from her.

Even Elann cracked half an awkward smile when Dug greeted her with a happy shout. Childbirth might be an absolute bastard, thought Lowa, but the gods of creation had done a better job with babies. She handed him back to Keelin reluctantly. He stared at her over the girl's shoulder as she took him away, bursting into tears after a dozen paces, which was satisfying.

"Right," said Lowa, breathing out. "I'll go first, then Mal, Adler, Elann and Maggot – in that order – tell Chamanca and Atlas what we've done so far to prepare for the Romans. Then Chamanca and Atlas will tell us what they've seen and we'll discuss how the new information changes our plans."

Part Two

Britain and Gaul
Late summer 55 BC

Chapter 1

Late one evening towards the end of the Roman month of August, Julius Caesar set sail for Britain with almost ten thousand legionaries from the Tenth and Seventh legions, plus two thousand auxiliary slingers and archers from Crete and the Balearic Islands.

Ragnall stood at the bow of Caesar's ship, the first to leave the broad Gaulish beach, listening to the creak of oars, looking at the golden light of the setting sun dancing on the wavelets. Rolling in their wake came eleven more warships like the one he was on, then eighty troop transport ships, then a swarm of boats crewed by merchants and adventurers eager for the glut of slaves and booty that flowed wherever Caesar went. Similarly minded seagulls swirled overhead, eager for the surfeit of human carrion that the great general had never failed to provide.

Ahead, the usually white cliffs of Britain were blood-red in the sunset. Home. Finally, after more than five years of exile, he was going home. Home is the true destination of all journeys, a drunken philosopher had told him once and now he could see his point. The moment he'd boarded that boat with Drustan all those years before and left Britain for Rome, he'd been at the beginning of a loop that ended where it started. Finally that loop was almost closed, and he was a returning king! He did not expect an affectionate reception, in fact the opposite, but they'd learn. In a few years the Britons would live in paved cities, with luxurious bathhouses and aqueducts bringing clean water into the middle

of thriving marketplaces that didn't reek of shit. Then they'd
thank him. King Ragnall, the man who bathed Britain in
clean water and the bright light of civilisation. He would
be remembered for ever in stories and statues all over the
land. He'd have to take a wife, of course. Might he forgive
Lowa? In a way it was her he had to thank for his current
position. He would see. Whatever he decided, he couldn't
wait to see her face when she saw him riding tall at the
head of the Roman army.

The furtive chat among the legates and other high rankers
was that Caesar was not taking enough troops because he
had only two legions, the rest having been left behind to
protect their conquered lands against the few remaining
rebellious Gaulish tribes. They didn't know what Ragnall
knew. To the south there was another ship heading for Britain
with a secret cargo that might ensure Britain's surrender
without any legionaries having to so much as hurl a pilum.

Night came, finally, and Felix led his legion from the trees
– twenty Maximen, thirty-six Celermen and a captive for
each of them. The single ship's tender could take only one
of the armoured giants at a time, so ferrying them aboard
took a frustrating age. Loading the Gaulish captives, carried
as strengthening fodder for the landing in Britain, was as
difficult, since they were chained three together by iron
poles and neck loops. He could have undone their shackles,
but they might have escaped. He could have killed some of
them to give his Maximen the strength to haul the ship
onto the beach and lift it off again, but he had only captives
enough to fuel his legion for the landing in Britain. So he
had to be patient. It was excruciating. As the first glow of
the false dawn began to lighten the sky, almost half the
Ironmen were still waiting to board. They'd been ordered
to leave in darkness and they were late. Caesar was not
going to be happy, although it was entirely his fault.

Felix had assumed they were going embark from a port, and that his legion would simply walk along a reinforced gangplank onto the ship. Mars knew that there were enough deserted ports around since they'd killed most of the Fenn-Nodens. But no, Caesar was so paranoid about word of the legion getting back to Rome that he'd insisted they set sail from a deserted cove. As if some Gaulish pleb was going to see them and go running back to the Senate! As if they'd believe him if he did!

At least, thought Felix, he'd learnt a lesson. He resolved that from then on he'd work out the largest number of captives he'd need to fuel his legion's missions, then double it. Triple it even.

A much greater consolation was that soon he'd have Spring's magic and he'd no longer need to heed Caesar's demands. Maybe by the time the sun set that night! Probably not that quickly, but it wouldn't take him long to find her . . . He'd make do as king of Britain first, where he'd produce more legions. He rubbed his hands together and grinned, imagining the troops that might be created by combining the girl's magic with his own.

The day before a centurion had told him, with a straight face, that they were in fact invading Britain to restore the rightful king – Ragnall! It amused Felix that Ragnall thought he might become king, that Caesar felt the need for societally acceptable excuses to invade these shithole territories like Britain and Gaul, but most of all it amused him that everybody – the general included – seemed to believe these excuses as soon as they'd been invented. Felix had thought the delusion was an act at first, but now he was pretty sure that Caesar was plain insane, so full of his own success and glory that he'd become disconnected from reality. Felix was very much looking forward to reintroducing him to it. When he took over, he'd keep Rome's hero alive for a year or so and humiliate him every day. Hades would thank Felix for taking Caesar a rung or two down the ladder of self-worship before he sent the conqueror to the Underworld. Ragnall he'd kill straight away. He'd never liked the British boy. Actually, he'd take a long while to kill him, but he'd *start* straight away.

His daydreaming was interrupted by a booming splash as a Maximan fell over while trying to climb into the tender. The mighty man lay in the shallows, face down, arms flapping. They really were useless without a recent kill. A few of his comrades lumbered over to help him. Felix hoped that the whole lot didn't end up drowning themselves.

Walfdan found the track again and stole towards the headland and the next bay along from the demons, where Maggot was waiting in the little sailing boat.

Something in the dark bushes rustled loudly and the Gaulish druid jumped, stifling a cry. It was nothing, a rabbit or some other scurrying creature. He tiptoed on, sweating and light-headed, turning every few paces. Every shadow in the nebulous twilight looked like a Roman monster.

He was not a brave man. He'd suspected that espionage would terrify him and he'd been right. It had been impossible to disagree with Atlas' suggestion that he spy on the Romans in Gaul, however, because being a coward was not argument enough and because the sharp-witted African had been right. Walfdan was a Gaul, he knew the country and its people and he'd been sailing since he could walk, so he was best suited for finding out everything he could about the invasion force and getting back to Britain ahead of it. Thankfully the British druid, Maggot, had offered to go with him, so he hadn't been alone when they crossed the Channel, then walked around the ports and discovered how many Romans were sailing and when. Felix's dark legion had been harder to find, but they'd followed the trail of deserted, blood-spattered villages and eventually narrowed down the location to one bay. At that point Maggot had said that Walfdan had better creep up on his own and see how many they were while he waited in the boat, since the jangling of his jewellery might give them away.

Squatting alone in a bush at the edge of the beach and counting the dark druid's demons had been the most frightening thing Walfdan had ever done. He'd always understood that the gods lent courage to people in preposterously dangerous situations. Apparently the gods were busy elsewhere that evening and Walfdan had found himself shaking like a chilly child, his guts heaving and threatening a impromptu evacuation. When he'd become briefly convinced that a Leatherman had spotted him, he'd nearly been sick.

So he was glad to be away and headed for the relative safety of Maggot and a small boat, but he would be a lot happier once they were safely out to sea.

Watching the inept attempts to right the giant, a feeling that he was being spied on crept up Felix's spine. He turned and saw Gub, leader of the Ironmen, standing nearby and staring at him, mouth open. Felix *hated* being stared at.

"Go away!" he commanded.

Gub looked around at the sea, the rocks, the beach and the trees, as if seeking somewhere to go. Not finding anywhere, he turned back to Felix and resumed his gormless vigil.

"Oh, just go up the path into the woods and see if you can find any wild boar or Gauls spying on us or something. Anything! Just go away and stop staring at me!"

"Sure thing!"

The huge man jogged away, armour clanging. Felix watched him go, hoping he'd have the nous to come back in time to get on the ship.

*   *   *

A sound made Walfdan turn. Just another rabbit, surely? But, no, this time it was really one of the huge demons – an Ironman – walking along the track towards him, its shoulders touching the trees on both sides. The druid was almost relieved after all the suspense. Finally, here was death and he could have a rest.

"Come here," said the beast in Latin.

"I will not," he stammered in Gaulish, staggering back on jelly legs.

The demon lifted its sword, a slice of iron not much shorter than Walfdan's boat.

The elderly druid spun round and pounded away along the track faster, he reckoned, than anyone his age had ever run before or would again. He'd seen the demons' speed and was sure he wouldn't get away, but by Toutatis he was going to give it a go. He expected a huge hand on his shoulder at any moment or a heavy metal blade through his neck, but he crested the top of the slope and pelted on, down the other side of the headland. Still not looking back, he tore along like a hare who's woken up and realised that the insufferably smug tortoise is miles ahead.

He left the road, crashed through the trees, tumbled down a bank and into the boat.

"Hello!" said Maggot.

"Demon . . . coming . . ."

"I see." Maggot shoved off with a foot, hoisted the sail in a moment and they were away, out onto the water just as the sun peeked over the horizon.

Walfdan looked over the stern. There was no sign of pursuit. He panted hard, then realised he was going to faint. He tried to calm his breathing but that made him feel fainter. The world swung in woozy circles. He'd run too fast. He wondered if his heart was about to give up. The irony of being killed by his flight from death pleased him. Then he wondered if that was, indeed, ironic. He'd never quite understood exactly what irony was, and secretly suspected that nobody else ever had either.

Maggot slapped him on the back. "Stay alive there! Or at least tell me how many demons there were before you die."

The slap seemed to help. Walfdan told Maggot what he'd seen, as the boat glided north-west towards Britain on a rolling run, the wind dead astern.

"That many, huh, and all in the one ship?"

"Indeed."

"Hmmm." Maggot pushed the tiller away from himself and the boat swung north-east. He pulled the sail to catch the perpendicular wind and the boat heeled over.

"What are you up to?" asked Walfdan, scrambling to join Maggot on the starboard gunwale and trim the dinghy. "The demon ship will set sail soon. On this course we're headed right for them. They'll surely see us."

The Briton ignored him.

"Maggot! You're taking us straight towards the monsters!"

Maggot winked, his grin brilliant in the morning sun.

Chapter 2

"They are not racing," said Chamanca, swinging off her horse.

"They're not," answered Lowa. The Roman fleet had been in sight since the middle of the night. Standing on the cliff top as the sun rose, you'd swear the mass of ships wasn't moving. Some had oars which they were hardly using, but most were sailing leadenly on the light south-easterly puff.

Chamanca nodded at the armada. "Atlas reckons it's two legions."

That tallied with what Lowa had heard from merchants and fishers. She'd know a more exact composition when Walfdan and Maggot returned.

"Ten thousand legionaries," she said. From this distance, the ships looked tiny and it was hard to imagine that they contained so many people.

"Same as we have," said Chamanca nodding, "but of course they'll have archers and slingers on top of that, cavalry, too, I should think, so they'll probably outnumber us.'

"Yes, and of course they'll have an unknown amount of powerful monsters, possibly powered by dark magic."

"True. But they don't have a Chamanca!"

"Thank Danu for her great mercies." Lowa regarded the grinning Iberian. She remembered when Chamanca had joined Zadar's army, soon after Lowa herself. So much had changed since then, but Chamanca looked the same. She still filed her teeth into points, still wore the same leather shorts and iron chest piece that seemed to expose more skin than they covered, and still made heads turn and jaws drop whenever she passed. Her flesh was as lean and firm as it had ever been, untroubled by a wrinkle or the tiniest patch of bobbled fat . . . Chamanca had been a good ten years older than Lowa when they'd met, but now she looked the same age. Perhaps a blood diet was good for the skin? Or perhaps there was something more?

"We still got no magic then?" asked Chamanca.

"Not . . . that I know of. Mal went to see Spring and she swears she remains magic free."

"Mal went to see her?"

"Yes."

"Not you?"

"I had a war to prepare."

"Sure you did."

"She could have come to me."

"She could have done."

Lowa sighed. "Chamanca, I have not had the time to repair the wounded feelings of a sulky child who blames me for something I didn't do. If she loved Dug so much that she's going to be this irrational about his death, she should at least have come to greet his child."

"Unless she hates the baby's mother so much—"

"Chamanca."

"Lowa?"

The Iberian didn't seem to have grasped to any degree that Lowa was her queen. Her other leaders spoke to her freely, interrupted her even, but she still felt that they respected her position. Chamanca's lack of deference was all-encompassing. Lowa usually didn't mind – the opposite in fact. Most times, it was refreshing to have someone she could talk to as an equal. But this wasn't one of those times. "If Spring wants to see me to discuss whose fault it was that Dug died – or who fired the fucking arrow into his head for that matter, or who knew in advance it was going to happen – then she is welcome. I am not going to chase after her for the joy of being accused of killing the man I loved."

"Spring is as skilled as you with the bow and will be nearly as useful as me in the battle to come, but she is young, so she is stubborn. I saw her yesterday. She is here, with the light chariots. You should visit her."

Lowa looked along the scorpions, hunched in a row a few paces back from the cliff edge, ready to shoot their giant bolts at the Roman ships. Mal, the scorpion commander, was walking towards her and the Iberian, inspecting his line. His hair and beard, she noticed, were freshly trimmed. She ran a hand through her own, probably wild, blonde hair, thinking that it was funny what people considered important on the day before a fight. She looked out over the approaching armada. It seemed larger now that the sun was up, or perhaps it was simply closer. Lowa nodded towards the ships. "You're right. I have nothing better to do today than to seek out a stroppy child and bang my head against her unshakeable bullshit. Where did you say she was? I'll go right now. If you could just stay here and ask the Romans to wait?"

The Iberian smiled, leapt onto her horse and galloped away.

"You all right?" asked Mal, reaching her at the end of his scorpion inspection.

"Never better," said Lowa.

"I don't want to tempt fate but, touch wood," Mal tapped his head and pointed out to sea, "it looks like our visitors might oblige and come right up under the cliff."

The Roman invasion had been heading straight for them ever since it had appeared and showed no signs of deviating. If the course was held, the vulnerable wooden fleet would be in range of the scorpions' heavy bolts well before it landed, and the legionaries would have to wade ashore on to a narrow strip of beach underneath a high cliff. The Maidunites had long, iron-tipped poles, chocks and heavy mallets ready to send a large part of said cliff down on to them.

"He's not going to land here. He can't have defeated all of Gaul and half of Germany in two years if he does things like that."

"True, but you never know." Mal tapped his head again. "He's never invaded by sea before."

"It is just possible that he's an idiot," Lowa conceded. "So make sure you keep your people back from the edge, and shoot only when they're within archers' range." She nodded at the archers massed inland, downhill from the scorpions, waiting for the order to run up and send a rain of iron onto the Romans below. There were well over a thousand of them, from the cavalry and the light and heavy chariots, their mounts and vehicles left on the road at the bottom of the hill. She wondered if Spring was with them. "If they do change course, I don't want it to be because some idiot shot his bolt early. And, of course, if they change course and they're in scorpion range but not archer range, see how many you can sink."

"Don't worry," said Mal. "My crews know what they're doing and so I."

Lowa nodded, mounted and rode away. Fully aware that she'd told Chamanca she didn't have time for anything but commanding her troops, she decided to go and see her son. The Romans were still half a day away at least, she had shouters all along the coast ready to tell her if anything changed, she'd been preparing for this for years and everything that could be in place was in place, so there was little else she could do. If Caesar turned north, as she suspected he would, and made a sensible landfall, it was

possible that she'd be leading an army into battle before the
end of the day. It wasn't what she planned, but planning
and warfare did not often go hand in hand. And, if she did
ride into battle and these demons were half as effective as
she'd been told, chances were she wouldn't ride out again.

And if she was going to die later, she wanted to see her
son first.

Ragnall yawned. By Jupiter and Bel, the crossing was a
dreary drag. The warships could have rowed to Britain
and back ten times by now, but they were held back by
the turgid progress of the overladen sailing boats. They
looked to Ragnall like a fleet of obese men floating on
their backs and holding up handkerchiefs, hoping to be
blown to lunch. At times he was sure they were going
backwards. Why hadn't Caesar learnt from the battle
against the Veneti that sailing boats were useless? Gaul
was shrinking behind them and up ahead the white cliffs
of Britain *were* growing, but only at the pace of a trodden-on
snail making for cover.

Caesar, Labienus, other generals and a couple of top legates
were at the stern of the boat, conversing importantly. Ragnall
wandered back to listen in. Everybody but Caesar was saying,
couched in polite terms and flattery, that their current course
was crazy. Judging by similar cliffs in Gaul, there would
be only a narrow beach at its foot, if the enormous tides
that plagued this part of the world had left a beach at all.
Moreover, any landing would be overlooked by the cliff,
from which any amount of missiles might be hurled.
Merchants spoke of a network of channels and beaches to
the north. It was there, said Labienus, that they should be
heading.

Ragnall could tell, however, that Caesar was frustrated
by the glacially slow pace of the sailing transports and
focused solely on getting to Britain as fast as possible. He

said that the men did not like being afloat, that most of the boats had enough supplies only for the half-day that they'd expected the crossing to take and that already the hindmost ships were sailing through clumps of bobbing turds from the foremost. It was undignified. Caesar's legionaries should not sail slowly through shit. The sooner they landed, the better. If there was no beach, they could sail along the coast until they found one. The Britons had no idea they were coming. The only missiles they'd face, said the general, might be the odd stone from a shepherd boy's sling.

"But Caesar," said Labienus, "they *do* know that we're coming and I am certain that they are watching us right now. We have hardly made our preparations in secret and the merchants—"

"We keep THIS COURSE!" shouted the general, face flushing and knuckles whitening. Nothing fazed Caesar, so what was this? Was he afraid of water? He'd said once that boats were beneath his dignity. Was he in fact scared of them? It was the only reason Ragnall could think of to make him behave like this.

Labienus spotted Ragnall eyeing the general and shot him an unequivocal "piss off" look.

So Ragnall pissed off back to the bow of the ship to plan his first couple of years of kingship. He'd reinstate the slavery that Lowa had banned. He understood the starry-eyed arguments disagreeing with human bondage, but the point that the well-meaning but naïve idealists missed was that everyone benefited from slavery. Without slavery, the stupid, uninspired and low-born would still have to work the land and fight in armies in exchange for food and a roof. With slavery, it was the same but better; their nutrition and lodgings were superior since people looked after things more carefully if they owned them rather than hired them (as you could easily tell by the condition of rental chariots in Rome). When there was no work or when they fell ill, the slave was still lodged and fed, while wage labourers were left to freeze and starve. From the slave's point of view, he or she was part of the family — part of that small circle of loyalty — so it was in his or her interest to constantly improve the position of the owners. Wage labourers owed no loyalty, so were more likely to steal a family's gold or spill their secrets. So slavery was good for everyone and it would be the foundation of Ragnall's Britain.

Something caught his eye. Was that a glint of metal at the top of the cliff?

"Get that scorpion BACK!" shouted Mal. The fools had pushed their giant bow right to the edge of the cliff for gods' knew what reason.

"Sorry, sorry!" said Gale Cossach and Taddy Ducktender, the scorpion operators responsible. They heaved the scorpion back into place five paces from the cliff edge.

Taddy's head was the shape and her hair the colour of a hazelnut, and her nose was wide and flat with a bobble tip. But she knew what she was doing. She operated the scorpion and carried out other orders with brisk efficiency. She was certainly not a typical beauty and her figure was different from Nita's — lean and defined while Nita had been soft and curved — but Mal found her breath-shorteningly attractive and she was the only woman that Mal had *almost* asked out for a drink since Nita had died. It would be a while before he did, though. Every time he thought about suggesting a liaison, Nita appeared in his mind, one hand on her hip, the other wagging a no, no, no finger at him.

Gale Cossach, on the other hand, was one disappointment after another. She was a big woman with a strongly boned, clear-skinned face that shone with confidence. However, contrary to her capable countenance, she always mucked things up. He wasn't sure if she forgot orders, lost interest in what she was doing or if she was just an idiot. She was always getting her scorpion stuck in ruts or gateways. Twice, she'd loosed one of the massive arrows by mistake and come within a sword's breadth of killing someone. He kept hoping she'd improve, but, as he'd realised in his years as a cart maker, people didn't change. The only reliable thing about unreliable people was that they remained reliably unreliable.

"It's my fault," said Gale, confirming Mal's suspicions. "I thought we'd get a better angle from the cliff's edge."

"You're right," said Mal, "you will get a better angle, but don't move until the ships are below us, got it? If they see us they'll never sail within range."

"You're right, I'm sorry."

"I did tell her," said Taddy, walking from the cliff edge, carrying one of the oversized arrows over one shoulder, "but she said she—"

Taddy tripped. She stumbled forwards, caught her foot behind her own ankle and fell. The metal head of the giant arrow she'd been carrying hit the scorpion's firing mechanism. With a THRUMMMMM! the loaded and primed arrow shot off into the sky, over the edge of the cliff and towards the Roman fleet

Mal watched it rise and fall in a graceful curve, the content of his gut performing a similar manoeuvre.

"Look!" shouted Ragnall. They all saw it. A huge arrow rose from the cliff top, flew towards them then plunged into the calm water a few hundred paces ahead. Ragnall saw Caesar talk to the ship's captain. The boat changed course to the north, parallel to the shining white cliff, still a good half a mile out to sea. The rest of the ships followed.

Little Dug was outside her tent sitting up on a rug, opposite a cross-legged Keelin Orton. The baby was waggling a three-legged, one-eyed wooden dog in one hand, slapping the ground with the other and giggling throatily at his nanny.

She was singing a song about a spider in a sweet, melodious voice that the little boy clearly adored.

Little Dug spotted his mother and scream-shouted with joy, bouncing on his fat little arse, flapping his short arms and laughing like a maniac. It was pleasing that he recognised her. As she was thinking how unusually big and round his head was and wondering if that would make him more intelligent, the boy managed to whack himself on the chin with the wooden dog. He stopped laughing and bouncing, looked at the toy in his hand and pushed out a low moan that grew quickly into a stunningly loud wail. Was there any other creature throughout the wilds of the world as loud as the human baby, Lowa wondered? As the volume increased, Dug's skin blossomed from pink to red.

"Your son, Graciousness!" said Keelin in the refreshing calm as the boy sucked in another lungful. She scooped up Dug and handed him to her. Lowa held him to her chest. Instead of screaming again he ground his face into her shoulder, rubbing saliva and snot into her cotton shirt. If any of Britain's Warrior queens had faced an invasion before with baby yuck on their battle threads, thought Lowa, then the bards kept quiet about it.

"Are you ready to go?" Lowa asked.

"As soon as you give the word, we're out of here on a fast horse with another couple of mounts in tow. But we won't need to flee, Lowa. You'll beat the bastards. The swanky shits will be corpses bobbing in the sea by the end of the day, you'll see."

"Why don't you check on the horses and do anything else you need to do? I'll look after him for a while."

"OK! He likes playing with that dog. Maggot gave it to him this morning." Keelin walked away, bottom swinging hypnotically.

Lowa sat on the rug, plonking Dug in front of her. She picked up the three-legged wooden dog. She'd seen it before, she was sure. Dug chortled, holding out his hands for it. She handed it over, the baby snatched it and she remembered. The same toy dog had been on the shelf in the hut in which she'd washed and changed on the day they'd massacred the tribe at Barton, before she'd gone to the party where Zadar had had her sister and her archer women killed. It was definitely the same one; she remembered throwing a slingstone at it and missing. How by Danu had it got here? She didn't believe in omens, she reminded herself, and did believe that the world would be a weirder place if freakish coincidences never happened . . . Still, if this freakish coincidence was an omen, it was not a good one. Or maybe it was? Omens were confusing, which was another reason for paying no heed to them.

She played with little Dug but he soon became whiney and Lowa's chief method of cheering him up – looking away then looking back – which had hitherto reduced him to fits of giggles – was no longer effective. She tried hugging him, but he arched his back and squirmed as if she were coated in poison. She waggled the dog, but he batted it away and howled.

"I am not good at this," she muttered to herself, and was about to yell for Keelin when the shout came.

"Romans changed course for the north!"

"Pissflaps" said Lowa, standing up with the boy. Dug stopped crying and poked a finger into her nostril. She prised his hand free.

Keelin came running as the shout was repeated.

Lowa kissed the baby on the top of his head, handed him to Keelin, leapt on her horse and galloped for the coast as Dug's howls grew fainter behind her.

Chapter 3

Walfdan shook his head. What had he let himself be talked into this time? He'd never claimed any mystical abilities – his druidic powers were limited to treating wounds and illnesses with stitches, splints and herbs – but he could feel evil radiating from the sailing ship like the stink from a rotting carcass, ever stronger as they approached, making him nauseous and terrified. Yet he held course. And why? Because Maggot had told him to and, for some unknown reason, following the orders issued by his strange new friends from across the sea was what he did these days.

The British druid was kneeling in front of the mast with a hand gripping either side of the little boat's bow, motionless, nose in the air like a dog, eyes closed.

The ship came closer and closer. Walfdan could see them now, huge heads in iron helmets and others encased in leather, watching them approach. He felt like a minnow swimming towards a circle of sharks.

Still he held the tiller firm, waves lapping the hull, sail taut in the mild but constant breeze, Maggot unmoving. Did he even know how close they were to the Roman ship?

They were fifty paces away. The only bareheaded person on the ship was a small, balding man, grinning at them hungrily. This was madness; they were sailing to their deaths.

"Maggot?" he murmured.

The British druid raised a finger, bidding silence. Walfdan shook his head again but held his tongue.

*   *   *

Felix smiled as the sailing dinghy approached his ship on a collision course. Its crew was two elderly men. At first Felix had thought they must be druids seeking coins for blessing the ship. But then they'd kept coming, even when they must have seen the Maximen and the Celermen. Why? Was their eyesight so bad that they didn't see that there were monsters crewing his ship? They didn't seem to be sinking or in any other obvious trouble, so it wasn't desperation that made them hold the course. Perhaps they were simply insane, two mad old men out for a jolly in their boat and coming over to say hello? It didn't matter. Whatever their intentions, Felix had his own plans for them. The journey thus far had been yawningly boring. A spot of torture would liven it up a little.

He could see them clearly now. The elderly man at the bow must have been freezing, dressed in only a leather rag and a silly amount of necklaces and other ornaments. The helmsman looked even older, with long white hair and beard. He stared back at Felix, terror in his eyes. The others' eyes were tight shut.

Eyes shut, as if . . .

"Helmsman, hard to port!" he shouted at his helmsman. There was something very fucking odd about that man and suddenly Felix was filled with an urge to flee from him. Their little boat was faster than his ship; there was no way they could outrun them, but . . .

Whump!

Felix staggered and gripped the side to keep his feet. They'd hit something in the water.

Whump!

The second blow came from the hull below him. They hadn't hit something, something had hit them! He looked over the side and saw a huge dark shape swimming down into the abyss. A whale?

WHUMP! The third, harder blow was followed by a

splintering crack. They were holed. Miles out to sea and their ship was holed.

"Kelter!" he shouted, "get below deck, find the hole and plug it with—"

WHUMP! CRACK!

Again? Felix beat his hands against the side in frustration. He looked about for the little sailing boat but couldn't see it. What he could see was a whale, just below the surface of the water, swimming directly for his ship.

WHUMP! CRACK!

"Hard to starboard, back the way we came for a bit, then to Britain," said Maggot, before tumbling backwards to lie still on the bottom boards. Walfdan dragged the tiller towards himself and the boat slice-turned through the water, the boom slamming across, over the prone British druid.

The sail filled and they whizzed away.

"Maggot?" said Walfdan. "Maggot?" He prodded the druid with his foot and got no response. He'd stop and tend to him soon. He didn't want to let go of the tiller with the wind so brisk and changeable, and he didn't want to stop sailing until they were well away from the monster ship.

He glanced over his shoulder. The ship was where they'd left it, sail flapping, and, it might have been his imagination, but was it listing? Just before he turned back to focus on sailing, a gigantic whale, far and away the biggest Walfdan had seen in a lifetime at sea, leapt almost clear of the water then splashed down on its side, sending a cascade over the demon ship.

Lowa reached the chariots on the road at the same time as Mal arrived back from the cliff edge. Behind him, the horse-drawn scorpions bounced down the broad field with their crews striding next to them.

"How many ships did you sink?" asked Lowa.

Mal shook his head, looking miserable.

"Don't blame yourself," said Lowa, "so long as you didn't actually do anything to prevent them landing under the cliffs."

"That's exactly what we did."

"How?"

"It was me," said a spry young woman striding bouncily up to them – she was called Taddy something, if Lowa wasn't mistaken. "I tripped and let off a bolt by mistake. I'm sorry."

Lowa had a sudden vision of a Roman soldier holding little Dug by the feet, lifting his sword and . . . Rage boiled from her stomach into her eyes, her world darkened and narrowed until only Taddy's stupid ugly fucking bolt-loosing face remained, smiling at her. Lowa drove her right fist into the woman's jaw, then a left into her ribs. Mal reached for her, but Lowa sent him flying with a kick to the stomach. The bolt looser was still standing, so Lowa punched her chin again. She went down.

The queen unsheathed her sword. Taddy was moaning, bloodied and crawling away. Lowa jumped onto her back, knocking her arms out from under her, grabbed her by the hair, pulled her head back and pressed the blade into her throat.

"Lowa!" she heard someone say. It was Mal. "Lowa!"

She turned to advise him to fuck off unless he wanted to die as well. He was clutching his stomach. Where she'd kicked him. She'd kicked her friend. A veil seemed to lift. Lowa took her sword away from Taddy's neck and laid the woman's head down. She stood. They were all staring at her, Mal, the scorpion crews and half a hundred assorted charioteers. The only person not staring at her was Taddy Ducktender, who was face down and sobbing.

Buggerfucktwats, thought the queen.

"Sorry," she said. "I . . . may have lost it a little there. But understand, all of you, this is not a speculative late summer raid by a tribe after your winter stores. The Romans will destroy our land. The men in those ships intend to kill us and enslave our children, and they are very good at it. In two years, outnumbered a hundred to one, they have conquered *all* of Gaul. They have sacked towns, massacred tribes and raped countless women, men and children. They are determined to do the same to us. If we let them, our children, their children, their children and on, for ever, will be lackeys of the Romans. They will dig and die in mines, slave on ships, fight and be killed in arenas, or − if they happen to be pretty girls or boys − be fucked a hundred ways until they're split apart and dying, all for the pleasure and amusement of Roman men. I see some of you turning away. You may be shocked but not I'm exaggerating. If anything I'm playing it down. These men are the nastiest bastards who ever walked the earth, and the best fighters. Now. Do you want the Romans to kill you and take your children?"

"No!" shouted a few of the onlookers, raising their weapons.

"Are we going to fight them and beat them and send them back across the sea to tend their wounded and warn the rest of the world not to fuck with the British?"

"Yes!" shouted everyone.

"Good. But do know that the fight will be hard. It will be worth it − and we have no alternative − but many of us will lose our lives. Never fear, we can win! But not if we fuck up and do things like fire a scorpion bolt too early. So everyone pay attention, *be careful with the details* and we will win!"

There were a few "Woos!" and "Yeahs!" and Lowa realised her little speech had not finished as rousingly as it had started. Be careful with the details − what had she been thinking? If any bards lived to tell the tale, they'd be leaving that bit out. On the bright side, nobody was staring at her in horror any more, they were all patting each other on the back and looking cheery and excited, so she'd rescued the situation.

She helped Taddy to her feet. The woman pressed a hand to her bleeding mouth, looked at it, then smiled. "I deserved that, my queen, I'm so sorry. Is there anything I can—"

Lowa put a hand on her shoulder "Don't do it again and fight well when the time comes."

Taddy nodded. Lowa turned to Mal and opened her mouth to say she didn't know what.

"Don't even apologise," he said. "Just remind me never to approach you from behind without warning. You and a horse – same awareness required."

"Thanks. Now, I think it's trumpet time."

He nodded, took a few paces away and shouted through cupped hands: "Trumpets ready!"

Shouts of "Trumpets ready" echoed around and everybody produced short, variably sized bronze horns, each with a wooden clacker in its mouth, mass-produced under Elann Nancarrow's directions. Mal handed one to Lowa. She held it to her lips and blew. Some ten thousand Britons in the countryside around did the same. The resultant noise was astonishing. It wasn't as piercing as baby Dug's wails, but it was so much louder, the largest sound that Lowa had ever heard, shaking the very earth.

She found she could only blow for a few heartbeats before the vibrations made her lips tingle horribly, but she rubbed her mouth, reapplied the trumpet and blew again. All around her people were doing the same, so the terrible trumpeting became quieter and louder, and colossal waves of sound rolled around the land and out to sea.

Music. So music was the first weapon they were using against the Romans, and shit music at that. Yilgarn Craton the Haxmite could have shown them how to get much a better tune from a horn – they were just blowing any old note and it was a mess – but nobody had asked him. The beautiful, the wonderful Jocanta Fairtresses had been right. The Maidunites under Queen Lowa were ignorant, arrogant and childish – like their queen. Fighting the Romans with music! The Maidunites were doomed. But Yilgarn wasn't going to let them drag the Haxmites down.

Undermine them when you can, then, when the moment comes, use the Haxmite soldiers well. He would heed Jocanta's words. He closed his eyes and pictured himself fighting Lowa and beating her in front of them all, Jocanta included. He'd punish her for cutting his chief's hair. She'd bested him before, yes, but it had been dark and she'd tricked him by putting a hand behind her back. He'd whip her next time, of course he would. Were her arms anywhere near as mighty as his? They were not.

Then, surely, Jocanta would see him by a different torchlight. She'd notice, finally, how much of a man he was and – no! no! no! He mustn't think like that. She was his queen, he was her guard. He was noble and heroic and must squash his grubby thoughts. But she'd never taken a man, he was certain of it. She kept companions, the old lady and the boy, but they were just that; companions and nothing more, no matter what the loudmouths said. Perhaps Yilgarn was the fellow she was waiting for? If he did well here and brought glory to the Haxmites, then surely he'd become more than her guard?

Chapter 4

"What," thought Ragnall, "by Toutatis' trumpet is that?" Everyone on the ship was looking about themselves, eyes wide.

The throbbing, pulsing wave of sound was astonishing. He'd heard war trumpets before, but nothing like this. The reverberating wail made his ears vibrate. Surely it must be thousands of horns? If Lowa had, what – twenty thousand trumpet blowers – how many soldiers did she have? Two hundred thousand? Four? Where had she got the troops? Perhaps it wasn't Lowa . . . he'd never been there himself but he'd always heard that Britain's south-east corner was a muddle of weak, peaceful trading tribes. That was why they'd done nothing to stop Zadar apart from give him gold. Perhaps he'd heard wrong?

The praetorians rowing the general's ship were obviously making similar calculations. Several were looking about worriedly. Even the super-tough-acting ones, who'd always given an air that they'd rather chop their arm off with a rusty sword than look weak for an instant, weren't looking as eager as usual. He saw one reach to his ears as if to block them and then seem to realise how pathetic it would look, and turn the manoeuvre into a double-handed scratch of his chin.

Only Caesar remained unperturbed, standing at the stern and looking ahead as if the blare of trumpets was birdsong.

A while later the coastal cliffs gave way to a wide estuary. Three of the rowing ships, including Caesar's ship with

Ragnall aboard, swung into the broad channel to investigate
while the others waited on the open sea.

The banks were deep mud, busy with seabirds strutting
about like newly made senators then poking pointy beaks
into the filth like longer-serving senators, thought Ragnall,
pleased with his satirical comparison. The northern shore,
to their right, was flat and featureless. Presumably there
was a salt marsh or another estuary beyond the mud shore.
The south shore, beyond the mud, was tussocks of grass
then woods. The air was sharp with the salt stink of
summer-rotting seaweed.

Ragnall could feel eyes watching him from the trees. By
the look on everyone else's faces, they could too. But the
only noises were the screeches and chucks of birds, the
creak of the oars and the slap of water against the hull.

The river narrowed. Much further and the ships would
be in range of projectile weapons from the trees on the south
shore. The mud looked too deep on both banks to land the
soldiers, so they wouldn't be able to do much in response
to a missile attack other than duck. The praetorians rowed
on. The channel narrowed. It felt like every Roman was
holding his breath, waiting for the arrows or the slingstones
to fall.

A whistle from the captain and that breath was exhaled.
Backing on one side and pulling on the other, the rowers
spun the ship.

Phew, thought Ragnall. There was nothing for them along
this river and finally they'd realised.

"Danu's tits," said Lowa. The Roman boat was going about
well outside everyone's arrow range – apart from hers, that
was. It was easy to see which one was Caesar. Even from six
hundred paces you could tell that the little red- and gold-clad
figure standing proud on the ship's stern was in command.

Lowa strung an arrow and stepped from the trees. She

aimed and loosed. Caesar bent over at the last moment. The man beside him threw his arms up and fell into the brown estuarine water with a splosh. There was a shout and the rest of the Romans ducked out of sight.

"Bel's cock," she said to herself. It had been too much to hope that the Romans would get trapped in the mud in range of her cavalry archers, but she was unlikely to get a clear shot at their leader again. The archers around her were muttering about the gods' favouring Caesar. She scowled at them, then ordered them to follow her and jogged back through the trees to the waiting horses.

Evening found Lowa, Chamanca, Atlas, Mal and Adler standing among the high littoral gorse, looking at ninety Roman ships anchored a good way out to sea, beyond the range of even Lowa's bow. Behind the three Warriors were the Two Hundred and Lowa's cavalry, with the rest of the army camped around the village of Taloon, a few thousand paces away.

It would be a good place to land – a spit of stony sand and a grassy salt flat wide enough for a large camp, with a marsh at one end and backdropped by a muddy estuary – but a bad place to advance from, the only access to the rest of Britain being across a river or through a marsh. If they wanted to land here, Lowa would let them. Then she'd keep them there.

"Why aren't they landing?" asked Chamanca. "I'm thirsty."

"Because they're waiting for their demons to do their work for them," said Maggot, riding up with Walfdan and Spring. Spring dismounted and helped Maggot from his horse. The druid was pale and looked half dead, but he walked over unaided.

"Welcome back," said Lowa. "News?" She nodded at Spring and the girl nodded back. It was the first time Lowa had seen her since the day of the wave – the Spring Tide – a year before. She was wearing leather shorts and a sleeveless cotton archers' shirt, swinging Dug's warhammer in one hand with her bow scabbarded on her horse. She'd grown in height and stature. She was a little taller than Lowa now, and there was a new sway to her hips.

"The demons' ship has returned to Gaul," said Walfdan. "Maggot crippled it and it was sinking when we last saw it, but still afloat."

"So they'll find another ship and head straight back?" asked Atlas.

Walfdan looked at Maggot, who nodded weakly. "We don't think so," said the Gaul. "Caesar has used every boat of any size in his invasion. We are somewhere between fairly and very sure that there are no boats left in north-west Gaul capable of carrying one fully armoured Ironman, let alone all of them."

"How did Maggot cripple their ship?" asked Lowa.

"Never mind that," said Maggot, his voice quiet. "Walfdan has something to tell you about the demons."

"Yes," said Walfdan. "Now, would you say I was a fast runner? Say you had to catch me, Lowa, and we started running from where we both are right now. How far would you say I'd get before—"

"Can you get to the point, please?" Lowa wasn't in the mood for a bardish recital.

"Ah, yes. I'm now fairly certain that the demons derive their power from the life-forces of others, which they take by killing them. I don't know how long the energy gained from another's death lasts, but Maggot agrees it's likely that it's not for long, and also that they get more and more energy the more they kill. Spring here says that, after a killing frenzy, a Leatherman caught an arrow that she shot, yet before the killing frenzy, she was able to shoot two of them."

Spring nodded.

So did Lowa. It was useful information, but it only

reinforced what they'd already guessed. Drustan and Felix, she knew, had been able to take power from killing and Maggot said that he also could, but that he never did. It was why Lowa had twelve chained men and two women – ten rapists and four murderers – ready for Maggot to kill and produce magic to combat the demons as a last resort. He hadn't agreed to do it, and Lowa had never liked the idea, but it was preferable to seeing all her people slaughtered by Roman monsters.

"It's possible they might have found another ship," she said, "or repaired theirs, and be on the way back already."

"That is indeed possible, although I consider it unlikely," said Walfdan. "Your shouters will see their ship in good time if they do return."

"I will keep the prisoners, just in case."

"What prisoners?" asked Spring. She had one hand on her hip with a look on her face that reminded Lowa of what she'd been like at that age – amazed at how badly adults ran the world and convinced that she would do an immeasurably better job.

"For Maggot to use if the demons land."

"Use?"

"As you used Dug."

"You'll kill our own to fight the Romans?"

"I'll kill murderers and rapists to save thousands more who aren't, yes."

"I see." Spring took a step towards her. "Good at sacrificing other people, aren't you?"

Lowa's mind went back a year. She saw Spring's arrow fly and Dug fall. She felt again the crushing weight of the sudden, overwhelming knowledge that the man she loved, the father of her unborn child, was dead. And here was the girl who'd killed him; no longer a girl, a woman now. The woman who'd killed her love, here with the nerve to suggest that it was Lowa's fault. She pulled her sword a hand's breadth from its scabbard and took a pace towards Spring.

The girl stood her ground, chin jutting, holding her gaze.

"Spring, go away, now." Maggot lifted a hand.

"I will not," said Spring, hefting Dug's hammer. "If this woman wants a fight then she may have one. I—"

"No, no, you will go."

"Oh," said Spring, looking confused and lowering the weapon. "You're right, I will. I've got things to do. Where's my horse?"

Lowa felt her anger dissolve as Spring mounted and trotted away.

She raised an eyebrow at Maggot. He shrugged.

Chapter 5

Spring stood on a hill above the village of Taloon. Nearby Pigsy was rootling around in a bramble bush while Sadie barked at it. Below her the majority of Lowa's army cooked and sparred and sharpened and did the myriad other tasks that prepared them for battle. She took none of it in. She was narrow-eyed and unseeing, debating with herself whether to go back down the hill and join them. She had a good mind to take herself and her dogs back to the farm, see how the army got on without her bow.

They were all idiots and Lowa was the biggest idiot of the lot, planning to kill Britons to stop the demons. Spring had stopped three of them without killing anyone.

"She doesn't want to kill anybody, you wee turnip brain," said Dug, walking towards her. As he spoke the trumpets blared from the army below – they were still all blowing them every now and then to persuade the Romans out to sea that they were more than they were – but she could still hear him. "She's doing it to save you all. All of it. She wants nothing more than to be with her son – and you, to a degree, she does love you – but she's devoted her life to making sure that you, and all the other ungrateful shites like you, aren't slaughtered by the Romans. And she didn't kill me. I walked down that hill and you fired the arrow. The only other person who knew what was going on was Maggot. But he's not to blame either. Nobody's to blame, least of all Lowa."

"Lowa is a dick."

"No, she is not. She's commanding a disparate army against the world's most powerful force and you're sulking because she didn't come and visit you when she was ploughing every single heartbeat of her life into building this army. Of course she wanted to see you. She wanted to spend more time with her baby, too, but she is the one person standing between the Romans and the destruction of Britain. She knows that, so, while she has the tiniest chance of saving you and all the other ungrateful badger turds, that's what she's going to do, all the time. You're thinking only of yourself, making stuff up, and irrationally hating the one person left alive who loves you. Have an objective mull through those positions and see if you can work out which one of you is the dick."

"Oh, just fuck off," said Spring.

Disappointment glowed in Dug's deep brown eyes and he vanished.

"Come back! I didn't mean it! COME BACK!"

But he was gone and she was alone. She sat down and hugged her knees. Both dogs lolloped up and nuzzled her. They smelled odd – disgusting in fact – but Spring was too miserable to wonder what they'd found in the bushes.

She'd show them all, she thought. But how . . . Well, it was simple. She'd stop the invasion. There was a way. But this time she wouldn't need to kill thousands, just one man.

"No, no," said Dug, looming over her again, hands on hips, "don't be so silly. There's no way you can do it and you'll die trying. You should listen to Lowa and—"

Spring closed her eyes. When she opened them he was gone. She stood up and looked about for her horse.

The trumpet salvo died as Lowa, Atlas and Chamanca arrived in the middle of the village. Mal, Adler and Maggot were waiting for her next to the village's centrepiece – a three-man-high carving of Epona, the horse goddess. Lowa was glad to see that Maggot was looking a lot more like one of the living.

"Right," she said, sliding from her horse. "Here's what's going to happen next. We are going to—"

"Lowa, before you start," interrupted Maggot, "this codger here would like a word."

Maggot's bangle-ringed arm jangled as he indicated an elderly man. The decrepit fellow shuffled forwards and lifted his head with obvious effort. Intelligent eyes looked out over a hooked nose in a leathery face. Behind him, Lowa noticed for the first time, were a gaggle of villagers staring at her with fearful defiance, and moon-eyed children clasping parents' legs. She recognised the old man; she'd met him the previous winter on a recruitment tour. He was chief of the Taloon tribe, and a cantankerous old fucker. He'd been reluctant to offer troops, and even more hostile to the idea that his village might be used as an base for Lowa's army in the likely event of the Romans landing nearby. He'd only reluctantly agreed when she'd reminded him that she was accompanied by two hundred heavily armed Warriors who didn't like it when she didn't get what she wanted. His name was . . .

"Hardward," she remembered. "What do you want?" She was inclined to dismiss him; she had a invasion to fight off, but her army was in his village. As he cleared his throat, she looked about. She'd been so focused on briefing her commanders that she hadn't noticed two smashed grain stores, several villagers with bruised faces and a hulking, sour-faced infantryman with his hands tied by rough rope.

Ah, she thought.

"Your soldier," Hardward indicated the bound man, "killed a Taloon man and badly beat his wife and sons – his very young sons – who tried to save him. One of the sons may die. Then he injured several more people who ran to the boys' defence."

Shit, thought Lowa. "I'm sorry."

"Other Maidunite soldiers have pillaged our stores and livestock. Three dogs defending property have been killed and four cats are missing, presumed eaten. I agreed – under duress – to supply you with troops, and I agreed that you might use Taloon as a base – again only because of your politely couched but clear threat of violence. You defeated Zadar and everybody said that a tyrant had been replaced by a good queen. It's now clear that you are no better."

Lowa sighed. She was standing next to the carving of Epona. Epona had been the name of her horse when she'd been in Zadar's army, when, under his orders, she'd sacked villages and shot countless arrows into people like Hardward and the farmer types cowering behind him. But she'd been following orders and she'd renounced that past. As a ruler, she was not anything like Zadar.

"I am sorry for your losses and, although I know it will mean little to the murdered man's grieving family, I apologise," she said, "particularly for the man who was killed and the violence to his sons and others. What was his name?"

"Jostan."

"And his badly injured son?"

"Erca."

"Maggot, will you tend to Erca?"

"Already have." The Druid waggled his fingers. "He will be fine."

"So you say." For an older man, Hardward did petulance very well.

"So I know." Maggot waited.

"You," said Lowa to the accused man, "did you kill Jostan and beat his family?"

"They tried to stop me taking rations for the men."

She recognised his accent, then the man himself. He was a Haxmite, one of the men whom Jocanta Fairtresses had unwillingly relinquished under Yilgarn Craton's command.

That was annoying, since they were already reluctant allies, but there was only one possible course of action.

"Did you kill Jostan and beat his family? Yes or no?"

"Yes."

Lowa sighed. "Adler?" she said, nodding at the stern young captain of the Two Hundred.

Adler nodded in reply and strode over to the Haxmite, unsheathing her sword as she came.

"No!" the murderer stammered. "They were just peasants getting in the way. You can't—"

Adler held her sword aloft. The murderer lifted his tied hands and shifted from foot to foot, watching her blade. She kicked him in the knee with her iron-heeled riding boots, cracking bone. He fell into a kneel, roaring with pain. Adler grabbed him by the hair, pressed the tip of her sword into the nape of his neck then thrust down, severing his spine. He flopped forwards, jerking, and was still.

"Right," Lowa said as Adler dragged the dead Haxmite away by his feet. She wanted to get this finished. "Everyone, make sure that everyone else knows that this man was executed and why it was done. I will talk to his commander, Yilgarn Craton. When we have repelled the invader, I will investigate the theft of grain and destruction of property myself and make sure that any surviving perpetrators are punished, reparations paid and damage repaired. Now, if you wouldn't mind, there's the matter of the large invasion of merciless killers who could make landfall at any moment."

"What will we do for food until you've finished mucking about with the Romans? Your army took it all." Hardward was unappeased.

"My quartermaster will ensure that nobody starves. Talk to her."

"It was not your food to take!"

Lowa was running out of patience. "Look, Hardward, I

have over twelve thousand soldiers here and near that number again in cooks, blacksmiths, healers and others. With that many gathered, there will be crimes. There will be murders. That's because we are human, and, Danu knows why, that is how humans behave. I am sorry that you and Jostan's family have borne the brunt and I advise the rest of your people to stay clear of my troops as much as they can, and to report any problems immediately to me or my generals. That's the best I can do other than leave, but if I leave, the Romans would invade unopposed. If that happens, they will kill or enslave all of you."

"So you say, but that's not what we've heard. We have a merchant who visits yearly from Rome, so we know all about them. They have gallons of wine, a surfeit of delicious food and fine clothes. They heat their giant, stone-built huts with hot water running from room to room in bronze channels. They have farming innovations which means they spend less time toiling in the fields and more time bathing in their hot water, gorging on piles of food and making love to each other. I could go on."

"Please don't."

"All these things they will bring here."

"Yes, for themselves. We Britons they will kill. You younger people," Lowa spoke up so the rest of the village could hear, "if they don't slaughter you, they'll enslave you. You've heard they have innovative farming methods. What do you imagine these are? Magic seeds? Crops that harvest themselves? Nope, sorry, the innovation is slaves. Slaves do the work while the Romans sit idle. They don't even whip you themselves – they have other slaves to do that. And when the slaves realise they shouldn't have let themselves be taken in the first place and rebel? They kill them, in their thousands."

"Queen Lowa, you are wrong. The merchants tell us of a life in Rome—"

"They have told you only half the truth, and barely that. They will tell you that Rome is a place of idleness and decadence. It is, but only for Romans. Slave markets all around their empire process tens of thousands every day. Caesar has marched through Gaul and left unimaginable horror in his wake. Hundreds of thousands of corpses rot in the fields and trains of slaves that would stretch from here to Maidun have been marched from their homes. I'm sorry my army does not behave perfectly, but raided supplies and one murdered man are the price you pay for us to repel the invader. A great many of my men and women are likely to pay for your defence with their lives."

"What you've failed to grasp, Queen Lowa, is that we do not require you to repel the invader. For us, *you* are the invader."

He had not listened to a word. Danu's tits, she hated people who didn't listen. She drew her blade. "All right, if that's how you feel. Everything else still stands – investigation, reparations and so on – but if you and your Taloons aren't out of this square in twenty heartbeats I'll kill the lot of you."

The old man looked at her sword, then into her eyes. "I'm afraid that you're rather proving my point."

"Nineteen heartbeats."

The chief shuffled away, shaking his head. His villagers followed him, flashing reproachful glares at Lowa. Here was proof that she was no Zadar. People who crossed him never got the chance to look reproachful. If he'd been commanding the army, the Taloons would have looked terrified, then they would have looked dead.

Lowa turned to Atlas, Chamanca, Mal, Adler and Maggot.

"Right," she said. "Here's the plan. Given how far south Felix was sailing, Maggot is sure that Caesar doesn't know yet that the demons have returned to Gaul."

"Sure as I can be of anything, but how can we know anything for sure?"

"Indeed. Thanks. So, my guess is that Caesar is holding off and waiting for his demons to attack us tonight, either to destroy us or freak us out so much that we're a pushover when he lands tomorrow. We're going to convince him that's what's happened. We'll keep it up with the horns, then, immediately after sunset, we are going to fake the noise of a battle. After that we'll blow no more trumpets. He won't see his own troops arrive on the shore, so Caesar will assume we've defeated them or that they've retreated, but he'll think that we were weakened fighting them and the legions will land at dawn. We will be ready."

"Why aren't we landing?" said a praetorian near Ragnall at the bow of the flagship. It was the middle of the day and they'd done nothing but look at a beach for most of the morning. The only excitement had been a few tiny figures appearing on the shore – most Romans' first sight of the exotic inhabitants of this wild, distant isle – and the regular wall of sound from the Britons' horns blaring out across the waves. "They haven't got an army," the praetorian continued, "they've just got a fuckload of trumpets."

He was not alone in the sentiment. For a good while everyone out of Caesar's earshot had been griping about being stuck on a ship when there was a perfectly good place to land right there. Ragnall had heard somewhere that all soldiers were whingers, but he was amazed how quickly they called into question the judgement of a leader who had not made one tactical error in nearly three years of campaigning. Ragnall didn't know why Caesar was holding, but he knew that there had to be a good reason for it.

"Ragnall!" called a praetorian from the stern. He made his way back and found Caesar scanning the coast, looking, oddly for him, less than utterly confident.

"Ah, Ragnall, good," said the general. "Say an army landed twenty miles to the south. What impediments might prevent them marching cross-country to the shore that Caesar is regarding right now?"

Ragnall didn't have a clue, he'd never been to this part of Britain, but that wouldn't be an acceptable answer for Caesar. "Ah, well, there's a wide river – the Tems – and several woods." He had no idea where the Tems was, but was pretty sure it wasn't far, and there were always woods.

"Mountains?"

"There are no mountains in southern Britain."

"Marshes?"

"Marshes . . . yes, some. I haven't really—"

"All right, all right, thank you." Caesar looked along the boat. Praetorians and legionaries looked back expectantly. He contemplated the shore. You could feel the impatience of the men, keen to disembark these crammed and unusual transportations.

"Give the signal to land," Caesar told Labienus.

Chapter 6

Chamanca and Atlas walked away from Lowa's briefing. Chamanca quite liked Lowa's plan. It meant she'd have to wait until the morning for blood, but she'd waited so long now that a little longer couldn't hurt, and besides she could do things with Atlas that were almost as good as the joy of blood. Yes, she thought, taking his arm in her hands. They'd go back to their commandeered hut now and—

"ROMANS COMING IN!" came the shout.

"Fenn!" said Chamanca. They ran back to the centre of the village. Lowa was there, giving orders.

"Adler, all cavalry including the Two Hundred will go to the beach. *Now.*" Adler ran off.

"Mal, the scorpions will form up to defend the path through the marsh, but be ready to move if the Romans carry boats over the spit, or swim, or cross the water between here and the spit."

"Can they not sail their ships round the spit?"

"No, too shallow and cliffs to the south. The only place they can land is the spit and the only way off the spit without swimming or floating is the path through the marsh."

"But what if—" Chamanca put a hand on his arm and shook her head. This was not the time to be questioning their general. And besides, Chamanca knew what Lowa was doing even if Mal didn't. The spit looked like a great place to land from the sea, but, once on it, the Roman army would be more or less trapped. Their options would be to go back to sea, or to come inland across water or up the narrow path through the marsh. Either of those latter options, and they'd be torn apart by scorpion and arrow fire.

Mal seemed to get her point, nodded to himself, and strode away.

"Atlas – infantry should not be needed yet. Tell them to hold by the village, to rest, sleep and eat, but to be dressed for fighting with their weapons ready. Ensure your company commanders are ready to run their men anywhere to defend a crossing, then come to the beach to join me and the cavalry.

"Chamanca," Lowa continued, "same deal with the chariots. They're to cover the path foremost, but keep an eye for anyone crossing the channel and be ready to move quickly to support the infantry with slings and arrows and *not* get in its way. Once they're in position make sure your deputy knows the plan, then get on a horse and join us on the beach. I have a role for you and Atlas."

Chamanca grinned and ran to find her chariots, blood lust fizzing in every limb.

The first ships ran aground, still a good forty paces from the shore. Ragnall gripped the rail and watched legionaries jump from the boats, swords aloft and roaring heroically. He shared their excitement. Ragnall knew that Britain was just Britain, a place of mud and beer and brutes, but to the legionaries this wild land was another world – unknown, exciting and, surely, terrifying. If he'd been one of them he'd have roared, too.

Their ardour was immediately dampened, unfortunately, when they found that the water was deeper than it looked. The tallest sank up to their chests. The shortest went under. Holding swords and shields aloft, some waded in while others helped their smaller brothers in arms. The next soldiers off the boats climbed down a great deal more gingerly.

On Ragnall's boat, Caesar's mouth was a line of frustration. Ragnall saw his point. Those cursed Gaulish boat builders

should have made transports with shallower draughts! He
followed the general's gaze to the shore, past the legionaries'
slow, ragged and painfully vulnerable advance. If a few
hundred archers appeared now, then surely they'd have to
retreat? Luckily, all was quiet. More and more boats swished
aground and legionaries disembarked more carefully.
However, on a nearby boat he saw a lone legionary become
frustrated by the delay and jump from too far back in the
boat. Ragnall shouted a warning, but too late. The legionary
splashed down and disappeared. His hands surfaced, but
weighed down by leather and metal, that was the best he
could do. A couple of heartbeats later his hand appeared
again, just one this time and further out to sea. He was
jumping for air and heading the wrong way. On the next
jump only his fingertips broke the surface. He was going
to drown. Ragnall shouted at the men still on his ship, all
queuing to leap off the front, but nobody heard him.

Jupiter's tits, Ragnall said to himself. He peeled his toga
over his head and dived off the side. He swum across with
the powerful, overarm stroke that he'd learnt on the Island
of Angels, and dived under as he approached what he hoped
was the turbulence caused by the drowning man's thrashing.
He found the man straight away, grabbed him around the
waist, and, staying underwater himself, hoicked him up
above the surface and marched him to the side of the ship.
After what seemed like far too long a time, the legionary
found a grip that held and hauled himself up. Ragnall leapt,
sucked in air and climbed onto the boat where he stood
naked save for his sandals. Luckily the waterlogged legionary,
the helmsman and a couple of crew were the only people
left onboard. The legionary found him a blanket.

While Ragnall had been rescuing the man, he saw
hundreds and hundreds – thousands – more Romans had
disembarked and were wading for shore, swords and shields
aloft. Here we go, thought Ragnall. This is a big moment.

The beginning of the Romanisation of Britain. Day One of the Reign of King Ragnall.

"Thanks for that!" said the legionary, high-pitched and happy. "Thought I was a goner, then. And you know what? All I could see when I was down there was my wife telling me how stupid I was. 'Didn't even get to dry land!' she was saying. 'You're so thick you can't even get off the right end of a boat!' I tell you, I was glad to be dying for a moment. Not that I'm not grateful that you rescued me, I am. And I do love by wife although, between you, me and the lantern post, she can be a right bitch. Now, I've got to be going so . . . oh, by fucking Mars!"

Ragnall followed his gaze, past the thousands of wading Romans. Cantering along the beach towards them were several hundred British cavalry riding in two well-ordered lines. The nearer line hurled spears and took bows from their backs as their first missiles impaled some of the keener shore-bound soldiers. He recognised the woman at their head, speeding up into a gallop, blonde hair dancing behind her, recurve bow pumping shot after shot into the wading Roman ranks – Lowa! And, right behind her, that was Chamanca and Atlas. These latter two dismounted. While the others all carried on with their bows, Atlas and Chamanca walked towards the sea, the African holding his axe, the Iberian her ball-mace and short sword. So she had survived the sea battle. He wondered where Carden was. He hoped he was all right – he'd been thinking of giving a role in his new Britain to the big man who might or might not have saved him from Ariovistus by catapulting him into a lake.

Behind the front row of archers picking targets and shooting directly into the soldiers, the back line of cavalry sent a volley of arrows upwards. The missiles peaked, paused and fell in among the legionaries.

Ragnall looked to the command boat – he should be getting back, he thought – but its oars were in the water and it was swinging south, away from him, along with the eleven other warships. So he could either swim ashore through the storm of arrows and join the fight or stay in the transport. He decided to stay where he was for now.

"Rather them than me!" said the helmsman, walking up to stand next to him. He was a stout man, bearded but bald, with hair sprouting from the neck of his sailor's jerkin. A Syrian, Ragnall guessed, from the east end of the Mediterranean. "They're getting their arses handed to 'em!" The Syrian nodded, as if agreeing with himself.

Ragnall did not dignify his defeatist comment with a reply. But he did have a point. Lowa and her Maidunites were slaughtering the legionaries. Ragnall had never seen the Romans anywhere near the trouble that they were in now. Even Caesar, he supposed, was prone to the odd error. Although, in the general's defence, it was his first sea invasion, and, more pertinently, if the Gauls had built him proper transport boats, the legionaries would be ashore and much more ready to defend against the deadly iron salvos.

They were getting there now. None of the Romans, Ragnall was proud to see, was attempting to return to the boats. Despite arrows stopping as many as one in every two, they waded on. Their courage was stirring. The first legionaries reached the shore and formed their shields into a defensive tortoise. Ragnall cheered. The helmsman gave him an "Oh, you're one of those, are you?" look, but Ragnall ignored it. On the shore the first tortoise advanced up the beach, becoming more hedgehog than tortoise as arrows zipped into shields. All along the shore, more impregnable tortoises were forming.

Ragnall bounced on the balls of his feet. He was thrilled, but confused. He wanted the Romans to triumph, but he also wanted the Britons to do well. Part of him hated watching the legionaries die, but part of him was glad that Lowa and her army were fighting so intelligently. There was no doubt about it, he was proud of his homeland. The British, as he'd pointed out repeatedly over the last two years, were not Gauls.

Atlas' first swing smashed two shields and severed a Roman arm. Chamanca dived through the breach in the tortoise's shell. The Kushite scanned left and right as he brought his axe down again. It was vital that their route back to their horses was left open. Their role was to kill a lot of Romans, quickly, then get out of there. They weren't seeking to win the war that day, just to give the Romans something to talk about around their campfires.

In front of him legionaries screamed under their shields then the shell fell away to reveal dead Romans, dying Romans, confused Romans – and Chamanca, sucking on a Roman neck. Atlas stepped in to dispatch the confused legionaries. The last of them was a reasonable fighter who dodged a couple of axe blows before an arrow took him in the chest, heralding Lowa's arrival.

"We're done," she said, nodding to the south, where the Romans' warships teeming with slingers and archers were drawing into a line and about to be in range of the British cavalry, then to the north, where a giant tortoise formation was advancing behind a brave man carrying a gold eagle standard. Lowa took aim, shot, and the aquilifer – the man carrying the standard – went down. Another snatched it up immediately, though, and the Romans kept coming, not slowed at all. The cavalry's arrows were having no effect on the shielded Romans and soon they'd be cut off from their retreat across the marsh. It was, indeed, time to go.

"Come on," said Lowa, and ran off.

Chamanca was still sucking away at the moaning legionary's neck.

"Let's go!" Atlas said.

She held up a hand to indicate that he should wait a heartbeat. He looked up the beach. A dozen or so of the

Two Hundred were galloping at the large tortoise, pumping impotent arrows into it, but drawing it away from their escape route. To the south, the Roman ships came into range and their archers loosed a salvo. At him and Chamanca. He crouched and reached for a Roman shield, but the Sobek-cursed thing was attached to a dead man's arm. He yanked, just as the arrow took him in the shoulder. It slid through skin, ripped muscle, grazed bone, ripped more muscle, burst skin and the head was out of his back.

"Fucking . . . Fuck! Pigs' cunts!" he shouted. Bel but it was painful.

"Let me . . ." said Chamanca, reaching for it, her bloody face a picture of contrition.

"Get off. Let's go like we already should have done. Come on!" They had to get clear before the next volley. He stood and ran, glancing over his shoulder. Chamanca was following. Every pace sent jets of agony pulsing along his arm, through his torso and head. They reached the horses and he swung up, kicked the beast and set off at gallop.

"Sorry!" shouted Chamanca behind him. It was, thought Atlas, gripping the shaft of the arrow with his left hand, a bit late for that. She'd had to stop for a drink and now he had an arrow through his shoulder.

He snapped the shaft, chucked away the feathered end, reached over his shoulder and grasped the head. He pulled hard, but it was slick with blood. His hand slipped, the edges of the iron head slicing his palm and fingers open. He gripped again, higher up the shaft so that the iron corners dug into his hand to give him purchase. He pulled and this time, the shaft came through his shoulder and out. Waves of agony pulsed through him. As he lost consciousness, he held the arrowhead to his nose. Was that shit he could smell on there? Yes, he thought as the world disappeared, he rather thought that it was, Sobek curse them.

*   *   *

Angus Watson   153

They were fleeing! The British were vanquished, galloping away inland and northwards. Rome had shown her might and Britain had been found wanting.

"A good start!" Ragnall said to himself.

"Do you think so?" said the Syrian helmsman.

"Well, we won."

"Did we?"

"Yes, of course we did. Look, the Britons are fleeing. That's what armies do when they've lost."

"That's a few horses, not an army. You heard the trumpets, there's a lot more where that came from."

"Possibly, but, like I said, a good start."

"Yeah? How many Britons did you see killed?"

"Um . . . well Atlas – the African who attacked the tortoise – took an arrow."

"Yes, that's all I saw as far as Britons wounded or killed went. How many legionaries would you say lost their lives? Two hundred? More?"

"Probably more . . ."

"So let me get this straight." The helmsman smiled. "Hundreds of Romans were killed and one Briton was injured, and that's a loss for the Britons?"

"It's more complicated than the butcher's bill – that means how many were killed or injured."

"I know what butcher's bill means. This is not my first war, young man."

There were two nasty scars on the man's left cheek and a chunk missing near his right temple, he was about double Ragnall's age, and as a ship's captain in the Roman navy, Ragnall conceded, he'd probably seen quite a bit of military action. No doubt he'd served in Pompey's famously bloody pirate wars. But obviously, like so many junior ranks, he didn't understand warfare and Ragnall would have to explain.

"The Romans' goal today was to land and establish a beachhead." He pointed at the Tenth Legion. They may have lost their aquilifer to Lowa's arrow, but they were jogging proudly southwards, their feet crunching out satisfyingly well-trained, regular beats on the British shingle.

"And the Britons' goal was to prevent the Romans landing. Now, the Romans may have lost more men, but if you know about war, you'll know that a general who's afraid of losing a few soldiers will not be a general for long. The Romans have landed, the Britons have failed to stop them, so the Romans have won."

"I see," said the helmsman.

"Good," said Ragnall, putting a hand on the sailor's shoulder.

"So let me get it clear," said the simple man, "it's a Roman victory if the Roman goal was to land and the Britons' goal was to stop them."

"Yes."

"Thank you for explaining."

"You're welcome."

"Thing is, though, and I'm sure you're right, but how do we know the enemy's goal? How do you know the Britons were trying to stop the Romans from landing?"

"Of course they were, it's obvious, they—"

"Are you sure? 'Cos I didn't see anything to suggest that they were. I saw them kill a lot – a *lot* – and I saw them fight well – very well – and then I saw them run off as if it had been their plan all along to put the fear of Mars into the legionaries then let the Romans come ashore."

"No, no, that's wrong. They were definitely trying to stop the landing. Of course they were. What else . . ."

"If you say so! You're a legate and I'm just a captain," said the grinning Syrian.

He really was an irritating little man.

Chapter 7

The bay's water was golden, smooth as a consul's table-cloth, punctuated only by the mast of the whale-holed sailing ship which had limped to shore, grounded, then been submerged by the rising tide.

Felix was waiting for Kelter and brooding. He'd been beaten by inferior druids. He cursed himself. He'd been so surprised by the leviathan strike, then so busy marshalling his men to get the ship back to Gaul – and by Neptune it had been a close thing – that he hadn't struck back. He could have killed a few captives and used the power to stop the hearts of the men on the boat – he was the stronger druid, he was sure – but by the time revenge had crossed his mind they were too far away.

But why had Lowa sent those druids and not Spring to attack him? Was she holding the girl back? Or had Spring sunk Caesar's armada to the north with a thousand whales? It was possible. He shook his head. He hoped not. If Caesar was killed and his army drowned, then Felix's scheme for ruling the world would need a major rethink.

Meanwhile, he was stuck here in Gaul, or at least his demons were. He'd sent some Leathermen north, in case Caesar had left any ships behind, but they'd returned without finding any, as he'd known they would.

He summoned Kelter.

"You called, boss?" asked Kelter, jogging up unmasked and smiling. In the setting sun his carbuncles shone virulently red and oozed disgusting yellow.

"You are going to kill one captive now, then row me and two captives to Britain in the ship's tender," he said.

"Sure," smiled Kelter, "but why aren't we all going?"

"Because there are no fucking ships and we've got to go and get one!"

"Let's go!"

"Right. Get the captives tied in the boat, and take your leather armour off but bring it with you."

"Why?"

"The captives? To fuel your rowing."

"No, why not wear my armour?"

"Because you'll need it in Britain, but your rowing will be more efficient if you're unimpeded." And, thought Felix, watching your muscles flex will give me something to do on the journey.

"Yeah, good point."

Felix smiled.

Yilgarn Craton found it easy to avoid the British sentries because he was one of them. He said he was off to check defences southwards and stole along the channel separating the Roman spit from the mainland. He congratulated himself on moving like a particularly stealthy shadow despite his muscular bulk. Dunes along the nearside of the spit hid the invaders' camp from view, but he could hear the yells, hammering and sawing that had been growing in volume since Lowa's ignominious retreat had gifted the Romans a beachhead.

When he was sure that no Britons were watching – their attention was focused on the Roman side of the channel anyway – he slipped into the water. He bobbed, aware that both sets of sentries might have slung a stone or shot an arrow into him at any moment. What he was doing was incredibly dangerous, but he was incredibly brave, plus Jocanta had asked him to do it. He would have cut his own hands off if she'd asked him to. He set off, his mind so engaged trying to work out how one might cut off both one's own hands that he was on the other side and out of the water in what seemed like no time.

You'd need someone else to help you, he concluded as he reached the top of the dune and saw the Roman camp. Well, they'd been busy. In their short time on British soil they'd build an entire town, wall and ditch included. What an efficient lot! Men after his own heart; and Jocanta's, she liked efficiency. She was right to throw the Haxmite lot in with this crowd – even more so now that Lowa had killed a Haxmite for some paltry offence, and then had the gall to tell Yilgarn to keep his men under control. He'd see her regret her lack of respect.

Either side of the camp, warships were drawn up onto the beach like a row of forts. Moonlight lit up the points of the huge arrows on scorpions lining their sides. The transports – more boats than Yilgarn had ever seen in one place – were moored a hundred paces out, silhouettes on the silvery sea.

He set off down the dune with his hands in the air. He'd gone three paces when someone very nearby shouted something which made him jump. He stopped, guessing that the shout had meant "Halt!" In about three blinks of an eye, a dozen legionaries had appeared from Bel knew where, all pointing spears at him. He'd heard that the Romans in Gaul were used to people surrendering, so surely they'd understand his intentions and not run him through?

They did understand. In fact they looked rather bored as they patted him down for hidden weapons, then gestured at him with their spears to follow them. They were small men, about Yilgarn's height, but all added together they didn't have as much muscle on their limbs as he did. He could have taken the lot of them, no problem, but he was following Jocanta's orders so he did what he was told, holding his chin high to that his captors would know that he was an impressive man, not to be messed with, and that he was walking into their camp at spear point very much on his own terms.

They marched through a gateway that bisected the cleanly constructed ditch, wall and palisade, then past rows of freakishly well-ordered, identical tents. A legionary pulled open the flap of one tent – how by Dwyn he could tell one from another, Yilgarn had no idea – and the others gestured with their spears for him to enter. He found more guard types and a table behind which sat a man wearing a ridiculous plumed helmet. The Gaulish tongue was nearly the same as the British one and the cockerel-headed soldier could speak Gaulish, or at least he thought he could. He was about as linguistically skilled as a four-year-old and he had a stupid staccato accent that didn't help things at all. He asked Yilgarn why he'd come. Yilgarn told him, repeating himself more loudly and clearly until the fool understood. The name Jocanta Fairtresses, chief of the Haxmites, clearly carried some weight even with the Romans, because the feather-headed fellow himself stood up and asked Yilgarn to follow him to meet Julius Caesar.

Yilgarn was led through the dizzyingly regular camp to a tent bigger than the Haxmite longhouse, and ushered in.

Because his own hair was so thick, black and curly, or possibly because he was a sympathetic man, Yilgarn always felt sorry for men who'd lost the hair from the top of their heads. The poor blighters had such difficult choices! They could carry on growing it from the back of their heads, which made them look old, they could shave it all off, which made them look thuggish, or they could comb the remaining hair over in an attempt to look hirsute which had never fooled anyone in the history of hairstyling. Julius Caesar, leader of the Romans and scourge of the Gauls, had chosen the latter method, which put Yilgarn at ease. It was hard to respect a man who looked like such a tit. He was tall, though, much taller than Yilgarn, as were all his black-clad guards. Those guys had some muscle. Nothing like Yilgarn's, though. He could have taken the lot of them.

Caesar spoke some gibberish in Latin. It reminded Yilgarn of a babbling child.

"Caesar bids you welcome," said the very tall and polished-looking young Roman next to the general, in faultless Island of Angels British, "and asks you to tell him who you are and why you have come here?"

Yilgarn told him, not sure whether to address the general or the translator. He settled for half and half.

He'd been concerned that the Romans wouldn't be interested in the help of the Haxmite tribe. He'd heard that they all were arrogant, effete little toffs with no time for real men like him. But they listened to him patiently as he told them all about Lowa's shameful attack on Jocanta Fairtresses, asked him questions that showed how well they understood Jocanta's grievances and generally treated him with the dignity he deserved. It was very, very different from the way Lowa Flynn had behaved towards him and his chief. (By Makka, if Lowa hadn't confused him with that one-handed trick, he'd have driven her to pain town in a cart made of agony, he really would have done.)

He left a long time later. The legionaries escorted him back to the channel, not at spear point this time. He swam across, climbed out unseen, stripped and wrung out his wet clothes, then marched back to camp, arms swinging, like the hero that he was.

"I do not understand," said Labienus back in Caesar's tent, "why these barbarians surrender so easily. Have they no pride?"

"Caesar has noticed," said Caesar, "that man will loathe his mild-mannered neighbour a great deal more fiercely than he will loathe a mass murderer whom he has never met. This childlike, irrational trait is stronger in barbarians. Given the chance and an excuse, he will slit the throat of a man he has known all his life, all due to some wrongly perceived slight from years before. So, Queen Lowa cut off this Yilgarn Craton's chief's hair — showing more clemency than Caesar would have done given the circumstances — and as a result Craton is prepared to deliver all of Britain, knowing that Caesar will enslave its people. This is why Romans rule and the brutish barbarians are their slaves."

Ragnall coughed.

"You are different, Ragnall, because you have learnt Roman ways. Your years among the Romans have improved you more than you can imagine. It is these improvements that Caesar brings to the barbarians. A few generations from now and these brutes, or at least their upper ranks, will be human."

"Indeed," nodded Labienus, "and moving on to matters martial, shall I have the men ready to march inland and fight at dawn?"

"No," said Caesar. "We hold here."

Labienus looked as if he was about to say something else, but he was silenced by the general's raised eyebrow.

Chapter 8

"And how long have you been mulling this plan around in your mind?" asked Dug. "Actually, make that mulling it around in your arse. This plan's been nowhere near anybody's mind."

Spring shook her head. Being dead had not helped Dug's analytical powers. "I'd have thought it was pretty clear. I ended the last war by killing one good man and thousands of other people. I'm going to end this one by killing one man who deserves it. Isn't this better?"

"Aye, if would be it you could do it, but you can't. You'll get yourself, Sadist and Pig Fucker killed, or worse."

"What's worse than being killed? And it's Pigsy and Sadie now."

But Dug was gone again. Guiltily, Spring felt a little glad. Her plan was full of holes and she didn't want anyone making her look into them. She just wanted to get it done. She crept through the night, grateful for the clouds scudding across the moon. Darting from cover to cover in the spells of moon shade, she skirted the perimeter of British watchers, her dogs padding quietly behind and lying silently when she paused.

There was only one path through the marsh that led to the beach, but Spring had spent whole days hunting waterfowl around the island of Mearhold, so was undaunted by wading through the morass's reputedly impassable muddy channels, her bow and hammer held aloft. The dogs took a little persuasion, but in the end they followed her, swimming when they could and dragging themselves unhappily through the mud when they couldn't.

Muddy, damp and cold, Spring peered through bushes at the edge of the beach, and silently asked Makka the god of war and Dwyn the god of tricks for inspiration. She needed it. She was near enough the Roman camp to hit a man in the eye with an arrow, but she might as well have been in a box at the bottom of the sea, the amount of chance she had of shooting Caesar. Since landing earlier that day the busy little Italian men had built a walled and ditched town flanked by heavily armed, beached ships; six facing her, five on the camp's far side. The oversized tips of scorpion arrows poked from the sides of each ship. Whatever else people said about the Romans —and she'd heard plenty — they did not muck about.

She'd imagined that the Roman camp would be more like, well, a camp, a collection of bivouacs and tents with Caesar strutting about in full view, giving commands and arranging crucifixions. That had been naïve, she realised. She could see a few guards on the palisade, and some people on the ships, but of the Roman general there was no sign, and she didn't imagine that he was about to walk out of the camp just to see if there were any assassins who wanted to take a pop.

Pigsy shuffled behind her.

"Shush!" she whispered.

Lowa found Maggot some way back from the beach, sitting next to Hardward on a log by a fire. Both had their hands cupped around steaming clay mugs. Maggot was wagging his finger and talking as Hardward nodded, but he stopped when Lowa came within earshot and said:

"Ah, Lowa, let me get you some tea! It'll make you happy and it'll make you pee." Hardward nodded hello as if he hadn't been such a dickhead earlier in the day.

"No, thanks. Do you know where Spring is?" Lowa wanted someone to join her firing arrows up and over into the Roman camp, and Spring was the only other person capable. That's what she was telling herself, anyway. It wasn't because she wanted to make amends.

"She went north then west with her dogs shortly after sunset. She thought she was sneaking off."

"Where was she going?"

"I don't know. To look at the Romans?"

Lowa shook her head. The girl was a liability.

The sun had been up for a good while when Sadie nudged Spring awake.

"Where's Pigsy?" she asked. Sadie looked back at her as if to say "Never mind that, where's my breakfast?"

"We'll eat later," said Spring, standing to peer from their bushy hiding place. "Right now I've got to . . . well, I'll be buggered by a badger."

Spring had crept up onto the dunes and dug herself and the dogs in behind the marram grass. It hid them and gave her a good elevated view of the camp. Now, walking towards her along the shingle, some way from the gates, were three figures. Felix, one of his Leathermen and a tall (for a Roman) balding man with shining gold armour and a red cape. Unless Spring was very much mistaken, the third man was Julius Caesar. He certainly fitted all the descriptions she'd heard.

She reached for her bow, drew, aimed and loosed. Instantaneously the Leatherman shoved Caesar out of the way and the arrow zipped harmlessly by. Felix and Caesar looked about for the would-be assassin. The Leatherman's gaze zeroed in at her hiding place. He leapt like a startled horse and came flying towards Spring at an astonishing pace, sword flashing from its scabbard and into his hand as he ran.

"Bollocks," whispered Spring, leaping round and running. She'd gone maybe ten paces before she heard the Leatherman behind her. She tossed her bow to the side, dropped and spun, whipping her hammerhead at his knee. He danced a step, avoided the blow and kicked her in the face. As she fell she saw Sadie leap. The Leatherman dropped into a crouch, thrust his blade upwards and opened Sadie's stomach. Guts burst out and the dog yelped horribly as she fell.

"Nooo!" roared Spring, thrusting the sharpened hammer end into the man's midriff. He batted it aside and punched her in the face.

She came to with the Leatherman straddling her, his hand in her hair and a blade at her neck. She struggled but his iron thighs had her gripped.

"I recognise the flight of your arrow," said the Leatherman, in Roman-accented Gaulish, muffled by his mask. "You killed my friend by the river." His tone was strangely chipper and matter-of-fact. He took the knife from her neck and gripped her by the chin. "They will want you alive, but I am going to kill you, to avenge him." She tried to shake her head but she couldn't budge. "But I cannot leave a mark, or my lie that you died of terror will not pass. So."

"Wait!" she managed before he shifted his hand to cover her mouth and pinched her nose shut with thumb and forefinger. She tried to suck in a breath but could not. She struggled, but he was immovable, so she stopped, saving her air and wondering what to do. She could hear Sadie yipping somewhere near her feet, quieter and sadder with each yip.

Lowa galloped north from the village, sick with worry. Nobody had seen Spring all night, but Maggot had said she'd gone north, and two others had seen a girl and two dogs heading for the marsh.

She rode on, cursing herself for not going to see Spring

after Dug's death — surely the reason for her surliness, which, if Lowa was reasonable, was not totally impossible to understand. But fuck reasonable! Lowa had a land to save, an army to rebuild, an invasion to prepare for . . . After this, after the Romans were gone, she swore she would make time for the people she loved. Which pretty much meant little Dug and Spring. She would delegate her powers and spend at least half her time with her son. She would rebuild the relationship with Spring . . . if the girl lived through whatever damnfool scheme she'd embarked on.

Spring heard a bark and had time to think "Stupid dog, you shouldn't have barked before you attacked!" before she sensed Pigsy leap. The Leatherman took his hand from her face and she gasped in air as his blade flew back to meet the new threat . . . and there it stayed. Sadie had slithered up, thrown herself forward with her final efforts and grasped the Leatherman's arm in strong jaws. He lifted his other hand from her neck to deflect Pigsy's leap, but it was too late. Pigsy clamped his teeth into the man's throat, puncturing the leather as if it was cotton, snarling and chomping. Blood gushing from his ripped hood, the Leatherman tried to pull his arm from Sadie's jaw. It held. Sadie growled and shook her head. He wrenched again and his arm came free, minus a hand.

The Leatherman screamed, grabbed Pigsy by the scruff with his remaining hand and pulled. His strength, Spring thought through all the horror, was amazing. He wrenched Pigsy from his neck. Half his throat came away in the dog's jaws. Spring saw vertebrae and the pipe of his trachea for an instant before blood cascaded and obscured the gore. He wasn't done, though. Holding Pigsy with his good hand, the demon, proving how just how far he was from human, stabbed the splintered bone of his other wrist into the dog's side, again and again.

"No!" shouted Spring. She heaved. As the Leatherman fell back she swung the hammer into the side of his head. He crumpled. Pigsy fell away, limp. Spring bounced to her feet and slammed the hammer down on the demon's forehead, denting it with a horrible crunch. Two-handed, she lifted the hammer above her head, as high as she could, and brought it down with everything she had. The Leatherman's head exploded like a rotten cabbage. She staggered backwards, blinded by his brains and blood. Someone gripped her from behind and said something in Latin as she passed out.

Chapter 9

"Have you seen Spring?" demanded Lowa, sliding from her horse before it had stopped, longbow in hand.

Chamanca looked at Atlas. "We haven't seen her," he said. "I'll ask around." The Iberian and the African were guarding the path through the marsh, along with Adler, the Two Hundred and the most capable of Atlas' infantry.

"Has anyone seen Spring!?" Lowa shouted.

Nobody had.

"Atlas, find me everyone who guarded the marsh last night,"

"They will be asleep."

"Wake them. Chamanca, help him. Find out if anyone saw Spring."

"Wait," said Atlas. "I sent some men through the marsh to look at the camp. One of them approaches now."

A slight, big-toothed, grey-stubbled man jogged up. Plaxon was his name. Lowa had fought next to him once shortly after joining Zadar's army. She'd progressed and he'd remained a simple soldier because, although he was a kindly, happy fellow, he was seriously thick.

"Have you seen Spring?" she said.

"I found her dogs," he said, looking at his feet.

"Yes?"

"In the dunes, near the demons' camp. They're dead. One's got its stomach slit, the other's been stabbed a lot. I checked, and they definitely are dead."

Lowa felt a ball of sickness rise from her stomach into her throat. "Any sign of Spring? Or anyone else?"

"No."

"No footprints, tracks?"

The man looked blank. "I don't know what—"

"Take me to where you found them, now."

The man nodded, turned round and started trudging back towards the marsh.

"We're going quicker than that," said Lowa, running past him and pulling his arm.

"Can I have the girl?" asked Felix, trying to sound like he wasn't more desperate to have her than he'd been to have anything ever before. "Keep her if you like, of course, but she'd be useful to power the Maximen for the row back from Gaul."

Caesar looked at Spring, held firm in the praetorian's arms. She'd already sent another praetorian to the medic's tent by pretending to be unconscious then smashing his knee with her hammer. Now she was tightly bound and actually unconscious after the knee-smashed praetorian had punched her. Another praetorian held her hammer.

The general looked the girl up and down. Felix followed his gaze. She had changed a lot. It was hard to tell with her head lolling and bedraggled hair obscuring her face, but when he'd last seen her she'd been on course to becoming a beautiful woman. Her figure had certainly developed well. Leather shorts revealed cleanly muscled legs – more like an athletic Roman boy's than a Roman woman's but Felix didn't consider this a bad thing, and under her archer's shirt she had a narrow waist and a well-shaped chest. Would Caesar want to keep her to himself? In Rome he generally preferred the wives of powerful men for bed mates, but in Gaul he had taken into his tent a few of the more attractive captives, both male and female, but generally young and physically fit like Spring. Or he could be planning to sell her as a slave.

Like all fabulously wealthy men that Felix had encountered, one of Caesar's favourite leisure activities was making even more money. A fresh, attractive barbarian, captured on British soil, would fetch a high price in Rome.

"I can't see that you'd have any use for a British girl," tried Felix, "we already have all the information we'll need from Yilgarn, and she'll fetch no great price since Rome's awash with British slaves from Zadar's days. The first generation of British slave children are about her age now, so there is a glut of girls exactly like her, but they're well-trained and won't require breaking."

Caesar ignored him, his eyes lingering on her thighs.

Ah, thought Felix, it's not a slave thing. "If you do keep her for . . . yourself," he tried, "please let me check her for disease first. They start them young here and women are passed round the elders of the tribe. When I lived here I found, by her age, almost all of the women were nastily diseased, with pus-filled, stinking—"

"Enough, Felix! Take her with you to Gaul and do what you will with her."

Felix tried not to show his excitement. As soon as they were at sea he'd eat her heart and take her magic. He'd collect his legion from Gaul and that would be the beginning...

"Praetorian," commanded Caesar, "follow Felix to his ship and restrain the girl on board." He turned as if to walk away, then turned back. "Actually, hold for a second. Why was she armed with a hammer? A very strange weapon for a woman . . . is there a story there? When she is revived, be sure to ask her, Felix."

"There's no need. Many British women use hammers. They are brutes."

"I'm not so sure, this one also fired an arrow, a long way and very accurately. That's a good point – where are her bow and quiver?"

"Got the quiver here, sir," said a praetorian, "it was on her back."

"And the bow?"

The praetorians looked dumbly at each other.

"It must be where you found her. Go back and get it." The praetorians set off at a jog. "And I will keep the girl so she can show Caesar how she managed to shoot an arrow further and more accurately than any of his Cretan archers."

"You don't need the girl to show you how it works," said Felix, trying not to sound desperate. "It's a bow. You slot the arrow, pull the string and let go. The simple fact is that British bows are better than Cretan bows. This one is probably made from Iberian yew. I can show your engineers how."

Caesar looked at Felix for a moment as if considering having him boiled in olive oil, then deflated a little and said: "Oh, very well. Caesar has more pressing matters. Take her. Interrogate her before you kill her. Caesar wants to know anything useful that she knows."

"Of course." Felix tried not to beam. "Follow me!" he said to the praetorian, setting off for his ship and the beginning of a wonderful new chapter in his life.

"We're here," panted Plaxon as they arrived in a steep dip in the dunes, shielded from all around by sand and marram.

Lowa nodded, struck dumb by a sadness heavy as iron. Dug's dogs Pig Fucker and Sadist, who had been her dogs, too, for a time, were dead. Both had their guts spilled and were abuzz with fat, black flies. The hounds were next to each other, but Sadist had crawled some way and left her entrails trailing five paces behind her. One of Pig Fucker's paws rested on Sadist's shoulder.

"Go," she said to Plaxon.

"Do you want—"

"*Go*."

He went.

Danu, the dead dogs were a heart-breaking sight. That stupid girl! She circled the dogs, analysing the sandy declivity.

By the quantity of brain matter spattered about the sand and stuck to the wide grass blades, one person had been killed, possibly by Spring's hammer. By the tracks leading up the dune, towards the camp, he or she – no, he, since the Romans didn't have "she" in a military capacity and the trail came from someone heavier than Spring – had been pulled away first, then somebody else the size and weight of Spring, wearing iron-heeled boots, had been dragged away by a large man holding her under the arms and leaving heel marks in the sand. So they'd taken her, unconscious or dead. She looked about for further clues and found Spring's bow, still strung. *Stupid girl!* she said to herself again.

She was alive, she knew it, she just knew it, but the Romans had her. She crept up the dune and peered through the grass.

On the far side of the camp she saw a ship's mast wobble, jerk and shift towards the sea. They were refloating one of their oared warships. Why? To take Spring away? Surely not. Why would they do that?

Nearer than the ships and more pressingly, two black-clad legionaries were walking towards her hiding place. She thought she was hidden, but one of them spotted her, touched his companion on the arm and pointed. Both came at a run. For the briefest of moments, Lowa considered fleeing. She didn't want to give them any reason for taking revenge on Spring. Then she thought, screw it. Killing so many of them when they landed had already given the Romans all the reasons in the world to kill any captives, so two more wouldn't make any difference. She had her own bow on her back, but since Spring's was already strung she used that. The leftmost one fell. She waited while the other wrestled

with the age-old decision when facing a ranged weapon —
charge or flee? He charged. Brave man, thought Lowa, and
shot him through the neck. She would also have shot him
if he'd fled.

Her plan had been containment. The Romans must be
aware by now that advancing from the spit was going to be
so costly that their only chance was to relocate or return to
Gaul and come back next year; probably the latter, given
the fact that summer was nearly over and launching a
successful invasion would be all the harder once the weather
turned. Over the winter, Lowa could prepare further and
the Gauls or Germans might just deal with the Romans for
them.

But now they had Spring? Screw them, screw their
tortoises and screw their ship-mounted scorpions, she
thought as she ran back to the marsh. She was going to
come back with her army, rescue Spring and kick the fuckers
off her island.

Chapter 10

"Heave, heave! You, fool, get off the deck! Are you fucking stupid? Stop making the boat heavier and help push it into the water, you arse! Heave the rest of you! Heave!"

The men were working as fast as was reasonable, and Felix knew that it was him being the arse, shouting at them like that, but he couldn't help it. He was desperate to be at sea and alone with Spring. By the time he got back to pick up his demons he'd have so much magic he'd be like a god!

"*COME ON!*" he bellowed.

He looked over to the praetorian. He still had Spring in his grip. He could hardly believe he was so close now. The silly girl had delivered herself to him! No, no, it had been the gods, for sure. They wanted him to have her.

"Felix!" He spun round. It was Ragnall. Tits! The silly boy could ruin everything. "Let me have a look at that girl," he said. His Latin was accent-free now, Felix noticed.

"No."

"Why not?"

"I don't have to give you a reason."

"I am Caesar's chosen king of Britain, you are on my island and I will see that girl."

"No! Praetorian, take her aboard the ship now." There'd been a time when he'd have been able to make all of them unite to carry out his wishes purely by thinking about it, as he'd done so often with Zadar's troops at Maidun, but he seemed to have lost that power. Had he used up too much life-force? Or perhaps pouring all his energies into his Maximen and Celermen had meant forsaking the control skill? He tried it, focusing his mind and willing Ragnall to go away.

Ragnall pulled his sword, unaffected. "You will do no such thing. I will see that girl."

"Will you ladies both calm down," said the praetorian. "I take orders from two men, neither of whom are you. I will put the girl on the ship, as Caesar has commanded —"

"Do it now! Now!" Felix was bouncing on the sand, all sense gone. He had to get the girl on that ship!

"— however, I will not put her on board before the ship is floating, because, Felix, as you pointed out so eloquently a moment ago, that would be fucking stupid. In the meantime, I cannot see why Ragnall should not—"

"Hello, Ragnall, hello, Felix. How are you both?" said Spring groggily, returning to consciousness at exactly the wrong moment.

"Spring! I knew it was you," said Ragnall.

"Praetorian! Kill them both! They are plotting in barbarian language against Caesar!"

The praetorian looked at Felix, shaking his head.

"We are plotting nothing," said Ragnall. "We were greeting each other in the British tongue. This girl is a British princess. Her father was King Zadar of Maidun, as Felix well knows. I'm sure you told Caesar, didn't you, Felix?" The druid looked at his feet. "You didn't? Well, I'm sure the praetorian will agree that the general will want to know that he has such a valuable captive."

The praetorian raised an eyebrow at Felix. Felix gibbered. The praetorian shook his head. "Ragnall, you're right, I will take her to Caesar. Felix, come as well and explain why you didn't tell the general who he had, and why you wanted her for yourself."

Felix breathed in to scream orders at the praetorian, but then deflated. He'd got as far he had by being the master of his temper and knowing when to back down. It wasn't the end. He would have the girl. There was only one thing he could do now.

"Hang on, let me have another look at her." He walked over.

"Not too close, Felix." The praetorian took a step back. "I don't like this at all."

Felix shook his head. "I didn't mean her any harm. I'm just in a hurry . . . and actually, Ragnall, now you mention it, I *do* recognise her. I am *so* sorry and thanks *so* much for realising who she was. She's much older than when I last saw her, that's why I didn't recognise her. Praetorian, please take her directly to the medical tent and have those bruises on her face looked at and have her checked for concussion. Then go on to Caesar. I certainly won't harm her now I know who she is, and I look forward very much to seeing her on my return and having a good old catch-up. Goodbye, Ragnall, goodbye, Spring!"

The druid walked away, grinding his teeth and trying not to scream.

"I am fine." Atlas shivered, disproving his statement.

"Fenn's tits," said Chamanca, "I will be seriously pissed off if you die because of your bull-headedness. Go and see Maggot, now." Toughness she liked. Stupidity was unappealing and Atlas was being about as stupid as can be.

"Maybe later – look."

Chamanca turned and saw Lowa running into the village centre.

"Adler," called the queen, "Atlas, Chamanca, Mal, to me!"

Atlas staggered as he stood. His skin, usually a shining brown-purple, was turning muddy grey.

"Sit down again, Atlas," said Lowa. "You," she pointed

at a nearby soldier. "Find the druid Maggot, send him here."

"There's no need," said Atlas. "I have put a poultice on the wound. It is all that can be done."

Lowa shook her head. "Maggot will be the judge of that." Chamanca could have kissed her. "Right, everyone gather in round Atlas. I want your opinions."

"On what?"

"On how we're going to defeat the Romans tonight."

As they discussed and debated, Atlas stayed silent. His eyes were bloodshot and flickering.

"Atlas," said Lowa, "you will go and lie down until Maggot—"

"Until I what?" said Maggot, jogging up, his adornments jingling like a cart decorated with bells, followed by "Ah" when he saw the Kushite. "Can you walk, Atlas?" he asked.

"Course I can walk." The big man stood, then fell back down.

"You and you," Maggot called to two burly onlookers. "Take his arms and follow me." The men helped Atlas to his feet. "This way, come on, it's not far."

Lowa resumed the discussion of the battle to come, but Chamanca wasn't listening. She was watching the African's broad back heading off between the huts.

Ragnall followed Spring and the praetorian to the physician. There were several ranks of medical tents and Ragnall insisted that the praetorian took her to the highest, the one for legates and other important people. He waited outside while the doctor worked on her wounds.

Seeing Spring again had hit him like a plank to the face. Even though he'd known her for only a few months, here was someone from his previous life, someone who'd known Lowa and Dug — and Drustan, his dead mentor and friend. Seeing someone from that world and that time surrounded by Romans and Roman things was like a dream in which people and situations from different places and times muddle together in bright confusion. The nostalgia radiating from Spring was so weighty that his breath caught in his throat and he had to swallow to avoid weeping. The look, sound, even the smell of the girl made memories swirl into his head, not just of things that had happened in Britain, but of how it had felt to be happy. Well, not massively happy – his parents and brothers had just been killed when he met Spring – but he'd been a child, an innocent, lost in the world and looking to older people for guidance. He'd grown up so much since then, and not out of choice.

"You can go in," said the physician on his way out.

She was sitting on a camp bed. There were five other beds and three tables in the airy tent. Two were draped with cloths, the other held an array of gleaming little bronze tools – miniature pliers, knives, saws and other implements that Ragnall did not recognise. Only one other bed was occupied, by the sleeping or unconscious aquilifer of the Tenth Legion. He was the hero of the landing, apparently. Plenty of other people had been as brave, but none of them had been carrying a great gold "Look at me!" eagle on a pole, so it was the aquilifer who'd been noticed and who qualified for the best medical care. That was how the army worked. Lying on the bed next to the aquilifer was his golden standard, the letters SPQR under the eagle's claws. The letters stood for "the senate and people of Rome". Ragnall felt proud to be part of something so proud and mighty, although arguably the motto "for Caesar" might have reflected the legionaries' motivation more accurately.

"What happened to him?" Spring asked, nodding at the aquilifer, her voice muffled. Her jaw was swollen and one eye bruised, but colour had returned to her cheeks and the sparkle was back in her eye. Her hands were tied in front of her, attached to her shackled ankles by a thin chain which ran off the bed and disappeared under it.

"Battle happened to him. Never mind that, though, what happened to you?"

"Got caught trying to kill Caesar."

"Ah. We don't like that."

"We?"

"I'm a Roman now."

"That's like a horse deciding that it's a dog."

"No, it's not."

"Yes, it is. Why did you come here?"

"Me, or all the Romans?"

"You first."

"To bring the Roman way of life to Britain. You should see Rome, Spring. Just saying its name now makes me feel warm, excited. It's amazing . . . and we can have it all here in Britain, we really can. Clean water everywhere, warm homes in winter, governed by a rule of law that's the same for everyone and not subject to the whims of kings and—"

"And why are all the other Romans here?"

"Same reason."

"Are you sure?"

"Yes! Why else—"

"Ah, here she is." Caesar swept into the tent, flanked by a couple of praetorians. "Good. Spring. May Caesar call you Spring?"

Spring looked at him blankly, so Ragnall translated.

"May I call him baldy cuntface?" replied Spring.

"She says she's honoured that you should speak to her at all," said Ragnall.

"Good, good. So, a princess."

"Sort of."

"Come to assassinate Caesar, but Caesar will not trouble with details for such an esteemed guest."

"And . . ." Ragnall wondered whether to tell Caesar about

Spring's magic. He was almost certain that he'd seen her give Dug the power to fight like a god . . . but then she'd claimed she couldn't use magic any more and she certainly hadn't in the battle against the Dumnonians, when it would have been very handy. He decided to keep quiet, for now at least. "And she's daughter of King Zadar."

"*Is* she? Not your close relative?"

"Not my relative at all, other than the daughter of the man who slaughtered my family, but – oh."

Caesar was smiling, looking from him to the girl. Oh, Bel's tartan trousers, thought Ragnall. He realised all at once what Caesar was about to demand, why he wanted it and that there was no reasonable argument against it.

"She's too young!" was the only thing he could think of saying.

Caesar peered at her. "Too young? She's well past twelve, is she not? She's sixteen? Seventeen?"

"Something like that."

"Good. More than old enough. We will keep her chained for now, but you will look after her. Caesar will send you praetorians to protect her. She will be trained and as keen as you were to be Roman by the time you marry this winter."

Ragnall looked horror-struck at Spring, who grinned back at him as if she'd understood every word and was enjoying his discomfort. Ragnall had been fantasising recently about marrying a sophisticated, high-born Roman girl. Spring might have grown into an attractive woman, but her expressions, the way she moved, everything about her still screamed that she was a savage ragamuffin who wasn't above trying to solve problems by biting people. It would be like marrying a wolf cub.

"Caesar, I will do your bidding, but . . . Spring was about ten when I last saw her, but even then she was angrier and more wilful than a wildcat yet she was . . . capable. She sparked and organised the revolution that brought down her father. Given a chance, she will kill you, and she will do her best to undermine our mission . . . I did not translate entirely accurately when I said she was honoured to be spoken to."

Caesar looked down his nose. "Ragnall, Caesar is not an idiot and he does not pass through an invaded land without picking up the most popular insults. British is close enough to Gaulish for him to know that the word 'cunt' is not an honorific. You will make sure that her claws are kept away from Caesar and you will marry her."

"She won't want to marry me."

Caesar looked at him as if a singing squirrel had burst from the top of his head. "What, by all the gods, does that matter? Caesar's own sister Julia had to marry that oaf Pompey when she was the same age as this girl. She is lucky to be marrying a dashing prince and not a fat blowhard like him. And you should be glad – she is beautiful beneath the bruising and she has spirit. She will be an entertaining wife. You will marry in Rome this winter. When the army returns, the rightful king of Britain will be at its head, the rightful queen at his side.

"When the army returns . . .? We're going?"

"This is a reconnaissance mission. It is too late in the year for a full-scale invasion; surely you have learnt enough by now to realise that? We leave today, before the autumn storms take hold. We will return next year with an invasion force."

Ragnall could not believe what he was hearing. A reconnaissance mission was a couple of men in a boat sneaking ashore and having a look around. Twelve thousand armed men who hadn't left their landing site was the opposite of a reconnaissance mission. Could Caesar be fleeing? Surely not. But if so, why? Was Lowa's army as huge as their trumpets had suggested?

The general ignored his confusion. "Caesar must go.

Gather whatever you must gather and bring the girl to the flagship."

"Yes, Caesar."

"And a piece of advice. Do not teach her Latin and do your best to prevent her learning it. She will be less trouble if she depends on you."

Caesar swept from the tent.

"What was that all about then?" asked Spring. "And when can I go home?"

Lowa crept up the dunes on her elbows, Chamanca at her side. She and her commanders had come up with many ideas about how to attack the Romans, but all of them were flawed. There were plenty of ways that they could harm the invaders, but if she was going to attack, Lowa wanted to kill or capture all of them, partly so that they wouldn't come back and partly so that she could rescue Spring. The only realistic tactics they could come up with involved the Romans leaving the spit and marching inland, which they showed no sign of doing. She hoped that inspiration might strike if she had a long look at their camp.

She'd brought Chamanca with her partly to help deal with any overly alert sentries, but mostly to stop her brooding over Atlas. Maggot had done all that he could, but the African's wound had become septic and already spread its poison too far into his body. Given his great strength, Maggot guessed that he might live for another moon, perhaps a little longer. One man was a small price considering the number of Romans that they'd killed, but Lowa wished that it hadn't been Atlas. He was arguably their best fighter and a good leader, and seeing someone as indestructible as Chamanca brought low reminded Lowa just how much they had to lose by taking on the Romans. Atlas had advised flight. He would not be dying now if Lowa had taken his advice.

She'd hoped that they might encounter a guard or two

for Chamanca to tap, but so far they'd seen nobody. It was so quiet that Lowa was certain there was something afoot, but when they reached the top of the dunes and saw what it was, it was the last thing she had expected.

The transports were inshore, legionaries streaming onto them. In no time at all, the transports were full, the warships were refloated and all were sailing away. As the last act of their first invasion of Britain, the Romans put their camp to the torch. Chamanca and Lowa sat silently atop their dune and watched it burn.

Chapter 11

Spring leant on the ship's rail as the sun set, watching the Roman camp burn through a blur of tears. She didn't give the tiniest rat's cock that she'd been caught. She was crying because she'd told Dug she'd look after Sadie and Pigsy and instead she'd killed them both.

"Don't cry, Spring," said Dug, squinting back at the burning base. "The dogs chose to save you and they're with me now."

"In the Otherworld?"

"Aye."

"So you *are* a real ghost and not just part of my mind!"

"No, I am in your mind, but you think I'm in the Otherworld."

"But then how would you—"

"Don't overthink it. The point is the dogs were glad to die saving you and they're glad to be back with me. It wasn't for nothing. It was a good idea to kill Caesar and you nearly did it. Now you might get another chance."

Spring looked over her shoulder. Caesar was perhaps six paces away, talking to a scribe who was scribbling furiously. It was a shame she was attached to the rail by a pace-long chain, with nothing lethal within reach to throw.

"What the badger's arse bristles is that man doing?" Dug asked.

"Talking."

"The other one."

"Writing."

"I'd wondered what that looked like."

"I know how to do it. The girl who taught me Latin showed me," said Spring, expecting Dug to be surprised, but he'd gone.

Spring and the Roman merchant's daughter who'd taught her Latin at Zadar's behest had invented a wide range of abusive terms. Spring had been within a heartbeat of unleashing the lot of them on Caesar back in the physician's tent, but then decided that it would be more interesting if she kept her linguistic abilities to herself. Already it had proved a good decision; she was enjoying Ragnall's discomfort around her, looking forward to his awkwardness when he told her they were to be married, and planning a whole range of suitable responses.

Back in Britain, the flames were dying. She wondered if Lowa was watching the same fire, whether she'd noticed that she was missing yet, and if she'd care even a little bit when she did.

The wind dropped and she could hear what Caesar was saying to the scribe. It was an account of his trip to Britain, sort of. She listened in, increasingly amazed. The general's story was detailed, plausible – and utterly fabricated. He finished off by saying how he had put the Britons to flight, burnt a number of villages and secured hostages. Due to a lack of space on the ships, only two of these hostages were returning to Gaul with him – Spring guessed he must mean her and Ragnall – but he'd be back to collect the rest.

No space for hostages? thought Spring. It had been pretty convincing until that part. Surely nobody would ever believe that you'd leave hostages behind because you had no space for them! There's always a bit more room on a ship and it was not a long journey.

They arrived in Gaul at dawn and rode to a Roman camp, Spring under Ragnall's and the praetorians' guard. Over the next days she was allowed to walk around their boring, regular camp a little, but she remained chained and was watched constantly by four praetorians operating in shifts of two. To stay fit and strong – ready to slay Caesar then escape – she jumped on the spot, lifted heavy things and performed all the exercises that Lowa had taught her. The stony-faced praetorians didn't seem to mind.

They were near the sea, but she was forbidden to go to the port area, presumably to stop her seeing the extensive shipbuilding that was going on to prepare for the next inva- sion. Even if she hadn't been able to listen to everyone talking about it, the constant stream of timber-laden carts that trundled seaward and returned empty gave the game away. She heard that these boats were to be larger than the previous lot, so that they might carry livestock, horses and elephants, and that they were to have a shallower draught, so that the next landing wasn't such a cock-up. She wondered what elephants were.

Ragnall forbade the praetorians from speaking when they were near her – he was paranoid about failing Caesar and letting her learn Latin – but they only stuck to his orders when he was there. The rest of the time, despite their tough looks, they chatted away like elderly sisters who hadn't seen each other for ages. Spring learnt that the men loved and trusted Caesar. They were confused about the recent trip to Britain, why it had changed from an invasion to a recon- naissance mission, and quite why the general had taken twelve thousand men on what had turned out to be a camping trip, then burnt the camp. Even Caesar's most zealous supporter among the four praetorians conceded that his hero had made a mistake – the clincher being that they'd come away with no loot – but they all agreed that it was his first error in three years of successful campaigning and he would set it right soon enough.

There were rumours that he would cross next year with

ten legions as well as these things called elephants that they all thought were pretty amazing. None of them ever mentioned Felix's Ironmen and Leatherman so Spring guessed they didn't know about them. She was dying to ask, but managed not to. The most difficult thing was keeping the horror from her face when they talked about her. Perhaps some women might have been flattered but Spring was disgusted. The things they said! Did men really talk like this when there were no women around? She was sure that British men didn't. Several times she nearly said something pithy and complicated in Latin just to see the looks on their faces, but she resisted.

One surprising thing she did learn was that the praetorians held Ragnall in some grudging respect. Not enough to not talk in front of her as he'd asked, obviously, but apparently he had killed a German king and that had impressed everyone. Spring knew all about Harry the Fister, or Ariovistus as this lot called him, from Atlas' tales. Killing him probably had been a feat, and she waited for Ragnall to tell her the story of how he'd done it, but he never did. She'd thought he was the type of man who'd be unable to refrain from talking about his own successes, but actually he never talked about himself at all. She didn't like him; he was a deluded dick who saw no flaws in Caesar's murderous warmongering, but he wasn't a show-off.

What he did go on and on about – and on and on – was Rome. He was frustrated that they weren't heading directly for the capital because Caesar had a local rebellion to crush, but he more than made up for it by constantly telling Spring every little thing about the city.

His only topic of conversation other than Rome and its inhabitants was Caesar, whom he idolised, just as he'd idolised Drustan when they'd first met, and then Lowa. Ragnall, she thought, needed someone to follow. Dug had once told her why people were addicted to things like alcohol and mushrooms. Their addiction, he said, was a comfortable place that removed them from the troublesome real world of decision-making, guilt and so on. That was why Ragnall always had to follow someone, she reckoned. He'd never had to make a decision in his life and had become addicted to being told what to do. Nothing had ever been his fault. It might be, she mused, why he never talked about himself and his successes. Just as he thought his failures were other people's failures, he probably never counted his successes as his own.

Eventually, over a moon or so in Gaul, she found herself coming to like him, a little. He was a traitor who'd joined the enemy. He was blind to the faults of those he idolised and followed them unquestioningly – something that Spring would never, never do – but he was not a bad man and there was a certain strength to him. She was his prisoner. He could have neglected her or beaten her or worse, but he didn't. Instead he spent most waking hours with her, explaining how Roman structures worked and how they all culminated in this wondrous city where they were going to spend the winter. Ultimately, his incessant enthusiasm was effective. By the time they headed for Rome, Spring was quite looking forward to seeing it.

Chapter 12

With the ship and crew that Caesar had provided, Felix crossed back to Gaul. The journey was achingly slow because the captain and slave rowers refused to believe that he could make things go very badly wrong for them if they didn't speed up, yet he found his legion stunningly unchanged. Felix's keen mind needed constant occupation, yet his creations could sit and stare unthinkingly into space and simply wait for him to return. He was fairly sure that some of them hadn't moved at all since he'd left. That irritated him on one level because he thought it proved that they were seriously unintelligent, but on another, more niggling level he knew that he'd never achieve the peace of mind needed to simply sit, yet these brutes could do it with ease. So, in one way, their minds were superior to his.

Since the crew of slave rowers had been surly on his way back and the captain disrespectful, Felix enjoyed his first order to the Celermen and Maximen: to kill half of the slaves to fuel the Maximen's row back, and to break the legs of the rest so that they might not cause any trouble until their deaths on arrival in Britain. Unfortunately they needed the captain, so he'd have to stay alive for a while, but Felix expected he'd be a good deal more deferential on the return journey.

After a faster but still annoyingly slow load using two tenders, they set off back to Britain with the Maximen rowing at an astonishing pace. As the boat surged through the swell, Felix kept a lookout for British druids in boats and ship-holing behemoths, but the sea was blissfully clear. He called over Bistan the Celerman and told him he was the legion's new centurion. Bistan took the news of Kelter's death matter-of-factly. Although they came from the same Sicilian village, the men were very different – Bistan was smaller, pale-skinned between his pustules, light-haired and openly friendly, while Kelter had been dark and cruel-faced. Bistan was cruel in character, of course – all of Felix's creations were – but he didn't look it or act it when he wasn't actually hurting someone, which made him more pleasant to talk to than Kelter.

Felix told Bistan his plan for the landing, instructed him to continue the watch and settled back to bask in the wonderful music created by the screams and moans of the broken-legged Gaulish slaves, piled in the boat's bow, now tied up after a couple had managed to scrabble over the side to drown. The sounds reminded him of childhood voyages with his slave merchant father and he soon floated into peaceful slumber.

Bistan shook him awake and said with a cheery smile that there was a fleet of ships to the north and a fire to the north-east.

It was the Roman fleet – the entire Roman fleet – heading back to Gaul with lanterns at bow and stern twinkling prettily above the black sea, away from the burning Roman camp.

"*Neptune's knob end!*" he said. For a fleeting moment he thought about carrying on to Britain and taking the island himself – surely he could conquer the oafs with his legion alone? – but then he remembered that Caesar had Spring. And, actually, he needed the general's legions. His troops were powerful, but they were few, and they were mortal.

"Turn the boat around," he said, clenching his fists so hard that they shook.

"Sure, boss!" said Bistan, like a carefree junior baker asked to put a couple more loaves in the oven.

The following day, his legion safely concealed in a new and unlucky woodland village, Felix went to see Caesar. After a little asking around he rode along a road busy with empty ox-carts trundling inland and plank-laden carts bumping in the other direction to the coast, and found the general in the middle of what had once been forest but was now stumps, detritus and industry. Some slaves stripped leaves, twigs, branches and bark. Some tended great fires. Others carried logs to carpenters for the more skilled job of sawing planks. Swivel-eyed overseers armed with whips strode about with bored-looking legionary escorts. The air was thick with woodsmoke, sawdust, the bellows of oxen, the shouts of workers and the screamed pleadings of a few slackers that the overseers were whipping to the bone. Caesar stood as a serene hub in the Underworld-like whirl, peaceful as if he were watching a parade of vestal virgins on a cool afternoon.

"Ah, Felix," he said, "walk with me." He headed off, picking his way over broken branches and circumnavigating hut-sized piles of burning foliage and twigs.

When they were out of everyone's earshot, Felix said: "What happened? Why—"

"The army returned because part of the plan failed. The part of the plan that failed was yours."

"But I was on my way. I saw you and you agreed—"

"Had you landed as we'd arranged on your first attempt, then this conversation would not be taking place. However, you will not be punished."

Not be punished! The man was amazing. The plan was that he'd wait until Felix returned to Britain. It was Caesar's plan and he'd even supplied the ship. Something must have happened or he must have found out something new.

Whatever it was, Caesar had returned earlier than planned, forgotten what had actually happened and decided that it was all Felix's fault. This was why he was so dangerous. A man might be executed for failure in any army. In this army you could be executed for landing the wrong role in Caesar's fantasies.

"Caesar will launch an invasion next year," the general continued, "for a full campaign. His reconnaissance has confirmed what he thought. The Britons are a tougher nut to crack than the Gauls, so he will require a larger nutcracker. Six legions, more cavalry, more slingers and archers, your legion and more. Out of sight of Rome, the entire war machine might be fully tested in the obliteration of the British."

"I see. Where will we winter?"

"Caesar's wintering is unclear – there is rebellion in Illyricum that he will have to stamp on – but you will winter with your legion in the marshes of Belgium. There is insurgency fomenting in those swamps which may hamper next year's invasion of Britain. You and your troops will end it. Travel quietly and swiftly from village to village and teach them the folly of resistance."

"Execute some as an example?"

"Execute them all as a solution."

Felix sighed. Another ball-achingly cold winter away from Rome did not appeal, but at least he'd have some fun.

"Certainly, Caesar," he said.

"Good, then farewell, Caesar shall see you in the spring."

"Right. Ah. There's one other thing. Do you still have that British girl you captured?"

Caesar looked into his eyes unblinkingly for so long that Felix felt sweat prickle under the skin on his brow. "You seem unnaturally interested in this girl," he said eventually. "You were desperate to have her on the beach in Britain. Why do you want her?"

"I knew her in Britain."

"You did not know her well. Unless you were pretending not to recognise her at first."

"She has changed from a girl to a woman, she looks completely different."

"Answer the question now and truthfully. Why do you want her?"

"You know that my sacrifices are more effective if I know the victim. I have known this girl since she was born, so—"

"No. It is more than that. Caesar can see your desperation. Perhaps she is the great British magician of whom you spoke, whose powers will enable Caesar to conquer the world? Perhaps you mean to take these powers for yourself?"

"No, Caesar, no, you have it wrong. The magician, like all those who can use magic, is a man of reasonably advanced age, not a girl. It is possibly the man who commanded whales to hole my ship. Women do not have the capacity for magic."

Caesar looked him in the eye for far too long again. Felix felt a treacherous bead of sweat leak from his bald skull and trickle down behind his ear.

"No matter," the general said eventually, "because you will not be going anywhere near the girl and you will make no attempt to see her."

"If that is what Caesar wishes, I will strive to—"

Caesar turned and walked away at speed. It seemed that their audience was over, so Felix set off back to his legion. Shortly afterwards he came across a large grass snake writhing on the open road, a female by her size, presumably injured by the woodcutters. He stamped on her head. It gave him a little boost and he felt a great deal better. He'd bide his time and he would have that girl.

Part Three

Britain, Rome and Gaul
55/54 BC

Chapter 1

"**B**ah bah bah!" shouted Dug "Aye . . . bah!" He pointed his forefinger to the sky behind her with his eyes so wide that there might have been a dragon coming in to land, and screamed even more loudly than he'd been able to last time Lowa had seen him.

She looked up. Nothing there. Who knew what the little oddball's developing mind was seeing? Maybe there was a dragon that adults couldn't see? Elann Nancarrow's cats were forever staring freakily at terrifying invisible beings. Maybe when people aged they lost the ability to see into other worlds? It was possible, she supposed. Lowa dragged herself back from ridiculous musing. She'd been on her horse all night and her mind was bouncing around like a storm-tossed sailing dinghy.

Keelin put Dug down on the rug, on all fours. The day was cold but sunny, and the baby was bundled into an outfit made of fox fur which made him look like a fat bear cub. He spotted his wooden dog on the far side of the rug, screamed with joy and crawled towards it wobblingly.

"See?" said Keelin. "Crawling."

"I see," said Lowa, as Dug's arms splayed and he face-planted into the rug. But he pushed himself up, looked at his mother, scream-shouted happily and carried on.

"He'll get better. He's later crawling than most, but I'm sure that's because of his whacking great head weighing him down. He's still the cheeriest baby I've ever seen. Even when he's crying you can see the smile in his eyes. He's the smartest as well. He knows things, that one. He certainly should be clever, with a head that size. His dad had a big head, didn't he?"

Lowa nodded and smiled. It was good to see new life, particularly because she knew what was coming next. She'd arrived back at Maidun that morning from another recruitment trawl. This time she'd been to the treacherous bastards in Dumnonia. She was that desperate. It had been depressing, whole villages populated by the elderly and children after so many of fighting age had perished under the Spring Tide. Thank Danu that most of them blamed their dead king Bruxon for leading the whole army to their deaths against Maidun, rather than blaming the queen of Maidun for drowning them. She'd still received the odd angry shout and thrown egg, though. She'd very nearly killed the first man who'd thrown an egg, but Mal had calmed her down and charmed the egg thrower so much that he had become her chief recruitment agent, mustering half a thousand on his own. So forgiveness did work sometimes, she guessed, although that half-thousand were pretty much all fourteen-year-olds who'd been deemed too young for the army the year before.

When she'd reached Maidun, Mal had run up to say that the merchants and fishers all reported that the Romans were preparing a much larger invasion fleet, to be ready early the coming summer. Then Chamanca had approached, wrapped in a woollen shawl, looking as if she hadn't slept for a year.

"Welcome home," the Iberian had said. "Atlas is still alive, the stubborn bugger. Maggot says anyone else would have died a moon ago. He will die tomorrow or possibly the next day."

"I will see my son, then I'll come straight to Atlas."

"Thank you. He'd like to see you. He is in his hut."

*   *   *

Lowa left Keelin feeding cow's milk and honey to Dug from a cored bull's horn fitted with a leather teat. The boy, guzzling happily, didn't seem to notice Lowa leaving.

The door to Atlas' hut was open. Lowa could smell death from twenty paces away. She knocked on the doorframe and Chamanca answered from the darkness. The stench inside was so strong that for a heartbeat she couldn't see. When her eyes had adjusted, she saw Chamanca sitting on a stool. She looked up at Lowa but didn't greet her or stand.

Atlas was on the bed, lying on his side, a thin woollen blanket over his shrunken bulk.

"Lowa, welcome," he said, his voice deep as a god's. "Chamanca, please will you offer our guest a drink."

"Don't worry, I just . . . drank." Lowa didn't want to breath in.

Atlas sniffed a weak laugh. "Don't be awkward, please. Death is merely a stage of the journey. Not an enjoyable one, I grant you, but there is no need to be miserable. Have you seen people grow old? It is not pleasant. I have no desire to age and weaken. I look forward to seeing what comes next. Now, take a seat. Chamanca, fetch Lowa a mug of beer, please. And have one yourself."

Sitting down on the stool next to Chamanca's, Lowa could see Atlas more clearly. His frail smile was twisted by the scar that she'd given him with a deer bone, when they'd killed her women and tried to kill her. Sometimes that evening seemed as if it were centuries ago and sometimes as if it had happened only moments before. This was one of those latter times. She felt a flash of anger that he'd killed Aithne, then reminded herself that he'd been under Felix's spell and he'd done his best to make up for it since, plus it was hard to hate someone so obviously near death. His injured shoulder was grossly swollen. A black, sewn-up wound ran across it, with a tube – a cow's vein, Lowa guessed – running from the wound into a wooden bucket by the bedside. It was hard to be precise, but it seemed that most of the stench was emanating from the grim bucket.

"I never thought I'd be Rome's first victim in Britain," said Atlas.

"The Taloon man and the Haxmite who killed him were the first victims of Rome's invasion," said Chamanca, sitting down with two mugs of beer and handing one to Lowa. "So stop trying to blow your own trumpet."

"Quite right, quite right," said Atlas. "I'll leave that to Carden. Where *is* Carden? He was just here."

Chamanca clamped a hand to her face, stood and walked swiftly from the hut.

"Tetchy, that one," said Atlas, "now, tell me, where is Carden? Off with his brother Weylin somewhere?"

"That's one way of putting it," said Lowa.

She sat and talked to him until he went to sleep. When she left he was snoring quietly and unevenly.

Chamanca was waiting outside, alongside Maggot and Walfdan. Lowa nodded a greeting and opened her mouth to ask if there was anything the druids could do for Atlas, but closed it again. They would already have done everything.

Chamanca went back into the hut and Lowa asked Maggot and Walfdan to return to the eyrie with her to discuss deployment of the new recruits, training schedules and other things such, like who would replace Atlas as the infantry commander.

They set off slowly, since Walfdan was not well and could not go any faster, and Lowa sent three onlookers to fetch Mal, Adler and the blacksmith Elann Nancarrow. One of the many things she hated about being queen, possibly the thing that she'd hated most initially, was that there were always slack-jawed dimwits who thought it was perfectly acceptable to stand and gawp at her as she went about her day. However, since she'd realised that she could use them as a permanent fleet of errand people and a source for food and water, she'd despised them less.

Chapter 2

"You said it was impressive." Spring wrinkled her nose. "You aren't impressed?" Ragnall raised his arms at the wonderful architecture and stunning carvings towering all around them. There was nothing like this in Britain, nothing close to it. It must have looked like a god's palace to Spring. She *was* impressed, she was just being annoying. "It kicks the arse off Maidun's wooden arena."

"That's got seats all the way round."

Ragnall sighed. They were in Pompey's theatre complex. Several years before, Drustan had given his life to transport Ragnall there to save him from being buried alive by Felix. Back then it had been a building site. Now it was a freshly painted, palatial amazement. He and Spring were standing in the middle of the main theatre, on an expansive marble-floored stage surrounded by a towering semi-circular tier of seating and a three-storey, balconied, marble-columned backdrop.

Ragnall wasn't the only one amazed by the gigantic edifice. All around them wealthy, well-dressed Romans had lost their usual "Oh I'm so bored, nothing impresses me" nonchalance and were gazing around wide-eyed at the newly opened wonder. Most of them were looking at the theatre, anyway. Quite a few of them were looking at him and the British girl, pointing and talking about them as if they were animals in Caesar's menagerie.

They were famous because, yet again, Caesar's adventures were the chat of the city, and they were the young barbarian royal lovers whom he'd rescued from the horrors of dark Britain. This time the Senate had granted a new record amount of holiday – twenty days of celebration – to honour the general's new victories in Gaul and Britain, even though he hadn't actually had any in Britain. Some people, most notably Marcus Porcius Cato, were calling Caesar a war criminal and saying that he should stand trial for his unprovoked massacre of the Usipetes and Tencteri. However, when most influential Romans were presented with the accusation, they replied *Twenty days holiday!* and carried on loving Caesar and lauding his adventures. The general himself was off east somewhere quashing a rebellion, which meant there was even more focus on the British couple.

The girl didn't help matters. The hulking praetorians who guarded them were something of a giveaway, but many rich young Romans had bodyguards and they might have gone unnoticed if Spring hadn't rejected the finest fashions and insisted on wearing her screamingly barbarian leather shorts and white cotton shirt. Many of the women glared at her exposed legs with outrage. Their male companions voiced their affronted agreement while taking good long looks at Spring's tanned thighs to fully assess just how offended they were. Spring was certainly one of the most attractive women in Rome that winter, and, given her outfit, probably the most visually appealing of all – to Ragnall, anyway, even though she was so annoying. He, despite his embarrassment at being assessed as a barbarian who'd "gone toga", was proud to be at her side and somewhat proud to be her betrothed. Everyone knew that they were engaged to be married and an auspicious date had been set in the new year. Everyone knew, that was, apart from Spring.

She pointed to the exquisite, columned temple that perched with tear-inducing majesty at the highest point of the theatre complex. From its apex an open-armed statue of the goddess Venus Victrix looked out over the marvels that man had made with pride, perhaps even awe.

"That stone hut with the lady on the top up there," asked Spring, "what's that then?"

"That is a temple to Venus Victrix, Pompey's personal goddess," said Ragnall.

"Oh, I remember," said Spring. "Shagging Venus, not to be confused with Mother Venus who Caesar reckons he's descended from."

"That's pretty much it." At least she listened to him and remembered things, thought Ragnall. "Isn't it beautiful?"

"I prefer woodland shrines."

"Do you want to go up and look inside?"

"Nope."

"All right, let's go through to the gardens." He added, in Latin, "And I'll come back and see the temple when I don't have to drag an ignorant child around."

Spring beamed at him and said: "I like it when you talk Roman, it makes you sound like a frog barking."

"Don't you mean a dog?"

"No."

They walked through the back of the theatre, past a gaggle of rehearsing actors hammily shouting lines at each other, through more marble columns and out into large, rectangular, colonnaded gardens. Exotic birds flitted between evergreen shrubs, past dancing fountains which reflected the bright paint on dozens of lifelike statues of actors and heroes. Behind the colonnades, Ragnall knew, were stylish salons and art galleries tastefully adorned with curios, pottery and paintings from all over the world. Pompey was famous for being a tasteless vulgarian, so he'd hired Rome's most fashionable decorators to fill his theatre with modish marvels and change his reputation. It didn't work, of course; people were saying he was still a fat ignoramus even if he had paid for a nice building, but Ragnall nevertheless thought it was the most amazing thing he'd ever seen. His yearning, burning desire to bring Roman ways to Britain blazed higher and stronger than ever before. They really could have wonders like this in Britain. Even more wondrous wonders! And he would be the man to bring them. *Ragnall's Theatre.* He liked the sound of that. It would be a good start.

"It's a funny sort of holiday," said Spring, bringing him back to the real world, "when the only people who've stopped work are the ones who don't do any work anyway. The people with the shit jobs are still beavering away." She nodded at two skinny Africans who were holding a huge ostrich plume to shade a tubby senator from the weak winter sun, then at a gang of slaves scrubbing stones and polishing pillars.

"But you've got to admit this garden is just wonderful? You've never seen these water things before." There was no word for "fountain" in British, because the British were too brutish to have thought of them.

"What are they for?" asked Spring.

"They're not *for* anything. They're just beautiful."

"Not as beautiful as the sea. Or trees or hills or cliffs or lakes or grassland or children or beaches or marshes or mountains or—"

Ragnall turned around, arms aloft. "Did you know this is the biggest building in the world?"

"It's not as big as Maidun Castle."

"Maidun Castle's not a building."

"But it's bigger."

"So are a lot of hills!"

"Exactly."

"For Jupiter's sake. How about this statue. It looks just like a real person. It's a million times better than any carvings in Britain."

"What's it for?"

"It's a demonstration of how amazing people can be! This

statue is a culmination of what man can achieve, when he
pools his strength and his learning, so that the greatest might
be freed from the mundane tasks like growing food and gathering firewood, and they can use their gods-given skills to—"

"Look, fish! In that pond. Now they *are* amazing. Can
the Romans make those?"

"Ponds? Who do you think—"

"No, fish."

"Can we make fish?"

"Yup."

"No. Nobody can *make* fish."

"Why not?"

"You can't make life."

"No? Well, until the Romans can I think you should stop
going on about how amazing they are. Life is the only thing
that's worth anything. Everything else – all your spurty
water things and stupid statues – are tagnuts on a badger's
ball sack in comparison to life."

"People here live much longer. Our druids can prolong—"

"Can your druids make life?"

"No."

"No."

They walked on through the gardens. People stared at
them, but Spring didn't seem to notice. She was looking at
the fountains. Ragnall was pretty sure she did like them.
As they neared the steps that led up to the Curia Pompeia,
the grand hall at the end of the gardens, he thought, well,
now's as good a time as any.

"You know we're going to get married?"

Spring stopped, turned and looked up at him. She still
had a somewhat childish button-mushroom nose, but her
overbite had retracted into full lips. The upper one was
particularly lovely, the shape of a recurve bow was such a
mesmerising red that she'd never need the paints that the
Roman women daubed on their faces.

"Why are you looking at my mouth?" she said.

"I'm waiting for you to say something about the fact we're getting married."

"If I'm entirely honest, I'd expected a proposal to be a little more romantic."

"We're in a romantic place?"

Spring looked around. "We're not. A wood is a romantic place, a riverside in certain lights can be—"

"OK, sure, but what do you think about marrying me?"

"It's a no. A very big one. Although you haven't asked yet."

"We don't have a choice. I'm not asking you to marry me. Caesar is making us."

"Making you."

"If you don't marry me he'll kill you."

"Then maybe I will marry you. But I won't mean it and there is *no* way we're shagging."

"I won't make you. I'm not mad about this either. The ceremony is in about a moon—" Ragnall paused as a small, dark-skinned female slave offered them wine which they both declined, "and it will be in public. Or at least there will be guests."

"Good. That'll be fun."

"If you're thinking of disrupting it—"

"Which I am."

"I told Caesar you would. He said that if you do, he'll have one of your toes chopped off every week, then your fingers, then your feet, then your hands, then he'll release you in the forests of Germany."

"Better behave myself then."

"Indeed."

"Right then. I suppose Caesar will – oh!" Spring staggered and Ragnall caught her arm. She was pale. They'd just reached the steps that led up to the Curia Pompeia.

"Here, sit down—"

"No. Sorry. Something just came over me. A nasty feeling," Spring said, looking up the steps at the meeting hall. "Did something terrible happen here?"

Ragnall shook his head. "I don't know."

"Maybe it's going to . . . This is a bad place. Let's go the other way."

Ragnall led her back towards the theatre. Within seconds she was fine again, chatting about the fish as if she hadn't just agreed to marry him then nearly fainted. Halfway back he spotted Clodia Metelli, walking with Pydna, the Macedonian girl who lived with her and with whom Ragnall had had a brief affair when he'd first moved in.

"Come and meet Clodia and Pydna," he said. "Clodia speaks a few words of British."

"Whup-dee-do," said Spring.

Chapter 3

The day was productive. Lowa never forgot that Atlas was dying in a hut nearby while a miserable Chamanca kept vigil, and she suspected the African was in everybody else's thoughts, but, rather than distract, it seemed to focus them all in dogged preparation for the next Roman invasion.

Among other ideas, Elann Nancarrow described a tool that might wreck the tortoise shield formations and Maggot devised a scheme for keeping Felix's legion contained. Adler reported that the cavalry were improving every day and Mal said he'd found an old hillfort in the south-east that would make a good base nearer Caesar's likely landing spot, and he outlined a novel scheme for improving its defences. The one thing they didn't resolve was a new commander for the infantry, because Lowa never brought it up. It seemed wrong while Atlas was still alive.

The one person who didn't contribute was the Gaulish druid Walfdan. He was quiet until the very end, when Lowa left to see how Atlas was doing and he asked to accompany her. It was a little annoying – the decrepit man walked at a slug's pace and Lowa wanted to get there before Atlas died – but she took his arm to speed him up and tried her best not to mind. She tried to talk to Walfdan on the way, but he didn't seem to hear her. He was not well; not a surprise given his age. Lowa wondered if he'd make it through the winter.

Atlas was unconscious, his breathing irregular.

"He will die soon," said Chamanca, "and I will return to

training the chariots. I am sorry that I missed your meeting, but you will be pleased with the charioteers. They have worked hard and—"

"It's all right, Chamanca, we can talk later."

The Iberian nodded. Lowa stepped in and put a hand on Atlas' chest. "Goodbye, old friend," she said. She searched for other words, or anything useful to do, but came up blank. The only thought that came into her head was that death was a huge pisser.

The queen left Walfdan with Chamanca, glad that the Iberian wouldn't be alone, and sent an onlooker off to find Keelin and her son.

She spent the rest of the day and the night with Dug, playing peekaboo, feeding him from the milk horn and stroking his breath-catchingly smooth skin. Now she was more used to it, she knew that if she hadn't had to be a Warrior queen she would have enjoyed looking after the little boy more often. She didn't even mind when she was woken by his screaming in the middle of the night. She rocked him and sang a song dredged from her childhood memories, again and again.

As she sat and sang, she considered something that she'd never thought of before. Her own mother must have done this for her, night after night. She had no memory of those times, of course she didn't, but she knew her mother must have loved her and cared for her and put her needs before her own. She pictured her mother suckling her as a baby in the village in the German forest, listening out for her cries at night and spending every day making sure her child didn't put her hand in the fire or cut herself on any of the number of sharp tools that were strewn about their hut. She remembered, so clearly, crouching with Aithne and watching the raiders kill her mother. Then she remembered Aithne's death.

And here she was, preparing for war and, very probably, her own death. She couldn't consider for a moment that the Romans might kill little Dug, it was too awful, but she wondered if her grown-up son would ever spare a thought for his long-dead mother. She'd just have to stay alive, wouldn't she? Which meant beating the Romans. She sat and planned in the candlelight while little Dug, quiet for once, held her fingers in his tiny grip and looked at her calmly with large, shining eyes.

Dawn came, along with Keelin, and found Lowa still sitting on the chair, the baby wrapped in fur, asleep on her lap.

"I bet you've had enough of him by now?" whispered his nanny.

"I'll keep him for a while. Come back around lunchtime."

Keelin smiled and headed out.

"Come on, Dug," she said when he woke. "Let's go and see if Atlas lived through the night. Seeing a baby might cheer him a little."

"It will cheer me a lot, I've always liked babies," said a deep African voice. Lowa looked up, startled.

Standing in the doorway, beaming like a well-fed puppy, was Atlas.

"What, by Danu's great big tits?"

"Can I come in and have a hold of the boy?"

Lowa nodded, he came into the hut and she handed Dug to him.

Atlas smiled and the child chortled, but then the African's face was grave. "It's not all good news, I'm afraid. Walfdan is dead."

"Oh shit. He didn't look well."

"He wasn't," said Maggot, standing at the door. "Can I come in, too?"

"Of course. What was it?"

"He was old, there were a few evil things going on inside that wrinkly skin-bag, any one of which would have finished him by the time the flowers bloom on the hills, but the thing that did for him eventually was a dagger in the heart from me."

"I'm sorry?"

"I killed him!" grinned Maggot.

"What?" She looked at Atlas, but he was occupied playing with the boy.

"Now I know you take a dim view of murder, Lowa, a fatally dim one, so although I don't like talking about this stuff, I'll explain."

"Go for it."

"As you will have worked out, magic is connected to life. A person or an animal can be alive or dead and there's a fucking massive difference between the two. That difference is magic."

"So Walfdan was dying, you killed him and transferred his life-force to Atlas."

"Nah. You can't transfer a life-force, or at least I can't, and I've never heard of anyone that can, and it would be a bit grim, wouldn't it? Atlas walking around using up another man's life? Yuck. And anyway, Walfdan was going to be dead within the moon so there wouldn't have been much point."

"So how did you—?"

"Death releases something which isn't life itself, but a force which I choose to call magic. 'Cos that's what it is. Some people can still use magic – it's to do with the inter-connectedness of everything, but I won't go into that now. I'm one of these people, so I can do a few tricks. About the easiest of all the tricks, strangely enough you might think, is taking the magic released by death and using it to kill something else. The infection from the arrow that was killing Atlas was a living thing. I killed it. And so here's Atlas. At least I think that's what happened. This is all –" he jangled his arm jewellery dramatically "– theoretical."

"I see. But you commanded the whales without anything dying?"

"Yeah, well, I'm not going to explain everything, am I? A man likes a secret or two. And, besides, haven't you two got an army to train? I'll take the baby for a bit."

"I don't think you will."

"Don't worry, I've already sent one of your peasant idiots to find Keelin, and, besides, I'm good with babies. I'm good with everyone."

He winked and smiled like a loon, which for some reason made Lowa trust him.

"Come on then, give him the boy," she said to Atlas. "We're missing mêlée practice."

Chapter 4

That winter Ragnall and Spring lived in a house that belonged to Caesar in a terrace of similar houses near the forum, in the least smart part of the Palatine Hill, Rome's richest neighbourhood. In many ways it was how Spring imagined most young wealthy couples lived in Rome – ten rooms, three slaves, all the wine they could drink and some very odd food – and in some ways it wasn't. The differences, as she imagined, were that she and Ragnall slept in separate rooms, her room's window had thick iron bars, there were always two great big men guarding her and she was often chained to something. It didn't stop her doing Lowa's fitness routine every day, though, and she whiled many hours away inventing new stretches and exercises. She didn't want to escape yet, but when she did, she didn't want to fail because she wasn't fast or strong enough.

She'd been in houses before, in the British towns of Bladonfort and Forkton, and had not been impressed. She now realised that they'd been fairly shit attempts to replicate a Roman house like the one she was living in, and conceded that maybe there was some point in persevering because despite herself, she liked her Roman house. It was clean. The chief attribute that the British imitations lacked was a regular supply of lots of water. On the journey south, she'd tried not to marvel too obviously at the colossal stone bridges and elevated man-made rivers that carried water from hills to towns. Due to those engineering marvels and the Romans' understanding of how the river system worked, there was a limitless supply of water flowing into her house, which meant that the slaves could clean effectively and, perhaps more importantly, pour all their waste away into an underground stream that flowed into the great central drain – the Cloaca Maxima – then into the river and off to the sea. It was clever. The one downside, the thing that prevented her resolving to set something like this up back at home, was that the whole stream diverting venture must have been such a massive arseache for so many people – so many slaves – to build. Using time that could have been spent lying on a hillside and watching the clouds, thousands upon thousands had sweated away, moving rock from one place to another. She was glad they'd done it, she liked her clean house, but not so much that she could ever have been bothered to put all that effort in herself or expect anyone else to do it for her.

And it wasn't like the water flowed to everyone. There were parts of the city which were more disgusting than the grubbiest parts of Bladonfort. She'd had to hold her breath down one street where they'd squelched through shit and rotting animal remains. It was the same at Maidun, of course. The people whose attributes best suited the culture – people with a degree of nous, a healthy body and a reasonable work ethic – lived in better, cleaner places. But in Rome, while the fortunate lived immeasurably more opulent lives than their peers in Britain, the unfortunate people lived in conditions that were worse than their British counterparts, which struck Spring as dumb. Why didn't the rich accept just a little less so that the poor could have a whole lot more? What was the point of all this advancement if it only benefited the few?

And the "few" were dicks. She'd started a game of counting how many people described her as "sordida" –a pejorative term for anyone who didn't wear Roman clothes, meaning grubby in both body and mind – but she'd given up because there were too many. Some people were interested, some were kind. Ragnall's friend Clodia had even spoken to Spring, with Ragnall translating, as if they were equals. But mostly? They were a shower of shitheads, sneering and shunning her despite not knowing the least thing about her.

There was also the position of women in Roman culture. On the surface, women seemed to have it better than she'd heard. The poor Roman women lived equally miserable lives to the poor men and the richest ladies were actually more luxuriously dressed and pampered-looking than their husbands. But – and it was a big but – women were viewed by the men, and by themselves mostly, as little more than decoration, accessories to bolster the glory of male achievement. Every single story had a man as the hero. Everyone with any power, from the two consuls to the guards snarling at the plebs not to loiter outside expensive shops, was a man.

Despite all of this, she understood why Ragnall wanted to bring the Roman world to Britain. It was a bonus that such a huge town didn't stink of shit, not everywhere anyway, and the public buildings were impressive. However, all in all, she preferred Britain as it was, and thought that most British men and all the women probably did, too. And if they wanted to copy Roman ways? Then they would, of their own accord. What they definitely didn't need was these pricks rowing across the Channel, walking round with their noses in the air, telling them how wrong they were about everything and killing them if they disagreed.

"Caesar's back in a couple of days," said Ragnall one evening as they sat eating a simple but excellent meal of deep-fried scallops and olive bread. The winter diet in Rome, she had to admit, was good. In Britain it was wheat or barley bread or, on special days, barley porridge with a chunk of salted meat or fish. In Rome many people went to a lot of effort to produce delicious, interesting food and so long as you avoided the freaky stuff like otters' noses and ocelot spleens, they succeeded.

Spring finished her mouthful and said: "Oh really?" She'd already heard her guards mention Caesar's return, and people on the streets talking about it, and heralds shouting about it in the forum.

"He wants us to marry while he's here."

"I see. And what does that entail?"

"First we pick you a matron. I've got someone in mind. Remember Clodia, the lady we met at Pompey's theatre?"

"Yup."

"Her."

"OK."

"Then we've got to get you a flame-coloured veil and a white dress. I think we've already got a cord we can use."

"A cord?"

"It gets tied with a special knot, which I undo in front of everyone."

"Everyone?" asked Spring, already planning to retie the knot into one that was impossible to undo.

"Not too many people, I'll just ask a handful, but it will be in Caesar's house so he might ask a few."

"Right."

"Then there's a dinner."

"Good."

"After that I'm meant to symbolically wrestle you from the arms of your family, to represent the rape of the Sabine women—"

"The *what*?"

Ragnall explained the historical event that they were to commemorate as part of the wedding ceremony. Spring was not impressed. "Then what?" she said.

"Then I think you get led through the streets by two boys, with another boy holding a torch ahead of you. When we get back here – I guess we'll use this house – you smear animal fat and wool on—"

"Hold on, hold on, this is all bollocks."

"It's tradition."

"Why don't we have a British wedding?"

". . . That *would* be more fun."

"Could you persuade Caesar?"

"You don't persuade Caesar of anything, but I might be able to make him think that it's his idea."

Suddenly Spring was properly happy for the first time since they'd been in Rome. She completely forgot that her ankle was attached to the table by a chain, as possibilities flared up in her mind. "Oh, it'll be *much* more fun. Who in Rome knows what a British wedding looks like?"

"Several tens of thousands of slaves?"

"Who that they're going to ask?"

Spring was glad to see a hesitant smile creep onto Ragnall's face. He wasn't so bad really. "You and me. I think I see where you're going . . ."

"We can do whatever we want! Like the custom of the bride being given a lovely new gold-decorated leather holster for her hammer and an aurochs' skin quiver of the finest arrows?"

"And the groom being given the host's finest white horse?"

"And the guests stripping naked and waving their cocks and tits at the departing couple?"

"They won't do that."

"They might!"

They thrashed out the details late into the night, drinking more and more wine. By the end of it, it wasn't that exciting at all, really. Ragnall had diluted and diluted her ideas until in the end they just had a nice day planned, not too different from the real British ceremony, rather than Spring's spectacularly hilarious series of wacky japes. But it was still by about a thousand times the best evening the two of them had spent together. By the end of it Spring was happy and drunk enough that she almost wanted Ragnall to ask her into his room. He didn't, though. Her praetorians led her to her room as usual, attached her chain to the bed and bade her goodnight.

The day came. They waited in the garden of one of Caesar's new houses for their guests, all friends of Ragnall since Spring didn't have any friends in Rome. Ragnall was in a toga which Spring thought was probably the most pristinely clean piece of cloth in the whole word at that moment, and she was in a sleeveless white cotton dress.

First to arrive were Clodia and Pydna, with whom Ragnall had lived for a while. He'd been amusingly cagey about them and went pink when they walked in, so Spring guessed he'd had an affair with one them – probably Clodia. Given the way she looked at everyone, Spring included, Clodia was up for anything. Next came a chap called Publius Licinius Crassus and his wife Cornelia Metella. He looked to be about Ragnall's age, but his wife looked, if anything, a little younger than Spring.

"Greet you," said Publius to Spring in faltering Gaulish, "my wife beaut I full." He indicated Cornelia, who took Spring's hand.

"Good moaning to yoy," said Cornelia, also attempting Gaulish.

"Good moaning to yoy too," Spring replied, pleased that they'd made the effort.

Cornelia looked delighted and in a flash Spring saw that she was indeed beautiful. Her face was broad, her eyes long and narrow, her thinnish lips twisted as if she were chewing, but these all managed to combine into an intriguing, inviting, bright attractiveness, as if she were enjoying the world and wanted you to come along on the ride.

Ragnall was clearly surprised and pleased at the next guest, a gangly fellow, maybe ten years older than Caesar.

"This," Ragnall said, "is Marcus Tullius Cicero, former consul and cleverest man in Rome."

"You," Cicero said in Latin, taking Spring's hand and bowing, "are the most beautiful barbarian I have ever seen."

Well, that's half a compliment if ever I heard one, thought Spring, but when Ragnall had finished translating she smiled gratefully and said in British: "And you are the tallest gnome I have ever met."

"She says your reputation precedes you, and she is more than honoured by your presence."

"Good, good, what a lovely girl. Now, Ragnall," Cicero gestured to two people who'd wandered into the garden behind him – a bearded man who looked about Cicero's own age, and a tall, skeletally thin woman daubed with far too much red lip paint and black eye make-up, "I hope you don't mind, but my younger brother Quintus Tullius Cicero has nipped back from winter quarters in Gaul for a few days, and he and his wife Pomponia were keen to help you celebrate."

They didn't look keen. When they were introduced, Pomponia peered over the top of Spring's head as if seeking more interesting company, then fixed a fake smile and headed for Clodia. Conversely and disgustingly, her husband Quintus looked at Spring all too much, and not in the eye either. He grasped her hand with one of his clammy paws and her arm with the other. He released her hand, but kept his other hand on her arm, stroking her bicep with his thumb. She yanked away and looked at him as if he was the piece of shit that she thought he was.

"I see the girl does not understand a Roman greeting."

"No," said Cicero senior, looking appalled at his brother. "Why don't you come over here, Quintus, there are some trees from Asia that you'll be able to identify for me."

"Sorry about him," said Ragnall. "He's a famous arsehole, as is his wife. People say they hate each other more even than people hate them, and that makes them even worse.

Don't get on his wrong side, though. I've heard he puts people who cross him in a leather sack full of snakes and chucks them into the Tiber. Strangely enough I knew another man in Gaul called Quintus, too, a fellow envoy. He was a prick as well."

"What a lovely person to have at our wedding!"

Ragnall chuckled. "I suppose Cicero told them that Caesar was going to be here. Everyone's trying to speak to Caesar at the moment, and Clodia told me that these two are social climbers."

"Great! Got to love a social climber!" They had social climbers in Britain, too, of course – the way people acted around Lowa was very funny – but the affliction seemed more common and desperately grasping in Rome.

"Well, my old mentor Drustan used to say that if you were in a group of people and there wasn't a twat, then the twat was you."

Spring giggled. "I like that. And we've got two, which means that we're double definitely not twats."

"Yup." Ragnall clacked his wine cup into hers and winked.

That was it for guests, other than Caesar himself. He was expected at any moment. Slaves brought drinks and food – "Steer clear of the mares' vulvas," warned Ragnall – and the others asked her questions about Britain, Ragnall translating. He altered her replies to say how much she was looking forward to Roman aid to recapture her throne, but other than that told them pretty much what she was saying. Clodia, Pydna, Publius, Cornelia and the friendly Cicero all listened politely, laughed when they were meant to laugh, gasped when they were meant to gasp and asked further questions that showed they'd paid attention to what she'd said and taken it seriously. Quintus Cicero and Pomponia were nowhere to be seen, presumably in another part of the garden waiting for Caesar to arrive.

Other than these latter two, they were kind, decent people, and Spring found herself having an excellent morning, both pleased and confused that there were good people in Rome when so many horrible acts had been committed in Rome's name. Then again, she thought, she was Zadar's daughter.

It looked briefly as if Caesar wasn't going to make it – some other urgent business – but finally he arrived full of smiles and joy, and presented Spring with a quiver of arrows and Ragnall with a sword. The arrows and the sword weren't nearly as good as Elann Nancarrow's – the arrows were too short for Spring's longbow and the sword not so lovingly forged – but the quiver was a delight. It was horse leather, she reckoned, but they must have found a really weird horse because its hair, which had been left on the outside, was striped black and white. Spring was genuinely touched, and she haltingly said "*Grat – ee – ass max – ee – mass*" to the great general. He looked surprised and raised an eyebrow at Ragnall.

"It's the only phrase she knows," he said. "I taught it to her specially so she could thank you. It took her about an hour to learn."

"Hmmm," said Caesar, treating Spring to a suspicious raise of an eyebrow. Other than that one look, he was a charming and attentive host. It was very difficult to reconcile him with the man who'd killed so many Gauls and was determined to massacre her countrymen.

She had vaguely planned on killing him at her wedding – she knew she ought to – but it looked like he knew it and there were always at least two people between him and her. Despite his smiles, she remembered, he had threatened to cut off her fingers, toes, feet and hands and dump her in the woods. She kept looking for an opening to grab a knife, dive across and finish him, but the opportunity never arose. If she was honest, although she definitely still wanted to kill him to stop the coming invasion, she also wanted to have at least a chance of getting away afterwards. There will be other opportunities, she told herself, not even half sure that it was true.

Caesar clapped his hands and decreed it was time for the ceremony. Ragnall asked Cicero to preside, which meant, he said, saying a few nice things.

They stood beneath a tree and Cicero spoke eloquently about the joys of marriage, about the island of Britain, including many of the things that Spring had told him earlier, remembered in perfect detail. He said that he believed the Roman way of life was the best possible, and that he hoped that Roman rule would bring all benefits of living like a Roman yet none of the potential horrors of conquest, and that Rome and Britain would be partners, rather than overlords and a subjugated population. Making these latter points, he looked pointedly at Caesar.

Ragnall and Spring said their vows to each other. They stuck pretty much to the standard British words since Ragnall was worried that Caesar understood more than he let on, but they omitted the words that would have made them husband and wife.

Spring found it odd, going through the ceremony with the kind, handsome Ragnall, surrounded by people who were happy, interesting and clever, even if one of them was a genocidal maniac. She'd never really thought about marriage, she'd just supposed it would happen one day, but she did realise that even if this wasn't a real wedding, it was about as joyful a day as she could imagine.

After the ceremony, Caesar bade them all farewell and left, unassassinated. Quintus and Pomponia suddenly reappeared – Spring had thought they'd gone, since they'd missed the ceremony – and followed him out. Spring slipped away to walk in the gardens. Lovely as the others were, she wanted some time on her own. She hadn't had much when Clodia appeared around a corner.

"There's a big wasp on your left arm," she said, looking Spring square in the eye.

Spring started and brushed at her arm. No wasp. She realised that Clodia had been talking in Latin and deliberately not looked at her arm so that Spring couldn't use that as an excuse for her reaction. She raised her head slowly.

Clodia was grinning. She peered about herself to check they were alone, leant in and said, "I knew it! I was watching you when Cicero was blathering on. You understood every single word!"

Spring smiled sheepishly.

Clodia leant in further and Spring breathed in a noseful of her headily floral scent. "Don't worry, I think that your secret is very funny and I'll keep it for you. Just be more careful, not everyone's as dumb as Caesar and his gang. Well, they're not dumb, they're very clever at analysing forests, just not so bright with trees, if you know what I mean. Like most men."

Spring nodded.

"And look, I won't speak any more Latin to you, but tell me one thing. Do you want Romans on your island?"

Spring looked around. They were alone. She beckoned Clodia further forward and whispered in her ear in Latin: "Please don't take this as a personal slight, I think you and all the guests are delightful and I'm grateful that you came to see Ragnall and me married, but I'd rather be beaten with a shitty stick for eternity than see another legionary set foot on British soil."

"Ha, ha! Magnificent! Your Latin is better than mine! By Venus, men are idiots. I like you very much, young Spring. It's too dangerous for us to speak more, but I do wish you well."

Clodia turned to go, then leant back in with a waft of perfume. "One more thing I have to know. This wedding's a sham, right?"

"Yes, but Caesar will maim me and leave me to be eaten by wild animals if I don't pretend to enjoy it."

"I see."

"But I am sort of enjoying it."

"Good!"

And Clodia was gone.

Spring enjoyed the rest of the afternoon even more. They drank several amphoras of wine and ate roast boar which Ragnall had arranged to be cooked in the British way and everybody said was delicious. After the feast, Cornelia played the lyre and they all sang. Spring hummed the verses, but sang along to the choruses tunefully but in a tortured language that sometimes sounded a bit like Latin. Everyone thought this was very funny, including, apparently, Clodia. The woman was an excellent actress. Spring had worried that she might give her the odd knowing look or wink which Ragnall might ask about, but Clodia didn't show the tiniest sign of having sussed Spring's secret.

They sang and drank late into the night. At one point, pissed, she staggered into another part of the garden to see if Dug was around, but she couldn't find him anywhere.

Chapter 5

They rode north through Italy, over cloudy mountains sodden, noisy and often beautiful with melting snow, and up through Gaul. The new Roman territory reminded Spring of parts of Britain after a ravishing by her father. The previous year's harvest had been pitiful and people were starving. As they rode by, black-eyed beggars lifted their arms in wretched supplication and mothers held screaming babies aloft. The legionaries didn't register their pathetic entreaties, but the endless miserable onslaught worked on Spring like a pilum twisting in her guts. She couldn't do anything since she was chained and manacled all the time, so she asked Ragnall to give away three-quarters of their rations. He gave away half. One of her praetorian guards commanded him to stop. Caesar had ordered that nobody was to give food to Gauls. Ragnall told the man to fuck off and handed almost all of their next meal to beggars while the praetorian glowered at him. Spring was proud. He would be a good husband to someone one day, she thought, but never to her. Their marriage had been neither a proper British nor Roman wedding, plus it hadn't been consummated which made it void in Roman eyes. You weren't considered to be properly married in Rome until you'd had a child, which Spring found odd, but she was happy to go along with it. She and Ragnall were exactly as married as two bards who'd pretended to wed in a play.

Word in the army was that the harvest had failed due to drought, and everyone seemed to accept this. Their self-delusion was staggering. The harvest had failed because everyone had been busy fighting the Romans, because so many had died and been enslaved that there was nobody left to tend the fields, and because Caesar had stolen so much food for his huge army. Anyone over the age of five, surely, could see this, but the Romans genuinely didn't seem to. "Terrible thing, drought," they'd say when they passed another pile of dead Gaulish men, women, children and babies. The babies always made Spring cry, but she did her best to hide it.

She talked to Ragnall about the Roman delusion.

"The Roman invasion may have contributed a little to the lack of food," he said, "but everything would have been fine if there hadn't been a drought. You can hardly blame Caesar for the weather."

"But there was no drought!" She shook her head.

"Really? Why would everyone say there was if there wasn't? Or were you over here measuring rainfall?"

"You were in Gaul last year. Was it very dry?"

Ragnall hesitated. "I think it was a bit drier than normal, yes. Look, the Roman experts say there was a drought. That means there was a drought."

She looked into his eyes. He really did seem to believe what he'd just said.

"What's more," he added, "in future, Roman farming means, storage practices and distribution methods – better roads, better carts, better planning – will mean that droughts won't have this effect. People might go hungry for a moon or two but nobody will ever starve again. I can see why these piles of bodies make you sad – you haven't seen real war like I have – but you can see them as a symbol of the old, bad Gaul dying. They're like the dead flesh being eaten from a wound by maggots. Things will be much better from now on, as they will be in Roman Britain."

"Ragnall, these people are dying now, in Roman Gaul. They're not symbols."

"Under the structures of old Gaul. It'll take a year or two before Roman ways bed in properly. Then they will see the benefit."

"The dead babies won't."

"They didn't have lives worth living."

There was no point screaming and her hands were tied so she couldn't strangle him, so she clamped her lips shut and fumed. She was glad he wasn't really her husband.

They journeyed on. Riding near them most days was Quintus Tullius Cicero. Despite having invited himself to their wedding, the old man didn't acknowledge Spring or Ragnall but he did ogle her regularly, which was about as comfortable as being lowered naked into a bath full of sexually aggressive eels. The lecherous goat didn't look nearly as grumpy as he had at the fake wedding because, Spring soon gleaned, his wife Pomponia had demanded to travel next to him with the legions, but Caesar himself had told her to get to the back of the marching order with the rest of the civilians. Quintus Cicero told the story to everyone who came close. His own wife being upbraided by the general was apparently the most excellent and funny thing that had ever happened. It did upset him, though, when people rode up and asked him about "Cicero". They always meant his famous older brother, seeming to forget that it was his name, too. It obviously galled Quintus to be reminded regularly that there was only one notable Cicero and it wasn't him. By the amount that it happened, she guessed that everyone knew this and enjoyed riling him.

Spring wondered who the civilians were that Quintus had mentioned and why they were following the army. She was waiting for Ragnall to tell her the story of Quintus' wife so that she could ask about the civilians, but he didn't, even though she knew he knew the story – he must have overheard it as many times as she had. In the end she asked him directly if he knew where Pomponia was and he pretended not to know. He was a strange one, Ragnall. He had committed the greatest treachery possible by betraying the land of his parents and he believed the wicked lies of the Romans, but he wasn't one to pass on gossip. Luckily, one evening as they crossed a bridge that had been erected in a morning by the astonishingly efficient engineers, it began to rain and he said:

"I hope this rain doesn't swell the river, for the sake of the following civilians."

"What civilians?" she asked. "And can you pull my hood up for me, please? Or unchain me so that I can do it?"

He rode closer, so that their horses bumped, and pulled the leather hood of her riding cape – a present from the older, non-dickhead Cicero brother (the Real Cicero, as Spring called him in her mind) – up over her head and said: "There are thousands of them, following the army. Some are wives, girlfriends and families of the soldiers, engineers and others in the army, but most are chancers, hoping to make their fortune by following Caesar. I've heard that some are carrying their own ships, broken down in carts and ready to assemble at the Channel."

"And you're still happy to support this Roman invasion?"

"Of course." There was no trace of doubt in his voice. "I'm stunned that you can't see it, even though you've been to Rome. Roman culture has *so* much to give Britain."

"These soldiers and your thousands of civilians don't intend to give. They plan to take."

Ragnall shook his head at her despairingly, then told her guards, in Latin, that he was riding on ahead and they should keep an eye on her.

When he was out of sight, she leapt off her horse and jogged along next to it, as she'd done all the way from Rome when he wasn't watching.

The main talk on the march and in the nightly camps, other than the excitement of invading Britain, was about what a marvellous time it was to be a Roman. The world, apparently, was about to come fully under the heel of the Roman sandal and its wonderful new trio of heroes – Caesar, Crassus and Pompey. Crassus was heading east to invade Mesopotamia, Pompey was consolidating Iberia in the west – albeit from a command post in his country house just outside Rome – and Caesar had the biggest adventure of all, into the unknown wilds of Britain. When Ragnall wasn't sulking about Spring's latest accurate observation about the Romans, he translated all this for her.

"But how can they say Britain is unknown when half the slaves in Rome are British?" she asked.

"Nowhere near half."

"A lot. Enough that they should definitely know a lot more about Britain."

"I guess they're not in the habit of conversing with their slaves." And he headed off again, sulkwards.

They arrived at the huge Roman pre-invasion camp, a frighteningly regular city of prim tent rows and efficiently teeming industry spread across the well-drained former farmland of north-west Gaul. The four praetorians that had guarded Spring since her capture marched off to undertake more manful duties and were replaced by only two. Presumably they thought Spring less likely to escape, now that they were in a camp surrounded by nothing but Roman men for several miles. These two were much more friendly, albeit in the bluff, rude manner that passed for friendliness among soldiers. Unlike the other four, they actually bothered to introduce themselves by name – Tertius and Ferrandus. They did it by pointing at themselves and repeating their names loudly and carefully as if Spring were a stupid child or a clever animal, but she still appreciated it.

*   *   *

Despite Spring's protests that she would love nothing more than a good walk after all that time on horseback, in fact he'd be cruel to deny her, Ragnall left her behind with Tertius and Ferrandus and headed for the coast. He was desperate for some time away from her incessant, wrong-headed prating.

The route was choked with carts, boat builders, mercenary gangs, legionaries and others all accusing each other of not knowing how to use the road, so Ragnall walked cross-country, through pillaged fields and denuded woods, five miles to Portus Itius, the launch site for the second invasion. Ragnall didn't know the Gaulish name for the place, and it was a shame that Publius Crassus, who always knew the Gaulish name for everywhere, wasn't there to tell him; not because he gave the tiniest crap about the seaside village's name, but because he missed his only friend in the Roman army. Publius had gone campaigning with his father off into the east, hoping to find Alexander the Great-style fortune and glory.

From his position on a low cliff top, Ragnall could just make out the remains of the Gaulish village in the centre of a long, open bay that swarmed with Roman activity. A river met the sea at the village, splitting a broad, pale sandy beach which was fringed with low, brown cliffs. At the far end of the beach, to the north, the cliffs soared upwards into the same type of white chalk cliff common on the south coast of Britain.

He took all this in with his peripheral vision while gawking at the astonishing amount of ships pulled up above the high-tide mark, in various stages of loading. There were hundreds upon hundreds of them. Almost all were the same design – transport vessels larger than the eighty from the previous year's invasion – each kitted out with oar-slots and benches for rowing as well as rigging for sails. Moored out to sea were even more impressive boats, huge multi-levelled things with row after row of holes for oars, towering mini castles fore and aft, prows wickedly pointed into metal rams. Their visible upper decks were lined with giant arrow-firing scorpions and platforms, presumably for archers and slingers.

Ragnall smiled. Nobody would call this invasion a recon-naissance mission. There was absolutely no way that this kind of power could fail to take Britain.

"Quinqueremes," said a jaunty voice behind him. It was Quintus Cicero. "My pig wife has caught up with me again so I ran off, telling her I was coming up here to survey the fleet. Guess you've done the same? She's all right, your piece, great legs and nice tits, too – a rare and welcome combina-tion – but I bet she's a bitch the second that the world isn't watching. Women, hey? Can't live with them, can't kill them."

Ragnall was torn between wanting to flee this boorish bull-shit and his fascination for the great boats. "Quinqueremes?" he asked.

"Five-decked rowing warships. Crew of six hundred in each; three hundred rowers, three hundred archers, slingers and scorpion crew. Those dirty Britons are in for a big surprise, if they can stop fucking their own daughters for long enough to realise they're being invaded."

"I suppose they are." Despite being at his wedding, Quintus didn't seem to have worked out that Ragnall was originally British.

"Tell you what, I can't wait to get among the women of Britain. Apparently you don't even need to rape them, they just lie down waving their legs in the air with their snatches open. That reminds me – that wife of yours, do you ever hire her out? I've got a two-hundred-year-old Macedonian spear that you can have for a night with her. I bet she'd love some Roman cock."

Before he had time to think of the consequences, Ragnall leant forward and said, quietly: "I catch you anywhere near her and I'll stick that spear so far up your arse that you'll be speaking Greek." It didn't really work as a threat, Ragnall realised as he said it, but it was the best he could do spontaneously and he could hardly say, "Oh, hang on, wait a moment while I think of a better insult".

Quintus purpled and muttered, "You grubby barbarian. How dare you seek to preach morals to me? You British fuck your own daughters!" So he did know Ragnall was British, he was simply untroubled by tact.

"No, we don't."

"We'll see when we get there. I'll make them fuck their daughters. I'll make them fuck their sons! And I'll take your sordid, copper coin slut wife and I'll—"

Before Ragnall knew he was going to punch him, Quintus was lying on the ground, blowing hard and holding his jaw. Immediately Ragnall realised he had made a big mistake.

Technically, Ragnall and Quintus were both legates and equal rank. In practice, Quintus was massively influential, famously cruel and vengeful and a hundred times more powerful. Ragnall was under Caesar's protection to a degree, but someone like Quintus would easily find a way to kill him, nastily, without Caesar finding out. He would be certain to take it out on Spring too. He could not have chosen a worse man to punch. He might as well have climbed into a bag of snakes and hopped to the river himself.

"I'm sorry," he said, reaching out a hand.

"Get back, get back! Praetorians!" hollered Quintus, scrabbling away. Thank Danu there was nobody close enough to hear him.

"Let me help you up. I'm sure we can put this behind—"

"Get away from me, or I'll have you killed today!"

Ragnall walked off and didn't look back. Spring's company suddenly didn't seem so unappealing. What's more, maybe showing her the ships would help ram home just how advanced and impressive the Romans were in every field. Apart from, he thought with an inner smile at how witty he was becoming, the field in which Quintus the Roman had just been such an offensive moron.

"Do you want to come and see some boats?" asked Ragnall, as if he hadn't banned her from leaving the boring tent just hours before.

"Yup!" she said. She held up her chained wrists to her new praetorians Tertius and Ferrandus and smiled.

Ragnall was strangely quiet and brooding on the walk to the coast. Spring wasn't bothered. She'd heard enough of Ragnall's Roman arse-kissing to last a lifetime, then a long stint in the Otherworld, then another lifetime. She concentrated on forgetting that she was a prisoner, that her wrists were chained together, that she hadn't killed Caesar yet and was unlikely to get a chance to, and focused instead on enjoying the walk. She missed everything about Dug, but possibly the long walks with him more than anything else. Her chief hope was to spot some rabbits, the funny little fat hares that they didn't have in Britain, but there were none around, probably, Spring reckoned, because the sun was too hot for them in the middle of the day. Or because the Romans had eaten them all.

"The countryside's better around mine," said Dug, striding up beside her, dogs following. "And walking is definitely more pleasant without your hands tied together."

Ragnall was ahead. Looking back, Spring saw that Tertius and Ferrandus were twenty paces behind, arguing.

"Where have you been?" she asked.

"Where haven't I been?" Dug raised an eyebrow.

"You haven't been in Rome."

"I don't like Rome."

"How do you know if you've never been there?"

"Do you like Rome?"

"Not one bit."

"There you go. I told you, I'm just made up by your mind. You don't like Rome, I don't like Rome."

"But that doesn't explain . . . oh never mind. How am I going to escape back to Britain?"

"Wait for your moment, then escape."

"Wow. That is cunning. Dwyn himself would be proud of that plan."

"OK. To begin, you might as well let them take you back to Britain. No point escaping while you're still in Gaul."

"True."

"Then, maybe pretend you're going along with their plans. Come over all Roman. Style your hair as if you're in a most stupid hair competition, claim there's nothing more delicious that wren foetuses floating in bulls' spunk. Wait for them to drop the guard, then nip off when you get the chance. These two new guards seem a lot slacker—"

"No way am I pretending to have gone all Roman. I wouldn't give them the satisfaction of thinking they've persuaded me that their way is better."

"They'll know you were faking it when you kill Caesar."

"Good point."

"And watch out for Ragnall."

"What do you mean? He's actually OK, just a bit too much in love with Rome."

"He's not 'actually OK', he's a treacherous bastard who's *a lot* too much in love with Rome. He'll turn on you if it suits him, or if Caesar asks him to. You be careful."

"Who are you talking to?" asked Ragnall, who'd slowed down to fall back with her.

"Nobody. Just practising for future arguments. Doesn't everyone do that?"

"I don't."

"Maybe you should."

"Well, this is new," he said when they arrived at the cliff top.

"They've dragged up all these ships since this morning?"

said Spring. There were so many ships on the beach that it almost made Spring cry. How could Lowa possibly hope to beat off this invasion? There were enough surely to carry every Roman who'd ever lived across the Channel. And the size of those warships with all their scorpions and archer platforms! Just one or two of them surely could obliterate any Maidun force that tried to prevent a landing, and there were twenty-eight of them! *How could the Britons possibly fight this?*

"Most of the ships were on the beach," said Ragnall, a smug note in his voice, "and the big warships were here, but that lot have arrived in the last couple of hours." He indicated their end of the beach, where civilian-looking types were swarming around carrying, hammering and shouting and doing all the bits needed to assemble a collection of ships on the beach.

"What a hassle. Why didn't they sail them here?" asked Spring.

"Some of them did, look." He pointed out to sea, where four large boats, not as big as the Roman warships but a good deal more sizeable than the Roman transports, were sailing for the shore. They had flat fronts, rather than pointy prows like every other ship Spring had ever seen. There were odd things moving on them, too. As they sailed closer, Spring could see that they were giant beasts, surrounded by crews of people with skin as dark as Atlas'.

"What are those animals?" asked Ragnall, in Latin.

"Elephants," said Ferrandus the praetorian. "Monsters, the worst you'll ever see. They make them drink saltwater and that gives them a taste for human flesh. I was a mercenary down in Africa once and—"

"You were never a mercenary in Africa," interrupted Tertius.

"OK, it was a friend of mine, but story's the same, so what does it matter? Why do you have to interrupt a story?"

"To point out that you're a liar."

"It wasn't a lie. I was being succinct. Paraphrasing myself to make the story shorter for the benefit of the listener. That's not lying. It's oratory."

"Oratory my cock. You don't know the first thing about—"

"Can we get back to the elephants?" interrupted Ragnall. The first of the transports had reached the beach. The reason for the flat front of the ship became clear as it was lowered onto the sand to become a ramp for the animals to disembark.

The first of the elephants was led out. Spring was very pleased with it. Its fantastically long, dangling nose was bracketed by magnificent tusks tipped with gold. Other than that, its great head, its mountainous grey wrinkly body and its thick, tree trunk-like legs were unadorned. It was wonderful, like a giant, massive-headed, shaved and elderly dog. Its grey ears were flappy and each as big as its head. This lead elephant was missing half an ear on one side, but Spring reckoned that that was an injury rather than the norm. All animals, in her experience, were symmetrical. She wondered why briefly, then got back to admiring the elephants.

"They kit them up for battle," said Ferrandus "put armour on them, great metal boots and little turrets with maybe four archers. When I fought against them—"

"When your friend fought against them," Tertius reminded him.

"Right, prick, yeah my friend. Anyway, they came stamping through, mashing men under their feet and ripping them apart with those horns. Try and get nearby with a spear, the archers in the tower shot you."

Ragnall translated fairly accurately for Spring and she thanked him.

The man leading the first elephant was almost as impressive as his beast. He had the same-coloured skin as Atlas, so Spring guessed he was a Kushite, too, or at least African, but he was much taller and skinnier that the Kushite she knew. He wore a thick yellow-brown fur around one shoulder, the giant paw of some beast still attached to it; a big lion, she reckoned, bigger than the ones she'd seen in Zadar's arena as a child. His whole look was slightly ruined for Spring by his big, bulbous bronze helmet. Everyone knew that bronze was softer than iron so you wore it only because you thought it looked good, so his big round helm was just silly. There was nothing silly about the long, thick, curving sword that was strapped to his waist, though.

"As I was saying," continued Tertius. "Nasty, nasty animals. They'll gore you with those horns or stamp on you or strangle you with that nose, then they'll eat you. Their skin's impervious to arrows, spears or any blade. Only way you can kill one is to stick a spear in its eye."

Ragnall translated for Spring, leaving out the bit about being able to kill one by sticking a spear in its eye. That interested Spring. Was he worried she'd escape and take secrets back to Britain? If so, that wasn't a great secret. It would be hard getting close enough to the beast, let alone getting it to hold still for long enough to line up a spear thrust into that little eye. Besides, she didn't believe they were so bad. She felt that they were kind animals. Was she getting vibes from them, or was it just that every large beast she'd ever met was a herbivore? She remembered the aurochs they'd killed, and its ancient melancholy. Surely the elephants were similarly peaceful beasts, not meat-eaters, cowed by centuries of—

There was a terrible scream from the beach. The second elephant, standing at the top of the ramp, had reared up on its hind legs and was waving its nose in the air, crying out in an undulating high-pitched wail that sounded like a cartload of trumpeters being pushed into a burning long-house.

Forelegs crashed down, the ramp splintered and elephant and handler fell into the shallows. There was a mighty thrashing and more shredding of wood as the bellowing elephant regained its feet. Its handler found his at the same time and held out a calming hand. The elephant whacked him with its nose and he went down. It looked about as if seeking someone else to kill, spotted a gang of merchant types and their servants who were staring agog next to their half-built ship, and charged. The merchants stood like idiots for a moment, then ran, all but one, a great fat bearded man, who stood and stared as the beast galloped heavily towards him.

Spring turned away. She did not want to see the next bit.

"By Jupiter!" said Ragnall.

"Well, fuck me backwards with a wooden spoon," said Ferrandus.

Spring opened one eye.

The fat merchant was still standing, staring at the elephant. The elephant was two paces away, calmly swinging his nose. Spring knew he was male because a penis the same length as his nose had been unleashed from underneath and he was pissing prodigiously. Sitting on his great neck, stroking his head, was the first African who'd disembarked, the one with the silly helmet.

"What happened?" she asked.

"Bronze helmet man happened," said Ragnall. "Now there's a fellow who knows his elephants and by Bel can he leap!"

"I knew they were kind animals really."

The sound of shouting reached them from the beach. The merchant was waving his hands and hurling abuse at the elephanteer. The African leant forward, lifted an ear flap and said something to his mount. The elephant raised its tusks then cracked one down on the head of the merchant, who fell. Helmet man said something else. The elephant reared up on his hind legs as it had done on the ramp, stamped on the merchant, then bounced on his front legs again and again, pulverising the man into a bloody mess on the sand. When there was nothing solid left to mash, the rider jumped off, issued another order and, with a great trumpeting, the elephant attacked the half-built boat with his tusks, feet and nose, smashing it to bits.

"You certainly know your animals, Spring," said Ragnall. "I'm not sure if I've ever seen a kinder beast."

Chapter 6

"My go now," said Adler.

"Thank Danu for that!" Mal had thought he'd have to give up rowing ages back. He'd kept going and somehow found new strength but that new strength had now become very stale indeed. The little boat wobbled precariously as he stood stiffly and swapped seats with the captain of the Two Hundred, but he was too exhausted to worry about falling out.

He slumped gratefully on the back bench, reached under it for the water skin and drank one big swig. That was all he allowed himself, in case they were blown or carried by tides out into open sea. Chances of that were slim, since the shore of Britain was closer than Gaul's now, and there was a constant south-westerly pushing them along – a south-westerly that could bring the massive invasion fleet across in half a morning.

Spying on the Romans, as Atlas had assured him, was much easier than you would have imagined, unless you stood out like a blackbird at a seagulls' party like Atlas did. That was why Mal and Adler had gone across, rather than Atlas or Chamanca. By vaguely pretending they were merchants – Mal slung a sack containing the water skin and a couple of woollen capes over his shoulder and that was it – they'd been able to walk all along the beach, right by all the Roman ships. They'd counted nearly six hundred transports, so Makka knew how many Romans were going to flood across the Channel, but it was the elephants that had really freaked him out. After they'd watched the second one ashore kill a man and destroy a merchant's boat at the command of its rider, they'd seen a further thirty-eight disembark. As they walked back, trying to work out how many soldiers would fit into all those boats, Adler said, "Screw it, let's just ask someone." So they approached a Gaulish loader and did.

"Six legions!" he'd replied. "So nearly thirty thousand men, plus a whole load of cavalry and slingers. The Britons are in for a treat, I tell you."

Lowa's army was about half that size. Mal couldn't see how they had a hope, and that was without considering Felix's dark legion. He'd only heard about that second hand, but if Atlas reckoned it was unbeatable, that was good enough for Mal. Or bad enough. Whichever way, they were in trouble.

"What are we going to do?" he asked Adler when they'd refloated their rowing dinghy and were a good distance from shore.

"I don't know."

"Flee?"

"No," she said.

"Well, at least we're in the same boat," he said, then gestured at the boat they were sitting in and chuckled. Adler raised one of her handsome eyebrows but remained stony-faced.

When Adler shook him awake they were across. She'd taken at least a double shift rowing while he'd slept.

"Thanks," he said.

"I didn't want to hear your 'in the same boat' joke again."

She hauled the boat up the shingle by its mooring rope while he pushed, red-faced.

*   *   *

They travelled inland to Lowa's new headquarters at Big Bugger Hill. Mal had found the place and organised its rebuilding. He was very proud of it.

It was the only hillfort in south-east Britain, but a year before it had been little more than a low hill, fallen into disrepair over centuries. It had only one ditch, following the contours of a sixty-pace-high mound and enclosing an area about a third the size of Maidun Castle – around the same expanse as Maidun's eyrie. There had been no palisade on the wall, and the ditch surrounding the wall was half collapsed, overrun with scrubby bushes and trees.

Mal had renovated and rebuilt the fort in, he had to admit to himself, a pretty ingenious way. Everyone else had been sceptical, but Lowa had understood and agreed, so his plans had been realised. By the time it was finished, all the doubters were convinced that it was the best thing that could have been done.

In every other hillfort you had your ditch outermost then a bank or wall of earth and rock inside that, with a palisade on top of the wall. In multi-walled places like Maidun Castle, from the outside it was ditch, wall, ditch, wall, ditch, wall, but Big Bugger Hill was smaller, with only a single ditch and wall. To make the most of the space inside, and make the single wall as strong as possible, what Mal had done – or, more to the point, what he'd had the now fifteen-thousand-strong Maidun infantry do – was to build an awesomely strong, six-pace-high palisade not on top of the earth wall as was the norm but *around* the wall, growing up from the bottom of the ditch, using the ditch as a deep foundation. He'd shored up the wall and filled in the gap between it and his palisade, so that all around the perimeter of the hillfort was a walkway twenty paces wide. Defenders could move rapidly around the unprecedentedly wide wall top and as many ranks of archers and slingers as you'd ever need could shoot down at the foe. To make the wall even

higher and safer from rams and ladders, Mal had dug a new
ditch all the way around, filled with the traditional spiked
timbers, as well as some newer ideas like concealed
ankle-trapping holes and three-pronged iron caltrops hidden
under soft soil at the ditch's base.

Lowa's addition had been a high, sturdy wooden
command tower from which you could see all the land
around, and she'd also greatly improved the road running
inland from Big Bugger Hill. Ostensibly that meant that
the fort could be supplied and garrisoned with great
rapidity, but the real reason for the road, known only to
Mal and a few others, was so that they'd be able to flee
effectively.

The one thing that hadn't changed about Big Bugger Hill
was its name. It was a shit name, everyone agreed, especially
for a hill that wasn't big. Mal had heard about seven different
stories from locals about how it had got its name, a couple
of which were truly disgusting. One thing everybody did
agree on was that it was unlucky to change a name, so they
were stuck with it. They'd have enough to deal with without
luck being against them.

As they approached, the wall towered higher. Mal thought
it looked almost as formidable as Maidun Castle. "You would
not want to attack this," he said.

"No," said Adler. "Not unless you had thirty thousand
highly trained, fiercely disciplined soldiers, more siege equipment that you could shake a spear at, a squad of gigantic
animals, one of which can reduce a ship to kindling in a
few heartbeats and a mysterious force of monsters."

They found Lowa in the camp's small central clearing, at
the highest point of the hill. They'd sent a shout to announce
their approach, so the usual leadership team of Atlas,
Chamanca and Maggot was waiting for them, too, along with

Lowa's child and his nanny. When she saw them coming, Lowa nodded to Keelin and she led Dug away by the hand. The little boy toddled off next to his nanny, free hand waving, chattering nonsense. He was a lovely little boy, thought Mal. Mal and Nita had never been blessed with children. Having a little wobbler like Dug of his own was another reason for him to make his intentions known to Taddy Ducktender. Or to test the water at least.

"Did you see Spring?" Lowa asked without preamble.

"We did," said Adler.

"We did?" This was news to Mal.

"She was on the low cliff above the beach, when we were watching the elephant rip the ship apart."

"They have an elephant?" asked Chamanca.

"Elephants. Forty of them. I've only heard about them before but I'm sure that's what they were, but I didn't know they were so big, powerful or well-trained. One of them fell from the gangplank and flew into a frenzy, but the rider leapt on it and—"

Lowa held up a palm "Tell me about Spring first."

"She seemed fine from what I could see at that distance. I'm—"

"How far were you?"

"Two hundred paces. I didn't get Mal's opinion because he was preoccupied watching the elephant and I was certain it was her, plus she was with three guards so I didn't want them spotting our interest."

"What type of guards?"

"Two black-clad legionaries and a man in a toga."

"Can you describe the man?"

"Early twenties, good-looking, quite fat. I was sure it was Ragnall initially, but on the return journey I questioned myself. I didn't know him well when he was here, and if it was him then he has been eating with gusto."

"All right, thank you. Back to the elephants."

Mal and Adler told them everything they'd discovered. Afterwards they stood in silence, Lowa with her lips pursed and fists clenched. Chamanca paced and Atlas shook his head. Maggot wore a relaxed smile, his jewellery jangling softly as he turned his whole frame to watch birds flit by.

"We have three options," said Atlas eventually. "We send a delegation now offering allegiance to the Romans and your rule as client queen." He turned the iron arrowhead hanging from a leather thong around his neck as he spoke. It was from the arrow that had nearly killed him. If a man wearing that sort of lucky charm is suggesting surrender, thought Mal, then our position is far from strong.

"No," said Lowa. "We won't be doing that."

"Option two is flight. With our army we could conquer Eroo without a fight and then, because the Romans will follow us there to prevent us returning, we build a fleet and cross the great sea to—"

"No."

"We cannot hope to win against such a force. With just the legionaries – men with training and experience that ours never could match – they will outnumber us. The warships will prevent us from hampering their landing, which they will undoubtedly fuck up less having learnt from last time, they are not idiots, and now we hear they have elephants. More than all of that, they have Felix's Ironmen and Leathermen. If we take option three, to stand and fight, we are condemning our men and women to death."

"If we don't, we are condemning them to dishonour," said Chamanca.

"Dishonour or death?" said Maggot brightly. "I'd prefer dishonour, but perhaps that's just me. Tell you what, though. Lowa and I have a plan to slow them up a bit."

Lowa nodded. "And we have several more schemes in place to send them back to Gaul which, gods willing, will save many of our lives and all of our honour. The one involving the Aurochs tribe needs to be modified. Atlas, have you encountered war elephants?"

"Are you asking me because I'm African?"

"Yes."

"Well, it so happens I have encountered war elephants."

"Good. Elann will be here tomorrow. You'll talk to her and . . ."

Queen Lowa spent a long time outlining her plans, making sure that her generals understood them, then sent them off to do their duties.

Chapter 7

"The ships have oars, so why can Caesar's legions not row to Britain?" Caesar smiled thinly.

Ten days after Caesar had ordered the fleet to sail, it was still beached on Gaul's shore. Given the circumstances, Felix would have beaten the chief boat builder's face into a pulp with a ship's mallet then shat into the bubbling hole where his mouth used to be, but Caesar seemed calm. He wasn't, though. Felix could see a vein throbbing at his temple. The shipwright had no idea that he was a hair's breadth from crucifixion. Felix stifled a smile.

"No ships can make way against wind and tide like this, with or without oars." Apiapandus the chief boat builder was a former merchant from a land to the north of Germany who'd settled in Ostia, Rome's port. He was considered to be the best, so Caesar had commissioned him to build the fleet. With his cap of blond hair, lapine face and a voice like a seal's, he didn't look like the best.

"Caesar asked you to build boats that can be rowed."

"The ships can be rowed, but they will not make way against a strong wind and a contrary current. Last year, before the commission, I wrote detailed descriptions of the ships' capabilities and limitations. I gave you these descriptions and you told me to build your boats. They are ships and they can do what ships can do. They are not magic carpets."

Caesar drew his sword. The magic carpet comment, Felix guessed, had signed the man's death warrant.

Apiapandus' eyes bulged preternaturally wide. "No! You cannot! Nobody could have predicted this freak current. I built what you asked! I—"

Caesar stabbed him in the stomach, pumped his arm to slice across and withdrew. Apiapandus grabbed the wound with both hands. A glossy pocket of gut peeked between his fingers of his left hand. Felix licked his lips. He did enjoy watching a man trying to hold his innards inside a slit stomach. Apiapandus, mouth silently opening and closing, staggered backwards and slumped into a canvas chair. Caesar followed him and raised his sword again. Felix thought for one horrible moment that he was about to deliver a mercy blow, but the general wiped his sword on the man's shoulder, returned it to its scabbard and turned, leaving Apiapandus sitting there blinking, holding his guts and dripping blood on the non-magic Mesopotamian carpet.

"This wind must be changed." Caesar didn't say why – he would never confess a weakness – but Felix knew that supplies were being consumed faster than their supply lines were replenishing them.

"I cannot reverse it," answered the druid. "It is a magic wind, created by the great British druid. I have sacrificed dozens of Gauls to no avail. Perhaps if I could slay the British girl, the more powerful magic—"

"The girl will stay alive. Caesar remains suspicious of your motives."

"Caesar, whoever is creating this wind is the great British druid, not her. It cannot be her, because women lack the wit to control magic. I can see a solitary figure on a hill looking towards us creating the wind and the current, but I cannot see his features and my magic does not have nearly the range to reach him. I want the girl purely because I have known her for a long time, so the magic gained from her death might enable—"

"She is to be queen of Britain."

"Fine."

"Fine?" The temple vein pulsed and the general's hand closed on his sword hilt.

"I meant no disrespect. Frustrated by our delay and my own impotence I grow complacently familiar. I apologise."

Caesar relaxed. It felt to Felix as if a large plug had been pulled to let the tension and terror flood out of the room. The general had his own magic even if he didn't know it, Felix was certain. The power emanating from him at the moment that had just passed was astonishing, and when Felix had tried to control his mind in the past, back when he'd been able to control most people's minds, he had been unable to.

"What else can be done to reverse this weather?" said the general.

There was one other thing Felix could do, but he was going to wait until the last possible moment to try it, because it might well kill him.

"Nothing," he said. "I would have a Maximan row me across. Properly fuelled, I am sure that one of them could—"

"But the British are watching the sea so you will be shot or sunk before you reach the shore. Do you think that Caesar is an idiot that he hasn't thought of—"

A scream cut him off. Both men jumped round, Caesar drawing his sword as he spun.

It was just Apiapandus, still slumped on the chair and holding in his own guts, some new agony visiting him as he died.

"It's a nasty way to go," said Felix.

"Indeed," said Caesar.

Chapter 8

Lowa found Maggot sitting cross-legged at the apex of the hill where she'd left him the evening before, looking out over the sea. He looked like a corpse. His skin was like century-old leather, even more wrinkled than it had been the day before, as if all moisture had been sucked from his body. His feather-strewn hair danced lightly in the wind that was still holding back the Romans.

Maggot was using his own life-force to hold the Roman invasion fleet in Gaul. The extra preparation time was invaluable to Lowa, but what she really hoped was that the massive force would run out of supplies and be forced to retreat. Maggot had said from the off that he considered that unlikely, but that the delay was worth giving his life for.

"Have the Romans gone home?" she asked.

"They have not."

"Will you accept sacrifices now? A soldier attacked a girl last night so he'll be dying whatever happens and I have two murderers who need executing. Take their lives."

"I've already got a sacrifice, thanks."

He meant himself. For twenty days now Maggot had made the wind blow as a strong north-westerly and the sea current flow in the same direction by slowly killing himself. The wind was a doddle, apparently; it was the current change that was sucking the life from him. Lowa had offered sacrifices every day and he'd refused, saying he'd tried killing and didn't like it, and, besides, he needed the life of someone he loved deeply and utterly to make magic this powerful, and the only person who fitted that description was himself.

"How much longer?"

"Before I die?"

"Yes." It was a callous question but she needed to know.

Maggot looked up at the sky and smiled. "Some time around the next dawn."

Lowa closed her eyes and shook her head. "And then the Romans will come?"

"Yup."

Lowa wanted to scream and shake him. "Stop now then! Save yourself!"

"Every moment I hold the Romans, the weaker they become and the better our preparations."

"But one day . . ."

"Will save some British lives. Lowa, I'm a lot older than I look, and I've done some . . . bad things. I want to die now, and I want to die doing this."

"Nothing I can say to change that? Like how useful you'll be when the Romans come?"

"No, it's my time now. I can't change that, but I can decide how I die and this is what I have chosen. It is the most use I could have been to you. From tomorrow, the Romans are your problem."

She saw that he was resigned and there was nothing she could do, and, in truth, the delay he'd already created had been very useful.

"Shall I stay with you? Or send . . ."

"No, I want to be alone, but before you go . . . I'm the last like me, and I want to tell someone what I know about magic, or at least what I've guessed, before I die. Might as well be you."

"I'm flattered," said Lowa, sitting next to the druid.

Maggot was so silent for a while that Lowa thought he'd

died already, but then he began, his voice as clear as ever but the mockery now gone from it.

"Magic comes from the link between people. Flocks of birds move as one because their minds are all linked, right?"

"Are they?"

"Yes. Think of the way a flock of thousands of animals speeds up, slows down, swoops, climbs and changes direction at exactly the same time, again and again, all while flying faster than a horse can gallop. It would take years to teach a crowd of humans to make just one of those manoeuvres, but birds do thousands every day. Fish, too. They can do it because they share a group mind."

"OK . . ."

"Animals' minds are linked in another way, too. Take your son. He could be the brightest toddler alive but put him alone in a wood and he'd be dead before sunset."

"True."

"He needs to be taught not to kill himself. But animals don't. They're *born* knowing not to fall into rivers. They know which mushrooms are safe and which aren't. Dug's only just learnt to walk and he's very bad at it. Cows know how to walk as soon as they're born."

"I guess."

"So animals' minds are linked in two ways; to all other living animals of their type, and to their ancestors through their mothers. The source of this link is life and the link is destroyed by death. Got it?"

"I think so."

"Good, because here's the important bit. Hidden away behind all our bullshit, behind our jealousies, our fears and our endless fucking *competition*, we humans have the same link. Human minds are linked in exactly the same way as animals' minds, but we're so very fucking clever that we worked out how to speak. We needed the link less and it withered. Writing made the link even more unnecessary and finished it off in most places, which is why British druids destroyed everything written and banned writing a couple of thousand years ago, and why a few of us can still use the link."

"To change the direction of the wind and kill people?"

"Yeah, well, it's more than just moving around in a pleasingly synchronised group and knowing not to hurl yourself into a river, isn't it? It's the magic force, for want of a better word, that underlies and connects everything. This magic is all around. We see it in people in two ways. For some it's passive, and it's busy the whole time without them knowing. Magic is strong in you, for example, which is why you can pull a bow that few big men can pull and slot an arrow up a bee's arse from a thousand paces. It gives Chamanca her speed and more."

Maggot coughed and swayed. Lowa raised an arm to hold him up but Maggot pushed it away. His touch was cold.

"So that's passive magic," he continued, "but for some it's active – as in they can use it a bit to change the world around them, like I can. So could Drustan, a little bit, and there was Reena, queen of Eroo, who I don't think used it as much as she could have done, and then of course there's Felix who's pretty adept, unfortunately."

"But using it kills you bit by bit?"

"Pretty much, which is why you use someone else's lifeforce. When someone dies, a whole wash of magic is released. Some people can redirect that force to, for example, kill an infection in a big African. The stronger their link with the person who died, the more of the power that they can use."

"But apart from Walfdan . . ."

"I haven't killed anyone? Well, that's not true, you didn't know me when I was younger, but you have a point. I can use quite a bit of my own life-force because I've got a lot more than most people. I used some to encourage those whales to attack Felix's boat — quite a bit, actually — and now I'm finishing myself off with this wind and tide."

"What about Spring?"

"I think she has some passive magic that gives her strength, so she can use a bow like you can, but the big magic, the real magic, wasn't ever Spring. It was Dug. He had more magic in him than I thought was possible, much more, but no connection to it. He was like a giant wooden barrel of whale oil sitting in a deserted hut for forty years. Spring came along with a tap and used his oil to light a couple of lamps."

"And when she killed him?"

"It was like she'd thrown the torch into the barrel. The greatest explosion of magic for a long time, perhaps ever, was unleashed. It destroyed a mountain and created the wave."

"How did they know what to do?"

"I helped."

"I see."

"And when you're dead?"

"Then Felix is the only one left alive who can actively use magic."

"There's nobody else?"

"Not that I know of. There is one more magic, vastly more powerful than Dug's, that makes the mountains and knocks them down, a magic which will obliterate the Romans and scrub away every trace of their existence."

"What's that?"

"It's called time."

"I see, clever. But not so helpful."

"Yeah. Now I've talked too long. Today is the end of my extremely long life and I'd like to spend the rest of it alone with my favourite person — me."

"Is there anything else you want?"

"Only solitude."

"All right. Goodbye. And thanks. This delay should save thousands of lives."

"Yup."

Lowa nodded and walked away across the springy grass, leaving the druid staring at the sea.

Chapter 9

Atlas rode alone to the forest of Branwin and the Aurochs tribe to fetch the cavalry of armoured aurochs to the east coast. He could have sent someone else, but he was keen to see the anti-elephant modifications that Elann had made to the giant cattle's armour, and, more than that if he was honest, he was keen for some time away from Chamanca. He liked her a lot, perhaps even loved her, but, he told himself, every man needs some time alone, particularly when that man has spent nearly every moment for the last half a year with a manically energetic Iberian who seems to have taken his near-death experience as a cue to cram as much living as possible into every waking heartbeat, and quite a few of the heartbeats when they should have been sleeping.

After three days of blissfully peaceful riding he found Queen Ula of Kanawan waiting for him at the edge of the forest, also on horseback. Atlas had met her on Maidun before the battle with Eroo and the Spring Tide. He'd been struck by her beauty then and she was much as he remembered. Her black hair was longer, and her simple but well-made brown dress was more like a woodlander's garb than what she'd worn at Maidun, but she still had the same unblemished, pale skin, full red lips and invitingly arched eyebrows. She was a very attractive woman. As, he reminded himself, was Chamanca.

"We got the shout that you were coming," she said. "Elann asked me to send someone to meet you and show you the way. I thought I'd come myself because I . . ."

"Felt like some time alone?"

"Yes!" Her blue eyes sparkled and she smiled the mischievous "You might be able to have me if you only gave it a go" smile that he remembered.

"I understand the sentiment," he replied.

As they rode along the woodland track, Ula explained how she and the Kanawan tribe had moved to spare land belonging to the Aurochs tribe. The Aurochs people had been greatly reduced by plague and welcomed the extra numbers. She'd intended for her own tribe to remain separate but allied to the Aurochs, but she'd got on so well with their new queen and their people had melded so easily that the tribes had united and the two women now shared the rule.

"There's a new queen of the Aurochs?" asked Atlas, leaning to flick a horsefly off his mount's neck.

"Relatively new. She's called Manfreena. It's a bit of an odd story really." Ula looked around as if to check whether anyone was eavesdropping, then put a hand on his bare forearm. "She was a traveller from Eroo who settled in the forest a couple of years ago, after the Spring Tide and before the plague struck. The old ruler and all his heirs died in the plague and the Aurochs asked Manfreena to rule. You'll understand why when you meet her."

Manfreena . . . thought Atlas. A woman called Reena had been queen to Manfrax, the king of Eroo who had invaded Britain and whose force of Fassites had killed most of Atlas' infantry, and she'd died with the rest of the Eroo under the great wave. Shortly after that, it seemed that someone with a name that was a mashing together of Manfrax and Reena, also from Eroo, had turned up in the forest of Branwin and become a queen. There, thought Atlas, was a coincidence.

"And you rule happily together?"

"Oh, we're very happy together." Ula's smile was, if

anything, more mischievous. "Did you ever meet Farrell, my old husband and former king of Kanawan?"

"I never had the pleasure."

"It wouldn't have been a pleasure. If there's a special area of the Otherworld reserved for the smarmiest, most self-obsessed wankers then he is now king of that area. Had you met him you'd understand why I'm so particularly happy to have met someone like Manfreena. Now, tell me. Is Lowa going to beat the Romans?"

Atlas wondered for the briefest of moments whether to tell Ula about Felix's demons but elected not to. Everything about Ula was normal and fine — very fine — but he did not like the sound of Manfreena. He didn't like coincidences.

"Lowa is as well prepared as she could be, given the limits."

"And her plan is . . .?"

There was no harm in telling Ula the outlines. If Caesar himself knew the outlines it wouldn't have helped him.

"She wants Caesar to come, she wants him to find there's nothing here for him but fierce resistance, and she wants him to leave. She wants him to appeal to Rome to fund another invasion, and she wants them to reject his appeal because there was nothing to show for the first two. Simple as that."

"But surely the Romans will return at some point? It's what they do, isn't it; fight and fight until they get what they want?"

"Possibly, but if Lowa's plans come to fruition, they will return to find an increasingly unified and determined Britain."

"And how will she achieve that?"

"There's a lot of detail. Simply put, she is a good queen and she is doing well. I am more interested in the aurochs. Are the adaptations to their armour complete? Have the cavalry learnt the new skills I suggested to Elann?

Ula answered and Atlas kept asking questions about the giant cattle as they rode on through the woods. All around them birds sang and squirrels leapt from bough to bough.

Chapter 10

Felix shook his head. It was weird, transporting yourself like that, and it was much more dangerous than he would have liked. Chances of appearing in front of a galloping horse or similar were high, plus the process always left one blind for a moment, so if you arrived near an enemy they had plenty of time to ram a sword into your spine. After twenty-five days of contrary winds, however, the Romans were nearly out of food. If they didn't cross more or less immediately they'd have to give up the invasion for another year, and Felix simply could not have that. He wanted Britain.

He shook his head again and his vision cleared.

Good. Nothing charging at him and the British druid was sitting cross-legged a dozen paces distant, facing away from him. Felix pulled his knife from its scabbard. The plan was perfect in its double-headed simplicity. He killed the druid, the wind and tide returned to normal. It had taken the lives of two dozen Gauls to send him to Britain, but this druid, Felix reckoned, was powerful enough for his death to fuel his journey back. He'd cleared a wide field in Gaul and left his legions to guard it to make his return safer.

"You're too late, you nasty little shit, I'm already dead," said the druid, weakly, without turning.

"You will be."

Felix strode forwards, lifted his knife . . . and the man's head slumped forwards into the ground. A trick? Felix stood motionless. The British druid didn't move. The Roman took a step back and looked around. Nobody. He darted in, stabbed the point of his knife into Maggot's lower back, then darted away. No movement. And no blood. The knife had gone in far too easily, as if he'd stabbed a pile of ash. Oh no, thought Felix.

He flipped the corpse over with his foot as easily as if it were made of dried leaves. The British druid was completely desiccated, all fluid gone, his eyes like raisins, lips like black, salted anchovies curled back from yellow, ovine teeth. He looked as if he had been dead for a thousand years.

Felix stamped on his face and it collapsed with a pouf! like a dried-up wasps' nest. He felt for life-force but there was none.

Fuck! he thought, but then the wind died. All was still for a few seconds, then the wind began to blow again, in the opposite direction. He ran to the cliff edge. The water below was aswirl with eddies as the natural currents re-established themselves. He looked across the sparkling sea to Gaul, so far away. Soon, very soon, that view would be full of ships.

He tramped off down the hill, grinning. He'd done it! It hadn't gone exactly to plan, but one thing he'd always congratulated himself on was his adaptability. If there was nobody around with enough life-force to transport him back to Gaul, then he'd simply find somewhere to hide until the Romans arrived.

Lowa felt the wind change. She told Adler to take over the infantry training, leapt on her horse and headed for Maggot's hill. Her inability to help Maggot through the pains of stopping the Roman fleet had upset her more than she would have liked, but by being first to his body and carrying it down the hill, at least she'd be honouring his life. She was still no great fan of the gods and was unconvinced that there was an Otherworld, but seeing what Spring had done, the wave in particular, coupled with Maggot's words the evening before had forced her to accept that there was more to the world that she could immediately see.

She dismounted, told her horse to stay and walked to the pile that had been Maggot. She'd expected it to be bad, but not this bad. He was no more than dried slivers of skin and flesh among his clothes and . . . were those footmarks? His body had been stamped on! She looked around and saw the trail of someone's recent passage across the dewy grass. She followed them to the cliff edge, where they turned and led away downhill, in the opposite direction to the one she'd come. She whistled for her horse.

"Good evening!" said Felix to the guard. It was the first time he'd spoken British for an age and was glad to hear it coming out correctly.

The guard spun. He was a nervy-looking fellow, not much taller than Felix himself, with white hair and moustache. "Wha— what? What you doing?" he asked.

Felix smiled. "I'm here to relieve you, friend."

Lowa saw a figure that couldn't be Felix, but looked an awful lot like Felix, talking to a guard. She reached for an arrow in her back-slung quiver.

Chapter 11

"Where is Ragnall the Briton?" demanded Quintus Cicero, speaking like a man with a mouthful, presumably on account of his bruised jaw. He glanced at Spring, chained to the bed, back to Tertius and Ferrandus, then, seeming to realise what he'd seen, his eyes swivelled back to Spring like deck-mounted whaling scorpions spotting a juicy target. His gaze slithered down her body and came to rest on her legs and Spring wished that she hadn't worn her riding shorts that day. She crossed them in an attempt to show him less, but his eyes bulged all the more.

"I don't know, do you know?" said Tertius, seemingly unfazed by Quintus' demanding tone. "Ragnall, you say . . ."

"A Briton, huh?" said Ferrandus. "Seems unlikely. Perhaps you'd like to go back to your own tent and leave Caesar's prisoner be?"

"Ragnall assaulted me and will face trial. I know he is billeted here with his barbarian whore, so I will wait." His slimy eyes were still fixed on Spring "You two will wait outside."

"Generally," said Tertius, "we don't like to ruffle feathers."

"Calm-water men, that's us," said Ferrandus.

"However," continued Tertius, "those words that you just said, the ones that you intended as commands? Well, they're not commands to us. Each word is interesting, and you do have a pleasant speaking voice, but for us, all those words together, they're just noise. Certainly not commands, is the point. What we did hear was you insulting

Caesar's prisoner. That, we cannot allow. You will leave, now."

"What sort of insolence is this?" spat Quintus. "I am Caesar's legate, I was governor or Asia. My brother—"

"What my comrade is trying to say," said Ferrandus, "and he's right for once, is that we are praetorian guard. We take orders from the praetorian centurion and Caesar, nobody else, and both of them have told us to guard this young lady. So that's what we'll do until either of them tells us to stop."

"You will do what I tell you!"

Tertius shook his head. "No, that's just the thing. We won't. You can try to order us about until your cock falls off, but nothing will happen. It's almost, sir, as if we didn't give the slightest fuck about who you are and what you've done."

"Oh, I see." Quintus seemed unfazed by what Spring thought was impressively tough talk. "And are you family men?"

"I'm not," said Ferrandus, "but Tertius here has two children. And another one on the way, isn't that right, Tertius?"

"Oh, Ferrandus," said Tertius, shaking his head.

Quintus smiled like a snake finding a nestful of unguarded chicks. "I am a very, very rich man with a vast network of clients. There are many men who owe me big favours and other men whom I can pay to do whatever I want. If I wanted to find a praetorian's family, for example, it would take moments. Now, I'm not one to harm children, nor, Juno forbid, visit horrors upon a pregnant woman. But, having said that, I am probably more used to getting my way than I am to not finding people's families, ripping foetuses from wombs and torturing the rest of them to death."

"Oh dear, Tertius, I think he'd gone too far now." Ferrandus took a step towards the legate. Quintus took a step back.

But Tertius put a hand on Ferrandus' arm. "No, Ferrandus.

Thanks to your tittishness, he's gone exactly far enough. We're leaving him in here."

"But——" Tertius silenced Ferrandus with a look.

Quintus beamed. "I'm glad we could come to an agreement. Let's be clear. If I think that either of you is closer than fifty yards to this tent any time in the next hour, I'll set my network in motion and next time someone asks you if you have a family, you will weep."

"Very well. Let me check her chains before we go," said Tertius, walking over to Spring's bed. "You wouldn't want her getting free."

Felix heard galloping hooves and saw the guard's eyes flick upwards. He dropped. An arrow thumped into the guard's chest and knocked him backwards.

Ha! thought Felix to himself as the dying man's energy flowed into him. Take me, he thought, take me – the world fell away and a new one rushed up towards him.

That, thought Lowa, looking down at the dead guard and sighing, answered one question. It seemed that magic users didn't need to kill the person themselves to take their life energy. The last she'd seen of Felix, he'd ducked the arrow meant for him and it had taken the unlucky soldier instead. Thank Danu, thought Lowa, that she was queen. A murdered guard with one of her arrows sticking out of his chest might have been hard to explain. Then she felt bad for thinking of herself first, and not this poor man whom she'd murdered by mistake. The knowledge that Felix would have killed him anyway was some consolation.

She'd approached the body cautiously, but had already known that Felix had disappeared. She hadn't seen it herself, but everybody said he'd vaporised into thin air after she'd killed Zadar. She had no idea how far he was capable of flying, or whatever the Bel it was that he did, but she presumed it was at least across the Channel because that was how he'd presumably got past her guards watching the sea and her sentries guarding Maggot.

The dead guard had a well-trimmed, freshly combed moustache. The thought that he'd never groom his facial hair again almost brought tears to her eyes. She wondered if he had children and pictured her own death and little Dug playing on, not knowing where she was . . . .

She stamped her foot, cursed this mawkishness that seemed to be worsening with age, and called her horse. The new wind would bring unwelcome visitors and she wanted to be ready for them.

Felix shook his head, blinked, heard somebody say something, shook his head again, and opened his eyes.

"I asked you what kind of demon you are." It was a blacksmith, a tall man with a narrow head, pointily arched eyebrows and such a double bush of nasal hair that Felix thought for a moment he had a moustache although he was clean-shaven. He was standing next to his anvil and forge, hammer in one hand, in the entrance of a lean-to attached to a large rectangular hut. His accent was British, not Gaulish. Felix had not expected to cross the Channel but it would have been nice. Still, this was better than landing in the middle of the ocean, inside a mountain or any other number of places even crappier than right next to a weird-looking British blacksmith.

"I'm no demon, friend, just a weary traveller."

"You're no traveller." The man's eyebrows jumped as he talked, like two tethered falcons making repeated, simultaneous attempts to take off. "I saw you appear out of nowhere. Just then!"

"No, no, you've got it all wrong, come over here and I'll show you what happened. You're clearly a decent fellow and I mean you no harm."

The blacksmith's eyebrows danced in crazy disapproval, but he came. He walked as if he had no knees, with a backwards lean of his body which allowed him to swing his straight legs forward. Felix was working on a ruse but decided not to bother. This lunk had the speed and gumption of a half-brained cow. As soon as he was close enough, Felix whipped out his blade and leapt forward to slit his gut open.

But the lunk proved to be fast. He grabbed Felix's sword hand with one great paw and swung the other fist into his face.

Felix's head reeled. "No," he cried, "stop! I saw a big spider on your—" The man punched him again and the world spun, then blackened.

Lowa dragged on her reins. Chamanca, galloping in the opposite direction, did the same.

"Maggot's dead, wind's changed," said the queen. "You're going the wrong way. We've got an invasion to see off."

"I know, but . . . I feel something. I think Felix is here. I can't explain it. Back in Zadar's day I always knew when the nasty little shit was near, and then in Gaul his magic made me stronger—"

"He is here." Lowa told her the basics as quickly as she could. This was no time for storytelling. "So, where do you feel that he is?" she finished.

"Along this road."

"How far?"

"I don't know. A few miles maybe."

"Go, but be careful. You will be needed in the coming days."

"He cannot harm me."

Lowa nodded. "Then go and kill him."

The two women kicked their horses and galloped off in opposite directions.

*　　*　　*

"Now, my little darling. You just stay there a moment." Quintus turned away to pull his toga up over his head. It was an odd display of modesty, Spring thought, for a man who, she was pretty sure, intended to rape her. She thanked Danu – and Jupiter, too, why not? – that Ferrandus had unchained her wrists. She jumped into a crouch.

He turned, fully naked and semi-tumescent. Spring gave him a look that said "I would have thought I deserved a full erection" and leapt into one of the kicks Lowa had taught her. The side of her foot smashed into his temple. He went down.

Spring was worried that he'd come round as she dug her fingers into his arms and hauled him onto the bed, but he didn't. She gagged him and tied him as firmly as she could, because what she had planned was probably going to wake him.

When Ferrandus had begun to unshackle her wrists, she'd thought: "I'll knock Quintus out, duck out of the back of the tent, find Caesar, and kill him." But, as she'd watched Quintus peel off his toga, she realised that he'd doubtless raped women before, and, things being left as they were, he'd do it again. She couldn't have that.

She checked the bonds. All good. She went over to Ragnall's side of the tent.

"Now, where does he keep that knife?" she said to herself.

Felix blinked while the world formed around him, for the third time that day. He was bound to a chair. That blacksmith had had the look of a man who knew knots, he thought, and indeed he did – there was no chance of escape. He was inside a capacious hut. Sitting opposite him on the floor in a pool of sunlight lancing down from a high window was a small girl, playing with two stones.

"Come on, Mr Sheep!" she said shaking one of the stones, her voice high and lispy. "Come to market with me!" She shook the other stone. "I'm not coming with you, you're not a sheep, you're a dog. A mean nasty dog who eats sheep. My daddy told me—"

"Uh, hello?" said Felix.

She started and looked up at him with big blue eyes. She bit her lower lip.

"What's your name?"

"I'm not to talk to you."

"That's not nice. Who told you not to?"

"My daddy."

"Where is your daddy?"

"Gone to see good Queen Lowa"

"*Good* Queen Lowa?"

"She *is* good."

"Where's your mummy?"

"She's in the Otherworld, waiting for me and daddy."

"I see. And what's your name?"

"Autumn."

"That's a lovely name. What are your sheep and your dog called?"

She looked at the stones in her hands. "They're just stones."

"Doesn't mean they can't have names, right?"

"I suppose not."

"How about Felix for the dog?"

"That's a silly name."

All the tents looked the same and soon she was infuriatingly lost. In the end, Spring decided there was only one thing for it.

"Where's Caesar's tent?" she asked a passing legionary.

He put a finger to his chin and looked at the sky, not seeming to mind either that there was a woman in the camp, or that she was wearing a man's toga hoicked up and belted with rope. Spring had decided that "prostitute who's borrowed her client's clothes" would be a less conspicuous look than her riding shorts and shirt, and it was better for hiding Ragnall's freshly cleaned knife.

"Are you in a rush?" he asked.

"Not really."

"Then the easiest but not the quickest route is to keep going this way until you come to the Seventh Legion's tents."

"How will I know when I'm there?"

"There will be guards asking you what you're doing."

"I see. And if I was in a rush?"

"Then you go the quick way. Just keep going in that direction." She followed his point over the sea of tents. "The best way to do that is to remember where the sun is. Face that way." She did. "So you see that the sun is diagonally in front of you, between your right shoulder and your face?"

"Yes."

"Well, keep it there as much as you can and you'll soon find Caesar's complex. The sun will move a little to your, um . . ." he pointed towards the sea, then at the sun and nodded, "yes, it'll move a bit to your right. But probably not enough to be relevant, or even notice."

"Great directions! Thanks!"

"You're welcome." He walked off, then stopped, pointed seawards and up at the sun again, and nodded to himself again before walking on, a satisfied jaunt in his step.

Spring headed off, weaving between the tents. Lowa had told her once that men's love of giving directions was so strong that it could override all other senses. It looked like she'd been right. Lowa was always right. She *should* have come and seen Spring after Dug had died, though. Having thought that, Lowa had had an army to build and a big collection of tribes to run. It wasn't a good excuse, but Spring was beginning to accept that it was, at least, an excuse, and just maybe she shouldn't have hated Lowa for putting the needs of the entire land before the wants of one girl.

At first Chamanca thought it was one of Felix's monsters coming along the road towards her – he was walking as if burdened by improbably heavy armour – but when he got closer she saw that it was just a man with bad knees trying to walk as fast as he could.

She pulled up ahead of him. "Have you seen a short, bald man with a sneer on his face?" she asked.

His upside-down Roman-five-shaped eyebrows danced as he blinked at her. "More balding than bald?" he said, "with hair round the back of his head? Cocky fucker?"

"That's him."

"I've got him!"

"You've got him?"

"Tied up in my house. He appeared out of nowhere and tried to knife me. I knocked him out and tied him up. I was coming to tell good Queen Lowa."

"*Good* Queen Lowa?"

"That's what we call her round here. She is good."

You don't know her like I know her, thought Chamanca, but she let it go. "Where is your house?"

"A way back that way on the road. You can't miss it."

"Is there anybody guarding him?"

"Not really. My daughter Autumn's there but I've told her not to touch him and I reckon he'll be out cold until I get back anyway."

"How old is she?"

"Five."

Oh fuck, thought Chamanca, closing her eyes.

"What?" said the man. His widening eyes and his creasing brow pressed his jiggling eyebrows into motionlessness.

"Nothing. Nothing to worry about. But I have to go now." She dug her heels into her horse and willed it to gallop as fast as it could. After a hundred paces she turned. The man was following her, arms swinging, coming as fast as his stiff-legged gait would carry him.

Spring thought about crouching between tents and waiting until Caesar emerged from his, but then decided that standing in plain sight was probably a more effective way of hiding.

"Spring!" cried a woman's voice, instantly proving her wrong. It was Clodia, loping towards her. For an urbane socialite, Clodia had a very rural stride. She wore an almost obscenely short, belted white toga, and her long brown hair was hanging free. The skin on her bare arms, legs and face was the same colour as her hair. She had spent a good deal of time in the sun since Spring had last seen her.

"What are you doing here?" she called, still a good ten paces away.

Spring smiled.

"Of course, you can't speak Latin, can you?"

Spring looked back uncomprehendingly. Clodia had been talking to a knot of toga-wearers who were now staring. All the nearby praetorians and normal legionaries had also turned at her call.

"Come with me into Caesar's tent. He'd like to see you, I'm sure, and there's a translator there so we'll be able to have a good talk. Gaulish is the same as British, isn't it? I'd love to hear what you've been up to. But what are you wearing? That's a man's toga. And it's dirty. You can't see Caesar like that. Come back with me to my place and we'll find something proper . . ." She lowered her voice, so that the watchers wouldn't hear. "Wait a moment, is that blood on your hem? Are you hurt? You look scared. Are you lost? Come on, take my hand." She reached out.

Spring leant away, and, because she was a complete idiot, dropped the knife. She squatted immediately and picked it up, but Clodia had seen it. She took a step back, opened her eyes wide in surprise, but not shock. She looked as if she'd just caught her preparing a thrillingly daring but harmless jape. Spring immediately thought of running, but there were several praetorians watching and an assortment of other Romans blocking her escape.

"Oh, Spring!" She looked about to check that nobody had come within earshot. "You naughty girl! And to think I was going to take you right in there!" She gasped and shook her head, mouth wide. "I can't let you kill Caesar, you wicked thing. Now, come with me to my tent, and you can tell me what's happened."

The child was simply the most winning little creature that Felix had ever met. He genuinely thought that, he wasn't pretending. He could almost feel tears developing at the thought of killing her. Which was great – such affection for his victim should fuel his return to Gaul easily.

"Why don't you make Felix the dog chase Spring the sheep?"

"Dogs aren't meant to chase sheep, silly! They're naughty if they do."

"Maybe Felix is a naughty dog?"

"No! He's a good dog."

"Tell you what, why don't you bring the sheep and the dog over here, sit on my knee, and I'll sing you a song all about the day that the sheep decided that enough was enough and it was time for the sheep to chase the naughty dog for a change."

She nodded and skipped over to him.

Felix thought he could feel his heart breaking, which made him very happy.

Chapter 12

The forest road emerged from the trees and curled up a grassy hill to the palisaded Branwin village. A couple of the Aurochs tribe heading for the woods with empty wicker baskets stared at Atlas as if they'd never seen a huge African with an axe on his back, then seemed to remember their manners and greeted him and Ula cheerily. Four aurochs near the road looked up as they approached, didn't find Atlas nearly so interesting and returned to their grazing.

From a distance the grazing aurochs looked like standard cows. Up close they were more impressive: immensely muscled, so tall that they were almost at eye level with Atlas on his horse, and with great horns that swept forwards, as if designed for charging headlong and ramming into the side of an elephant. Atlas found himself nodding. They weren't nearly as big as elephants, maybe a quarter of the weight, but size wasn't everything in a fight, as Chamanca proved so very often.

Outside the wooden village wall was the blacksmithing complex built for Maidun's master smith, Elann Nancarrow. It lay in a hollow that hid it from view until you were right on it, although the smoke pouring up from five forges had given away its location as soon as they cleared the trees. There were smiths at each forge, including Elann at one of them, several leatherworkers and others carrying out the various tasks that contributed to the production of the beasts' armour. At the edge of the thronging industry were several large, neat stacks of shaped plate iron and dozens of elongated conical horn tips.

Atlas caught Elann's eye and raised a hand in greeting. She looked at him briefly and he was fairly sure she nodded before returning to her work.

"Doesn't exactly gush with emotion, Elann Nancarrow," said Ula as they rode on towards the settlement's open gates.

"No, but she's the best smith."

"Her son Weylin came to Kanawan once. He wasn't the brightest."

"He wasn't, but Kanawan captured him and he escaped. What does that say about Kanawan?"

Ula chuckled. "Fair point."

Atlas thought back to the day Weylin had arrived on Maidun Castle, lied about what had happened at Kanawan and been executed by Chamanca on Zadar's orders. Atlas and Weylin's brother Carden had sat and watched while Chamanca strangled him. They'd all excused themselves their behaviour under Zadar because they'd decided that Felix had put them under a glamour to do Zadar's bidding.

It was a convenient excuse that made sense, but Atlas wondered sometimes if it was true. He, Carden, Chamanca, Lowa – all of them – had complacently murdered dozens of men and women at Zadar's command. He hadn't felt like his mind was under anyone else's control at the time. However, it did seem unbelievable that Carden had been able to watch the slaying of his brother so impassively unless he'd been under some sort of magic control, and none of his friends now seemed like keen murderers (apart from Chamanca).

But did that mean that they were being controlled by Felix's magic when they'd sacked towns or attacked inferior forces knowing it would be a massacre? Or were groups of people capable of atrocities because other people's complicity normalises one's own behaviour? The legions murdering their way through Gaul were surely not under any glamour. If you plucked any one of them away from his mates, Atlas reckoned, and asked him if the legions' relentless rape and murder was acceptable, he would probably have broken down and repented. Atlas was sure that most individuals weren't inherently evil. But when everyone around you was doing evil things, maybe that became the norm and . . .

"Ah, here you are now!" An Eroo accent snapped him from his reverie. Ula slipped from her horse, skipped up to the woman walking towards them, gripped her arm and kissed her full on the lips. It was like watching a teenage girl greeting an exciting new boyfriend of whom she was fiercely proud.

Manfreena smiled at Atlas. Her eyes were so close together that it made him blink, her skin so white it was surely a little blue, her grey hair patchy, her two remaining teeth black with rot, and her large ears jutted at right angles from her head. Villagers all around smiled indulgently at the couple then up at Atlas.

Something, he thought, was wrong. It was possible that a beauty like Ula could be smitten with a woman who'd win the ugliest old crone competition at most fairs, and it was possible that the villagers were all very happy about it – their tribe's god Branwin was the goddess of love and this was her forest, after all. It was incredibly unlikely, but it was possible.

But what clinched it for Atlas, what made him sure that there was something extremely odd afoot, was that he'd seen Manfreena before. When the Eroo army had landed on the beach two years before, shortly before the Fassites had followed and slaughtered Atlas' men and women, a druid had danced a jig to curse the Maidunites. This was the same woman; Queen Reena of Eroo, druid wife of the tyrant Manfrax, who was meant to have perished under the Spring Tide.

* * *

Spring sat on a prettily tasselled chair in Clodia's tent, centre-piece of Clodia's own little fenced camp, and told her what had happened since the wedding, leaving out what she'd done to Quintus, then asked her what she was doing. The socialite explained that she had been allowed to follow the army with her own little legion of slaves and guards in return for a *whopping* donation to Caesar's war chest.

"Being decadently rich doesn't solve all your problems," Clodia explained, "but it does make life more *interesting*." Spring considered that she'd got to the same place without spending any coins, or owning any of the other goods like salt and lumps of iron that were money back in Britain, but didn't mention it. "But, anyway, that's enough of me going on about myself. We'd better get you back to Ragnall."

"Couldn't you . . .?

"What?"

"Let me escape? Help me get back to Britain?"

The big eyes again. "Oh, no. Everyone notices me, Spring, and about a thousand people saw me with you. If you disappear now I'll be in trouble. Besides, you're assuming that I'm your ally. I am not. I'm a Roman and you're a Roman captive. You're my captive. I have recaptured you. I'm really in the army now. Thrilling, isn't it?"

"I don't think it's that thrilling."

"Oh, don't sulk. Come on, let's go."

She stood up and Spring followed in her floral-scented wake.

The feeling that Felix was nearby evaporated shortly after Chamanca had set off up the road from his captor. She guessed what that meant, but refused to acknowledge it. She galloped the horse as hard as it would go, without a thought for the return journey. She arrived at what had to be the place – a solitary blacksmith's dwelling – leapt off and sprinted into the hut, sword in hand. The short blade was more useful in enclosed spaces than her ball-mace.

She'd known what she'd find and she found it. Felix was gone. Autumn was dead.

She'd seen thousands of corpses, made hundreds of them herself. But this one hit her, even though she'd never seen her alive. Little Autumn, the innocent girl with no involvement in all this British and Roman nonsense, had had her life cut short before it had really begun. The comparison with Spring was obvious. It was more than the name. Just a bit older, and Autumn would have had Spring's nous and she wouldn't have gone near Felix. But the gods, presumably, had decided that they didn't give a fuck about letting little Autumn grow any older.

Chamanca picked up the girl and laid her on the bed. It wasn't difficult to make her look comfortable and she hoped that somehow this would soften the blow for the blacksmith returning to find his murdered daughter. There wasn't a mark on her because, Chamanca guessed, Felix had suffocated her. That would have been a frightening way to die . . . She shook her head and left the hut.

The blacksmith was already in sight, marching up the road towards his misery, straight-legged, arms swinging. He was fast, despite his handicap.

Chamanca looked up to the blue sky. "By Makka the god of war, Fenn the god of fear and Danu the mother, I swear I will avenge this girl and all those innocents killed by the druid Felix. No matter what comes in my way, no matter what pain it might cause me, I will kill Felix and I will ensure that he suffers much, much more than that poor little girl."

Chapter 13

By the time Felix reached the assembly outside Caesar's tent the general had worked himself into a frenzied but eloquent stream of oration. His freshly built wooden speaking platform was squeaking under bouncing heels as he waved his arms and elucidated his plans to the plume-helmeted generals, senior centurions and toga-wearing legates. In between the dramatic language and heroic claims, Felix heard that two legions were to stay in Gaul under command of Titus Labienus, and six legions – almost thirty thousand infantry – along with two thousand cavalrymen and their horses, were to cross the Channel, leaving at sunset that very day. The previous year's reconnaissance had identified the perfect place to land and make camp under protection of the warships.

If anyone took exception to the word "reconnaissance" to describe the previous year's aborted invasion, they didn't show it.

"What about the elephants?" someone muttered.

Caesar peered about to see who had spoken, but couldn't. "The few elephants that you may have seen are here as an aid to the engineers. They are not war elephants." A few eyebrows were raised. Everyone had heard the story of the elephant pulping a merchant and splintering his ship. "Each of the beasts can bear the burden of twenty oxen, so we are testing their use as siege weapon transporters, camp constructors and builders of bridges. They are not to be described at any point, by anyone, as war elephants. This will be a victory for Roman men, not African animals. In fact, given that Caesar has employed the animals on a temporary basis as a favour to a friend, they will not be recorded as part of the Roman force."

Felix smiled. He knew about Jagganoch and his elephants. During his war with the pirates a decade before, Pompey had captured a pirate king from the Yonkari empire. The Yonkari had conquered much land in Africa but few Roman explorers had reached it because it was beyond the near impassable sand sea. Pompey had taken a liking to the pirate, or, more specifically, to his descriptions of man-eating war elephants larger and fiercer than any Roman had seen before, and freed him on the understanding that he'd send back his son Jagganoch with a herd of the beasts. Pompey had never expected to see the elephants – he had so much booty that he didn't care – but the king had been true to his word and some time later Prince Jagganoch of the Yonkari had arrived at one of Pompey's estates with a crowd of slaves, a squad of elephant Warriors and forty armoured war elephants, which, going by the descriptions of history, were indeed larger and fiercer than Hannibal's elephants that the Romans had faced a hundred and seventy years before, and the Persian animals that Alexander had defeated and then employed a couple of hundred years before that. They were also more trouble.

Pompey kept the elephants on his estate, but had been astonished at their expense; not so much their food, which was far from cheap, but the cost of the damage. As well as destroying buildings, they killed and ate horses, oxen, slaves and anything else that Jagganoch considered might be useful to their training. However, because Pompey was such a joker, as part of the previous year's wranglings between him, Crassus and Caesar about how they were going to share the leadership of Rome, Pompey had insisted that Caesar take the elephants on his next campaign as a condition of the deal that allowed him free rein north of Italy. Caesar had escaped his pledge the year before, but Pompey had cornered him that winter and he'd been unable to wriggle out of it.

So they had the elephants. While others had complained of the murder of a merchant on the beach, Felix guessed that Caesar had been encouraged by it and decided that he would definitely take Jagganoch and his troop across to Britain. However, he had sensibly decided to keep the Africans and their elephants in their own camp, clear of the legionaries. It was fine to kill the odd merchant, but if the elephants started stomping on Romans then even Caesar's fiercely loyal troops might have complained.

The general finished his briefing, asked if there were any questions in a tone that made it clear that there would be no questions, and beckoned Felix to follow him into his tent.

"This is a glorious day," said Caesar, pouring water from a long-necked bronze jug into a plain wooden cup. "Tell Caesar the state of your legion."

"The thirty-five Celermen and twenty Maximen are in full health and are ready to sail. I myself found a way of travelling to—"

"Just the essentials, thank you. The wind has changed and there is no time for storytelling. The northernmost ship on the beach is yours. Take it to wherever your legion is waiting. Your part of the plan is the opposite geographically to last year, but the same in essence. You will follow the fleet, see where it lands, then make landfall twenty miles to the north. The ship's crew are expendable so expend them as you need. You may also take as many captives as you require – talk to Labienus about that. Once landed, make a good camp and remain there until you receive orders from Caesar. Kill anyone who sees you and stay out of sight of the Roman army. You will not fail this time."

"I will not."

"You will communicate in Britain by sending your head Celerman, only at night. Have you replaced the one killed by the British dogs?

"Yes. Kelter was killed, Bistan is the new leader."

"Right. While you are camped, kill anyone who sees you. You should avoid killing Romans, but if a patrol discovers you, their deaths will be blamed on the British. Understand?"

"I do."

"Good."

Felix turned to go, then stopped. "There was one more thing . . ."

"If it's about the British girl, the position has not changed. She will be vassal queen. You will keep clear of her."

Felix nodded and left.

He strode away through the sea of tents, wondering which one was Spring's. He could have found out and circumnavigated her guards by transporting into her tent, possibly, but it was not that precise a magic, and the girl would be certain to knife him before he knew where he was. She was not incapable; the gossip about her castration of Quintus had zipped through the camp like a winter pox. He bit his lower lip and told himself that he'd have her soon enough.

Unless, of course, she used her magic to escape. He didn't know why she hadn't done that immediately. Perhaps she didn't know how to? Perhaps, like him, she could use her magic only for certain tasks, and these tasks changed? Or perhaps she had some design of her own which meant she needed to stay with the Romans? The latter seemed the most likely. So what was she up to?

Jagganoch punched the slave on the back of the head. "Polish harder! In smaller circles, you fly-blown jackal's vomit." The buck-toothed fool nodded rapidly and returned to his frantic rubbing of the bladed iron tusk cap. By Sobek, how Jagganoch hated the pathetic man. He despised all slaves. No matter how badly he treated them, as long as he fed and housed them they seemed content. Even worse, if he did show them the tiniest kindness – by speaking to them, for example, even if it was to insult them – they would fawn contemptibly. They were so much less than him and he hated them for accepting it. Had he been born a slave rather than prince, he would have killed his master and become a prince. These worms? They would rather lick his boot after he'd kicked them than rebel.

Bandonda trumpeted from the neighbouring ship. He knew all the elephants' calls, but he knew his own Bandonda's best of all. The animal was frustrated to be cooped up again like a common farm animal. Jagganoch felt the same, stuck on the beach surrounded by midget Romans. Soon, though, they would be in Britain and they would be let loose on the milk-white savages, to gore and trample.

"You'll be wanting to have a look at the aurochs' armour, I'm sure," said Manfreena in her strong Eroo accent, Ula still clutching her scraggy arm.

Atlas nodded and the three of them walked back through the village, past smiling Aurochs tribespeople. He couldn't remember feeling more uneasy. The village was clean and in good repair and the people were cheerful. Yet in the middle of it all was this Eroo witch. Perhaps she'd survived the wave, perhaps she'd taken part of her husband's name to commemorate him, perhaps she was genuinely loveable. But it all seemed so unlikely.

Elann did not look up as they approached, but carried on beating her hammer on iron.

"Atlas, hold on a minute," said Reena, "and bend down and touch your toes for me."

"What?" He remained standing.

"I thought so. Ula, hold him."

The queen of Kanawan was quicker than Chamanca. Before he realised that she'd moved, Ula was behind him, with one of his wrists in each hand, her fingers gripping so tight that it felt like they'd broken the skin.

"You've got magic in you," smiled Reena, "not your own. There's an evil in you that's been killed by magic. It means I can't control you like all these good people. Shame, I was hoping that you'd lead the aurochs' charge into Lowa's camp and chop her to bits with that big axe of yours, but it's not a real problem. I'd take the magic out of you to control you, but you'd die straight away if I did that." She grinned. "Hang on, that's no bad idea. I'll take the magic out of you. Kneel."

Atlas strained to pull free, but Ula lifted and twisted his wrists and forced him down on his knees. The strength that Manfreena was giving her was amazing. The druid put her hands on his head, then stood back and jigged with her arms by her side, kicking her knees high, as she'd done on the beach two summers before.

Something rose from deep inside Atlas and he thought he was going to be sick, but instead it felt like an invisible vapour pouring from mouth, nose, eyes and ears.

"Throw the body deep in the woods," he heard Manfreena say. Ula's grip released and he slumped.

"I will take it." It was Elann Nancarrow's voice. "Bones burn hot."

Part Four

Britain
54 BC

Chapter 1

"It's an impressive bit of getting-togetherness, I would reckon, to gather this many ships and have them all sail at the same time. A clever thing to achieve," said Spring, looking behind them and nodding.

Ragnall was suspicious. Ever since Spring had maimed Quintus Tullius Cicero she'd behaved impeccably, even praising the Romans and asking him to translate her words for anyone nearby.

He peered at her, searching for signs of sarcasm. As was now usual, he didn't see any. She was looking towards Britain, smiling peacefully, hair blowing in the wind. There had been no repercussions from her attack on Quintus so far, and Ferrandus and Tertius had both sworn she'd acted in self-defence. But their testimony would mean nothing when Quintus was back on his feet. He was a powerful man and apparently he was recovering quickly. Ragnall reckoned Spring's new "well, I do think the Romans are quite impressive" stance was intended to pull as many people as possible onto her side before Quintus resurfaced and sought revenge. It was a sensible policy but unlikely to work.

"Will the elephants disembark at the same place as us, do you think?" Spring nodded to the four large ships a mile to the south, silhouetted in the moonlight.

"I shouldn't think so. It was only a merchant that the elephant killed, but it still wasn't popular. I suspect Caesar will keep them well clear in case they squash someone who matters." Ragnall said this to get a rise out of Spring. On the journey up from Gaul she'd flown at him when he'd suggested that some people's lives were less valuable than others. Now she just nodded.

"And Felix?"

Far to the north, well beyond the furthest boat in the massed fleet, was a solitary winking light.

"How do you know it's him?"

"Just a guess."

"I don't know anything about what he's doing or where he's going."

"I see," said Spring.

It was maddening, standing on a warship that was part of a fleet stuffed to the gunwales with men, beasts and monsters all bent on attacking her island and her people, and being unable to hamper them. She could probably have knifed a couple of praetorians. Ferrandus and Tertius had become much less vigilant now that they were sort-of partners in crime, and Ragnall seemed to be buying her "I like the Romans now" spiel. However, it would be a massive waste of all she'd put up with to kill just a couple of Romans before getting killed herself. Besides, she liked these praetorians. No, she had either to do for several thousand of them, assassinate Caesar, or take some piece of information to Lowa that was so valuable it would let the British win the war. So far she'd come up with precisely zero ideas of how to do any of these things. There was nothing to do but bide her time and keep an eye out, while wary that Quintus or his cronies might strike at any moment. She deeply regretted castrating him. She should have killed him.

"I'd like to go to sleep now," she said to Ragnall. He told her guards in Latin and Tertius went off to fetch her a blanket. He came back with two.

"It's one blanket each," said Ferrandus.

"I'm giving her mine," Tertius replied.

"You're a dick," smiled Ferrandus.

"You're a twat." Tertius handed over both blankets. Spring nodded thanks, made gestures to show that it was a warm night and she never felt the cold anyway so she only wanted one, and handed one back. Tertius tried to make her keep it, but she insisted and eventually he took it, looking a little glad.

She was woken at dawn the next morning by centurions' shouts ordering men to the oars. The wind had dropped and they'd drifted off course. All over the fleet oars were slipped out. At almost the same time every boat began to row, on one side only at first. The armada turned ninety degrees and headed for the shore like a multitude of spindly legged larvae crawling on their bellies across the salty sea, ready to savage and gobble up anything in their way.

Near the coast the transports hung back while the twenty-eight warships lined up parallel to the empty beach with a ship-length's gap between each, two anchors out at either end to hold them in place. It was low tide, and there was a good hundred paces of white-yellow sand between the sea and the low trees and scrub that fringed the beach. Archers crammed up onto the warships' platforms and scorpions lined their shoreward side, missiles primed and crews ready. To trim the boat, the rowers had all been ushered to the seaward side where they sat mostly looking bored, some bickering about who was taking up whose space.

"What's going on?" asked Tertius, waking with a yawn.

"I guess we're waiting to see if the Britons will send their army onto the beach to get cut to ribbons by the warships," said Ferrandus. "Do you reckon they will, Ragnall?"

"I shouldn't think so."

"Clever lot, are they?"

"I wouldn't say that, but they did send Caesar packing last time."

"Well, there you go," said Tertius. Spring was pleased and a little surprised at the note of pride in Ragnall's voice. Perhaps he hadn't gone totally toga-wearing? "And what's that warship that's hanging back? Hang on, that's the flagship."

"Yes," said Ragnall. "I was on the flagship last time. I would be again if it wasn't for the girl with us. They've got one archer in Britain who can fire a bow like you wouldn't believe. Of course it is a special bow, but she can—"

"She?"

"She. Queen Lowa, in fact. She's been training with it for ever. Last year she *just* missed Caesar from about four hundred paces away, and only because he bent down. I guess they're worried that she'll do that again so they're hanging back."

"Ah, the famous British Queen Lowa. Do you know her then?" Tertius asked.

"Know her? I . . . well, a gentleman doesn't like to say."

"You fucked Queen Lowa? Yeah? Well, I've done Cleopatra. Twice. Up the arse," said Ferrandus.

"I never said I did." Ragnall smiled like Quintus had in the tent. Lowa had taught Spring a move where you thrust stiffened fingers into someone's throat, killing them. Spring imagined herself doing it right then to Ragnall, but instead she smiled, showing some interest because she'd heard him say "Lowa", but otherwise displaying her blank-faced incomprehension.

"Hang on," said Ragnall, "speak of the demon . . ."

A blonde woman in a white shirt and leather shorts exactly like Spring was wearing trotted out onto the beach on a prancing, head-shaking horse. It was Lowa! Spring resisted the urge to shout with joy.

Facing the southernmost warship, the queen raised two

fists then lengthened the longest two fingers of each hand. She rotated northwards, flicking her fingers at each boat so that they could be sure the message was meant for all of them. At one point Spring was sure that Lowa looked straight at her. She waved subtly.

"That two-fingered gesture means 'Fuck off,'" Ragnall informed the Romans.

"We guessed," said Tertius.

"She's a beauty," said Ferrandus.

"You can't tell that from here, you dog. She could be a bloke in a wig from this distance." Tertius shook his head.

"That's what you're hoping for, isn't it? An island entirely populated by well-hung blokes in wigs."

"As long as they kill you as soon as you step ashore, I don't care who lives there."

"No hermaphrodite barbarian is going to kill me!" Ferrandus gave his chest a single beat. "I'll chop their cocks off if they so much as look at me. Why aren't we shooting her, anyway?"

"She's outside our range," said Ragnall.

"Of the archers maybe," said Tertius. "A scorpion would reach her, but they'll be holding back until a lot more of them are on the beach, and then they'll mince them."

"It's actually possible you're right for once," said Ferrandus as Lowa slipped off her horse, slotted an arrow, lifted her longbow and drew. She pointed it at their boat. Spring and Ragnall ducked.

"What are you doing?" laughed Tertius. "She'll never reach—"

There was a scream, then a splash.

"She's only hit the fucking helmsman!" squeaked Ferrandus.

There were a succession of thrums as scorpions shot their missiles although nobody had given the order. Spring peeked over the edge. Lowa was back on her horse, trotting northwards along the beach, still raising and lowering an arm to deliver her two-fingered message to the Romans ships. One scorpion bolt missed her by a few paces, but the rest were miles off.

It looked like other ships assumed the general order to shoot their bolts had been given and more and more were loosed, until a whole flock of hefty wood and iron missiles were zooming in elegant arcs towards the little rider on the beach.

Lowa did not seem to notice. She trotted along, happily signalling at the Romans. And one point she tweaked the reins and the horse stopped. An instant later a scorpion bolt passed so close it must have shaved the hairs off the animal's nose. It ploughed into the sand and threw up a huge fan. Lowa trotted on as if nothing had happened. The scorpion salvo ended and there was a pause for reloading. Lowa raised her longbow again. Spring didn't duck this time. It was too much fun watching thousands of Romans all dive for cover.

Lowa lowered the bow, flicked her fingers one last time, then galloped from the beach.

"Wow," said Dug, sitting on the side of the boat. He nodded down to the corpse of the helmsman that was floating by, face up, a long poplar arrow shaft sticking out of his heart. "I'd say that was one–nil to the Britons."

"Maybe," said Spring, "but the Romans have got a lot more where he came from."

Chapter 2

"That was close," said Mal, peering through the gorse, over the dozens of scorpion arrows littering the beach, to the line of towering warships. Each of them was several times larger than any boat Lowa had seen before. Together they looked more like a chain of wooden, cliff-sided islands than a line of ships. How could they stop a force which had weapons like these?

She shrugged, but the size of the warships and their firepower had rattled her. Mal and Adler had told her about the warships and their missile power, and Mal had insisted that it was an idiotic idea to ride out onto the beach and goad them, and it had been, but at least she now knew for certain that any troops sent to oppose the Roman landing would be slaughtered.

"So what do we do?" Mal asked.

"That solitary boat heading north must be Felix and his legion. I'm going to take the Two Hundred to have a look at them, and see if Elann's new arrows have any effect."

"Are you sure? We heard what they did to the Tengoterry cavalry."

"The Tengoterry charged them. We won't. We'll shoot from a safe distance. If the arrows work, we'll carry on shooting. If not, we'll retreat. Quickly. They cannot be as fast as horses."

"Are you sure that's a good plan?"

"My mind's made up." She'd thought this through and she knew the risk. From what she'd heard it was possible that the demons could outrun horses. That's why she was going herself.

"Fair enough! And the four elephant ships heading south?"

"Atlas should be back with the aurochs soon. Until then I'll send Chamanca with the chariots to either hold them until I need the chariots, or to lead them north."

"Makes sense. Shall I get back to Big Bugger Hill and make sure the scorpions are ready?"

"No, have a deputy oversee that. I'd like you to stay here with the remaining three hundred cavalry split into squads of sixty, and shout to me at Big Bugger what the legions are doing. They'll send cavalry patrols of their own inland. If they send them out in groups of fifty or less, kill them. Groups of more than three hundred, stick some arrows in them and retreat. Anything in between, use your judgement. Do you know where all the false roads and hidden tracks are?"

"I think so."

"Make sure all the riders do."

"So, in essence, you want me to discourage Caesar from leaving the shore."

Lowa looked around. Nobody else was in earshot. "No. But that's what I want him to think you're doing."

She sprinted back to her horse and Mal watched her go. In seven years, Lowa had matured into a fair, respected and effective ruler. She'd been better than most from the off, but as the years had gone by she'd developed a toughness and a way of reacting to situations that showed a wisdom well beyond her thirty or so years. But she still ran everywhere like a child.

He peered back through the gorse. The Romans were coming in. Transport boats filtered in between the warships, which, one by one, moved closer to the shore. The transports had a shallower draught than the previous year's and had been constructed so that they could be disembarked more easily. The legionaries leapt from the broad landing planks without getting their sandals wet, and immediately formed shield tortoises before advancing up the beach and creating a perimeter. Other legionaries unloaded catapults and assembled them in a matter of heartbeats, while yet more carried small barrels from the boats and loaded them into the giant slings. The catapults fired and moment later circular wooden crates of oil were landing in the gorse all around Mal. They burst, spraying oil. The Maidunite didn't need to wait until archers disembarked and dipped arrows in burning pitch to work out what was going to happen next. Sometimes running was the right thing to do.

On horseback once more, he watched the gorse burn. As the smoke billowed and shifted in the wind, he glimpsed thousands of Romans, busy building their camp. They were fearsomely efficient, and this time they'd chosen a much better spot for their bridgehead base. The cleared gorseland would provide a vast area for a camp. To the south, it was flanked by a broad, shifting and impassable river delta. To the north there was marsh, also impassable, and limited access along the beach – almost none at high tide but plenty when the tide was low. To the Romans' west, leading inland to the rest of Britain, the way was clear.

Lowa cantered north, Adler at her side, the Two Hundred following behind. They were going on a demon hunt. Each, Lowa included, carried minimal provisions, a sword, a recurve bow and Elann's demon-slaying arrows designed to fly faster and pierce the thickest armour. Their shafts were ash, heavy and tough but difficult to form into the long, dead-straight dowels required. Their long, sharp heads were the finest, most painstakingly smelted and hammered iron and the feathers the very best a goose had to offer. Each one took a day to make. Lowa hoped it had been worth it.

The plan was to hit Felix's legion fast and hard, then return to Big Bugger Hill. In a perfect world they'd kill all the demons and remove the most troubling part of Caesar's force before taking on the rest of it. She expected that they'd kill some of them before having to flee. The other possibility was that the demons were faster than horses, and would kill all of them. So her choice, hers alone, was putting two hundred men and women in terrible danger. But what alternative did she have?

Of course, there was one very obvious alternative that would save them all.

It wasn't too late. She could march up to the Roman camp, make an alliance with Caesar, then help him conquer the rest of Britain. Caesar would have to accept her offer. Her army might be smaller than his, but she had fifteen thousand infantry and nearly fifteen hundred chariots, so surely he'd be grateful to have those for rather than against him?

And then Caesar would have Britain. Every Briton – every living man, woman and child, and countless people yet to be born – would be slaves of Rome. But did it matter to most who was in charge? Why did she give a crap? She may have spent most of her life in Britain but she'd been born in Germany. What did it matter to her if the Romans took Britain?

A lot. It mattered an awful lot. The argument that the majority of people didn't care who ruled them didn't work here, because under Lowa they were free and increasingly prosperous but under the Romans they would live like animals, allowed only enough resources for survival while the surplus was shipped off back to Rome so that men might build palaces and ponds for their pet fish. Britons slaving so that carp might be comfortable. No, that must not happen.

She rode on. One thing cheered her. When she'd ridden onto the beach, she'd spotted Spring waving at her, next to Ragnall on the railings. She knew from Atlas and Carden that Ragnall had turned traitor, but she didn't believe for a heartbeat that Spring had. She must be biding her time, looking for her moment. It warmed her just to know that Spring was alive, and it encouraged her. Hadn't Spring saved them all before? Then Lowa remembered the cost of that victory. If Spring was to be their saviour again, what could the price possibly be? She shuddered. It had taken Dug's death last time. There was a new Dug now . . . She shook her head. It didn't bear thinking about.

Ragnall left Spring outside the tent for once, guarded by Ferrandus and Tertius, to watch the camp being built. She knew he'd done it so that she'd be awe-struck by the Romans' amazing camp-building skills and, very annoyingly, she was reluctantly impressed. By running round like well-regimented blue-arsed badgers all day, by nightfall the Romans had converted the heathland behind the beach into a large, excellently defended camp. They called it a camp, but it was more like a town − a city even.

When they'd finished their ditch-digging, palisade-raising and tent-erection, instead of clapping each other on the backs and breaking open a few hundred casks of ale as the British would have done, the legionaries set to training, sharpening swords, polishing armour and generally being useful. They were *so* efficient.

"Aye, efficient and deathly boring," said Dug.

"How can it be boring to be busy the whole time?"

"Doesn't give you any time to think."

"But thinking makes people unhappy."

"Aye, that's true, I suppose, but it's better to be thinking and unhappy than not thinking at all."

"You reckon?"

"Aye . . ." He did not sound convinced.

Chapter 3

Out of sight of the rest of the fleet, Felix ordered his twenty Maximan to kill the first twenty captives.

The Maximen slaughtered the Gauls in various ways — they did love to experiment — and returned to the oars. The ship surged north up the coast then west along the River Tems at speeds that a low-flying seabird would have been proud of. Felix remembered the river. It was the same route he'd taken all those years ago on his way to becoming Zadar's druid. He'd hated the scenery then — the low, tree-fringed mud and sand banks, the choppy brown-grey water, the pointless gulls — and he'd been resentful at having to leave Rome. Now all of it excited him. Get ready for a new master, he told the gulls. Prepare to be firewood, he told the trees.

He turned to the captives, piled in the back of the ship. When they'd seen the Maximen chop, bash and twist the first twenty to death and toss them into the sea like chum, they'd yelled and strained at their chains for a long and fruitless time while Felix enjoyed ignoring their pleas. They were well secured and eventually they'd settled down.

Before they'd set off, he'd been about to order the Maximen to break their legs like the last lot to stop them leaping overboard, but he'd realised just in time that it would be handy to have them walking once they got to the other side, so instead they should be chained up. Secure in the stern, some stared defiance, some whimpered, some were catatonic with horror.

He shouted for the rowers to halt. It looked like a good place to land with firm sand and a wide enough expanse of it that they'd be out of missile range and he'd see any attack coming well before it reached them. He scanned the shore for a good while. The Maximen stared at him dumbly, holding their oars in readiness, and wavelets slapped against the hull. Finally he was satisfied that it was safe and he commanded the helmsman and the Maximen to row for shore. He had to shout for them to slow down – the speed they were going, the ship would have exploded when it hit the beach. They cut their pace a great deal, but even so he nearly flew off his feet when the prow wedged into the sand.

Felix ordered everyone to disembark. By Hades, he liked being the main man, the one everyone looked to for orders, even if was just this little gang. How much better would it be when he was king of the world? He climbed carefully over the bow, scanning the treeline for trouble and finding none. He dropped onto the compact sand and sniffed the salt air. Oh, it was grand to be back.

Lowa gulped. Atlas and Chamanca had not exaggerated. Walking up the beach were twenty gigantic, armoured men. Their size was amazing, but what really caught the eye was the fact that they were carrying a ship on their shoulders. She recovered her cool. These were the Ironmen. Twenty of them, as reported. Lowa was queen of the Maidunites and not one to be fazed. She'd expected these armoured giants and here they were. That was that.

Next to the Ironmen she counted thirty-five springy brown figures – the Leathermen. They were running about like well-rested and recently fed children, goading along a large group of shuffling, chained captives. Behind them was a gang of men who were probably sailors. By the way they were pointing and larking excitely, they were also surprised to see men carrying a ship. Leading the lot of them was Felix. He was a good few hundred paces distant, but she'd have recognised the bastard's swagger anywhere.

She pulled herself backwards out of her bushy observation post and ran through the woods to the clearing where her horse, Adler and the rest of the Two Hundred were waiting. It was time. Either Elann's arrows would be sharp enough to pierce the Ironmen's armour and fast enough to hit the speedy Leathermen, or they wouldn't.

"Give the orders," she said to Adler. "String bows, ready arrows and follow me."

Felix saw branches shake at the edge of the beach. Could have been an animal, probably it was a deer or something, but maybe it was a British watcher.

"Bistan!" he shouted.

"Yeah, boss?"

Yeah, boss? He'd been too slack with this lot. His next load of demons would have respect drummed into them. "Five Celermen, including you, kill five captives then head for the trees there," he pointed. "Capture anyone you find and secure them in the spare chains. Do not kill or maim them."

"You got it!"

Bistan and four others ran over to the captives, slashed the throats of the five nearest, then ran for the treeline as fast as diving falcons.

They were fifty yards from the trees when the first cavalry-woman burst from the foliage, followed by dozens more armed men and women on horses. The Celermen flew at them but a swarm of arrows flew at the Celermen. They dodged and ducked faster than Felix's eye could follow but one Celerman fell. Riders poured from the trees shooting arrow after arrow. Another Celerman went down. The other three reached the Maidunites and leapt at them and finally

Felix found the breath to shout: "All Celermen and Maximen, kill the captives and attack! ATTACK!"

By the time Lowa had nocked her third arrow, two were down but three were on them, blurred brown figures, blades flashing as they hacked and slashed. She searched for a target, but they were too fast. She was more likely to hit her own. She slapped her bow into its holder, unsheathed her sword and tried to follow their movements. It was impossible. A flash here, a blur there – that was all that she could see of the foe. Men and women screamed and tumbled from their horses, blood spraying. Riders flew from their mounts, whether bucked or thrown by the Leathermen she could not see.

Something leapt for her and she slashed instinctively. The blade connected and her attacker whumped onto the sand. It was a human-shaped creature, entirely cased in brown leather but for a slit for its eyes and the slit across its throat from her sword. It bucked and blood gouted from its neck, then it was still. It couldn't possibly be human, but it seemed that it could be killed like a human, although not easily; her sword strike had been lucky, not planned.

She looked up and down the ranks. Only a few heartbeats had passed since they'd first sighted them but the Leatherman attack was over. Five of the demons had died, but far too many of her own force had been killed or injured. There were over a dozen riderless horses and at least that many soldiers were clutching wounds.

She heard "ATTACK!" shouted from the beach. Felix was pointing at them. The Ironmen and Leatherman ran at their own captives, weapons aloft, presumably to kill them and fuel themselves.

Lowa blew three short blasts on her whistle, the signal for instant retreat. From the damage that five of them had done, the Two Hundred would be obliterated if they took on the demons. However, the speed the Leathermen had come at them, they were faster than horses. They were in serious trouble and her defence of Britain had not started well.

"North along the treeline!" she shouted, pulling reins and kicking her own mount. Their best chance was along the grass between the beach and the trees, then around the west end of the forest. The trees might hamper her retreat, but on good ground in the open and over a long stretch surely the horses would be faster than the demons?

Before they'd gone a hundred paces, the demons were gaining. Now that the remaining Two Hundred were clear she saw around twenty corpses and five dead horses on the beach, and those were just the ones she could see at a glance. How could they kill so many so quickly? Someone struggled woozily to his feet from the midst of all the dead and she felt a ridiculous flash of joy that one of her riders had survived. But it was a Leatherman. It shook its head, spotted the fleeing cavalry – looked straight at her, it seemed – and leapt into pursuit, swinging its arms and perceptibly catching up in just a few heartbeats.

The rest of the demons were still gaining. They showed no signs of slowing. They would be on the backmarkers in no time, killing those then chasing down and catching fleeing riders until there were none left, exactly as her cavalry would have done if they were pursuing routed infantry. If this carried on, they'd be picked off one by one and killed. If they turned to fight, they'd all be killed but they'd take some of the demons with them.

"Big badger's bollocks," she said to herself.

She thought of little Dug, toddling along with his arms in the air, babbling happily. She pictured him sitting down and playing with his three-legged wooden dog, looking up when someone came into the hut, seeing that it wasn't his mother and going back to his playing. And now it was never going to be his mother coming into the hut. He'd never see her again.

She jammed the tip of her whistle into her mouth and blew out the orders. The Two Hundred obeyed like the disciplined, superbly skilled cavalry they were. They yanked on reins, pulled horses round and arranged themselves into a double line around Lowa, arrows nocked, bows drawn, blades shining keenly at their hips.

"Hold!" she shouted.

The Leathermen were coming fastest, the Ironmen thundering a good fifty paces behind them with a mighty clanging like stampeding iron oxen. The monsters obviously responded to simple orders like "Attack," Lowa thought, but this charge had no strategy. Good, she thought. Maybe their lack of discipline would help Mal and the others defeat the demons that were left after the Two Hundred's last stand.

"Hold! Two salvos on my command then swords!" she shouted. They were a hundred paces away . . . Sixty paces.

"Shoot!" The thrum of so many bowstrings was a wonderful sound. The arrows flashed through the air, the Leathermen ducked and weaved like a school of fish. Several went down. As they unleashed the second salvo she saw one Ironman fall. Maybe the arrows could pierce that thick armour? If arrows could penetrate it, then so would a good sword thrust.

"CHARGE!" she yelled. She slotted her bow into its holder, lifted her blade and slammed heels into her horse. Around her the Two Hundred did the same. They surged forwards, men and women screaming in joyous, raging defiance as they galloped at the demons.

Chapter 4

Yilgarn Craton had seen a giant hut once, when he'd had the honour of guarding Jocanta Fairtresses on her visit to a fair at a causeway town. The giant hut had looked exactly the same as a normal one, but everything – the door, the roof, even the wooden uprights and twigs that made up the wall – was ridiculously bigger than it should have been. From a distance it had pleased Yilgarn. The people gawping at it up close looked strangely tiny, which he found amusing. Up close, he'd hated it. It had made him feel tiny too and Jocanta had teased him.

The new Roman camp that had sprouted in one day from the heath brought back all these feelings because it reminded him of the giant hut. It looked just like the previous year's camp, only everything was freakishly larger; the encircling ditch was deeper, the walls were double the height, the gates were twice as massive. Inside, the tents were the same as last year's, but there were many, many more of them.

It was overwhelming. His head became lighter but heavier at the same time and he thought he was about to vomit and possibly shit himself. He stopped walking and bent to touch his toes. That usually helped.

One of the escorts yapped at him in Latin.

He swallowed. It was passing already. Those eggs at breakfast had smelled funny. That's what it was. He'd never liked seagull eggs – who the Bel liked fishy eggs? It wasn't nerves. Other men might have been intimidated by this gigantic base, but not Yilgarn. He swallowed again and pictured Jocanta congratulating him on his deeds, then walked on through the camp, rolling his shoulders even more than usual and flexing his biceps. All the Romans stopped to stare as he passed, no doubt taking him for some British hero – which he was. And he'd be a Roman hero, too, before long. It took more than a couple of minging eggs to beat Yilgarn!

They didn't bother with the plume-headed centurion this time; they took him straight into the middle. By the amount of black-clad men and snooty fuckers wearing a lot of bronze, it had to be the commander's camp. Clearly he was expected and so he should have been. He had a lot to tell the combover general.

Atlas' eyes felt like they were gummed shut. Finally they came unstuck and sprang open. The light was like spears through his head. He tried to lift a hand for shade, but nothing happened so he closed his eyes. He tried to wiggle his toes. Pain bolted through his body and limbs.

He opened his eyes again, slowly this time.

He was in a hut. Something noxious was cooking on a stove. So his nose worked but he'd have preferred that it didn't. There was noise to his right. Ears were also good then. He tried to turn his head but had to settle for swivelling his eyes.

Silhouetted against the lancing windowlight, facing away from him, was a squat woman with a ball of curly hair, busying herself with something on the bench. After a long while, she turned and came to loom over him.

She was maybe seventy years old, but sure on her feet with bright eyes, a look of concern on her face and an iron knife in one hand. The knife might have been worrying, but the look on her face told Atlas that she was no torturer.

"Can you move?" she asked. She spoke in the same accent as Dug had, meaning she was from Britain's northern wilds.

He blinked.

She shook her head as if annoyed with him, and bustled out of view, only to reappear moments later with a wide-necked wooden jug. She grabbed his cheeks, squeezed his mouth open with surprisingly strong fingers and glugged in a small amount of liquid from the jug.

He swallowed. It was water mixed with honey, apple and other ingredients that he didn't recognise. She nodded, said "Hmm" in a satisfied tone and tipped the jug again.

He looked up at her and blinked a few times, hoping that she might tell him who she was, what had happened, where he was, why he couldn't move and so on, but she didn't. Glug by glug she emptied the contents of the jug into him, then lumbered over to the corner to stir the foul-smelling pot, then returned to whatever she was doing on the bench, her back to him.

Atlas blinked in frustration. Had he been in the woman's position, he'd have not only explained what the Sobek was going on, but also established a rudimentary method of conversation – one blink for yes, two for no, three for "Can you scratch my arm please?" and more. But, no, she had things to be doing and no time for the man with questions and a maddeningly itchy arm. She carried on as if there wasn't a massive African Warrior taking up a significant portion of her hut. He watched her for a while, then went back to sleep.

Chapter 5

"No, no, don't kill them all! Don't kill any more!" shouted Felix, running towards the massacre, but he might as well have been ordering a passing flock of birds to fly down out of the sky and dance a jig for him. All of them – Maximen and Celermen – were frenzied, leaping about the bodies of horses and people and hacking at anything that moved. Idiots. They'd killed all the Gaulish captives on the beach in their excitement and now they were finishing off the British. The only other people left for sustenance were the seven crew. They'd need more fuel than that!

"Save some of them! Gub! Bistan!" he shouted pointlessly. Some of the Celermen were chasing fleeing horses away along the beach now, for the love of Mars. Animals did almost nothing for the magic that powered them. They needed humans and they were slaughtering them all! It was like the legionaries landing and immediately gorging themselves on every single morsel of rations they'd brought with them before they knew what foraging was available.

Felix slowed as he came to the prone Maximan. A lucky shot had found his eye slit. He put the sole of his sandal on the giant's shoulder and shoved. No response. The Maximen were tough, but put an arrow through their brains and they died. He pulled at the arrow and it came out with a shiveringly unpleasant sucking sound. The missile was a marvellous bit of design and ironwork, he had to concede, better than anything the Romans had. Elann Nancarrow's work, no doubt. He'd have to try to make sure she remained alive when he took the land. She'd designed and forged Tadman Dantadman's armour, the prototype for the amazing armour the Maximen wore. Other smiths had replicated her designs. They'd been skilled, but none of them had been the innovator that she was, and besides he'd had them all killed to keep the secrets of his legion. When he captured Elann he'd see if she could do anything about the eye slits. A mesh of iron, perhaps?

He found four more Leathermen killed by the vicious Maidunite salvo, all of them head-shot. Felix prayed to Diana that that was it, but he knew it wouldn't be. He expected to find more dead Leathermen among the corpses ahead — but surely no more dead Maximen? He also hoped that the one Leatherman he'd seen leap up from the site of the first skirmish and run off to join the main battle had been Bistan. From the way he'd run he thought it was, but with those hoods it was impossible to tell them apart with any certainty.

At the main battle ground it looked like a herd of horses and a crowd of people had been butchered ready for roasting then chewed up and scattered all over the place by a multitude of marauding foxes. The Maximen and those Leathermen who weren't off chasing horses were pawing through the bodies, looking for survivors to kill. There weren't any.

"Bistan!" he called. "Bistan!"

One of the Leathermen came tripping up, soaked in blood, carrying what Felix guessed was a human thigh bone, but it could have been a smaller bone from a horse. "Yeah, boss?"

This time Felix was relieved to hear it.

Lowa gripped Adler around the waist and the horse thundered along beneath them. She'd been staggering around trying to work out where the Bel she was when the captain of the Two Hundred had grabbed her, pulled her onto her horse and galloped away, dodging Maximen, flying from the beach and plunging between dunes that had hopefully obscured their escape. She'd only just managed to grasp all this, because she was only just managing to grip on to consciousness. Her right shirt sleeve was sodden with blood. She guessed it was from her head, which was spinning about like a stone in a whirling sling.

She tried to remember what had happened. She'd shot a Leatherman with her second arrow and a few more had gone down, then the demons had hit them. She'd been knocked from her horse immediately, possibly she'd killed the Leatherman that had done that, then she'd taken on an Ironman. The next thing she remembered was being pulled onto Adler's horse.

"We have to go back," she managed.

"They're all dead," said Adler. "We go back and we are, too. You're needed. We're headed for Big Bugger Hill."

"No."

"You are needed. There's no sense dying here."

Lowa didn't feel that she deserved to live after leading the Two Hundred to their deaths, and if her best-trained, most talented men and women had been wiped out killing just a few of the beasts, what hope did the rest of them have? But Adler was right. Shitty as it felt, it made sense for them to return to base. What was more, she thought with a pang of guilt, there was a little boy at Big Bugger Hill who she was desperate to see.

She gripped Adler's shirt and looked back to check that they weren't being followed.

They were.

A solitary Leatherman was sprinting down the forest path behind them. He was a hundred paces back and catching.

"Adler . . ."

The captain glanced back. "Danu's cuntfluff," she said.

"Indeed," said Lowa. "We'll have to stop and face him."

"I will. You'll keep going."

"No. The two of us will have a better chance."

"You're injured, you'll get in the way. You have to go back and command Maidun and Britain to victory. I do not . . ."

"Adler, no, it's too much, I—"

"I'm doing it. You never know, I might beat him."

Adler stood up on the galloping horse's back, turned, put her hands on Lowa's shoulders and sprung over her head.

"Kill the Roman bastards for me!" she shouted, unsheathing her sword as she flew.

Lowa galloped on, between the trees, knowing that Adler was right again, she had to return and command the army. Still, she squeezed her eyes tight in rage and shame for leading so many to their deaths.

Chapter 6

Ragnall was surprised. They had an unassailable base here on the coast. They'd landed only that morning and he'd seen no reconnaissance patrols head out. Surely the best course was consolidation and caution? So why was Caesar commanding the centurions to prepare five legions to march inland at dawn the next day? No doubt it was the right thing to do, but Ragnall couldn't for the life of himself see the reasoning behind it.

"King Ragnall?" Caesar said when he'd finished explaining the marching order to the plume-helmeted centurions and they were striding away. Ragnall raised a hand. "Ah good, there you are. How is the queen?"

He hesitated for a heartbeat. A few centurions had turned their heads at the words "King Ragnall". Their looks combined unpleasantly into a waft of mild but universal hostility. They had a point, Ragnall had to concede. It was odd to hear himself and Spring referred to as king and queen, to be awarded with the rule of the entire province-to-be when they hadn't done anything to earn it. In Rome a man strived for position. Yes, there were great families and being born into them was an advantage, but in the end a man stood on his merits. Caesar, Crassus, Pompey – all these had schemed and battled a long, lonely slog up the political ranks. There had been kings way back in Rome's past, but they'd understood the folly and unfairness of the system and got rid of them *nearly five hundred years before* and replaced them with elected officials. That was how much more advanced they were than the British.

But they weren't in Rome, they were in Britain on that chilly summer's evening and he and Spring really were going to be king and queen.

Baths on Maidun Castle. That was the first thing he'd have built. Big, hot, marble baths, right next door to his palace on the eyrie. His palace. He'd burn Zadar's – Lowa's – little hut and have it replaced with a marble palace as huge and magnificent as Pompey's theatre. Or something more huge and magnificent, why not? He'd heard of a triangular tomb in Egypt that was the tallest building in the world. Not for long, he thought. The Britons would need a project to work on, a symbol of the new order. It might as well be Ragnall's Maidun Palace.

"The queen is well, my general, and she sends her congratulations on your successful landing," he answered.

"Caesar is pleased. Now Ragnall, Caesar knows that young bucks crave adventure and burn to join the fight" – Ragnall nodded, thinking that he had no burning need to face the likes of Atlas and Chamanca in battle – "but you will abide in the shore camp to protect the queen and ensure that she remains with the Romans. You will not let her return to the Britons. Do you understand?"

"Yes. O Caesar, I hesitate to bring such a trivial matter to you, but there is a potential problem. The queen was attacked by—"

"Good," said Caesar, waving Ragnall away. He'd stopped listening after "Yes." "Where's Mumarra?"

"Here!" Caesar's chief engineer, a lanky, toothsomely smiley fellow stood forward.

"Tomorrow the army will require three identical battering rams, each thirty foot long with a diameter . . ."

Ragnall walked away. Caesar would be giving orders late into the evening, then he'd retire and fall asleep immediately. He didn't have time to deal with Ragnall's problem – or Spring's, more accurately. Quintus hadn't been at the briefing, so obviously he wasn't on his feet just yet, but he didn't need to be on his feet to give orders. But surely he wouldn't attack Spring now that she was queen and under Caesar's protection?

Then again, men like Quintus had such resources and influence that they were very unlikely to be tried successfully for any crime, and revenge on the girl who castrated him was probably incentive enough for Quintus to take a small risk.

"You've got to go now," said Dug, "while they haven't got you chained."

Spring shook her head. "I'm staying here until I have something to take to Lowa."

"You've got yourself. That'll do. Go."

"Oh yes, she'll be jumping with joy to see me. Got myself caught, got the dogs killed . . . No, I have to have something, to know something useful – or I have to have killed Caesar."

"You and your bow would be very useful right now. You might turn a battle. The war even. On top of that, if you stay here any longer, Quintus will kill you."

"I've beaten him once."

"Aye, and just him. He'll come with ten men next time. And another thing, Lowa loves you. She's having a shitty time of it and—"

"Lowa loves me! Now I've heard it all."

"She does. She couldn't visit you after I died because she was having a baby and then she had an invasion to ward off. You're a great girl, Spring, the best, but you've got to start trying to see things from other people's point of view."

"I do see from others' point of view! All the time! And besides, I can't go without your hammer."

"Where is it?"

"I don't know, I guess the praetorian who took it still has it."

"You can get Elann to make you a better one *if* you get out of here now."

"I suppose you're right . . ."

"I am."

"OK. I just need to pack my—"

"Talking to yourself again?" asked Ragnall, dipping through the tent's flap, followed by Ferrandus and Tertius. Tertius was carrying a length of iron chain.

"Only way I can get a decent conversation."

"Hmmm. Well, sorry about this, but Caesar's ordered me to chain you up so you can't escape."

"That's a fine way to treat your wife."

"I'm sorry."

"But what if Quintus comes? I won't be able to defend myself."

"You'll be chained by the ankle only. You'll still be able to do what you did to him last time."

"I won't."

"Why not?"

Spring raised an eyebrow and realisation dawned on Ragnall's handsome face. He'd been taught a lot on the Island of Angels, and he was a good-looking man, but he was not bright.

"All right, but you know what I mean. And Ferrandus and Tertius will be protecting you."

"Fat lot of good they were when he came before." She looked at the two guards. They'd heard their names mentioned and she guessed they guessed what she was talking about, because they looked suitably abashed.

"They'll kill Quintus rather than let him past next time. He threatened Tertius' family before. That's why they let him pass."

"So what's different now?"

"I've told them to kill Quintus if he won't go away and that Caesar himself will protect them and their families if they do."

"Is that true?"

"Probably."

"Well, I still think it's a stupid idea to chain me up. I swear I won't try to escape. Why would I?"

Ragnall looked at Spring. She tried to give him her most innocent, trustworthy look.

"No, I'm sorry," he said, shaking his head, then, in Latin: "Ferrandus, chain her. Ankle to the bed frame. Make sure there's no way for her to escape."

Ferrandus nodded and stepped towards her, chain rattling.

Chapter 7

Jagganoch walked along the middle of the walled town's central street, keeping his footsteps silent, and listening. There was a raised walkway on the side of the road for pedestrians to keep the road free for carts, but men like Jagganoch walked down the middle of the road, always. Had there been any carts, they would have had to make way for him.

The town was deserted when they found it, but who knew what demons dwelt on this island on the edge of the world? A thousand imps might spill from side roads any moment, slavering for his fine African flesh, far superior to any they would have tasted before.

It didn't look like a home to demons, though. It was all rather mundane. The huts lining the road were stout, large and well-built. The crafters had been proud of their work and had finished it well, without feeling the need for the frivolous embellishment and childish sculptures with which the prissy Romans encrusted every building. In fact, the prosperous little town was not dissimilar to his Yonkari homeland, far away across many lands, two seas and the great ocean of sand.

Already he preferred this land to Italy. The countryside around Pompey's estate near Rome had two types of dwelling: giant stone ranches, homes to one family and its staff and slaves, and dilapidated shit-stinking hovels of impoverished Italians, apparently driven from their lands by the richer families. The poverty had offended him. The poor were more productive if one allowed them a modicum of dignity, his father had explained once, and Jagganoch agreed. Common people were the same as animals. If you kept your peasants healthy, well fed and comfortable, they behaved better, worked harder and didn't stink of shit. The Romans were too stupid to realise this. Instead of using their wealth to make their poor more productive, they built their walls higher and planted gardens so they didn't have to see or smell the vile creatures.

He looked up. The village might not be unusual, but here at the edge of the world the sky was much lower. The god Sobek had made the earth on the reverse side of his curved, round shield when he laid it down after defeating all the other gods. So in the land of the Yonkari, which was the centre of the world, the sky was at its highest. In Italy the sky was lower and here, right on the fringe, it was only a few hundred feet above his head. He'd seen skies this colour in Africa, but never this low. A lesser man might have been oppressed. Not Jagganoch. He shook his fist at it and resolved to travel further, to where the sky met the land. Whatever British gods were looking down from that low sky, Sobek had already beaten them once and he would do again if they dared to impede Jagganoch.

There was a great crash behind him, but he didn't turn. It was the elephants clearing huts for a place to sleep. The beasts would be ill-humoured tomorrow. They always were when he cut their rations. Caesar had promised that there would be plenty to eat in the villages of Britain, but this town's storage sheds had been as empty as its huts. As if to confirm his concerns, Bandonda trumpeted. He was angry, and hungry.

They'd brought enough fodder for only two days, or four days on half-rations, as he'd ordered. Caesar had told him to stay south, away from the legions, until he was summoned. But nobody told Jagganoch what to do and certainly nobody summoned him. The next day he'd walk his elephants north, find the legions and demand supplies. If they did not accede, they would see what angry and hungry elephants could do, especially elephants that had been trained by many generations of Yonkari elephant wranglers to eat human flesh.

His father had told him to obey Pompey and Pompey had handed his command to Caesar. He'd done what the Romans had told him to so far, but in his heart he felt that he could obey only orders that came directly from his father, and his father was a long way away, across many lands, two seas and the great ocean of sand. Here there was nobody to command him.

Another elephant trumpeted and at the same time there was a noise ahead and to the right – a footstep. He held his pace and didn't turn. Imps and demons were surely not meticulous enough to use the cover of noise when tracking their prey. No, this was a human. Just one, he thought, and light. A woman or a young man. He gripped the knob of his wooden club harder. The weapon had been carved from a branch of the hardest wood, its head polished, its shaft whittled down to a pole and fired until it was stronger than iron. It was more than a weapon; right now it was a walking and investigation cane, used to help his stride and poke anything that he didn't want to touch – dog shit, for example, to see how long the town had been deserted. It could also be thrown a long distance, and used as a straightforward club. Jagganoch was superbly skilled with it. Many times revengeful Romans, their kin killed by his elephants, had run at him with swords, expecting to find easy victory against a man with a stick. Instead they had found easy death.

He was close enough to hear his stalker's breathing now. It was a woman. No matter. He was as happy to kill a woman as a man. He passed the alley that she thought concealed her and heard a small excited intake of breath – he knew that sound, it was the noise of a top predator. He made it himself before a kill; lions did the same before they charged their prey. The woman would be on him in moments. She was in for a surprise.

Chamanca slipped behind the hut as the bronze-helmeted Africa walked past. He was a fine-looking man. He was a good deal slimmer than Atlas, but the lion skin over his shoulder left one of his arms and part of his torso bare, so she could see his excellently defined muscles rippling over each other under their covering of velvety, dark brown skin.

As well as the lion's pelt he was wearing a legionary's leather skirt and sandals, but instead of a sword he had a long mace. He was carrying it like a walking cane, but she could tell from the wear around its shaft that it was used as a club.

She wasn't meant to attack and, up to now, she hadn't been tempted to, because her own mace, sword and teeth would have been little use against the gigantic war beasts. She'd seen elephants in Iberia and been impressed, but these were much bigger. They were going to be a problem.

But it made all the sense in the world to kill this man, who appeared to be the leader and had made the mistake of walking off on his own. He looked like he was full of delicious blood, too. That was a bonus.

He passed and she padded out after him, silently. He did look formidable – lithe and strong – and she considered stabbing him in the spine to immobilise him. But where would the fun be in that? She leapt.

Chapter 8

Felix walked among the massacred Britons. The sharp stink from their eviscerated stomachs was eye-watering. He knew it would have disgusted most people, but he sniffed deep and shuddered with pleasure. He liked a number of smells that others found unpleasant – rotting flesh, unwashed men and women, stale urine – but his favourite was freshly spilled guts.

He found four more dead Celermen, meaning that he'd lost eight on the landing – nearly a quarter of them. He was surprised and upset that so many had died. More surprisingly, another Maximan had been killed in the mêlée. One of the Maidunites had rammed a sword through the gap in the armpit and into his heart. Well done, Felix thought. The killer had identified another weak spot in the armour that the captive Elann would have to strengthen.

So he was down to twenty-seven Celermen and eighteen Maximen, not even five hundred paces from the shore and they'd met only a fraction of the British army. On the bright side, Felix considered, since this lot had killed two Maximen and eight Celermen where the entire Usipete and Tengoterry army had killed precisely none, he guessed that this had been Lowa's elite force, the equivalent of Zadar's Fifty, and his little squad had destroyed it. Yes, he'd lost ten men in the process, which was too many, but it was unlikely that they'd have to face such skilled soldiers again. Next time he'd have the Maximen attack first, arms raised to protect their eye slits, followed by the Celermen, and he shouldn't lose another one. The lesson on the beach had been expensive but valuable.

The next problem was that they'd killed all the magic fuel, save for the seven crew members from the ship. It wasn't the end of the world; it just meant they'd have to find a village within an hour or so, before the life-force of these latest victims wore off.

As Felix pondered all this, Bistan came striding through the gore. "One got away!" he announced cheerily. "A woman on a horse. Another woman held up one of the Celermen so long that her friend escaped."

"Mars!" cursed Felix. "How— Actually, never mind." It was good that one of them had escaped to tell the rest of the British about his legion. Hopefully they'd be terrified into surrender.

He looked about for a living horse. There was none, so in the end he left the crew, two Maximen and two Celermen guarding the ship, climbed up on Gub's shoulders and told the rest of his legion to run behind them, westwards along the coast. In every part of every country he'd ever been to, there had always been coastal villages so they were bound to come upon one soon.

Bouncing along on Gub's shoulders was exhilarating, like running with a pack of hunting animals. The sun was lowering behind them, stretching their shadows longer as they ran across the alien land. Over the sea to their right, the evening rays cast a delicate blue, tending to rust.

But soon he began to worry. They hadn't seen a soul. The crops were gone from the fields and there was no fruit on the trees. When they did come upon a village it was deserted, not so much as a chicken scratching the barren dirt, the grain sheds open and empty.

The second village was tucked into a rocky crevice by the sea. By the time they strode down its steep but neat cobbled street, it was dark, they were a good ten miles from the ship and the power gained from the Maidunites had worn from all the Celermen and Maximen except Bistan. Gub had begun to struggle under Felix's weight and in the end the druid had dismounted to trudge along with the rest of them.

"And my energy will be gone soon, boss," the head Celerman cheerily reported to Felix. "I can feel it ebbing out . . . yeah, I think it's gone now, actually. What do you want to do?"

"Search the village again!" he shouted. Surely there were a couple of stubborn old people hiding in a hovel?

"There's nobody here, boss, we've looked."

"All right, tell everyone to muster. We'll walk back to the ship. But you won't."

"Where will I go?"

"Head south-east. If you find an opportunity to fuel yourself, take it. Find Caesar. Tell him where we are and that we require expendable men."

"OK!" Bistan ran off to do as he was bidden.

Chapter 9

Jagganoch felt the ground shift under the woman's weight and heard her breathe as if she'd been shouting. She leapt and he dropped, tossed up his slender club, caught it by the handle and spun. If it had smashed her ribs, as intended, that would have been that, but somehow she melted round his strike, landed and jabbed a hard little fist at his face. He rolled with the blow and swept his club back, catching her calves and sweeping her off her feet. She fell back, sprang on her hands and leapt in a backward somersault. Her speed and athleticism was impressive.

She crossed her hands over her torso and uncrossed them in a flourish, unsheathing a ball-mace and a sword. Her teeth were filed to points. She was small in stature and dressed like the serving wench at an orgy, yet she radiated power. For the first time in a fight since he'd been a child, Jagganoch took a step back.

"You're quick," she said.

"You're quicker."

"I am."

"But I am stronger," he smiled.

"I doubt it."

"Iberian, by your accent?"

"Clever man."

"You are also beautiful."

"I am," she agreed.

"Perhaps we should make love instead of fighting?"

She grinned and shook her head. "I am flattered but no

thank you. I already have one African. You are superfluous and will be culled."

All the time Jagganoch was looking for a moment of distraction, a way in, but there was none. The Iberian was bouncing on her heels, poised like a riled snake.

Jagganoch smiled. "I had not expected to find interesting opposition on this island."

"There are plenty more like me. Thousands."

"Then where are they? Why am I able to take this town unmolested?"

"We're luring you all in for the kill."

"It is I who will be killing today."

Jagganoch swung his club.

Chamanca lifted her sword to meet the blow, but it was more powerful than she'd thought possible. Her sword was whacked from her grip and sent spinning. She swung her mace, intending to press him back and catch the sword as it fell, but he brought up his club handle hard, very hard, and she had to leap back to avoid it. He jumped back, too, and the sword clattered onto the road.

He was very good. Not as good as her, but he was stronger. It was possible that he might beat her. Unlikely, but the offer to make love instead was beginning to seem more appealing.

"Why do you fight for the Romans?" she asked. "They are monsters."

"As am I." He came at her, darting forwards then back, swinging left and right with his club.

She dodged and blocked, but he was wearing her down and she saw no gap for the counter with her mace. She'd become used to fighting with two weapons. She considered dropping to smash his knees or crush his balls, but if that went wrong she'd be at his mercy. She couldn't remember ever having to think this much during a fight.

He broke the onslaught and stood back.

"You look worried," he said. "Perhaps you instead would like to change sides? You could ride into battle with me on my elephant Bandonda. There is no greater feeling in the world."

"I will ride on your elephant with you, if it is against the Romans."

He shook his head, smiling, and Chamanca darted in. He saw, but too late. She hammered a punch into his guts and cracked her ball-mace into his temple. He fell, unconscious. She jumped onto him and sank her teeth into his neck. Oh, it was good, it was *very* good. Saltier and hotter than Roman blood.

Engrossed, she heard the footsteps almost too late. A dozen of them, maybe more, charging. She sprang to her feet, snatched up her sword and sprinted away. She felt missiles whizzing, and dodged. Two clubs like Jagganoch's whistled past. She ran on, scurried up the side of a hut, bounced off its roof, over the town wall and away. She would have loved to have stayed and played, but she had work to do.

Felix and his legion arrived back at their landing site after several hours' walk to find two Maximen, two Celermen, no ship and no ship's crew.

"Where's the ship?" he asked.

"Done gone," rumbled a Maximan.

"What?"

"What he's trying to say," said one of the Celermen who'd stayed behind, "is that the ship is gone."

"I guessed that. But why? How?"

"We were tricked, I'm afraid," said the Celerman. "Almost as soon as you were gone, the tide came in — and by Jupiter did it come in, never seen anything like it. I thought it was a flood or another great wave, but the sailors said it was normal."

"Yes. Big tides here. And?"

"And they said they needed to anchor the ship to stop it drifting off. They told us it was dangerous for people who didn't know the sea, and told us to wait above this line of seaweed," he pointed at a dark line in the pale sand, "so we did. The crew all went to the ship and climbed aboard. The water came higher and higher, then the ship was floating. They pulled up that leather thing—"

"The sail."

"That's it. They pulled that up and off they went. That way." He pointed out over the moonlit, empty sea.

"On the bright side," said the Celerman, "they were true to their word about the seaweed. We stayed above it and the water came right up to it, but not over it. Did you find any people on your trip, or any food? We're all pretty hungry here."

Chapter 10

Lowa stood alone on her command tower, high above the palisade on Big Bugger Hill. All across the wide plain to the north, lit up rather fetchingly from the east by the rising sun, was the Roman army.

It could not be called a surprise assault. There were thousands of men, all marching in neat, boring squares. To the east was cavalry and to the west of centre was a battering ram, towed by oxen. The ram looked pretty much exactly the right size and weight for smashing her new hillfort's gate. She counted five legions, which meant they'd left one legion of five thousand men guarding the ships.

She looked along her palisade, lined with dozens of scorpions and hundreds of archers. It had looked formidable the day before, but in the context of twenty thousand men marching towards it looked like exactly what it was – a wooden wall that could be knocked down.

The front line of the Romans was approaching her longbow range. She stretched her arms up above her head, clasped her hands and bent over to one side, then the other.

"Badgers' spunk trumpets, that's a great look," said a voice that she'd once known very well. She turned slowly.

"Dug," she said, suddenly feeling faint and grabbing the tower's wooden wall. It was her head wound, she told herself. He was leaning against the wall at the other side of the tower. "Are you a ghost?" She wanted to run over to him, but held back.

"No, not a ghost, just part of your mind talking to you. I guess you've conjured me up to reassure yourself."

"No, you're not part of my mind. I have plans, I don't need reassurance. And I don't hallucinate. You're a bloody ghost . . ."

"I'm not."

"My love, you're lying." She'd always been able to read him. "Go deep into my mind and just maybe there's a part capable of creating a vision of the man I love in a time of duress. However, nowhere, *nowhere*, would you find any part of me that could ever come up with the phrase 'badgers' spunk trumpets'."

"Ah," he looked abashed. "But you still love me?"

Lowa smiled. "That's not the point. What are you? Don't get me wrong, I'm glad to see you, although this possibly isn't the best time." She glanced at the Romans. They were still just outside her bow range. "I know that you're not part of my mind. So what are you?"

"It worked on Spring."

"What did?"

"She believed I was in her mind."

"I bet she didn't. She's just more indulgent of you than I am. Look, we don't have long. I miss you and want to hold you and I'm so happy to see you because perhaps it means that one day I'll be with you again, but you always had terrible timing. The Romans are attacking." She looked over her shoulder. The front ranks were coming to the edge of her bow range. "Tell me quickly, why have you come?"

"Our son is in danger from one of those demons."

"He's here, in the fort. Do you mean we're all in danger from demons?"

"I saw a vision. There were people around but I could only see him, then there was a shout – *'Demons attacking from the north-west.'* Shortly afterwards . . . little Dug was killed, by a demon."

"Oh, piss." Lowa had a vision of her routed army, of herself crawling broken-legged and hearing the words *Demons attacking from the north-west*. "Why have you told me this?"

"So you can save our son."

Lowa sighed. "I'll do my best to save everyone, him most of all. I have to fight now. I love you, Dug. Please come back to me after this, assuming I'm not already with you. Although, actually, can you do anything useful? How about scaring Caesar?"

"I love you as well," he said, and he was gone.

She turned to face the Romans. They were in range. She slotted an arrow, drew and shot.

Two heartbeats later one of the two oxen pulling the battering ram went down. The archers and scorpion crews lining Big Bugger Hill's palisade cheered. A couple of heartbeats later, she loosed another arrow and hit the second oxen, which toppled more slowly with a pained lowing, soon drowned out by more British cheers.

The Roman legionaries stopped as one and the squares of men nearest Big Bugger Hill raised shields to form impenetrable armoured boxes around themselves. They waited and the British watched as something that looked like a longhouse on wheels — a shield for the battering ram, presumably — was rolled forward, and a couple more oxen were driven in from the back lines.

During this lull, Lowa looked around for Dug again but he wasn't there. Seeing him had filled her with a joy that she hadn't felt in a long while and at the same time pissed her off massively. Why hadn't he appeared to her before? And why couldn't his warning be less cryptic? She would do her best to keep little Dug safe, and she'd listen out for the *Demons attacking from the north-west* shout, but really she could not be focused on him, not today, with twenty-five-thousand-plus men marching at her wooden walls and fifteen-thousand-strong army.

She wondered how Chamanca was getting on with the second phase of their plan for the chariots. And where the Bel was Atlas with those armoured aurochs? There hadn't been so much as a shout from Atlas since he'd headed to the Aurochs tribe. Where was he?

Chamanca liked driving chariots, particularly these lighter, faster ones, and particularly when she was at the head of eight hundred of them charging at the Roman camp as the sun rose.

Some Roman foragers were out early. They spotted the chariots and ran for cover that was just a little too far away.

"Shoot them!" Chamanca commanded, without slowing or turning. She heard bows thrum behind her then squawks as several dozen arrows found targets.

"Did you get one?" she called back to her crew, a young woman called Yanina. Yanina had been Chamanca's driver at the battle against the Dumnonians on Sarum Plain, when she was only a girl. She'd been a good driver then and she was a good fighter now.

"I got two."

"Excellent."

Chamanca had picked the girl to share her chariot firstly because she'd done well on Sarum Plain, probably saving Chamanca's life when she'd deftly driven the chariot clear of a crowd of clinging Dumnonians, and secondly because she was good-looking. If a woman as beautiful as Chamanca had to have someone else in her chariot – and Lowa had insisted that she did – then it needed to be someone who complemented Chamanca's appearance. Yanina had been terrified at first, remembering that the Iberian hadn't been exactly kind last time. Now that the girl was fiercely trained and much more capable, however, Chamanca didn't feel the need to whack her. She even felt able to treat

Yanina almost as an equal, and she could tell by the new swagger in the tall girl's rangy stride that she was proud to be so closely associated with the fiercest Warrior in Lowa's army.

The wall of the camp loomed out of the sea mist and Roman trumpets blared through the still morning. The big gates in the centre of the south wall swung shut. There was no rattle in the neck of a Roman trumpet; they were all the same size and the trumpeters blew the same clean, single note. The British trumpets' music, with wooden clackers in their mouths, all whatever size the bronzesmith had decided to make that day, all blown to the individual blower's personal tunes, always swelled and throbbed like a swarm of gigantic insects. The Roman ones sounded like the honk of defiant but harmonious geese. Chamanca preferred the British ones.

A hundred paces from the wall she shouted, "Jump!" and felt her chariot lighten and speed up as Yanina leapt off. She wrenched on her right-hand rein and turned for the coast.

"Take care!" Yanina shouted behind her. Chamanca shot an evil look over her shoulder and Yanina grinned back. She had been too kind to the girl. Some discipline would be called for after the attack.

A couple of slingstones flew from the walls and landed ineffectively and soon there were several hundred British arrows suppressing the Roman defensive missiles. She glanced at the gate – still closed, which was good. She wasn't sure how many legionaries were going to charge out and she wasn't looking forward to finding out.

Half the chariots – four hundred of them – followed her to the shore, minus their passengers, and half the chariots stayed with the disembarked crews, adding to the deluge of arrows raining down onto the wall and into the camp. Soon they'd be adding fire arrows to the standard ones.

Ahead of her, she was glad to see, the twenty-eight Roman warships were still near the beach where they'd guarded the landing and camp construction. The hundreds of transport ships bobbed behind them, peaceful in the early-morning mist.

The trumpets woke Ragnall.

"Whassat?" he mumbled.

"That was your signal to let me go." Spring was sitting upright on her bed, fully dressed, as if she hadn't slept. "Lowa's attacking. She's sure to take the camp. If you let me go now I'll put in a good word for you. Make sure she kills you quickly."

Ragnall pulled his toga over his head, ran a hand through his hair and strapped on his sandals.

"You stay here." He ducked out of the flap.

Legionaries were running eastwards, buckling their armour.

"What's going on?" he asked Ferrandus, who was sitting on a canvas stool outside the tent, trying to clean muck out from under his fingernails with the tip of his sword.

"British are attacking."

"Any more details?"

"Nope. Go and have a look for yourself if you want to find out more. They don't think about people who need to clean their nails when they make these swords, do they? Or maybe it needs sharpening . . ." Ferrandus poked the tip into his palm.

"You're not worried?"

"Nope."

"But you said—"

"The British are attacking? Yes, and my orders are to guard Queen Spring. If the Britons breach the walls then I need to think about moving her. Until that happens, well, I could run up and down waving my arms shouting 'What's going on? What's going on?' like a prick, or I could sit here and get something useful done."

He returned to his nails.

Ragnall ran in the same direction as everybody else, then stopped when an arrow thwocked into the ground by his feet. The running legionaries lifted shields over their heads and ran on as more arrows fell. Ragnall ducked behind one and tried to follow him to where thousands of legionaries were massing, ready to storm out of the camp, presumably.

"Sir?" said the shield-carrying legionary, looking over his shoulder at Ragnall.

"Yes?"

"This is a one-man shield. Would you mind fucking off?"

Ragnall did as he was bid and sprinted back in the direction he'd come until he was clear of the falling arrows. A flying spark caught his eye, then another and another. Fire arrows. He was outside their range but he ran back a little to be sure, then stood and watched as the burning barbs rained down.

They were effective, each landing with a bright little splash of flame. The tents they landed on quickly went up. He couldn't see the mustering legionaries, but he heard horrible screams. It sounded like the little exploding missiles set people alight effectively, too.

Spring had identified the chain's strongest and weakest links and focused on rubbing the former on the latter. She thought she'd made some headway but it was hard to tell. She put the weakest link under the bed leg and sat heavily on the bed. That only embedded the chain into the earth. She wrapped the links around a bed leg then around her wrists, braced her feet against the edge of the bed and pulled.

To her great surprise the chain snapped with a ping and

she fell back. She gathered up the chain, still attached to her ankle but no longer to the bed, and found that a different link had broken – not the one that she'd worked at for ages. There's probably a lesson there somewhere, she thought. She jumped over to Ragnall's side of the tent and rummaged about in his pack for his knife. You didn't want to be escaping without a knife.

At the shore Chamanca yanked her left rein. The horse skidded on the sand as it turned to the north, then galloped along the beach in between the lapping waves and the high wooden wall of the Roman base. Chamanca bounced along, repeatedly flicking reins on the horse's back to remind him of the ongoing need for speed.

This was the dangerous part. Theoretically, there would be no defenders on the Roman camp's seaward, eastern wall because it was protected by the ships. Indeed, she could see nobody on the wall. So far, so good.

Out to sea, people were running about on the ships, but none of the dreaded scorpion bolts flew. As Lowa had reckoned and Chamanca had hoped, while not using the giant bows they'd let the tension out of the draw-twine to avoid overstretching it, which meant she and her squad had a few dozen heartbeats before they cranked the twines back and a deadly salvo of scorpion missiles flew their way. It was going to be tight.

She reached the point where she was sure she was in range of the most northerly warship, dragged her chariot to a halt, grabbed her bow and quiver of special arrows and leapt out. Around her two dozen other charioteers stopped and dismounted, too. Fifty paces back along the beach another two dozen were doing the same; fifty paces back from them were another two dozen, and so on. Five of the chariots in each group carried sealed buckets of pitch. The charioteers with buckets grabbed them, twisted them down into the sand, prised off the lids, chucked in a handful of dried grass already mixed with slivers of highly flammable dried dog's nose fungus and struck flint sparks onto it.

Chamanca dipped her arrow into the burning pitch and loosed it at the northernmost warship. The burning missile rose slowly and looked like it would never make the distance, but it flew as far as Elann had promised. Instead of the usual iron head, each arrow had a bulbous, freakishly wide arrow-shaped pod with a thin wooden skin. This pod was packed with wool soaked in the finest whale oil on the inside, and then wrapped in wool and a whale-fat glue on the outer. This outer wool was soaked in burning pitch by the dip in the bucket, then shot. The arrowhead would burst on landing, unleashing its small but fiercely burning little cargo.

Chamanca shot ten arrows into the northernmost warship then surveyed the damage. Small fires were burning all over it. Sailors with buckets were seeing to several of them, but they hadn't spotted all and even if they had they'd never be able to get to them — especially the three high up the mast which Chamanca naturally assumed were her shots. The ship was doomed.

"Next boat!" she shouted, and her gang shifted their aim to the next ship along. Each group was to target two warships and any transports in range before fleeing. She fired three arrows and looked along the line. Several of the warships were fully ablaze and the rest were well on the way. Four more arrows and Chamanca was happy. All the warships were burning merrily, as well as a few dozen transports.

"Hurl buckets, then south!" she shouted, mounting up and flicking the reins. Charioteers slung the burning buckets at the wooden palisade.

Her horse sped along. To her right, flames from the buckets of pitch licked up the silent seaward wall of the Roman camp. To her left the ships burned. The cart's wheels

fizzed along the packed wet sand, faster and faster as
Chamanca whipped the reins. It was exhilarating. The goal
of the attack was to remove the base camp's defences and
reduce the Roman supply line from Gaul, while leaving
them enough transports to flee in. That goal had been
achieved. She hadn't been a fan of Lowa's plan initially
– it didn't involve nearly enough blood drinking – but
now that it was done she felt a new thrill, of being part
of a tightly organised, minutely planned, diligently
executed exercise. For the first time, she had some appreciation of the Roman hive mentality. Of course in this
particular hive exercise she was queen bee, and she wouldn't
have had it any other way, but still, on the whole—

Her gleeful self-congratulation was instantly cauterised
as she rounded the corner of the camp.

"Oh, Fenn," she said.

A multitude of legionaries had flooded from the west gate
and formed their boringly impervious shield tortoises. They
were marching in dreary order towards the four hundred
light chariots and twelve hundred charioteers who'd stayed
on that side of the Roman base. Smoke was billowing up
from the merrily burning camp, but that was scant consolation for the position that the Maidunite light chariots
found themselves in. Because the legionaries were the least
of their worries.

They'd known the fort's garrison would come, so the plan
at that point was to mount up and flee back westwards,
passengers peppering any cavalry pursuit with arrows.
Marshland meant there was no escape along the coast to the
south.

That point had been reached, but the plan to retreat had
been thrown in the air, stamped on then fucked from behind
by the arrival of forty war elephants, galloping in a line
towards the camp. They were armoured in iron skull plates,
iron boots and bladed lances extending their already fear-

some tusks. Mounted on each was a mini walled wooden fort holding a driver and four dark-skinned archers. These latter were pouring arrows at the brave British chariots that charged them.

It was a beautiful manoeuvre; the chariots swung round in front of the elephants, the crew of each firing arrow after arrow, but it was ineffectual and doomed. The arrows that found unarmoured flesh had little or no effect on the animals' thick hides. A few archers in the mounted towers were hit, but the Africans had a better shooting position, lofted as they were, so were taking a heavier toll on the chariots. As drivers and horses were struck, so chariots slowed and stopped. The elephants ploughed through them, heads dipping and bucking, iron-capped tusks shunting and splintering wood, impaling and destroying men, women and horses. Out of the couple of hundred chariots that had attacked the elephants, perhaps ten fled back to the main body of the Maidunite light chariot squad, blood-soaked monsters galloping and trumpeting behind them. It looked like a fleet of full-sailed triremes chasing down a handful of fishing smacks. One elephant had a horse impaled and kicking on a tusk, but it ran as fast as the others.

The other charioteers who'd stayed to shoot arrows into the base were trapped between the closing jaws of two forces – elephants on one side, legionaries on the other. They were loosing swarms of arrows in both directions, but their missiles were sticking in the shields of the legionaries, hardly noticed by the elephants and not finding the African archers ducked down in their turrets. It galled Chamanca, but there was only one option ("Or is that no options?" said Carden's voice in her head – as he'd said to her moments before he'd died).

She blew three short blasts on her whistle, the signal to retreat, then two longer blasts, which meant "to the east". The only possible escape lay along the beach to the north, back along the fort's burning eastern wall. The chariots might make it. Anyone on foot was doomed.

The Iberian wasn't going to retreat yet, though. She'd ridden into this battle with two people on her chariot, and two of them were going to ride out of it. She slapped the reins and sped towards the Maidunite chariots as they thundered towards her, between the closing jaws of the Roman legionaries on one side and the African war elephants on the other.

The air between Big Bugger Hill and the enemy was thick with the arrows from five thousand Maidunite archers, shivering up from the wall, slowing and then pelting down onto the multitude of Romans. They had no noticeable effect on the steadily marching ranks, other than turning the tortoises into hedgehogs.

The Romans had no catapults, no towers, no scorpions, just men and a battering ram. Lowa scanned the land around. She could see no clever plans, no jinks to the left or right, no cavalry looping round the back. She was confident that there was nothing going on that she couldn't see because she had shouters hidden all over the place. The Roman plan seemed simple – break the gate, come in, kill the Britons. And this was the tactical genius that had crushed Gaul? Maybe their success was down to superior equipment, training and doggedness, she thought, because they still came. The battering ram was ten paces from the gate, five . . .

"FIRE!" shouted Lowa.

Spring found the knife eventually where he'd hidden it in his bedclothes, grabbed the striped horse-skin quiver that Caesar had given her and had wriggled nearly all the way under the back of the tent, when something yanked at her ankle chain.

"You'd think," said Ragnall, hauling her back in, "that after the last time you escaped under the tent that we might have done something to make it more secure."

"Actually, you did," said Spring as she slid on her stomach back under the heavy leather tent side. "It was much harder to get under this time. Ferrandus and Tertius made it tighter. You shouldn't blame them." She blamed herself. If she hadn't dallied finding Ragnall's stupid knife she would have been well away.

Back in the tent she stood up. Ragnall was holding the chain and shaking his head: "Where the Jupiter did you think you'd go?"

"Home. I've had enough of this now and I want to go. My place is with the Britons. So is yours. Come on, let's stop mucking around and get out of here. With all the noise outside nobody will notice."

"My place is not with the Britons. The Britons killed my mother, my father and my brothers. When the Romans take Briton that won't happen any more to anyone. Law will rule and nobody will have to suffer as I did."

"Everyone suffers. You think the Romans are good and kind?"

"The Romans are just. Under them a good man can live a good life. In the Britain I knew the good were tortured, enslaved and killed – by your father."

"But Lowa is in charge now. The good are living their lives and the country is at peace – at least it was until you and your dick friends crossed the Channel."

"Spring, I know you're young, but try to understand. Lowa might be good. I happen to disagree with that, but let's say for the sake of argument that her rule is as just and fair as the Romans' will ever be."

"It's better."

"OK, it's better – doesn't matter. The point is, with things left as they are, without the Romans taking over, Lowa will be queen only until the next Zadar comes along, kills her and takes her place."

"No way. Nobody could kill her."

"Then she will get older and die. This is obvious stuff, Spring. The way Britain is ruled now, bad kings and queens will come again. It's inevitable, it's what happens when power is a free-for-all. The selfish, ruthless, cruel and the aggressive are in charge."

"And sometimes the good win out, like Lowa."

"True, sometimes they do – sometimes. But it doesn't have to be so arbitrary. In Rome the people choose who's in charge. It's not faultless and they have their troubles, but it's a thousand times better than the rule-free system in which the biggest shit floats to the top."

Annoyingly, he had a bit of a point. But he was missing the main one. "No. Voting and all that stuff may well work for the Romans and maybe we should try it here, maybe we really should, but it ought to be our decision, not forced on us by plume-headed idiots from Italy. If we want to, we will work out our version of it – one that includes women, perhaps? It's none of Rome's business what we do here . . . Actually that's a point, do you really think the Romans care at all what political system we have in Britain?"

"You've changed the subject. We were talking about how much better it is to have annually elected leaders. Are you conceding that argument?"

"Just answer me. Do the Roman care what system of rule we use?"

"Yes, that's why they're here!"

"Is it? Or are they here to pillage the land, to further the *glory* of Rome, to make Rome richer, to build more big silly buildings so silly people with stupid hair can walk around marvelling at how marvellous they are while people in Britain are enslaved and worked to their deaths in fields and mines and all the profits from their sweat are Romeward-bound?"

"Rome will be enriched by the conquest of Britain, but it's a side effect. You say Lowa's the best ruler ever?"

"Yes."

"Is she richer than she was before she was queen? Does she have a bigger hut, more shiny possessions and finer clothes?"

"No!"

"You're lying. Of course she does. Rulers always take from the people they rule. It doesn't mean they're ruling badly, it's a reasonable reward for improving everyone else's lives. But just imagine Britain covered with aqueducts so we all have that delicious clean water you drank so keenly in Rome. Better fields, better storage, theatres, plays, philosophy, writing and—"

"No. If we want it we'll have it. It shouldn't be forced! Say you loved the game Capture the Fort and I didn't – would you make me play it?"

"Hang on a minute." Ragnall stuck his head out of the tent flap, still holding Spring's chain, and had a word with whoever was guarding. Spring wasn't sure if it was Tertius, Ferrandus or both of them.

He brought his head back in. "The east and the south of the camp is ablaze."

"Oh?"

"They'll tell us if we have to move."

"Right."

"Now, where were we?

"I was asking if you'd make me play a game that you liked and I didn't."

"Of course not."

"Exactly! The Romans should go home! They shouldn't try to make us play their game!"

"But I'd explain why it was a good game and I'd suggest that you played it."

"Exactly again! If you told me about your dumb game,

I'd listen to you and maybe give it a go if you were persuasive enough. Rome could do exactly that. They could send embassies here, they could invite British delegations to visit Rome. They could fill them up with dolphin legs and pig's wings and all that other stupid food, show them the gladiators and the mosaics, let them bathe until they smell like flowers. Then let them *decide*. Instead they've come over here to kill everybody until the only people left are the ones who aren't brave enough to fight and pretend to agree with them. They don't want to change our lives – they want to take them!"

Ragnall shook his head. "It doesn't work like that, Spring. You're too young to understand—"

"Who's changed their argument now? And I'm not too young. You're too stupid. So don't come. Stay with your new idiot friends. I'm still going." Spring yanked the chain.

Ragnall wrapped it around his fist. Spring reached round to the back of her leather shorts and brandished his dagger.

Ragnall's nostrils flared and the blubber that had accumulated around his once square jaw quivered.

"I will kill you if you don't let me go." She stepped forward.

Ragnall stretched a hand out to take the knife. Spring swished it out of his reach. He made a grab for it. She spun around him, stuck a foot out and pushed him over it. He stumbled and fell into the back of the tent.

"I'm warning you, Spring," he said, clambering to his feet.

"Warning me what?"

"Give me the knife or I'll take it."

"Come and try. I'm a trained soldier from Lowa's army. You're a fat traitor. Come for the knife and I'll kill you. Stand aside, let me out of the back of the tent and I won't."

He advanced, more carefully this time, stance wide, arms out.

"I don't want to kill you, Ragnall."

He grabbed at her knife hand. She swept in, darted a short but hard punch into his jaw and melted away. It was easy, like fighting a practice dummy.

"Let me go."

He stood back, holding his jaw and blinking at her. "You bitch," he said.

"I could have broken your nose. I could have crushed your windpipe, or stabbed you for that matter in your gut, heart or neck. I don't want to. I don't want to kill you. You're not bad, you're just stupid. Now let me go."

Ragnall roared and leapt. Spring ducked round him and punched him on the temple, hard this time. He fell on her bed, dazed. She vaulted onto him, legs clamping his arms to his sides. As the fug cleared, his facial expression morphed from stupefied to enraged.

He struggled and bucked but she squeezed her knees, tucked her heels under the camp bed's metal frame and pinned him with ease. She'd repeated Lowa's exercises and her own constantly improving routine almost every day since captivity, often several times, and she'd jogged most of the way from Rome to northern Gaul. Ragnall hadn't. She was half his weight, but she was a good deal stronger. With her feet holding the bed frame he wasn't going anywhere, but still he writhed, face reddening. She squeezed her thighs until his red face started to turn purple and his efforts weakened. She relaxed her grip a little.

"Get off me or I'll—" he spat.

She crushed her legs together, gripped him by his hair and pressed the tip of the knife into his windpipe.

"Go on then. Kill me," he spat.

She didn't want to kill him. She didn't know what to do.

Lying on the bed, Atlas woke often, day and night, always in pain, always maddened by not knowing what was happening with Lowa, the Romans and the squad of aurochs riders that he should have taken to join the fight Sobek knew how long ago. Often the curly-haired old woman was out when he woke, and he'd lie awake until she returned and gave him the same honey and apple drink. Then the pain would subside and he'd go back to sleep.

Nothing was clear, but soon he was awake for longer periods and the drink seemed to be losing its flavour. After what might have been a day, or a year, he couldn't tell at all, movement returned a little and he could move his digits, then speak. Finally he could ask questions, but it didn't help as much as he'd hoped.

He'd been brought to her by Elann Nancarrow, the woman told him. Her name was Nan; that was it, no elaboration. They were in Nan's hut, which was somewhere in the Branwin forest. He asked her to tell him all about the Aurochs tribe and Manfreena and why Elann had brought him to her even though she seemed to be under Manfreena's spell. Nan said she didn't get involved with other people's business. She shored up this latter point by asking him no questions at all, not even his name. When he asked her something that she didn't want to answer, such as what was wrong with him, or how long it would take him to recover, or what was in the honey and apple drink, she'd turn away and get on with her work. That work was comprised solely of spending a lot of time in the woods, tidying the hut far more than could possibly be necessary and cooking foul-smelling stew.

One morning Nan helped him sit up and spooned some of the stew into his mouth. It tasted worse than it smelled, like she'd gutted a dozen squirrels and cooked the wrong bits. Even though he was ravenously hungry, he struggled to swallow what might have been a rat's kneecap and shook his head when Nan offered him a second bite. She said

"Tsk" and gave him some honey and apple drink. He went back to sleep, exasperated that the old crone was doing nothing to help him.

Chapter 11

Chamanca vaulted over the front of the chariot and landed smoothly on the horse's back. She slashed back one side and then the other with her sword, severing the leather ties that attached the animal to the chariot's yoke, gripped its mane and dug her heels in.

"Around the camp to the north on the sea side!" she yelled as she approached the fleeing Maidunites. With good fortune some of them would make it.

A heartbeat later and the Iberian was among the thundering Maidun chariots, jinking reins to dodge in between them. It reminded her of avoiding the landslide during Rome's battle with the Nervee in Gaul, but this time she wasn't energised by fresh blood and she was reliant on an animal responding to her commands. She was glad that she'd spent so many hours riding the little horse, and that Lowa had had the wheel blades removed from the chariots. The blades had always been more for show than anything else and often injured more friends than foes in normal warfare. The one thing they were great for was massacring unarmed, fleeing people, but Lowa wasn't planning on doing much of that.

A moment and an age later, Chamanca burst out of the chariots onto bare heathland. It was a hundred paces to the Maidunites on foot. There was no point in them running, they'd never make it, but they were also doomed where they were, with legionaries marching steadily towards them from one side and elephants charging from the other. Every other army Chamanca had seen would have run, but not

Lowa's brave light charioteers. They stood, firing arrow after ineffectual arrow into their attackers. Some were shooting fire arrows at the elephants, which Chamanca thought would have stampeded the reputedly skittish creatures, but the well-trained beasts didn't seem to notice them.

Two burning darts hit one elephant's little wooden fort and set it ablaze. Chamanca hoped for a moment that that elephant might run amok and cause havoc with the others, but the archers leapt and slid down the elephant's rump. The driver jumped onto the beast's neck, reached around behind himself and severed leather thongs. The turret crashed down in an explosion of sparks and the elephant charged on.

The legionaries stopped forty paces from the Maidunites, but the elephants kept coming. The Romans, sensibly, didn't want to be trampled along with the Britons. The charioteers realised this, tossed their bows aside, unsheathed their swords and charged the Romans, screaming battle rage. Chamanca's heart swelled with admiration as she galloped towards them.

As the Maidunites rammed the shield wall of the legionaries, the elephants hit the Maidunites' rear and galloped on, trampling enemy and ally alike, shaking their heads, bladed tusks slicing limbs and heads from Maidunites and Romans.

Chamanca spotted her chariot crew, slashing a legionary's throat then rolling to avoid a sweeping elephant blade.

"Yanina!" she called. Yanina looked up and spotted Chamanca. A Roman took advantage of the distraction to whack a shield into the young woman's face. She went down. The legionary's sword went up.

"Fenn's tits!" said Chamanca, digging her heels into her horse.

Lowa watched as all along the wall and throughout the body of the fort at Big Bugger Hill, British men and women struck flints into buckets of pitch. A thousand archers put aside their quivers of standard arrows and reached for incendiary ones. They dipped the heads in the burning mix, lifted their bows, strung, drew and shot.

Dotted among the archers in the body of the fort, two dozen catapult crews lifted sealed buckets packed with wool and whale oil, and covered in wool soaked in pitch. They placed them carefully into the scoops, lit them with torches and let fly.

On the wall, Mal's sixty scorpions leapt as they unleashed their mighty bolts.

Burning arrows and great balls of fire sailed up over the fort's wall, onto the shields of the nearest legionaries. Further back in the Roman ranks, beyond the range of bows and catapults, scorpion arrows struck shield tortoises, smashing great holes and maiming swathes of soldiers.

Another thousand fire arrows whizzed into the air and down into the legionaries.

The vanguard of the Roman attack dropped burning shields and ran, many themselves ablaze. The hut on wheels that had housed the battering ram went up, its draught oxen bellowing in horrible agony.

"Standard arrows!" shouted Lowa. "Scorpions continue!" All along the British defences, captains repeated her orders. The four thousand archers who'd paused while the fire arrows flew resumed their shooting. Their missiles tore into the shieldless Romans. After the second salvo there were no legionaries within arrow range left standing.

Mal's scorpion arrows flew, smashing more tortoises. Realising their vulnerability, the centurions shouted commands and the legionaries jogged neatly out of reach.

The rest of the Romans – most of the army – stood behind them, still in their tidy squares. At the rear was a small group on horseback. One of those men was, presumably, Julius Caesar. Her missile attack had just killed an entire legion – nearly five thousand men and one sixth of his invasion force. Lowa wondered what he was thinking.

A surprisingly sensible and never-before-heard internal voice told Chamanca to flee immediately and live to fight another day. With the elephants on one side and the legionaries on the other, her chariot mate Yanina and the other dismounted light charioteers who hadn't fled were doomed. So was Chamanca if she stayed around a heartbeat longer.

Chamanca told the voice to piss off. She'd decided to rescue Yanina and that's what she was going to do. Once she had the girl, she had a reason to leave the field. Without the girl, she would be running away, and Chamanca the Iberian did not run away.

She galloped behind three elephants which were carving and stamping havoc in the mass of Britons and Romans. She noticed that they didn't have boots on their back legs, so as she passed she leant over and slashed their rear tendons. She hadn't expected great results, but the animals scream-trumpeted, their back legs collapsed and they crashed onto the ground, crushing soldiers from both sides.

There were two figures struggling on the ground ahead of her. A legionary, sitting on Yanina, was trying to force his sword point into her chest. Yanina was holding the sword back by its blade, bloody handed, legs thrashing.

The Iberian leant over the side of her mount and cracked her ball-mace into the Roman's face as she galloped past. She pulled the reins around. The clever little horse turned very swiftly, probably keen, Chamanca guessed, to be away from the battle.

Yanina was up and waiting. Chamanca scooped her onto the back of her horse and galloped on.

"Thanks!" Yanina cried as they speeded up, gripping Chamanca around her bare midriff, hands slippery with blood.

"Hold tight," said Chamanca, kicking her heels. She pulled the reins to the right to take them out of the fighting, but the crew of one of the downed elephants was up and had spotted them. They reached for arrows, strung them and aimed at the fleeing women.

Yilgarn Craton was not a fan of fussy warfare. For most of his life he'd considered any suggestion that he might follow any sort of plan as a direct insult to his hero-hood. Run at them, attack them with all you've got. That was how men like him fought. When he'd battled as Jocanta's champion, and when he'd led her troops into battle that one time, he hadn't had a plan and he'd won every fight.

He was, however, grudgingly impressed by Lowa's strategy. She'd lured, what, four or five thousand Romans in – not most of them by any means but a good proportion of their army – by pretending that her only defence was an absolute fuck load of arrows. Well, that's all they've got, the Romans must have thought, and it has no effect on us, so we'll march merrily up to her wall under our shields. But then, when they were all crammed in, Lowa had let them see her real defence and it had worked an absolute treat.

Yilgarn wished he'd known about the fire scheme when he'd gone to Caesar. He'd known that Lowa expected the Romans to stay in their camp for several days before marching inland, and he'd told Caesar that, but that's all he'd overheard that time he'd walked behind the queen as she made plans with Mal.

So, yes, Lowa's plan was clever. However, inspired when Lowa had explained the strategy to all the captains, Yilgarn had devised a plan of his own. He had his three hundred Haxmite troops stationed all round, ready for the right moment. And now his moment had come. He reached into his pouch, pulled out his little trumpet and blew. This would show Lowa, he thought, who the greater Warrior was. If she somehow lived through her forthcoming defeat, a defeat at his hands, he'd find her and they'd have it out, a fair fight this time, no hand behind the back tricks, a good, proper—

Something hit his head very hard. He staggered. That almost knocked me over, he thought, and whatever it was feels extremely odd. *Why can't I see?* he wondered. Then he wondered no more.

Lowa looked to the source of the thin blast. Smoke billowed clear and she saw the squat figure of Yilgarn standing on the wall blowing his little trumpet. Immediately she regretted letting him live. She'd known of his treachery the year before because he'd been seen coming back from the Roman camp. This year he'd been useful. She'd fed him the line that she expected Caesar to tarry at the coast, watched him go and deliver it, then seen Caesar march inland immediately, exactly as she'd wanted.

And then she'd let Yilgarn back into the army, thinking to use him to deliver made-up plans again. The notion had crossed her mind that he might do more than simply report her plans to Caesar, that he might sabotage her, but he was so valuable as a planter of false information and so lacking in nous that she'd gambled that he wouldn't. The instant she saw him blowing that stupid little trumpet she knew she'd lost the bet.

She flipped up her bow and shot him in the head. But it was too late. As she strung a second arrow she saw Yilgarn's Haxmites, spaced evenly all over her defences, ruin everything. Several shot fire arrows into the buckets of pitch, sending flames bursting over her troops and the wall. A few of them lobbed torches into the buckets of whale oil piled up next to the catapults, which exploded with great gouts of flame. She saw one creeping up on Mal, hatchet in hand. She shot him, but there were many more, lashing out at the scorpion crews with swords and pushing the giant bows off the wall.

The Maidunites reacted well. There was a swift counter and within perhaps twenty heartbeats all three hundred Haxmites were dead, and already men and women were running to douse the wall, but it was all too late. Almost all the scorpions and all of the catapults, as far as she could tell, had been destroyed.

She'd wiped out one Roman legion, but the other four were fully intact and ready to march on her barely defended fort.

"Put your hand in my mouth!" Chamanca commanded.

Thankfully Chamanca had slapped the idea of questioning orders out of Yanina a long time ago, and the girl immediately jammed a hand between the Iberian's waiting teeth. Chamanca lapped the girl's palm, already bloody from her fight with the legionary, then bit into the pad at the base of her thumb and sucked as the four African archers loosed their bows. Four arrows flew as warm blood flowed down Chamanca's throat. Time slowed. The missiles came at them like fat pigeons. Chamanca whipped up her sword and slapped them out of the sky. She steered the horse at the archers with her legs, blade in one hand, mace in the other, Yanina's bleeding hand clamped in her mouth. The archers saw what she planned and tried to escape, but for Chamanca they were no faster than statues. She sliced open two of their heads and clubbed the other two. The world whooshed in and time returned to normal speed and she galloped off. She took one last, long suck at Yanina's hand then opened her mouth.

"You can have you hand back. Are you injured?" she shouted.

"Never been better," said Yanina quietly but firmly in her ear, linking her hands around the Iberian's midriff again, pressing up against her back and resting her chin on her shoulder.

They skirted the corner of the Roman camp and pelted along the sand, sea and burning ships on one side, burning wall on the other. The heat tightened Chamanca's skin, blood from the girl's injured hand ran down her stomach and into her shorts. She was wildly happy. There was no situation in the world, not one, that wasn't improved by a few gulps of blood.

The few Roman sailors who had escaped the warships and swum ashore were clustered in the shallows, away from the heat of the burning wall. None tried to impede their passage. Chamanca guessed they weren't in the mood to give death another chance so immediately.

As they neared the end of the camp, she saw out to sea that her chariot attack had succeeded in its goal of burning the warships and half the transports. Judging by what she'd seen on the other side of the camp and the seaward wall, they'd destroyed a good bit of the Roman camp, too. She looked back along the beach. She and Yanina had been the last of the Maidunites to escape, but there was no pursuit. Many had died, but she wasn't going to let that dent her mood. They'd won! She grabbed the girl's hand, held it to her mouth for another suck of blood, and galloped on.

Spring despised Ragnall, but he was right.

"I can't kill you," she said, "you're too harmless."

His eyes widened in anger and he shouted, "Ferrandus, Tertius, to me, quickly!"

"Big badgers' bollocks" said Spring, lifting the knife from Ragnall's neck.

The two praetorians ducked into the tent. If they were surprised to see Spring straddling Ragnall on the bed and brandishing a knife, it didn't show.

"Yup?" said Ferrandus.

"I caught her crawling out of the back of the tent," said Ragnall. "Your chain wasn't good enough. So first wrap her in this chain and secure her so she can't escape again, then go and get a better chain."

Ferrandus looked at Tertius, lifting his lower lip into a "What do you reckon?" expression. Tertius nodded.

She climbed off, considered attacking the praetorians for a moment but quickly dismissed the idea. She didn't want to hurt these good men.

Looking apologetic, Tertius gathered the chain, then both he and Ferrandus attached it around her arms. They tied her legs together and fastened her feet to the bed with a short length of rope. She tested the bonds. There was no give in them. It was strange to think that such nice men as Tertius and Ferrandus knew how to tie someone up so that they wouldn't escape.

"And now get some better chain," said Ragnall.

"She will come to no harm while we're away," said Tertius. "I will look after her."

The praetorians left and she was alone with Ragnall.

He rubbed his temple where she'd punched him, then his jaw. He touched his ribs on both sides, wincing. The leg squeeze must have bruised him, she thought.

He looked at her. She'd seen that look on other men. Quintus Cicero, for example.

"It's not my fault you got hit," she said. "You shouldn't have attacked me."

He advanced, shaking his head. She strained at the chain and rope to no avail.

"You should have let me go! You should have come with me! It's not too late, I'll tell Lowa that you—"

"You and Lowa," he growled, "you're as bad as each other." He raised a fist.

"Ragnall, no, you're not yourself. You'll regret it if you—"

He swung at her. She dropped back onto the bed, lifted

her bound feet and kicked her heels into his chest. He staggered back and fell on the other bed. He lay there for a few heartbeats, panting, then sat up, looking even angrier than before. He leapt, knocking her kick aside this time. She tried to roll away, but he turned her onto her back and scrabbled until he was straddling her, as she'd been straddling him not long before. He was heavy, and smiling horribly.

"Ragnall, no! Stop! I'm sorry I hit you, but you—"

He punched her in the mouth. It hurt a little. She looked up at him, eyes wide and pleading. It had no effect. He punched her again and again and again.

Spring rolled her head with the blows, as Lowa had taught her, but after the third it began to hurt properly. She hadn't expected this. He wasn't strong and he was a bad puncher, but he was heavy and he was putting weight into his work.

"Stop!" It was Tertius. He grabbed Ragnall by the shoulders, yanked him off Spring and hurled him to the floor. She heard Ragnall exhale in pain and craned over to see Tertius kick him in the stomach. Ragnall curled into a ball. Tertius glanced at Spring, shook his head and unsheathed his sword.

"No!" she said.

The praetorian put his sword away. Ragnall scrabbled to his feet and fled from the tent.

Chapter 12

Mal found Taddy Ducktender cradling Gale Cossach's head in her lap. Her friend was either unconscious or dead. Judging by her pallid, greyish skin, it was the latter. When this was all over, Mal decided, he'd ask Lowa if he could lead the revenge raid on the Haxmite tribe.

"Come on, Taddy, there are a few scorpions intact and I need you," he said, putting a hand on her shoulder.

She looked up, her blood- and soot-stained face beautiful in her hazelnut helmet of hair, and nodded. She laid her friend down gently, walked over to the corpse of a nearby Haxmite, pulled her sword from his chest and said, "I'm all yours."

Despite the very recent deaths of several scorpion crew, almost all of whom had been friends, Mal smiled. He'd just been reminded why they had to defeat the Romans.

The fires on the palisade wall were all doused, and no real damage had been done to the structure. They were lucky. As Mal and only a few others knew, the inside of the wall was packed with flammable material. If any of the Haxmite fires had set that off, then Mal himself would have perished along with Lowa, Taddy and all the other Maidunite defenders on the wall.

There were bigger problems. Of sixty scorpions, fourteen remained operational. Three were being fixed and the rest were smashed beyond repair. All the fire bucket ammunition for the catapults had been destroyed, and nearly all the fire arrows were burnt. Relatively, not that many Britons had been killed, leaving out all three hundred Haxmites, but the Haxmite insurrection had been a complete success and might well do for them all yet, because the Romans would be coming soon and they had nothing that would stop them.

Mal crossed over to the palisade edge to see what the enemy were doing. They were still body-collecting. Scores – hundreds – of dead legionaries littered the churned farmland in front of the fort. Pairs of unarmed legionaries walked among them, searching for the injured and bearing them away, well within British bow range but unmolested. Lowa had allowed this. When she'd signalled that the Roman stretcher-carriers could come forward, Mal had been impressed and surprised by her magnanimity. It was the right thing to do, of course, but she didn't have to do it, and it gave the enemy a close and relaxed view of their defences. Now he looked at the size of the Roman army, he realised with a swelling of depression that she was probably just being practical. They were massively outnumbered and, objectively, their chances of winning the war were slim to none, so Lowa was probably being merciful to the Roman injured in the hope that they'd be kind to captive and wounded Britons. On the plus side, the lull in action also gave him, Lowa and the rest of them time to rearrange the defences and get as many of the scorpions back in action as possible. He got back to it.

A while later he was startled by a trumpet blast. A Roman rode forward, bare-headed to show that he was a non-combatant. He was a stiff-backed man with an off-centre patch of white at the front of his otherwise black hair, as if he'd been shat on by a bird. He looked up at Lowa's command tower and raised his sword. Lowa raised her bow.

The Roman rode away. The battle was back on.

What would Dug have said? thought Mal. Something along the lines of *great big bags of badgershit*.

*　　*　　*

Jagganoch pulled the long blade from the third crippled elephant's neck. The noble animal sighed mightily and gushed blood as he died. Had he been at home in Africa he would have nursed all three injured beasts and they would have had a good chance of returning to health. Here, on this cold shore, that would have been impossible, so he'd finished them. Three more elephants had been killed by the British charioteers, making six dead in total. He'd been surprised. He had not expected the milk-white people in their silly vehicles to kill any of his magnificent animals.

Around him, at least, his remaining elephants were finally eating properly, gorging on the dead. An elephant would pick up a dead or nearly dead person by the ankle with his trunk, swing them into his mouth, and suck and chew the flesh and blood from his bones. He would usually have watched them, it was a sight to see, especially if you fed them a living specimen, but right now he had work to do.

He'd gathered the survivors from the crews of the three injured elephants so that they might watch in shame as he put down the beasts. They looked at him now, rabbit-eyed. Perhaps the British were in fact braver than his own men.

"And this was all done by the same woman?" he asked them. His narrowed his eyes at the fools. A rider had never, ever, got behind Bandonda, and never would.

"A small woman, dressed in very little. She was a goddess, I think. I saw her rescue another woman. She picked her from the ground as if she weighed nothing, then four archers fired arrows at them. On horseback, she hit the arrows away as easily as if they were apples hanging from a tree, then killed the archers with a blade and a mace before any could jump out of the way. Oh, she was a goddess."

"Then she rode away?"

"Yes."

"And you did not follow her?"

"I was on foot, she was on a horse. I had no bow. I could only watch her go."

Jagganoch flashed up his club and drove it into the underside of the man's chin, knocking him over. The others jumped away and the driver lay, clutching his destroyed jaw and staring wildly at Jagganoch.

He probably faced a slow, horrible death from infection. The man had angered him, and what use was an elephant driver with no elephant? But Jagganoch was not without mercy. He would do the same for the man as he had for his elephants. He raised his club for the death blow, then changed his mind. He whistled to Bandonda, who ambled over immediately, the ground rumbling as he came.

"No, no!" the man with the broken jaw managed.

Jagganoch smiled, pointed at him and ordered Bandonda the to eat.

He turned to the others and the worms shuffled away, looking at their feet, trying to avoid catching his eye and risk the honour of being eaten by Bandonda.

How he hated them. Looking at them, shuffling and inadequate, flinching as Bandonda sucked the meat off their screaming comrade, he considered giving them all to his mount. But no. Among these devil milk skins, Romans as well as British, he needed all the Yonkari that he had and, besides, he did not want Bandonda to be sluggish from overeating on the return journey. Despites centuries of being trained to eat flesh, the Yonkari elephants reacted badly to too much and it was best to keep them mostly on their natural diet of roots, fruit, grass and bark.

He gazed eastwards, in the direction the woman had flown on her horse. She'd beaten him in a fair fight and she'd killed three of his elephants, so she was good, but she was no goddess. Next time he met her he would break her limbs and feed her to Bandonda.

* * *

Ragnall stood on the smouldering wall surveying the scene
of dead men, women, horses and elephants. On the far side
of the field, the bronze-helmeted African leader put down
three injured elephants. It was not an everyday sight. Seeing
such incredible and fascinating events and, even better, being
part of them, was one reason – perhaps the main reason –
why Ragnall had joined Caesar on his campaign and become
a Roman. The exotic and the epic excited him. Surely, he'd
told himself, he was born to live in the thrilling Roman
world, not the boring British one. If his life had run as his
parents intended, he would have returned from the Island
of Angels, married Anwen and helped his elder brothers
with the mundane machinations of managing a medium-sized
tribe until mortality claimed him. That would have been it.

Zadar had put paid to that by slaughtering his family and
changing the course of his life for ever. There were moments
when he allowed himself to thank Zadar for freeing him
from the shackles of background and parental expectation
that held so many others back. But more and more he was
realising that Zadar had ruined his life, and he would have
been happier, much happier, as one of the top cows in the
small field of Boddingham.

The battleground didn't thrill him; the idea of being king
of all the British tribes appealed no longer. Nothing about
being Roman excited him any more. He wanted to go back
in time, save his tribe from Zadar and live the comfortable,
easy life he was meant to live.

Out on the plain, the African leader whacked one of his
own men with a club then called over an elephant to eat him.
Ragnall hardly noticed, because he was clenching his fists and
thinking that the person who'd ruined his new life was Zadar's
daughter, Spring. Since he'd saved her life – saved her life!
– she'd belittled him at every turn. He'd been a hero when
they'd found her, he'd been Ragnall the dashing new young
Roman who'd killed the German King Ariovistus. Now, every

day, he felt less of a hero in her presence. She questioned everything he said and somehow she'd managed to dig at everything he thought. Everything! She was always wrong, but her arguments aggravated him like sand in his sandals. Little by little, he'd begun to doubt his convictions and like himself less until finally he had come to loathe himself. He hated his toga, his cut hair, his excellently shaved face and his childish pretence that he could just choose to be a Roman.

More than that he hated that he'd been beaten up by a girl. Most of all, he hated that he'd attacked her when she was tied up. He was a coward who'd lost a fight with a child then attacked that child when someone else had restrained her. Few people hearing that story were going to be rooting for him.

He could picture everyone he'd ever loved – his parents, Anwen, his brothers . . . Drustan – all watching him from the Otherworld, all shaking their heads in sanctimonious disappointment. Sanctimonious? Maybe not. Let's face it, rarely had disappointment been so justified. He was a failure as a Briton, as a Roman, as a person.

He clenched his fists. Tears sprang and sobs shuddered through him. Where had it gone wrong? He'd been the golden child of his tribe! He'd been the best pupil on the Island of Angels! When had he become the sort of man who lost a fight to a girl half his weight and attacked her as soon as she was defenceless?

He knew when. It started when Zadar – and Lowa – had massacred his tribe. Then it had got worse when Lowa had made him fall for her and then tossed him aside like a gnawed bone. As if to reinforce his point, out on the battle-field the elephant flung away what was left of the man it had been chewing on.

Now, finally, when he'd been happy again, Spring had come along and spoiled it all. It was all their fault! He wiped snot from his nose and tears from his cheeks. He wasn't going to cry any more.

First Zadar, then Lowa, now Spring. They were in some Bel-driven scheme to ruin his life . . . That was it! He was a plaything of the gods. They all were. Perhaps one god had control of Zadar's bloodline and another was running his, and losing. Zadar's god had killed his family, used Lowa to make him betray Anwen, made Drustan believe he could control magic when really it had been Spring all along. Yes! The god that was controlling him was losing, but maybe through no fault of its own. Ragnall himself was meant to act! His god was giving him these thoughts even now. It was time for the next move in the game and for once it was going to be Ragnall who made it. And that move was clear. He had to kill Spring.

He couldn't do it himself. Caesar would be angry, there would be an investigation, Tertius and Ferrandus would tell all and Ragnall would be shamed and crucified. Then there was the practical side, of course. First, she was a better fighter. He shouldn't let that upset him. He was a thinker, not a fighter; she was a brute and he was pretty much a genius. But he didn't want to be bested by her again. Second was her magic. He'd seen no evidence of magic since they'd met again, and guessed – hoped – that she'd lost it. Surely she would have used it to escape if she could still control it? But if her life was threatened, it might just surface.

So, he couldn't kill Spring himself. But he knew a man who could, or at least who would have a much better chance of ending the spiteful girl's life.

He smiled, happy to have a project. He climbed down off the wall and walked into the camp, heading for the legate's sick tent. If Quintus Cicero wasn't there any more, they'd know where he was.

While the Romans regrouped, Lowa went to send her son away. There were two points she had to weigh up in making the decision. On one side were twenty thousand or so Romans about to storm her wooden wall, its defences greatly weakened by the Haxmite treachery. On the other was the dream of a ghost. It wasn't much of a contest. She'd heed Dug's warning, she'd listen out for the shout *Demons attacking from the north-west*, but soon this fort was going to a bad place for an eighteen-moon-old child. It was time to remove him.

"Now you be a good boy for Mummy," said Lowa, pulling down Dug's little cotton dress so it wasn't so rucked at his shoulders.

"Haaarbs!" said little Dug, pointing at the horse that was to carry him and Keelin away to the south and then west.

"Horse," said Lowa. "Horse."

"Haaaaaarrrbs!" shouted Dug, with a throaty giggle and a cheery scream.

Lowa picked him up and hugged him tightly to her. He smelt of warmth and life. He hugged her back, then grabbed her ear in a fat little hand and pulled.

"No, Dug, not Mummy's ear," she said, reaching up and prising his paw free. He was strong. Behind him Keelin mounted the horse. Lowa squeezed him one more time and handed him up to his nanny.

Dug smiled uncertainly down at his mother, wrinkling his nose and showing his sharp little white teeth. His eyes were huge and brown in his oversized head.

"Goodbye, little Dug," she said. "Look after Keelin."

The queen turned and jogged away. She could almost feel the child sucking in air behind her and she hadn't gone far when a wail to waken the dead rang out. She didn't turn. She didn't want the boy to be upset, but she was also glad that he was so sad to see her go. A little voice said yes, but he screams like that if you take away the stick he was playing with. Lowa told the voice to bugger off.

Back on the tower, she saw that the Romans were coming. One legion had been all but destroyed by her incendiary attack, but four more were marching at her. They were outside even her range, but their shields were already up.

She looked across the hills to the east, towards the Roman base camp and their ships. The sky over there remained stubbornly blue, unblemished by smoke. Caesar had brought five legions here, which meant he'd left one defending the camp, possibly alongside his elephants. Shouters had reported that the African beasts were heading north, towards the camp. Had they repelled Chamanca's assault before they'd managed to set the camp and the ships alight?

She scanned the land around. She would have heard from her shouters, but it was good to see for herself. The Romans hadn't encircled the fort, they were still coming only from the north, and there was no sign of Felix's dark legion. The latest shout about the demons, from her best shouters who were skilled at throwing their voices in only one direction, said that they were still on the coast. Lowa didn't know why they had stopped there, but she hoped they stayed.

The Romans advancing towards Big Bugger Hill had found only one of her hidden shouters, which was a testament to how well they hid, since they must have walked right over several of them. Simshill the shouter's final shout – "Shouter Simshill discovered!" – had been a poignant one, made worse because Lowa had known her. She was a merchant whom Lowa had persuaded to join her army as a shouter because of her excellent voice. Yet another life Lowa was responsible for throwing away...

She looked to the east again. Was that a tendril of smoke rising up into the summer sky or just a weird cloud?

Back on the plain she saw that a handful of Roman cavalry had come within her longbow range. Idiots, she thought, wondering how many she'd get before the survivors galloped out of range, and wishing she had Spring with her. She would have taught somebody else to shoot the longbow, but she knew that nobody would take to it like Spring, and, besides, it was Spring's bow and she didn't want anyone else touching it. The queen had brought it with her from Maidun, telling herself that it was a spare in case hers was broken, but really she was hoping beyond hope that she could somehow free the girl and give it back to her herself.

Chapter 13

Without fresh kills, Felix reckoned that his Maximen and Celermen were probably right up there with the most dreary creatures in the world. They were never conversationalists at the best of times, but at least when they were vibrating with the power of others' deaths they did interesting things. Now they were just sitting about under the trees, where grass met the sand, staring into nothingness, as stimulating as a pot of slugs. A few of them had walked about a bit earlier, but that had angered Felix because he'd noticed that none of the fucking idiots would cross the high-water mark of dead seaweed. They were terrified of the tide rushing in and drowning them. They'd happily charge an army of any size, but they were scared of dead marine plants. Jupiter's tits, thought Felix.

So he was overjoyed when a centurion turned up, followed by a century of eighty legionaries on foot. Their leader dismounted, removed his helmet and tucked it under his arm.

"Centurion Lucius Aurelius Dolabella reporting, sir! With the first century, second maniple, sixth cohort, Seventh Legion!" He smiled in readiness, then furrowed his brow and said: "Sorry, that's wrong. We were moved. They didn't tell me why and I still don't know. It's first century, *fourth* maniple, *fifth* cohort, Seventh Legion. No, wait, that can't be right, there are only three maniples to a cohort so we can't be in the fourth. By Diana, it's confusing. Sorry! We're here and we're a century, that's the point. Sorry."

Dolabella was probably not even in his twenties, yet he had hair like an old man's – dry, orange-brown and naturally curly, but combed furiously so that the top of his head looked like a minute, precisely ploughed field. He had a long, thin and bony nose, no chin and a small mouth, all of which combined to create a face like an inquisitive rodent's. He was taller than Felix, but he seemed smaller. He had the look of a high-born young man, but shit high-born. The kind of man that Rome's greatest families produced every now and then to their dismay. It was traditional to send sons like him off to their deaths in the furthest flung corners of the empire. And here he was.

"What are your orders?" asked Felix.

"They come from Caesar himself! He spoke to me! He is attacking the Gaulish fort, and he wants you to cover any possible retreat. He said he hoped I'd give my all, and that I was to tell you that I'm completely at your disapproval. No! Sorry! Disposal! My men and I are completely at your *disposal*."

Felix smiled. "We'd better get going right now then."

"Yes, there is one thing. We got really very lost on the way to you, so we took a jolly long time getting here, so . . . there's a good chance the battle's already *started*. I am sorry. But I am sure that I know the way back."

"Then let's go."

"Yes, and one more thing. We were with one of your leather chappies – Brutus?"

"Bistan."

"That's the fellow. When night fell last evening, he went off to find the route. He wasn't back this morning so we carried on and found you as much by mistake as anything else . . ."

"And no sign of Bistan?"

"No. He went north. Or possibly west. Probably not north or he'd be here. Are we north, here?"

Felix shook his head but smiled as well. He genuinely didn't always like ordering people's deaths. But sometimes he did.

Lowa knocked three of the cavalry from their horses and stuck one more in the leg on the extremities of her range as he tried to gallop clear. The Maidunites cheered each dismounting and she got a long "Oooooh!" for the leg shot. It was good to hear them confident and cheery after the Haxmite treachery.

She looked back to the east. There was definitely smoke coming from the direction of the Roman beachhead. Could have been some oblivious forester in the woods in between her and the camp, of course, but it looked further away . . .

"Roman camp ablaze!" came the shout.

The Maidunites cheered. Lowa smiled and beckoned her shouter over.

"Shout that again," she said, "and ask every shouter who isn't hidden to spread it through the land." The shouter did so and the words "Roman camp ablaze!" were repeated twice from all directions, then again more faintly, then again almost imperceptibly. It was a good sound, thought Lowa, a shout going out, even better now that she'd decreed each shout was repeated, hopefully to avoid the misheard shouts as they'd sometimes had in Zadar's day, which had had both hilarious and tragic consequences.

She watched the tiny figures at the back of the Roman army to see their reaction. One of them rode up to the foremost and it was a joy to know that at that very moment a translator was telling Caesar what the shout had said. A glance to the west − yes, there it was − would confirm the words and it pleased Lowa greatly knowing that Caesar was certain to be rattled − mostly by hearing that his camp was on fire, but also because he'd have just realised that the barbarian British had not only killed an entire legion with almost no loss to themselves, but also had a more advanced system of communication than he did.

"Roman ships destroyed!" came the next shout. The Maidunites cheered more loudly.

The queen's shouter looked at Lowa, eyebrow raised. Lowa nodded and the shout went out again.

Chapter 14

Mal had thought the Romans would retreat on hearing their fleet and fort were ablaze to rebuild their bridgehead. Lowa had disagreed. Annoyingly, she was right. Shortly after the second shout, Mal saw riders gallop up to the little command group at the back of the Roman army. Shortly afterwards the Romans trumpets sounded and the remaining legions rolled forwards. All four of them.

All the archers that could fit on the walls were there and ready. Three partially broken scorpions had been fixed and the carpenters had managed to create four more from parts of smashed ones, so there were twenty-one scorpions primed and ready to shoot. Roughly one per thousand Romans, Mal calculated.

The Romans rumbled forwards. Shields went up to form their tortoises well outside scorpion range, not that shields would help them much against a scorpion arrow. He saw that they had a new battering ram, at least that's what he thought the great wooden shed on wheels must be. He walked over to the left of Big Bugger Hill's wall, the part over the gate nearest the approaching ram, and told the three scorpions there to prepare to shoot it.

Behind him, the body of the fort was emptying. All the Britons who couldn't fit on the walls were pouring out of the south gate on the far side of the fort from the coming Romans. He had a while before the Romans were in range. He asked Taddy to shout for him if the Romans started running and walked around the wall to check the retreat was working as well as Lowa had intended.

On the south wall, he shook his head in wonder. If you could call a retreat glorious, this was it. For a couple of thousand paces away from the hillfort, along the flat land between two low ranges of hills, Lowa had ordered two wide, parallel roads to be constructed. On the westward road a stream of empty carts was bouncing towards the hillfort. Each was light but well made, drawn by four horses. On the eastern road, the same type of carts were trundling away, each one carrying thirty troops.

Nearest to Mal, fifty paces behind the hillfort, the western road looped round to become the eastern road. Here was the mounting area. Two wide bridges allowed troops to cross without hampering the flow of the carts, and meant that both sides of the cart could be loaded with passengers at the same time, so that they hardly needed to slow down. The whole idea had apparently been Dug's – the big, dead one, not the child. He and Lowa had often sat late into the night coming up with ways to defeat the Romans. Mal smiled. Dug had always been one for buggering off away from a fight as fast as possible and this rapid, brilliant way of removing as many people as possible from a battle as quickly as possible was truly the work of a brilliant coward. It was just a shame—

"Mal! Mal!" It was Taddy Ducktender, hollering from the far side of the hillfort. "They're coming!"

"You should have let me kill him," said Tertius, leading Spring outside to the better light as Ferrandus ran up with warm water, cloths and pots of who-knew-what to clean and treat her cut, swollen face.

As they eased her into a chair she said: "I shouldn't have. You'd be in trouble and he's not a bad man. He's had a bad time, that's all." She had to hold her hand back from slapping herself in the face when she realised she'd spoken Latin. But neither of them seemed to have noticed.

"What's all that smoke?" she asked in Latin, thinking never mind, she really wanted to talk to someone other than Ragnall, even if opening her mouth hurt her entire face. She thought that her secret would be safe with Tertius and Ferrandus anyway. If, indeed, they actually noticed that she was suddenly speaking their language.

"Burning. Quite a big British attack apparently, or at least an effective one. All the warships and half the transports are gone. Couple of hundred garrison troops killed, mostly by the elephants that are meant to be on our side, so they're saying."

"You don't seem too upset."

"Not our job to be upset!" said Ferrandus. "But this," he said, moving his head around Spring's face and peering at her like a crow looking for the best place to peck an apple, "this it is our job to be upset about. Are you injured anywhere else?"

"No."

"You'd tell me if you were?"

"I would."

"Good, and these aren't so bad. What did he hit you with? A cushion? If all the British men are as tough as him we'll have this island by lunchtime tomorrow."

Spring giggled. "It's the British women you need to worry about."

"If they're all like you, you're right."

"Most of them are even more frightening."

"Talking of frightening," said Tertius, "I'm going to go and find Ragnall."

"Don't hurt him," said Spring.

"I don't take orders from you," said the praetorian as he walked away, still apparently unfazed by her sudden linguistic ability.

*   *   *

He came back a short while later. "Not great news, I'm afraid." He caught Spring's eye. "But you're looking a lot better! It's like nothing happened! Ferrandus might be a complete idiot when it comes to almost anything else, but he does know how to patch people up."

Spring giggled again. She hadn't felt like such a little girl since the peaceful times with Dug. She knew he was lying; she must look like she'd lost a fight with a bag of hammers, but Ferrandus' cool water presses and herbal salve had reduced her swollen lips a great deal and made everything a lot less sore.

"What's the bad news?" she asked.

"I caught up with Ragnall at the medicine tent," replied Tertius. "When he'd gone a doctor told me that he'd been asking . . . Hang on a minute! Why are you speaking Latin?"

"Ah," said Spring. "That." She felt heat spread up and through her cheeks.

"Juno's big brown arse!" laughed Ferrandus. "I hadn't even noticed. I've been chatting away to you! Have you been able to . . . Of course you have! You've been able to understand us this whole fucking time . . . ever since the beginning, right?"

Spring grinned and nodded then greatly enjoyed watching the two men looking at each other, their mouths open in unison, both saying "Fuck!" then looking at the floor, trying to remember what they might have said.

"Don't worry," said Spring, "you've both been perfect gentlemen. Not like the first lot."

"How long have you been able to speak Latin?" Ferrandus was shaking his head.

"Maybe ten years?" said Spring.

"And Ragnall doesn't know?"

"He doesn't."

"Well I'll be . . ."

"Would you mind . . ."

"Keeping it quiet?" said Tertius. "Sure. Ferrandus won't spill your secret either."

"I don't take orders from you, but by happy coincidence I'm not going to tell anyone," Ferrandus pouted.

Tertius smiled. "Yes, well, to business. Ragnall was at the medical tent looking for Quintus."

"Hercules' piss," said Ferrandus. "Blokes don't like it when little girls beat them up. Apart from Tertius that is, who loves it."

"Not as much as you like little boys who——" Tertius looked at Spring. "Ah. Sorry."

"It's OK, it really is. I do think you Roman soldiers are all very strange, but I'm used to it now."

"So then," said Tertius, "he got us to tie you up, and then he attacked you when you were helpless?"

Spring wrinkled her nose. A scab cracked and she felt blood trickle.

"I'll take that as a yes," said Tertius, as Ferrandus leant forward and dabbed her newly opened wound with a cloth. "Sorry to ask, I just wanted to be sure of what the fucker is guilty of before we hunt him down and pack him into his own scrotum."

"No, you should leave, he'll probably be on the way back here already with Quintus and a gang. You should both leave."

"Nope," said Tertius

"Seriously. They'll kill you to get to me, but they'll still get to me. If you're not here, same thing happens but you don't get killed. Makes sense, no?"

Both men looked at her, shaking their heads. "No," they said in unison.

"Then let me go. Take me to the edge of the camp and set me free."

They looked at each other. Tertius shrugged and Ferrandus nodded. "All right."

"You're going to free me?"

"Yup."

"Oh good! That is good. Just let me get my—" She stopped and looked at the praetorians. They both looked very sad. Realisation dawned. "What will happen to you if I get away?"

"Possibly washing-up duties for a week," said Tertius.

"Or, more likely, crucifixion," Ferrandus added.

"Idiot!" Tertius punched him on the arm.

"Well, it's true, isn't it?"

"I've another idea," said Spring. Escape had been right there, but she couldn't let these men die for her. "There's somewhere in the camp you can take me where I should be safe."

"Where?"

"To the one other person who knows I can speak Latin."

"Who's that? Caesar?" said Tertius.

Spring shook her head.

"Ah!" Ferrandus slapped his forehead. "I bet I know who it is."

"Who?" Tertius pursed his lips.

"Remember that posh bird who brought her back after she castrated Quintus? That one with legs all the way from her feet to her cun— Sorry. The one with the legs?"

"Clodia Metelli?"

"Give that praetorian a truffle-stuffed mare's vulva," said Spring.

Chapter 15

As soon as the Romans were in range of the scorpions, they sped up into almost a sprint, while maintaining their tortoises. It was what Lowa would have ordered, too. The quicker they came, the quicker they'd be in the shadow of the wall and safe from the scorpions.

Mal shouted: "Shoot!" The scorpions bucked and twenty huge arrows flew at the Romans. One missile bounced off the top of the wheeled roof protecting the ram without doing any damage to the ram or its draught oxen. Two others dropped short but the rest scythed into the Roman ranks. Many fell but others stepped over their comrades' destroyed bodies and filled the gaps with their own shields. The formations that had been hit were a little more ragged, but their pace didn't slow for a heartbeat. They came within arrow range, and Lowa gave the order to shoot, even though she knew it would have little effect on the shielded legions.

By the time Mal had the second bolts primed, several hundred legionaries and the battering ram were at the wall, safe in its lee from scorpion fire. The archers were raining standard, non-burning arrows but these were finding few fleshy targets. Lowa's arrows were spearing feet and ankles revealed under shields, but none of the others had anything like her accuracy.

Under the protection of shields, she could see legionaries clearing away the caltrops and other devices that filled the ditch. She wondered if that was common practice or whether

Yilgarn had tipped them off to the unusual number and variety of traps. The latter, she suspected.

"Shoot scorpions! Pour fire on ram!" shouted Mal. Scorpion bolts slammed into legionaries further back. Men and women stationed over the gate hurled the few remaining fire buckets onto the ram's protective roof, followed by their last salvo of fire arrows.

The moment this second volley of scorpion bolts was loosed, the legionaries parted, leaving a clear swathe open for a couple of dozen carts, each pulled by four oxen armoured in thick leather, all galloping towards her wall.

What in Bel's name was this? The carts were piled high with what looked like earth. Was it earth? Or was it some incendiary material that Lowa didn't know about? Great Danu's shits, she hated a mystery.

Behind her the fort was empty of Maidunites. Carts were waiting for the troops on the wall. The transports carrying the rest of the infantry away to safety were already out of sight. Way beyond them, surely clear of danger, were Keelin and little Dug.

The Roman carts came into her range. She shot the front right oxen of the foremost cart between the eyes. It stumbled and went down, but the other three kept driving forwards and the cart kept coming, albeit a great deal more slowly. There was smoke rising from the hooves of all the oxen. The Romans must have stuffed red-hot iron barbs into their feet, she realised. That was one way of keeping an animal running as it strove to escape the pain, although not great if you were planning for that animal to walk again.

The other Maidunite archers had no effect on the beasts. Lowa shot a second animal on the foremost cart and that stopped it, but the rest, goaded by the legionaries on either side, crashed into the wall.

Lowa tensed for the explosion and a tower of flame, but nothing happened. The mighty palisade, which had taken hundreds of men and women a year to build, stood firm against the assault.

She peered over the edge at the mass of flailing oxen and smashed carts. It *was* earth – or little more than earth, anyway. Each cart had been packed with boulders, wood and soil. She looked along the clear swathe between the legionaries. More carts were coming, at least double the number that had already hit the wall. Lowa saw their plan.

There was a shout from the Romans. Twenty paces out, all along the wall, men popped up from behind shields and slung stones at the Maidunite archers. Several archers were hit, but by the time Lowa or anyone else had taken aim the slingers were back behind shields. The archers all strung arrows and watched, ready for the next slinger unveiling, but a small group popped out, took out a few archers and ducked back behind shields before any of them were hit. This happened again and again. It was like the game at fairs and festivals when you had to hit one of six woollen rats with a mallet as they appeared briefly from their holes, except these rats could kill you.

With each reveal, more and more archers were hit by stones. Lowa saw a young man she knew – he'd been an apprentice baker when she'd recruited him – stagger and fall from the wall. With the archers trying to spot where the next gang of slingers would rear their heads, and ducking to avoid their salvos where they did, the number of arrows shot at the legionaries was much reduced. They took advantage. Many dropped their shields and rushed in with poles, spades and spears to finish off the oxen and pile up bovine carcasses, crashed carts, earth and rubble against the wall. With the amount of debris hurtling towards the fort, it wouldn't be long before they could just run up on to the wall. Clever, she thought, shooting one of the ramp-building legionaries, then another.

A slingstone whizzed past her ear and she fell to the

ground as several more whooshed through the space she'd occupied moments earlier.

It was about time, she thought, to—

"Demons heading for Big Bugger Hill!" came the shout. Followed by "Shouter Touchnight discovered!"

"Makka's tits," said Lowa, fear lurching through her. They weren't the words that Dug had said would herald her son's death, but they weren't far off. But she had to forget about that and focus on the battle

She peeked over the palisade. The Roman ramp was already halfway up the wall. Had she intended to keep the fort, there were a couple of things she might have done about it. As it was, the plan had always been to flee and the time had come. She shouted the order, Mal repeated it and the archers streamed off the wall and out of the gate to the waiting carts. The only ones who didn't run immediately were the couple of dozen who'd been instructed to remove a few key planks and set fire to the dried twigs and grass that was packed throughout the wall's interior.

Lucius Aurelius Dolabella's troop contained enough men for the Maximen and Celermen to have two each – one to fuel the journey, and one for the attack. Felix shouted the order and held Dolabella at sword point while his Maximen and Celermen killed one and crippled one man each.

Dolabella gibbered at the sight of his men being massacred and disabled. Felix apologised for the inconvenience and, while the death-fuelled Celermen chased down a couple of the faster-running legionaries, he told Dolabella who he was, about his legion and how he'd created them, and how they were working for Caesar.

When he'd finished, Dolabella said: "A secret mission! How exciting!"

They ran inland, the Maximen carrying wailing legionaries. Dolabella led the way on horseback like a true hero of old, Felix galloping behind him, grinning and looking around to see if he could spot Bistan. Where could his head Celerman have got to?

To Felix's surprise, Dolabella not only found the way to the battle, but took them to probably the best vantage point, a hill to the west where they were hidden from the Roman army but could see the British position and their route away from the Romans.

The battle was over. The fort was ablaze and the Britons were retreating to the south in fast carts along a broad road. It gave him a little thrill to see a mounted blonde figure riding alongside the carts – Lowa. They were clear away from Caesar's legionaries, who hadn't yet passed the fort, and there were only a couple of thousand retreaters in view, so he guessed that the main body of the army was long gone. That didn't really matter because his men would be able to chase down and kill all the ones he could see, and that included Lowa.

"Dolabella, get off your horse."

The idiot boy did as he was told.

"Come over here." Felix pointed to the nearest Celerman. "You, hold him."

Dolabella looked worried but didn't try to flee as the Celerman took his skinny arms in strong, leather-encased hands. Felix put his own hands round Dolabella's neck and pressed his thumbs into his windpipe. The centurion's eyes bulged as Felix squeezed with all his strength.

As the boy goggled and tried to breathe, his reddening eyes staring terrified into Felix's, the druid was surprised to feel an erection growing in his leather riding trousers. Even more of a surprise was a sudden and powerful urge to press against the boy and lick his face as he died.

Why the Hades not? he thought. Pretty soon he'd be king of the world, so he might as well get used to doing exactly what he wanted all the time. He thrust himself against the centurion's shuddering groin and lapped his face from chin to eye. He licked again, this time lingering on the lips, all the while squeezing his neck and grinding his hips against his victim like an enthusiastic older man on a drunkenly compliant girl at a dance.

When it was done, Felix stood, panting, watching the British army retreat. His skin prickled with a mixture of excitement and something else, something he hadn't felt for a long time . . . It was shame, he realised. Oh yes, there was shame there, for sure. Frotting young men as he murdered them was not what his father had brought him up to do, and it was a pretty long way from societally acceptable behaviour, even in Rome. Surely it was his imagination, but he thought he could feel disapproval emanating from the hooded Celermen. But neither others' disproval nor his own shame was going to stop him. The feeling was too good. Ideas of what else he could get up to flooded in, but there was work to be done, so he held them back. For now.

He gathered his troops around.

"In a moment, I'm going to order you to kill the remaining legionaries, and attack that." He pointed to the fleeing column of Britons. "However, there are three important things to remember. Are you all listening?"

Iron helmets and leather hoods nodded.

"Good. First, is that the Maximen will be first to attack, the Celermen behind them. As you've seen, the British have good arrows, very good arrows. If they begin to shoot before we're among them, then the Maximen should raise an arm like this," he held a protective forearm across his forehead, "to protect the eye slits in your—"

"Which arm?" Gub's voice sounded out, all the more booming from inside his thick iron helmet.

"The one that's not holding your sword."

"OK!"

Felix shook his head. "Second, when I blow on the whistle

twice, you will stop the massacre, even if there are more men and women to kill." He did not want them running amok at the Roman legions. "Got it?"

They all nodded.

"Sure?"

More nodding.

"Good. Third thing. There is a blonde woman on a horse called Lowa. She will have a bow which is very dangerous. Avoid her arrows, and, more importantly, catch her but do not kill her. Got it? Hold her unharmed, or as unharmed as can be."

They all nodded.

Felix smiled and climbed back on his horse. "Right. Kill one legionary each and FOLLOW ME!"

He galloped towards the fleeing British, leading the charge while they were well out of range, knowing it wouldn't be long before his legion caught up and overtook.

Lowa pulled her horse to a stop, leapt up and stood on the well-trained animal's back, looking at the burning fort and scanning the low wooded hills to either side. There was no sign of Roman pursuit; neither Caesar's infantry, nor cavalry, nor Felix's legion.

But where were the demons? Judging by when Touchnight had shouted they should have seen them by now. Perhaps Caesar had held them back? Or perhaps . . . perhaps they had unseen scouts that had divined the direction of their flight. Perhaps the demons had been sent to head off the retreat. Foremost in the retreat were little Dug and Keelin.

Sudden fear for little Dug gripped her. Without thinking, she kicked her horse and galloped up the line. The carts were fast, for carts, but on horseback she was much faster. People shouted at her as she passed but she didn't hear them. She had to get to her son.

Then she heard the shout she'd been dreading. "Demons

attacking from the north-west!" It came from behind her, nearer the fort, and it meant that the demons were attacking the rear of the retreat that she'd just left. Little Dug was at the head, but those were the *exact words* that his ghost father had claimed would precede his death.

She was torn. Her place was where she knew the demons were attacking, back behind her, leading the defence. But she already knew what she was going to do.

Pleading with the gods to let her get there in time, as the carts of infantry archers turned to meet the foe, she kicked her horse and sped westwards, away from the attack.

Chapter 16

As the three of them marched through the Roman camp, Tertius puff-chested and threatening on one side and Ferrandus watchful and ready to pounce on the other, Spring chewed the inside of her cheek, looking up each new road or gap between the tents, expecting to see Ragnall, Quintus and a gang of legionaries charging at them. She was fairly confident that Clodia would take her in. Yes, she'd returned Spring to Ragnall the last time, but things were different now and she was sure that Clodia would understand. She hoped she'd understand.

Around them all the fires were already extinguished and the camp was sensibly abuzz with its usual well-ordered business. Surely, Spring thought, immediately after a massive attack there should be an air of desperation in the camp, or at least mild panic. But no, panic would be irrational and the sensible course of action was to pragmatically carry on, so that's what they were doing. Many of them had been killed that morning, yet, other than the smoke still rising from the remains of the east wall, anyone waking up late and leaving their tent would think it was just another day in the garrison. By Toutatis, she thought, these Romans were marvellously efficient and boring as boring could be.

Finally they arrived at Clodia's quarters.

"Fuck me, she does all right for herself this one, doesn't she?" said Ferrandus.

Indeed she did. Next to Caesar's tent complex, Clodia had the same little wooden stockaded camp as she'd had in Gaul, complete with gate and four gate guards dressed in newer-looking, shinier and more colourful versions of legionaries' armour. Instead of legionaries' gladiuses they were armed with long, curved swords.

"Nice swords," said Ferrandus to the guards.

"Queen Spring of the Britons, to see Clodia Metelli," said Tertius.

A gate guard raised an eyebrow at Ferrandus, then turned to Tertius, nodded and headed into the enclosure. He came back moments later and said, "In you go then."

"Spring! Spring!" Clodia came loping towards them across an immaculately swept courtyard. Smart little tents lined the walls to either side and ahead was her own great purple and white construction. Clodia was wearing a simple, short white dress, brought in at the waist by a broad leather belt with scabbards on either side, each holding a curved dagger with a jewel-encrusted hilt. "I am *very* glad to see you. I wasn't sure if you'd come across the sea and— Oh, but look at your face! What *has* happened? Come, come into my tent. I'm sure we can work out some kind of sign language so you can explain. You praetorians – Secundus and Ferrandus, isn't it – you can stand guard if you like?"

"Tertius," said Tertius.

"Tertius, how silly or me, of course." She smiled winningly.

"I'd rather we came in—" started Ferrandus, blushing a purple to match Clodia's tent.

"And I'd rather you didn't. I admire your dedication to the girl but she looks like a gladiator who's just had the thumbs-down, so your protection isn't *that* effective, is it? Do stand guard, though, if you'd like. She'll be fine with me and you can dart in if you hear screaming."

Clodia walked backwards into her tent, beckoning Spring with both arms like a farmer encouraging a calf into a stall. Spring nodded at her praetorians that everything was all right and followed the Roman woman through the wide porch.

Spring's first thought was that Dug would have liked Clodia's tent because it was cleverly ventilated. Outside the air was thick with the heavy tang of burnt palisade and ship, but, despite four open roof vents that allowed the faintest of breezes to shimmer the drapes, Clodia's vast tent smelt of fresh and floral incense. It was the same scent, Spring realised, as the one that Clodia wafted wherever she went. So Clodia had paid people to create a fragrance for her tent that matched her personal perfume. That pretty much summed up for Spring all that was impressive and awful about Rome.

Clodia poured two silver cups of watered wine from a long-necked silver jug and handed one to Spring. Smiling at the girl, she unbuckled her dagger belt, dropped it clatteringly onto a table that might have been made of bronze, then sat on a purple couch and tapped it with a palm to indicate that Spring sit next to her. She did. Clodia crossed her long, deeply tanned legs and leant in, wafting a briefly stronger wave of that musky floral scent. Spring blinked.

"Tell me what happened," the socialite gasped, sounding thrilled.

Spring told her. Clodia made appropriate concerned noises and shocked faces throughout. At the end she said: "So you want me to protect you, because my brief acquaintance with you is more important to me that my years of friendship with Ragnall?"

Spring nodded.

"And you hope that, after meeting you twice, I'm prepared to take on a man as powerful as Quintus Cicero and risk all this?" Clodia waved her hand to indicate the riches surrounding them. Spring followed her gesture and took in the giant vases, intricately painted screens, lustrous golden furs and other luxuries that Clodia had decided were essential invasion kit.

"If you wouldn't mind?" asked Spring.

Clodia leant back, her mouth a taut line. Her eyes sparkled as a corner of her lips lifted into a mischievous smile.

Lowa crested a hill and the front of the long column came in sight. It was marching on, no demons in sight. She could even make out Keelin just back from the head of it, some four hundred paces away, trotting along carefree, holding a bundle that was surely little Dug.

She'd been a fool. She'd believed a ghost, a figment of her imagination, and she'd deserted her army in its moment of need on a paranoid dickhead's errand. What had she been thinking . . .

No, there, sprinting from the trees, was it . . .? It had to be. No normal man could run that fast. It was a solitary Leatherman, heading straight for Keelin and little Dug. Lowa did not have her recurve, only her longbow, which was too long to shoot while mounted. She dragged the reins, commanded her horse to stay still and leapt to stand on its back. She nocked an arrow, drew, followed the Leatherman's course with the arrow tip, compensated for his speed and the wind, and loosed.

The demon ducked, the arrow sailed over his head and he ran on, closing on Keelin and Dug, certain to get there before Lowa. She dropped, slammed her heels into her mount's flanks and shouted at it to gallop as fast as it could.

The Maidunites had seen their ambusher. Other arrows launched. Six cavalry sallied out to meet him, swords ready. Others gathered round Dug and Keelin. After the Two Hundred's last stand on the beach, Lowa had drummed the danger of the demons into her troops and it looked like they'd taken her seriously. It was as good a defence as could be offered by their numbers.

The Leatherman tore into the six cavalry, spun, leapt, hacked and sliced and ran on moments later, leaving four of the Maidunites unhorsed and the other two slumped in their saddles. He reached the knot of riders surrounding her son and jumped into it, sword flashing. One went down, then another, then she saw Keelin fall, still holding little Dug. The demon loomed over them.

Lowa hurled her bow, jumped from her galloping horse, rolled, snatched the bow from the air and an arrow from her quiver and fired at the demon's back.

He went down. Whether he'd dived on to her son or been hit by her arrow, she did not know.

She ran to the site of the skirmish, jumped over an injured, kicking horse and found them.

Keelin was lying on her back, little Dug next to her.

"Hello," said Keelin.

"Mum!" said Dug.

Next to her son lay the Leatherman, her arrow sticking out of his back. She nocked another one and shot it into his head.

"That's the first time he's said 'Mum', isn't it?" asked Keelin.

Lowa nodded, then looked around frantically. There did not seem to be any more demons around.

"Keep him safe, will you?" she said, already turning to run to her horse and gallop back to the attack on the rear.

Atlas heard the second shout, "Roman ships destroyed!" more clearly. It was a relief to hear that Lowa was managing without him, but maddening not to know more. So the fleet and the camp were burnt, but at what cost? And what of the rest of the army? For all he knew Caesar's legions, elephants and demons could be tearing into the outnumbered Maidun forces at that very moment.

"Did you hear that, Nan?" he asked the old woman, who was bustling at her bench. She didn't reply or even acknowledge that he'd spoken.

He tried to sit up and managed only to lift his head. He let it fall back with a sigh.

Chapter 17

Lowa's horse was lame by the time she got to the battle site because she'd pushed it so hard, but the fighting was over. The dead and parts of the dead were spread across the valley, horses and men strewn between and across broken chariots and carts. Their injuries were horrifying, the worst she'd seen on a battlefield, even though in her youth she'd regularly fought beside Atlas, whose speciality was cleaving people from shoulder to hip with an axe.

Huddles of survivors were dotted around, crouching over friends who were moaning, screaming or silent.

She rode past one dead Maximan, a sword protruding from the eye slit of his bucket helmet. He had a giant sword in one hand and was holding a man's leg attached to part of a torso in the other. He was the only enemy dead she could see. The armour was almost identical to that worn by Tadman Dantadman the day Dug had killed him in the arena. Was Tadman the forerunner of these monsters that Felix had created, or had they already existed? Surely they had to be more than six years old? Or were they men, twisted and grown by magic generated by the slaughter of Danu knew how many? Focusing on questions like that stopped her from confronting the horror around her. So many had died in such a short time . . .

Sickening waves of guilt flowed up from her stomach. She should have been here. She should have met the assault. But then her son would be dead. She couldn't have stopped all these people from dying and she probably would have been killed herself. And there was the shameful knowledge that, given the choice of saving her son or all these friends, allies and subjects, she would have chosen her son every time. She had chosen her son.

She asked around and found Mal. He was sitting on a shattered cart. Lying on the ground in front of him was the throat-slit corpse of Taddy Ducktender, the woman Lowa had punched for letting the scorpion bolt off early. Seeing Lowa, Mal laid Taddy's head down and stood. He seemed strangely calm.

Never explain, never apologise was a maxim she'd heard. It was meant to be particularly useful for rulers, and most of the time she agreed with it. This wasn't one of those times. Mal and her troops needed to know why she'd missed the battle. She explained where she'd been and apologised.

"And little Dug is safe?" said Mal

"As far as I know, yes."

"And he would have been killed if you hadn't gone?"

"Yes."

"Then you did the right thing."

"Thank you, Mal." She put a hand on his arm and he nodded. "Tell me about the attack here."

Mal shook his head wearily and pointed at a hill to the west of the smoking remains of the fort.

"The demons ran down that hill. We spotted them in time to turn the carts, hand out arrows and string bows, but the Ironmen led their attack and Elann's arrows did nothing more than dent their armour. We might as well have been shooting at rocks."

"Where were the Leathermen at this stage?"

"Sheltering behind the Ironmen."

"How ordered was the Ironmen's attack?"

"Not at all. Other than Ironmen first, Leathermen second, they had no order. But they didn't need order. Before they reached us, I gave the signal for the heavy chariots to attack their flank from those trees." He pointed westwards. "The Leathermen saw the threat and ran to neutralise it. Before the chariots had a chance to swing round and bring their bows to bear or dismount their infantry, the Leathermen were among them. They were even faster than the Ironmen. They leapt from chariot to chariot, killing the crews with astonishing efficiency. Rather than tire and slow down they appeared to speed up."

Mal closed his eyes and Lowa could see he was struggling not to weep. She held out a hand to him.

"Sorry." He pushed her arm away, sniffed back his grief and carried on. "When they were almost on us, I led a charge. Up close, the armoured giants looked even bigger. They're not human, Lowa. Men don't get that big. They hit us and they ran through us. They didn't even try to parry our attacks. They ran through us, chopping our people apart as they came. It was bad. I was knocked aside – only Danu knows how their blades missed me – then they were past us, among the archers. They lifted and smashed the carts as if they were toys, killing dozens. We killed just one. Taddy put a sword through his eye slit."

"That was well done."

"It was, but the beast killed her with his arm blade as he died." He nodded down at her body and shook his head.

"How many Leathermen were killed?"

"Ten in total, I think, two by infantry arrows and eight by the heavy charioteers."

"Why did the attack stop?"

"There was a double whistle blast. They withdrew immediately and ran back the way they'd come. Each of the giant men took two captives, one under each arm. Given what you said about how they get their power, I ordered archers to shoot those captives."

"You did the right thing."

"Did I? It didn't feel right, and we didn't hit many of them."

"Did you see the whistle blower?"

"Yes, it was Felix. He was with a man in a gold chest plate and red cloak, Caesar, I guess, and several black-clad legionaries. All were on horseback. When the monsters ran off up the hill Felix rode with them. The others headed back to the fort."

"Any idea why they retreated?"

"No. They could have killed us all."

Lowa looked about. The number of corpses made her catch her breath as much as the stink of spilled guts. "Any idea of our losses?"

"Nothing accurate, but the heavy charioteers say half of their chariots − about three hundred − are destroyed and maybe three hundred charioteers are dead. Many of the survivors are injured. For the infantry, deaths are around six hundred, and injuries . . . I don't know. A lot." He looked down at Taddy, dead on the ground. "I . . ." Finally his tears came. "I'm sorry . . ." he managed, turning and walking away.

Lowa felt sick. This was a defeat. It was her fault. Soldiers she could fight, but these things . . . What could she do?

Quintus Cicero was surprisingly genial when Ragnall found him at his collection of tents. He already knew that Spring was sheltering with Clodia and intended to head there as soon as he was able to walk.

"Stay with me until then! It will be a couple of days at most," said Quintus. "The doctor johnnies told me to drink wine to dull the pain between my legs and that is what I have been doing. I suspect they mean to dull the anguish of losing my manhood, but really there is none. Although that may be because I have been following their advice. You there! Bring more wine and a cup for the king of the Britons!"

On his way to see Quintus, Ragnall had begun to doubt his plan of encouraging the man to murder Spring. On the one hand he had to stand up for himself. He owed it to his ancestors to win this game of the gods. All he'd done so far was to be pushed about by others. Killing Spring was the start of pushing back. On the other hand, he was encouraging a man he despised to kill a young woman.

He was confused, and the drink was very welcome. He downed the cup in one and sat down next to Quintus.

"Ha!" Quintus raised his cup in salute. "Bring more wine for the king and me! More!"

The following afternoon, while Quintus slept off the morning and lunchtime's drinking, Ragnall walked into the camp. It was brighter than usual and sounds echoed boomily in his head. He was drunk, but not that drunk. He'd been right. Drinking had been exactly the right thing to do. It hadn't resolved his quandary but he no longer cared about it.

Stopping to eavesdrop here and there, he learnt that the five legions had returned overnight after attacking a fortress which the British had burnt before the legionaries could take it. Almost an entire legion had been lost in the first attack, and the rest of them had returned to the camp with no gain. Very few British had been killed and they'd retreated intact.

Meanwhile, the British chariot assault on the ships had destroyed all of the warships and half the transports. The mood in the camp was a strange mix of subdued and bellicose. Some were whispering that there was nothing but death in this wild land, that they should cram onto the remaining ships and return to Gaul. Others were exercising and sparring with swords, eager to return to battle.

Soon all began to flow into the centre of the camp, for Caesar's address. Ragnall joined them and stood in a crowd of legionaries, auxiliary soldiers, smiths, cooks, quartermasters and others.

The general climbed up on to his speaking platform and the men cheered as if he'd just won a great battle. He waved, nodded, gestured for silence, then congratulated the troops on two great victories. His words punctuated by much manful cheering from the crowd, he described how the legion left behind to guard the camp had shown its mettle in repelling the cowardly chariot attack on a supply centre. Meanwhile, the other five legions had successfully conquered the south-east of the country. Yes, they had lost some boats, but this was due to their inferior Gaulish construction. There had also been some fire damage to the camp, but it was already repaired.

"First," Caesar finished, "we will rebuild this camp, larger and mightier so that it may serve as a Roman town and the link between Roman Gaul and Roman Britain. Then, country-men, the legions will march inland and shine the light of Roman glory on this benighted isle!"

Ragnall walked away with the masses, much cheered by Caesar's words. He hadn't thought of the British chariot attack as cowardly, after all a relatively small number had attacked a stout fortress garrisoned by five thousand men but, when you thought about it, the hit-and-run method of attack was pretty spineless.

He headed back to Quintus' camp. Hopefully he'd be awake by now and they could resume drinking.

"Caesar demands you pay compensation to the families of those that your elephants killed."

Jagganoch bristled. He took orders from nobody apart from his father, and his father was Sobek knew how many miles away. The little general was afraid of him, that much was certain. If Jagganoch had needed to see the general he would have gone by himself. Caesar had ridden to the Yonkari camp hidden among a gaggle of large men in black leather armour. The guard was pointless. Had Jagganoch wanted to kill the general, they would not have stood in his way.

"I have none of your sestertius coins to pay the families of the men who threw themselves under the feet of my elephants as we defeated your enemy. And I would claim from them reparations for the six elephants killed. Had not your worthless men got in their way, none of the noble beasts would have died."

"The legionaries would have defeated the chariots without you. You acted against orders and caused the death of Romans, and for that you must pay. However, given that your intentions were to defend Rome and strike against her enemy, Caesar will not take anything that you already have. Your reparations will come from your portion of the proceeds of the invasion."

"Fine." Jagganoch cared nothing for his "portion of the proceeds of the invasion". If he wanted something, he took it.

"Now you will return to your base in the south with your beasts and await the order to move inland."

"There is no food. The land is stripped. My elephants and troops were promised bountiful farms and slaves. There are none of these things."

"Even now ships are crossing from Gaul directly to your southern base. You will have all the food you need shortly. Until then, you will show the same fortitude as the legionaries and live on half-rations. Is Caesar clear?"

Jagganoch had no choice but to bide his time and agree with the little man for now.

"Caesar is clear," he said.

Chapter 18

Lowa, Chamanca and Mal sat at a table in an otherwise empty tavern. They were in a walled town, in and around which her infantry were billeted for the night. Lowa had sent its inhabitants north with their food and valuables as soon as Caesar had landed. She'd done the same all over south-west Britain. For several days' ride into Britain, there was nothing for the Romans: no food, other than a few ducks and hedgehogs, and no people, other than Lowa's army.

"Right," said Lowa to her remaining deputies. "Gains and losses. Chamanca first."

"Where is Atlas?"

"We will come to him."

Chamanca and Mal reported the figures of Britons lost and Romans killed. It was bad, particularly for the infantry and scorpion crews, but it wasn't terrible and the Romans had lost many more. Mal, however, had not taken it well. His tone was flat and any liveliness that had begun to return after Nita's death was. Lowa guessed that Taddy, the woman whose corpse had been at his feet, had become his lover and her death had hit him hard. She didn't have time to ask about it, though, let alone console him.

"We face three Roman forces," she continued. "First are the six legions and the cavalry, now five legions. They have returned to the bridgehead base at the coast and will not come inland for a good few days as there is no forage. If they'd brought enough fodder for an inland campaign from Gaul, they would have stayed at Big Bugger Hill and waited for their provisions to be carted to them before continuing inland. So they will have to wait for supplies from Gaul. Given their reduced fleet, that should take a while.

"Now, the elephants. They are reduced to thirty-six at most, and, according to shouters, they have returned to their base at the coast. We will keep watching them. They may prove to be a problem."

"Because Atlas hasn't come back with the Aurochs?" said Chamanca.

"I have sent a dozen riders to the forest of Branwin to find out why."

"I will go myself."

"You will not, Chamanca, I need you here. You crippled three elephants, you say. How?"

"On horseback, no chariot. Without the aurochs, that is the way to fight them."

"Good. So you will take charge of the cavalry and teach them how to bring down elephants."

Chamanca nodded.

"And then we have the demons. Shouters report that they have returned to their original landing site, Corner Bay, a day's ride to the north-east from here.

"So that's their forces. Here's our plan. While shouters keep a close eye on all the Romans, I will lead our infantry back to the newly fortified Saran Fort, halfway between here and Maidun and on the edge of the area we have cleared of people and forage. If we are lucky, the Romans will decide that there's nothing for them in Britain and they will leave. However, having come this far for a second time, with so many more men, I do not expect Caesar to give up so easily. He will march inland.

"Now, the demons. Mal, you think Caesar made Felix call them off today?"

"I do, but before you go on, I have an idea for the demons."

"Yes?"

"The demons think that they have us terrified, and they'd be right."

"I am not terrified!" said Chamanca.

"So they won't be expecting us to attack them," Mal continued. "I will take a small force of fifty for a night raid on their base. If the gods are with us, the Ironmen will be out of their armour. We will kill as many as we can before they wake up."

"When they'll kill you," said Lowa.

"Probably." Mal held her gaze.

"You don't have to do this."

"I want to. There are people in the Otherworld I'd like to catch up with."

Lowa sighed. It was a good idea, but Mal and whoever went with him would be unlikely to make it back.

"I won't help you escape, Spring," said Clodia. "I am a Roman and you're a Briton, so you're my enemy, aren't you?" She gripped Spring's knee and smiled. "If you were a happy little peasant farmer who yearned for her hillsides and her sheep then I might let you out because I'm kind, but you're not, are you?"

"No."

"No." Clodia shook her head, wafting a floral scent from her shiny hair so intense that Spring could taste it. "You are a beautiful barbarian princess with every intention of fighting against the Romans, using information that you've gathered during your time with us, aren't you?"

"Yes. Apart from the beautiful barbarian princess bit."

"Oh, Spring, there's nothing more boring than a beautiful girl who claims that she doesn't know she's beautiful. You've seen the way people look at you and you're not stupid, so no more of that. So, moving on. As well as intending harm to our war machine, you humiliated and insulted Ragnall, who is officially Roman, and you castrated Quintus, who is definitely Roman, and an attack on any of us is an attack on all of us."

"They both asked for it. Anybody would have done what I did."

"Spring, my sweet, no, they wouldn't, but that doesn't matter. They're Romans and you're not. Maybe you'd get away with assaulting Ragnall because he's not a real Roman and you hardly hurt him. Quintus, however, is a senior legate with a good deal of influence and you castrated the old goat. Possibly Caesar might be able to explain to the consuls, the senate and the people why he didn't allow Quintus to punish you for that, but it would be an effort and I don't think he'd bother. I believe that you acted in self-defence. I believe both men were in the wrong. I'm particularly disappointed in Ragnall, who seems to have been ruined by his time in the army. However, they are Romans, you are not, so it doesn't matter whether you were acting in self-defence or if you planned your attacks for months with the specific aim of undermining the Roman war machine. I should hand you to Ragnall and Quintus immediately."

"Really?" asked Spring.

Clodia stood and poured herself some more wine, then held the jug out at Spring with an inquisitive twist of her head.

"No, thank you," said Spring. "Can you send Tertius and Ferrandus away when Quintus comes to get me? They'll defend me and I don't want them being killed too."

Clodia laughed, replaced the jug, walked back over, stroked Spring's hair for a short but, for Spring, exquisitely awkward few moments, then sat back down. "So there's no reason to help you, but I've never liked reason. You can stay here in my compound, in my tent with me."

Spring's eyes widened. Was this what the knee-touching and hair-stroking had been leading to?

"Not like that, don't worry. I'll have your own bed set up." Clodia put her hand back on Spring's knee, which rather weakened her reassurances.

"Can Ferrandus and Tertius stay, too?"

"They are commanded to guard you?"

"Yes."

"Then they'll have to, won't they?"

"Oh, thank you!" Spring leant in and hugged her.

Clodia laughed and pushed her off gently. "Calm yourself, Spring, there's a condition attached."

"Which is?"

"You have to tell me everything. All about your life from the start, and everything you know about Britain and its people, particularly this Queen Lowa. In fact, let's start with her then we'll get on to you."

Spring leant back. Did Clodia want information to help the Romans?

"Oh, don't worry," said the socialite, seeing the look on Spring's face. "You don't need to tell me anything that might help Caesar. I want to know about Britain because it fascinates me. That's why I'm here. Not to fight, but to learn. There is nothing better in life, Spring, than to discover the world around oneself. Will you indulge me?"

"If you like. I am a good talker."

"Good. We will start immediately. Wait here while I tell your loyal praetorians what's happening and have someone find them a tent. And, while I'm gone, drink that wine. I cannot bear conversing with sober people."

"OK!" said Spring as Clodia swept from the tent. She looked about for somewhere to tip the wine.

Ragnall couldn't free his arms no matter how much he struggled, Spring's legs were too strong, but when she stood up and towered above him, his arms remained pinned by his sides as if still clamped between her powerful thighs. She laughed at his pathetic attempts to free himself. As she laughed, she changed from Spring into Lowa, then whipped off her leather riding shorts with one tug and thrust her naked hips forward.

Where her vagina should have been was a penis, as big as Heracles' from back in those early days at Clodia's. She wiggled her hips and it slapped weightily from side to side. He watched, mesmerised. She took it in her hand and leant over him, so the tip was above his mouth. He thought, no, she's not going to . . . But she did. A couple of spurts that made him blink at first, then a great wash of piss straight into his face. He thrashed his head from side to side, but couldn't stop it going in his mouth. He wasn't really trying to. It tasted like the finest white wine and he stopped struggling and opened his eyes and Lowa was urinating straight into his mouth and he was gulping it down like a thirsty man guzzling sweet water and looking her in the eyes and she was nodding, half a smile on her cruel, beautiful face. He didn't try to move as she crouched down, straddling him again. She squeezed her legs, clenching him, and he quivered with pleasure as she guided her girthy cock towards his waiting mouth. She put a hand under his head to lift it, but she didn't need to, he was eagerly craning forwards, straining to open his lips wide enough . . .

And she was gone and he was awake. He moaned with shame when he realised that his own real-life penis was burstingly erect, then moaned again as the tendrils of his hangover found his brain and penetrated deep into it, choking it with pain and filth. He pressed his hands into his eyes. Those evil women had found their way into his dreams. They had humiliated him time and time again, and now this! There was no escape.

But there was, of course. Today was the day. Quintus was going to kill Spring. Lowa would be dead soon after that. And then, surely, his dreams would be happier?

Chapter 19

Elann and Nan took an arm each and helped Atlas outside. He slumped down into a low-slung but sturdy wooden chair, exhausted. How, he wondered, was he going to get out of this chair? Let alone defeat the entire Aurochs tribe and Manfreena the druid, then get two hundred armoured aurochs to Lowa's army before it was too late?

The clearing around Nan's hut was green and leafy, with what seemed to be an unnatural number of butterflies all flitting through it in the same direction to some unguessable common destination. Elann stood nearby, silent as usual. Nan had shuffled off into the woods again. It was great to be out here, free from the noisome air of the hut, with the sun on his face, even if it wasn't in the most convivial company. As he waited for his strength to return sufficiently so that he might speak, he wondered which god it was who'd decided to make a joke out of his life. Dwyn, the British god of mischief perhaps? Who else would find a man who could hardly talk and give him the two least talkative women in the world for company?

"I thought Manfreena had you under her spell?" he managed eventually. Elann looked at him then looked away and Atlas remembered that you needed to ask her direct questions, not just make a statement that invited embellishment.

"Why are you not under Manfreena's control?" he asked.

"I don't know," said Elann.

Slowly, Atlas discovered that when Lowa had sent Elann

to the Aurochs tribe to make armour for their giant cattle, Manfreena had welcomed her and delegated people to help. Elann had known immediately that Manfreena was a druid who had both the Aurochs and Ula's Mearhold tribe under her spell, and that she was likely to use the armoured aurochs against Lowa rather than giving them to her, but Elann had been sent to make armour for the aurochs, so that's what she did. On her visit to Big Bugger Hill, she hadn't told Lowa or anybody else about Manfreena because nobody had asked. It seemed to Atlas that Elann was blind to everything that didn't directly concern smithing. Even on the day that Zadar had died and Lowa had become queen, hammer blows had rung out from the blacksmith's hut from dawn till dusk as Elann had carried on smithing.

However, she'd acted out of character by carting his unconscious body to Nan, a druid who lived in the woods, whom Elann knew from her younger days. Atlas guessed she'd done it because he had been a good friend of her dead older son, Carden, but, no, she said it was for her dead younger son, Weylin. Atlas was one of very few people who'd treated Weylin almost like an equal and she'd appreciated it.

"Well, I'm grateful," said Atlas, "but maybe you could have found a more communicative druid?"

"Are you unhappy with Nan's care?" Elann asked, surprising Atlas with an unsolicited comment.

"No. Although she ignores my questions, her food is disgusting, her hut stinks and she's away most of the time."

"The chair you're sitting on is her bed."

"She sleeps outside?"

"She doesn't choose to and at her age she shouldn't. But there's only room for one person on her bed in the hut."

"Oh."

"And she is almost totally deaf."

"Ah."

"Yes. The drink she's been giving you is to purge the evil

magic with which Manfreena riddled your body. These ingredients are rare, so she spends much time in the woods searching for them."

"I see."

"The stew is a stronger cure, containing ingredients that are even more difficult to find and unpleasant to prepare. Her hut does not usually smell like that."

Atlas shook his head.

"She speaks only when necessary because she's worried how she sounds, since she can't hear herself."

"Oh no. You must take me for an ungrateful shit."

"I do. But you're a man. Men are shits. So are women." As Elann was saying all this, Atlas was flattered at the same time. He was pretty sure that this was the most she'd ever said to anybody, her own sons included.

"I'm sorry to have been ungrateful to Nan, but I have been very ill and I need to—"

"Shits always try to blame their shitty behaviour on anything but themselves."

"All right, I'm sorry. But can you help me get those aurochs and their armour to Lowa?"

Elann paused for so long Atlas wondered whether she was going to answer him at all. Finally, she said, "I have made some modifications to your axe which will enable you to defeat Manfreena, if you don't fuck it up. But we cannot do anything until you are stronger. Eat more of Nan's stew."

"I will. Do you know what's in it?"

"I do. It's best that you don't."

Mal crouched in the trees a hundred paces from the demon camp. An eye-wateringly foul odour filled the air around like a thick fog. Originally he'd thought it came from the corpses of the Two Hundred which had been left to rot above the tideline, but he knew now that the gag-inducing reek came from the camp itself. If anything confirmed that the demons needed to be exterminated, it was their monstrous stench.

His volunteer fifty were hidden along the treeline. Almost all had lost friends or lovers at Big Bugger Hill to the demons, were itching for revenge and unafraid of consigning themselves to the Otherworld. Mal was looking forward to seeing Nita again. No doubt she'd ask him quite why he'd taken so long to join her and who the Bel was this Taddy he'd been chasing after. But he'd still be glad to see her. And Taddy too . . . how was that going to work?

A large, dark cloud obscured the moon and the time had come. Mal hooted like an owl. He felt shapes rise in the darkness all around him.

They ran from the trees, silent in their soft leather foot covers. He willed his feet to stay light, praying he didn't step on a twig, or, worse, run into a demon sentry.

They reached the tents unimpeded. As planned, men and women peeled away, some ducking into the first tents they came to, some running on with him. He was heading for the newly built hut which reconnaissance had identified as Felix's, taking care not to trip on guy-ropes.

There was a scream, a shout, another scream. Mal sprinted, all pretence at stealth gone, sword in hand. A shape blocked his way – a giant man. Mal thrust with his blade, but the shape melted to the side, flailing a backhand punch which Mal sensed more than saw. He ducked and stabbed and was surprised when his blade struck home, into flesh. So the Ironmen did take their armour off, he thought, as he thrust, up under ribs and into the creature's heart. It fell with a sigh. Mal ran on, to Felix's hut. The door opened as he raised his arm to push it. It was Felix. Mal slammed his blade into the druid's chest.

Felix ran down the hill, then he sprinted into Rome's forum. He couldn't find anyone. They'd all gone. He was the only person left in the world! Finally he had power but they'd all gone! He knelt on the marble tiles, looked around and it was an empty Maidun Castle, spinning around him. He screamed.

His scream morphed into another scream and he was awake. And people were screaming, in his camp.

He leapt from the bed, tripped on his blanket, untangled it from his feet and rushed out, naked into the night air. He saw the man and the sword at the last moment and turned, but the blade sank into his chest.

"This is for Taddy," said the man. "And you didn't kill Nita, but it's for her, too. Wouldn't want her to feel left out."

Felix wondered why the man's face was dirty, then realised that the camp invaders must have muddied themselves camouflage. He gasped, the man smiled and pumped his blade in and out. Felix could feel the metal inside him, tearing his lung to pieces. Then his attacker's head was gone, replaced by a stump spouting blood. The headless assassin fell back and the sword went with him, sucking out of Felix's chest. He would have fallen too but strong hands held him up. It was a Celerman.

"You all right, boss?"

"Get me . . ." He coughed blood. That wasn't good. "Set me down, gently." He sucked in the life-force flowing from his attacker, but it wasn't enough. "Get me live captives, quick as you can."

For the next two days Spring told Clodia everything. The Roman was infinitely more interested in Britain than Spring had ever been in anything. She questioned and probed and theorised as her eyes danced with the joy of knowledge. Spring rather regretted not making more of her time in Rome. She should have found out much more about the city and its people, she realised, not so that she'd know how to defeat them, but simply for the satisfaction of knowing. She resolved to be as inquisitive as Clodia from then on.

While Clodia took her daily rides up and down the coast – the ones that her guards had told her were too dangerous but that she went on anyway – Spring sat with Ferrandus and Tertius, questioning them about their own lives. They seemed surprised at first, and hesitant, but soon they were gabbling away and Spring realised that she'd be able to learn pretty much everything about Rome without going back there, which was a relief.

For now the whole Roman army was holding on the coast, being supplied from Gaul, repairing the few ships that could be repaired and rebuilding the camp. They were enlarging it so that the new ships and the mended ones could be *taken out of the sea and kept safe within the camp's walls*. Spring had thought they must be joking or exaggerating, but Ferrandus her assured that, no, this was exactly the sort of crazy project that Caesar liked to undertake every now and then. The gates were widened and heightened and such mighty gate towers built that five hundred men guarded each gate, all the time, with thousands more ready armed and on call. Spring was rather proud that the Romans were going to so much bother to keep out little old Lowa.

Caesar's tent complex, next to Clodia's compound, was to stay in the same place as the whole camp was rebuilt, still the hub. However, on Spring's second day there, two toga-wearing legates marched in and ordered Clodia to dismantle her temporary home and move it to a site that had been cleared for her, next to the stables by the new north wall. Clodia, smiling all the while, asked the legates to follow her into her tent. Shortly afterwards, they'd walked quickly from the compound, both red-faced. Clodia's box stayed where it was and nobody else came to tell her to move.

Spring asked, but Clodia wouldn't tell her what she'd said to the legates.

Spring was enjoying herself a great deal in the mini camp. She was mindful that she needed to escape at some point soon, but Clodia insisted that her ankle was chained to something the entire time and her guards were permanently on watch. They weren't as useless as they looked. There was no massive rush, though, as the army wasn't going to move for a while. They were still waiting for the transports to fully resupply the army, and work was ongoing in the gigantic camp.

Then, in the middle of possibly her most fun chat with Clodia yet, on the morning of the fourth day, Ragnall and Quintus arrived.

Chapter 20

Clodia's flamboyant guards might have guarded Spring effectively, but they were no match for Quintus' squad of ten legionaries and six Cretan archers. Swords to their necks, the guards stood aside as the toughs kicked open the gate and ran in.

Ragnall followed. Quintus limped in behind him.

Tertius and Ferrandus brandished swords, ready to fight, but the Cretan archers' bows were drawn and aimed.

Spring held up her arms and gestured for the praetorians to stand down. She glanced at Ragnall and he felt his resolve shake. He looked away. No, she had to die. She was bent on ruining him and he had to stop her. He would make his own destiny from now on. In memory of his parents and for his own sake, Zadar's daughter had to die. He knew he was right. It had been difficult, but spending the last few days drinking heavily and talking to Quintus had helped. Alcohol opened the mind, and Quintus had helped him see his predicament from a Roman man's point of view. The Britons were fools to allow women so much power, because they twisted it and used it against decent men like Ragnall. It had been happening all his life and it had to stop. He had to harden his heart and stop treating women as equals. Spring had to die.

"Give me your swords," said one of Quintus' toughs. The praetorians looked at Spring. She nodded. In unison they flip-tossed their swords, caught them by the blades, and handed them to the legionary.

"Hands on your heads," he said.

They complied as Clodia emerged from her tent, looking, Ragnall had to admit, fantastic. She spotted him.

"Oh, Ragnall, you poor thing, you look simply awful. What has happened to you? Why don't you ask your fellows to leave, and rest here for a while. You've had a terrible time, it's clear. You need to recuperate. Stay here. I will make you feel better."

Her lovely smile and the invitation in her voice might have stopped a charging elephant, but Ragnall's days of being wowed and pushed around by evil women were over. Over! From now on he'd be tougher than a charging elephant.

"I don't need to feel better," he said, "I need a Roman man to see justice visited on his barbarian attacker."

"Ragnall, she is your wife. You know what happened."

"She's not my wife. We didn't marry properly." Tougher than a charging elephant, he told himself. "But even if she was my wife, she is a barbarian who attacked a Roman and she must face justice."

"If I might cut in here," said Quintus with a smile, his voice as quiet and calm as a giant wave heading for shore, "Ragnall, I'd like you to leave. I don't want you to see this."

Ragnall looked at Spring, for the last time he hoped, and strode from the compound.

Atlas walked from his bed, out of the hut and sat in the chair. Nan smiled and nodded. "You'll be right soon!" she said, reddening as she did so.

The short journey had exhausted him, but it was encouraging nonetheless. It was only that morning that he'd stood unaided for the first time. After Elann's talk, he'd been wolfing down Nan's stew and he did feel a lot stronger. He felt sick most of the time, too – the stew was vile – but definitely stronger.

As he mustered the strength for the return journey to the bed, Elann appeared.

"Manfreena has enchanted twelve Maidunite cavalry who came looking for you," she said without preamble. "We will move against her as soon as you are able."

Atlas looked at Elann. She was stocky but child-height, with black eyes bulging from a head almost as large as her torso. Her disproportionally massive hands were flecked with countless pink burn scars. Her dark hair wasn't cut short, it was burnt short by constant forge accidents.

"Why will you help me?" he asked.

"Get better. I'll be back every day until you're ready." She turned and walked away, leaving Atlas confused in his chair.

Spring's first thought, once she'd stopped Tertius and Ferrandus from sacrificing themselves, was how awful Ragnall looked. In the few short days since he'd fled their tent, he'd lost much of the fat he'd gained in Rome. His usually pristine toga was wine-stained and hanging off him like a cloth draped over a pole. His eye sockets were so sunken and black that it looked like he'd found Clodia's make-up trunk and used all of it in one go.

She was about to say something to him, something kind, something helpful, but Clodia came out and did it herself, in a much better way than Spring could have. But Ragnall rejected Clodia's offer and called Spring a barbarian, which was just weird, considering they came from the same place so if she was a barbarian then so was he.

When Quintus sent Ragnall out, things got scary. Ragnall had had the chance to kill her before, when he'd been in a rage, but she'd never thought for a second that he would. Quintus, she was certain, would not think once, let alone twice, before chopping her head off or crucifying her or something else horrid. The only bright lining was that he wouldn't be able to rape her first. Although, of course, he could get someone else to do it. *Oh no*, she thought, *that's probably what he's going to do* . . . Surely Clodia wouldn't let him? But what could she do?

Clodia stood in the entrance to her tent. Quintus regarded her calmly, legionaries at each shoulder. His six archers still had their bows drawn and arrows nocked, one of them pointing at Spring, one at Clodia and the other four at Tertius and Ferrandus. The praetorians were glowering with rage, alert and ready to leap into action, but they were unarmed with their hands on top of their heads, so she hoped they weren't going to try anything.

"Why don't you come into my tent for a moment so we can talk about this?"

"Thank you, no," said Quintus. "Can you go into your tent and stay there, please? I'd like to have a word with young Spring here."

"But surely—" Clodia tried.

"Now," interrupted Quintus.

Clodia looked at the legionaries and the archers, sighed and ducked into her tent.

The legate turned to the praetorians. "You two, sit on the ground."

"And keep your hands on your heads while you do it," snarled a legionary. They looked about as far from happy about it as Spring had seen anyone ever look, but she nodded frantically at them, trying to look confident, and they did as they were told.

Quintus turned to her for the first time and looked at her with his incongruously avuncular eyes. Spring felt like she had spiders running all over her skin. He beckoned her over. She went quickly, keen to prevent Tertius and Ferrandus from trying anything. He walked to Clodia's summer seat, an ornate iron bench with room for two, sat down, and tapped the cushion next to his. Spring sat. Quintus took her hands and looked into her eyes.

"I want to thank you, Spring," he said, "from the bottom of my previously black heart."

Spring peered at him. She could see no duplicity. He looked sincere.

"Um?" she said.

"I know you can't understand me, but I'm going to tell you this anyway. I didn't like what I was. I thought about sex all the time, and I took it whenever I wanted it. I always hated myself immediately afterwards, but I couldn't stop. I had dozens of comely young slave girls and boys in Rome and I used them horribly. Some of them pretended to like it, possibly some of them even did, but mostly I could see that they hated it and they hated me. I'd feel so, so bad afterwards, but I'd soon forget and I'd do it again. All men get these urges."

No, they don't, thought Spring.

"And then I came for you," he continued, "which was simply unforgivable. I used the excuse of Ragnall hitting me, but I deserved that hit. And now I'd like to thank you from the depths of my heart for chopping my balls off."

She almost laughed. He did not seem to be joking.

"I mean it, I really do. I don't think about sex at all now. I'll be a much better man from here on, a better soldier, and, ironically enough, a much better husband to poor, poor Pomponia." He chuckled. "Well, hopefully. She's still a fearfully unpleasant woman but I daresay much of that is my fault because I was a much worse man. But I'm not any more, all because of you!"

So are you going to let me go? Spring wondered.

Quintus chuckled. "Now, having said all that, you may have made me a better man, but you still castrated me, and for that you have to die."

Chapter 21

Felix ordered his Celermen to chain the new prisoners while Maximen stowed the provisions. They'd intended to use captive Britons as magic fodder, but they had only the ones that the Maximen had carried from the battle. Luckily there was an army of Romans nearby, and in a group of people that size there were always some who needed to be punished and others that commanders wanted to be rid of for a variety of reasons. A selection of these were sent to Felix daily, the unwanted guarding the miscreants. While the Celermen chained the criminals, he'd give their guards a couple of amphoras of the strongest wine and ask them to drink with him. Once they were relaxed, the Celermen would restrain them. Drinking with them was usually a bore since they were mostly boorish men, but he had to incapacitate them to ensure none escaped and talked about the secret legion.

Thinking of escapes . . . It had been close, far too close, but the Celerman had brought him a captive in time and Felix had mended his own injured chest. Thank Mars he'd managed to shift so the man had stuck him on the wrong side, and only destroyed one lung instead of his heart.

He'd cured the wounds of several others, but four Celermen and six Maximen had been killed. Six Maximen! From the British perspective, it had been a successful attack. All fifty Maidunite raiders had died, but they had given their lives expensively. One of them had very nearly killed Felix himself. He'd never had a wound like it before and he had not enjoyed it one little bit.

It would never happen again. He'd been certain nobody would attack his unbeatable legion and he'd been a fool. They probably wouldn't strike a second time, but from now on he'd light up the camp every evening like Rome on a Triumph night, and have one third of his men on a rotating, constant guard. One third of his twenty-three remaining men. Twenty-three, down from sixty at the start of the previous year . . . It was bad. He would certainly not tell Caesar that he hadn't posted any guards.

Thank Jupiter some of the Celermen had woken in time. Used well, his twelve Celermen and eleven Maximen could still destroy any army. If Caesar let him, of course. He'd been incensed the general had called off his attack on the retreating Maidunites. Felix had had to obey, though, his legion was powerful but it couldn't take the Britons alone. Once they'd defeated Lowa's army the chance to kill Caesar would come, and Felix would be ready.

Quintus' guards grabbed Tertius and Ferrandus and held blades to their necks.

The legate stood and unsheathed his sword. Spring jumped back, putting the bench between them. Quintus advanced.

The compound gates crashed open and black-armoured praetorians rushed in.

"Swords and bows down now! All of you!" shouted a man who epitomised the word "beefy". By his golden helmet, Spring realised he must be the praetorian centurion, the only man apart from Julius Caesar who could give orders to Tertius and Ferrandus.

One of the archers was too slow. The centurion's sword flashed, smashing the bow and opening his throat. The Cretan went down with a gurgle.

"Stop, stop, everybody calm down," Quintus raised his hands. "There's no need to—"

And the only other man whom Tertius and Ferrandus

took orders from marched into the compound, Clodia looking hot at his heels.

"Quintus is right," said Caesar. "There is no need to. Everyone stand down." He glanced at the dying archer and his eyebrows flicked, in what looked like distaste rather than surprise. He turned to the legate. "And what is happening here, Quintus? What business do you have with Clodia Metelli and the queen of the Britons?"

"None, Caesar. In fact I was just going."

Caesar nodded once.

Quintus limped out, followed by his troops, the Cretan archers carrying their dying compatriot.

Chapter 22

Ragnall walked into Caesar's little tent town in the middle of the tent city, next to Clodia's stockaded compound. The praetorians let him through as if he were expected. He had come to join the army. Having nothing to do all day was driving him mad, and he envied the industry and the camaraderie of the Roman soldiers. He'd had a dream the night before in which he'd explained this to Drustan, who'd told him that lack of achievement was causing his misery. The secret to happiness, the elderly druid had explained, was to impress oneself every now and then. The path to impressing oneself was endeavour, and the army would provide Ragnall with plenty of endeavour. Moreover, it would stop him drinking so much.

He'd woken and known that Drustan was right. He needed to do something, to be a part of something, and the army was the obvious solution.

Caesar was pacing in a canvas-sided courtyard, dictating to scribes. "The Britons have no corn nor other crops, they live on milk and meat. They shave their entire bodies other than their upper lips and heads, where they grow the hair long. Their shaved bodies they dye blue. They have no sense of love or marriage, instead woman are shared between groups of men, especially brothers and fathers—"

He spotted Ragnall, held his finger up to indicate that he should wait, and continued: "We will come back to the British later. Back to the campaign. To repair the storm's destruction the legionaries worked day and night. They

brought the repaired ships ashore into the enlarged camp
to avoid further ravages from the weather. More ships arrived
from Gaul and these too were taken into the camp. The
Britons, fearful of the might of the Romans, remained at
bay while Caesar consolidated his foothold."

The general waved a hand to indicate he was finished
dictating for now and strode over to Ragnall.

"Hail, king of the Britons! You are looking well. Not so
fat."

"Thank you, Caesar. I would like to march inland as a
legionary."

"You cannot. You will be king, Caesar has decreed. Your
queen must not be disappointed."

"The queen is dead."

"Is she? She looked alive earlier today."

What was this? Was he joking?

"Clodia Metelli is her keeper now,"

"But I thought—"

"Ragnall, Caesar does not care for the details of domestic
disputes. He understands that you argued with your wife.
This happens. It will happen again. Although Caesar is no
great paragon when it comes to matrimony and should not
seek to lecture, he advises two things. First, do not take
these spats seriously. Second, keep your arguments private.
To have one's public business known by all is noble, to have
one's private business known is not."

Ragnall nodded. So Spring was alive. He was glad. He'd
been ashamed of his role in attempting to have her killed.
But at the same time he still wanted her dead for all that
she'd done to him, and for her father's murder of his family.
He was confused. Again! It was exactly quandaries like
this that made him want to be a soldier. Forget Drustan's
"impress yourself" lecture, Ragnall simply wanted a simple
life.

"Please, Caesar, can I be a legionary? I want to be part

of the victory over Lowa and . . . I want something to do. Inactivity is driving me mad!"

Caesar raised his eyebrows, then nodded, as if he'd asked himself a question and decided an answer. "Caesar understands. Idleness is a curse. You cannot be a legionary because they are trained and you are not. They will be in battle soon, and an untrained man is a liability. However, I have something for you. Caesar should have left you with the cavalry after he defeated the Nervee. You may rejoin them. Report to Labienus and tell him Caesar's bidding."

"Thank you." Ragnall turned to go.

"Wait. You are troubled, Ragnall. Caesar senses that you are somewhat . . . lost."

"I . . . well . . . I suppose . . ." Ragnall was surprised at the personal observation.

"There is only one person who can help you find yourself again. You know who it is."

"No." Ragnall didn't have a clue. "Is it Labienus?"

Caesar blew a small laugh through his nose. "No, fool, it's you. You need discipline and exercise as a framework, but within that you must force yourself to have the confidence to be the man you want to be, not the man that you believe others expect you to be. Caesar went through this process when he was several years younger than you, but he had the advantage of a Roman upbringing. It is time you caught up. The cavalry will help. Farewell."

"Farewell" from Caesar meant "Go away," so Ragnall went, eyes wide in surprise and joy at receiving such personal advice from probably the greatest man in the world. He would do it, he'd do for Caesar, and for Drustan too. He was lucky to have their advice, and receiving direct instruction from two such fine men on the same day was surely no coincidence. He would heed their words. He would become a better man.

Part Five

Britain
54 BC

Chapter 1

Caesar dismounted, looked around slowly, turned to Felix and raised half a disdainful lip.

Felix saw his point. He had forgotten how squalid his camp had become. Because it made training more fun and because they had a surfeit of captives, Felix had allowed his Celermen and Maximen to make some kills the morning before. They were messy murderers and reluctant house-keepers, so body parts, guts and sheets of skin were strewn over the ground and draped over tents and training equip-ment like clothes at an orgy. Although he liked it, Felix knew the stench of the dead wasn't to everybody's taste. The captives chained nearby added to the smell, as did the dozens of corpses not far away along the tideline.

On top of all this, since the day was hot, the Celermen and Maximen who weren't on guard were naked. Other than the pustules all over the Celermen's heads, they were fine specimens of leanly fit and very muscular young men. Felix thought they looked fantastic strutting about free from their armour, but the Roman army's view was that male nudity should be left to the perverted Greeks.

"Follow. Caesar will talk to you somewhere that does not stink like the latrines of Hades and looks like a Spartan's wet dream." He strode away.

Felix trotted behind the general's long stride across the beach and out on to a grassy spur that probed the wide estuary. The day was still. Sun sparked off the sea and Caesar's gold-plated armour, and seabirds glided lethargically overhead. Felix hoped that enough supplies had come from Gaul and it was time, finally, to stop dallying. The sooner they conquered this backward land, the sooner Felix could reveal his plans and stop chasing after Caesar's toga tail.

As they arrived at the end of the spit, the faint echoes of a shout drifted across the water.

"What was that?" asked Caesar.

"You have good ears. It was a British shout reporting our position. I've searched for the shouters but they are tiresomely competent at concealing themselves and we haven't winkled any out yet. They're also good at throwing their voices in certain directions, so we hear them only out here when the wind is in the south or west."

"How do these shouters operate?"

Felix told the general about the network of shouters set up by Zadar to yell messages across the country, how they could direction their voices, use codes to cut certain areas out of a shout, and so on.

Caesar nodded throughout with uncharacteristic patience, and when he was finished said: "You will use the speed and stealth of your Celermen to capture as many of these shouters as you can. Bring them unharmed to Caesar."

"We will try."

"You will *do*."

"Sorry, yes, of course."

"Do they have an emergency shout, to inform the network that they are captured?"

"Yes, I think they do."

"Ensure that none are able to make this shout."

"That will be difficult."

"Yes."

"But it will be done," Felix added.

"Good. Now, the legions are marching west," said Caesar. "You will shadow the army to the north, keeping contact through your man Bistan."

"Bistan is missing."

"How careless, but no matter, any of your Celermen will do, it is not a taxing duty. Ensure they come at night. The British are dug into a fortified position some hundred and fifty miles west of our beachhead. Scouts report a barren country between here and there. You should not meet any opposition. Caesar will continue to send you those who meet his displeasure to fuel your troops. He commands you to remember that these are Romans and our allies, and should be treated as such. Are these men being fed?"

"Yes," lied Felix. When food was scarce, why feed doomed men? If they needed to march he would give them sustenance, however.

"Good. Now fetch Caesar's horse. He will never again come within two miles of your mephitic camp."

Lowa leant on the north-east wall of Saran Fort, next to the high, intertwined banks and gates which made up the eastern entrance. There were no clouds, the moon had not yet risen and the bright stars stretched from one wide horizon to the other. She wasn't normally given to whimsy, but so brilliant and enveloping were the stars that she could almost feel that she was up among them, floating and free from the terrible burden of responsibility she bore for those who'd already died and for those who were going to.

The smell of smoke and the background carousing of her army kept her thoughts anchored to the earth. The aroma of freshly cut wood from the new gates reminded her of the day that the old gates had been destroyed, when Zadar had sacked the place. She remembered it well. The double walls had been high but rampart-free and so collapsed that a horse could charge up them. Zadar's Fifty, his elite cavalry to which Lowa had recently been elevated, had ridden up the first wall, through a shallow point of the ditch and onto the interior wall. They'd galloped around the edge and shot arrows into the fort until the defenders surrendered. It had been fun, an exciting sport. She hadn't considered for a moment that these were real people with families and lives that she was spitting with iron and wood. Her only concern back then had been her own and her sister's survival.

And now here she was, back in the same place, striving for the survival of every tribe on the island. The links between geography and time, she mused, were often odd. People changed and the land remained.

Over the last two years Mal had restored and enhanced the fort so that it might be their headquarters if Caesar marched inland. If this fort were breached then they'd retreat to Maidun Castle's superior defences; assuming that retreat was possible and there was anybody left to retreat.

Saran's ditches were now deeper and steeper and full of spikes and devices that would stop cavalry doing what Zadar's had done a decade earlier, and Mal had topped both the outer and inner walls with broad wooden palisades. It was now a decent fort.

Thinking of Mal, Lowa sighed. Shouters reported that his raid had thinned the demons' numbers. His attack had to be considered a success, even if all those who took part had perished. As commander of the army, she was grateful for his sacrifice. But she grieved for him as a friend.

"You've still got me," said Dug, leaning on the spiked palisade next to her.

"I wish I had."

"I live on in the people whose lives I've affected. Since my death wiped out three armies with horrible intentions, that's pretty much everyone in Britain forever. But, most strongly and importantly, it's you and Spring."

"Well, that's great, but I still wish you were here. Spring, too. What is she doing? Is she even alive?"

"She's all right, and you'll see her again."

"There's no sign of her."

"You'll see her soon."

"There's no sign of the dozen riders that I sent to the Aurochs tribe to find out what the Bel had happened to Atlas either."

"What are you going to do?"

"What can I do? There's something going on in the forest of Branwin, enough to detain Atlas and twelve of my best troops. I've sent twenty more today because I want those aurochs. I'd like to have sent greater numbers, but I need them here to face the Romans. All I can do is hope that Atlas is alive, because if he is, I know he'll be doing every bloody thing he can to bring us those beasts."

"What's your plan with Caesar?"

"I hoped he'd take the message of one legion and half his fleet destroyed, and no food or people for hundreds of miles and piss off back to Gaul. He hasn't, though. He's on his way here."

"Determined fucker."

"Isn't he?"

"Reminds me of someone." Dug grinned.

"According to the shouters, the demons and the elephants are still at the coast. The five or six legions he's marched inland are almost double our numbers, and they have more training and vastly more experience. But we've been training hard ourselves, we've got some good ideas—"

"All of them mine."

"Some of them yours. Plus we know the land and we have more to fight for. So I think we can win. I just hope the demons and the elephants stay where they are. I guess he's left them behind because he wants all the glory to go to the legions. I think that's why he called the demons back at Big Bugger Hill. That suits me, I'd much rather fight men. Chamanca has a plan to defeat the elephants, but I'd rather they stayed away until I've worked out what's happening with the aurochs. And the demons? We're chipping away at them but it's costing a lot of lives and even then we've been lucky. Properly commanded, I think they could defeat both Roman and British armies on their own."

"Maybe Caesar's scared of them himself? Maybe that's why he's left them back east?"

"Maybe. I hope so."

They stood without talking for a while, listening to the cries and squawks of nocturnal animals outside the walls the noises from and within the camp.

"Dug," said Lowa eventually, "when I die, will I be with you?"

He didn't answer. He was gone.

Chapter 2

The cavalry was comprised of men from a range of places including Italy, Iberia, Illyricum, Helvetia, Asia, Sicilia and Gaul. They accepted Ragnall more readily and treated him more civilly than the Roman legionaries ever had, even though he'd been preoccupied and less than chatty.

In a squad with fifteen others, he rode along valleys, through woods and over hills, searching for supplies. They found only deserted farms and empty villages. The Britons had stripped every grain of barley from the stores, every piece of fruit from the trees and bushes, every bucket and rope from every well. Even the wildlife seemed to have deserted the land. It was eerie, with not so much as the grunt of a pig or the tweet of a robin to pierce the silence.

The desolation suited Ragnall's mood. Caesar's idea of him gaining confidence to be his own man had sounded great at the time but instead, riding between fruitless searches of buildings and stores, he had even more time to brood about how much others had ruined his life. Drustan's idea of achieving something was all well and good, but all this riding around was achieving nothing. His hatred of Spring and Lowa grew anew as he considered all the things that had gone wrong for him because of them. His yearning for their deaths was rekindled and, as dreary day followed dreary day, it burnt stronger than ever before.

When he wasn't wishing death on Spring and Lowa, he thought about becoming king, and decided that he'd be a good one. His plans for rule had so far been selfish and he would change them. He'd still have a palace built, but a smaller one than he'd first imagined, no larger than the palaces in Rome. He would be under Rome's control, he had no illusions about that any more, but not entirely. He'd told his friend Publius back while campaigning in Gaul that he hoped that Britain's songs and stories and way of life would be preserved, while incorporating the myriad advantages of Roman culture. As king, he would ensure that happened. He pictured British men in splendid, newly built baths, singing the old songs and bards composing new ones to praise their king.

The cavalry rode on, enthusiasm for the search dwindling ever further as they realised that they were never going to find anything. It didn't really matter. Extra supplies would have been useful, but there was plenty of food and other supplies coming from Gaul. The fleet might have been depleted but it rowed and sailed back and forth night and day, fully laden on each return journey. The effectiveness and efficiency of the Romans was simply astonishing, and soon Ragnall would be using it to benefit Britain. Sooner, if they weren't following already, Caesar's six legions would be fully stocked up and would advance in the wake of the scouts.

"It is five legions, truly," a fellow cavalryman from Asia told him one day as they rode along the man-made bank that bisected a wide, lifeless marsh. The man spoke in passable if oddly phrased Latin: "The British kill one whole legion with fire. Thousands of man burnt."

"But we still have six legions . . .?"

"Troops moved from other five legions, so to pretend we have six. Gone legion, bad morale."

Ragnall nodded. It was probably at least partly true, knowing Caesar. When he was king, Ragnall resolved that he, too, would have the courage to change the story of the past to improve the present and the future. First of all, he'd remove any mention of Lowa from all the bards' repertoires.

Shouters had told Lowa of the Romans' progress all the way, so it was no shock when the Roman army marched into sight. According to her network, the elephants and demons still hadn't budged from the coast, which was something of a surprise, but a welcome one.

Lowa pulled everyone back into the fort. It was busy within the walls, but it wasn't cramped, largely thanks to innovations of Dug's which Mal had implemented. There were strange-looking three-storey longhouses which housed the men and women of the army, and astonishingly deep storage pits shored all the way around with timber to prevent collapse. She hadn't seen Dug since they'd discussed the aurochs. In the quiet nights she missed him. In the days she was too busy – and still exasperated about where the Bel Atlas and the aurochs could be. She'd sent more scouts and shouters to the forest of Branwin. None of them had returned. Had the elephants been coming, she would have send a larger force or perhaps even gone herself to investigate the hold-up, but, with the African animals still camped on the Channel coast, she had more pressing concerns.

The entire Roman army camped on the Downs Road directly north of Saran Fort that night. Before dawn the next day, instead of swinging south from the Downs Road and besieging her with all six legions, Caesar sent one legion south and marched on with the other five. His intention was clearly to pin her in place while he searched for supplies. In a few days' march, he would indeed find land that she hadn't stripped and evacuated. If he was very lucky, or, more likely, if he tortured some locals, he would find the huge caches of food taken from Britain's south-west corner. So the latest Roman strategy was a good one.

However, she had a good reply to it.

Lowa watched as the single legion began to dig its camp. She waited until she heard from shouters that the other five legions were still marching away, and she told her captains to prepare the army. She waited until late morning, when shouts confirmed that the five other legions were well clear to the north. Then she gave the order to leave Saran Fort and attack.

Chapter 3

Atlas trudged along the path that curved up the hill to the Aurochs tribe's village, his Elann-modified axe over one shoulder. He hoped that his slow speed made him look confident, but in truth he couldn't have gone any faster. Not that he could see anybody around to pass judgement. This time the hill was deserted, neither villagers nor aurochs to be seen. Smoke ascending and the hammering from Elann's forges hidden in the hollow up to the right were the only signs of life.

When he was three-quarters of the way up the hill, further than he'd walked since Manfreena had laid him low, the Aurochs tribe trooped from the gates in the wooden palisade. His legs felt as if they were made of iron, but he walked on, manoeuvring his axe into position.

The villagers filed left and right, formed a semicircle and waited for Atlas. Manfreena and Ula walked out and stood in the middle. Silently, they all watched his approach. They looked calm, some were smiling. It was unnerving. He would have preferred it if they'd been shouting hatred. As he neared, he recognised some of the smiling spectators as Maidunite cavalry. He guessed that Lowa must have sent them to find him and that the new Aurochs queen had managed to warp their minds.

"Here's a surprise," said Manfreena cheerily. "You!" She nodded at a nearby villager. "Go and fetch Elann. I'd like to hear why this walking corpse wasn't burnt on her forge. Ula, would you mind finishing him off?"

"No problem." Ula's smile widened, her eyes flashed and she strode towards him.

Atlas shifted the axe on his shoulder. He'd hoped to get closer than this. He pointed the end of the handle at Manfreena and flicked the release catch. The iron bolt shot from the axe's shaft, passed through Manfreena's left ear with a small explosion of blood and flesh, flew between the village's open gates and disappeared.

"Ah," said Atlas. In the plan, that bolt hit Manfreena in the narrow gap between her eyes, she died, the glamour fell from the village and that was that.

Ula stopped and looked back at Manfreena. The former queen of Eroo held her hand to the side of her head, felt about with her fingers and found that most of her ear was missing.

She smiled. "Have you got anything else?" she asked.

Atlas dropped his axe and fell to his knees. He didn't have anything else. Not even the strength to stand.

"Ula?" said Manfreena.

The queen of Kanawan jogged up and kicked Atlas on the side of the head. He couldn't block or dodge. He fell, thinking that it was good she was bare-footed. One of Lowa's iron-heeled kicks would have killed him. On the other hand, he considered as he lay there, this way was going to take longer.

He managed to clamber up on to all fours. He felt more than saw Ula walk around him and pull her leg back. The kick to his stomach lifted him from the ground, turned him over and landed him on his back. By Sobek, he hated magical strength.

He lay where he was. He couldn't lift his arms or move his legs. He felt Ula kick his feet apart, then walk away. He wondered what she was doing, and did not like his conclusions. It was going to be a running kick to the bollocks, or possibly she was going to leap and come down and mash her knee into his groin. He didn't relish either idea much. He tried to shuffle his feet back together but he couldn't.

"Wait a moment, Ula," he heard Manfreena say. "What's this coming up the hill?"

Atlas managed to tilt his head so that he could see.

Hobbling on a stick towards them up the road, her white curly hair aglow in the sun like a dandelion-seed ball and with a smile on her face to match the mad cheerfulness of the Aurochs tribe, was Nan.

Chapter 4

The Maidunite infantry streamed out of the fort, formed up into their hundreds and marched towards the growing foundations of the Roman camp. The Romans saw the threat, dropped shovels, picks and other camp-building equipment, snatched up pilums and shields and arranged themselves into battle lines.

"By Juno, it's exciting, isn't it?" said Clodia.

They were watching from the edge of woods on a hill to the west, all on horseback, ready to scarper the moment any British paid them too much attention. Ferrandus and Tertius had been against the plan to have a peek at the British fort, in fact there would have been a fight between them and Clodia's guards, but Clodia had smiled at them, suggested that the two praetorians be wholly in charge of security for the trip, and tensions had cooled.

Now it looked like they were going to see a lot more than the British fort. Spring shuddered as British and Roman infantry formed up, three hundred paces between each. Behind the British were the walls of Saran Fort. Looking out from the centre of the wall, next to a trumpeter, was a blonde woman holding a longbow.

Spring hoped it was going to be different from the last British battle she'd seen when a force could have stayed in a hillfort but didn't — at Barton, where she'd watched Zadar's army massacre an entire tribe. She ached to be down there with them, but unfortunately Ferrandus and Tertius knew that. Her hands were tied with a leather cord, and leather thongs attached her to both praetorians.

"Why aren't they attacking each other?" asked Clodia. She was wearing her short white dress with the broad belt and its double jewelled daggers. Her hair was perfectly coiffed to look like it hadn't been, her graceful limbs a flawless and sun-kissed bronze. If there was ever a Roman mural painted of Lowa on horseback, thought Spring, then it would look more like Clodia than the British queen. Not that there was anything wrong with how Lowa looked on the back of a horse; she was just more athletically set than the Roman ideal of feminine beauty, her hair saw only ever the briefest attention from a comb, she wore boyish leather riding shorts and tough, iron-soled boots, her skin was permanently pale, and she always had scabs on her knees and elbows.

"The Romans will be waiting for the British to attack," said Tertius. "That's how they like to fight. But they're happy attacking, too, which they will if – oh, hang on, here we go."

Clacker-mouthed trumpets blared in alarming cacophony from the Maidunite lines. The front ranks of the British infantry charged, yelling and waving swords above their heads. Roman shields lowered to meet the onslaught.

"And they looked so disciplined on the approach," said Ferrandus. "But that's your barbarian for you. He can march like a cockerel, but control goes to shit when the battle starts. They're like children. It's sad, really. Just you watch how the legionaries deal with this. First up, a salvo of pilums will kill a good many of them and put the shits up the rest. Then the barbar will hit the Roman shields, maybe dent a couple but no more, get bounced back a couple of times, then, once they're dazed and exhausted—"

"Hold up, Ferrandus," said Tertius. "I hate to interrupt

one of your patronising lectures because you do enjoy them so, but take a closer look."

Ferrandus peered down at the attacking Britons, then said: "Ahhhh!"

"Yes," said Tertius. "Exactly."

"What? *What?!*" Clodia peered at the men in birdlike enquiry.

The two praetorians were too rapt to answer. Spring could see why. Only the front few rows of Britons were attacking. Their charge looked ragtag at first glance, and it would look messy if you were facing it, because the front-running Britons were indeed a mess of men and women waving their arms and yelling. But the attack was far from ragtag. They were all running at approximately the same speed and they were as evenly spaced as the most disciplined marching legionaries. If you looked closely you could see that there were three distinct lines. In the first, the Britons were armed with swords and shields. The third line was armed with long spears. The second line had scabbarded swords, but they were also dragging long iron poles with crosspieces that looked like stretched anchors. What, wondered Spring, could they be for?

Behind them, several hundred strange chariots were sweeping in from right and left – unusually broad vehicles with high platforms. Towering on the platforms over each driver, strapped into place by legs and waist, was an archer. Their bows were plain, not the recurve ones that cavalry used, and almost as long as Spring and Lowa's longbows. Standing high gave the archers the space to use full-powered bows.

Following theses weird chariots were thousands of infantry in ordered lines.

"Fuck me," said Tertius. "We could be about to see something here."

"What?" cried Clodia.

"Shush and watch," said Spring.

Clodia pouted at the girl's impertinence, but did as she was told.

When the howling Maidunites were twenty paces away, the Romans hurled their pilums. Spread out as they were, the British dodged the missiles and Spring didn't see a single one of them hit.

A good number of the British let fly with slings. All along the Roman front line, shields banged down with a fearsomely synchronised clap. The second, third and fourth legionary ranks lifted their shields overhead to form the standard, impregnable tortoises.

Three paces out, the running, howling Maidunites stopped running and howling and formed into three tidy lines. Behind them, the chariot archers drew and loosed, aiming high. At that moment, the second row of the infantry lifted their ten-pace-long iron poles with two-pace-wide crossbars at the end, and slammed them down on to the Roman tortoise.

The heavy metal crosspieces smashed through the tortoise roof. Holding the poles, the Britons ran back, yanking shields from Roman hands and pulling men off their feet. The front ranks of the Romans fell apart in a muddle of shields and men. A moment later the arrows landed, with beautiful, horrible accuracy, tearing through leather and ripping flesh. Long spears flashed out from the third row of the Maidun infantry, impaling those not hit by the archers.

The front three rows of Romans were destroyed. The next few lowered their shields as the second salvo of arrows swished down towards them. The Maidunites lifted their cross-barred poles again and charged the Romans like besiegers with mini battering rams. The shield wall was destroyed again. Again the arrows fell and spears lashed into the defenceless Romans.

"I thought the Romans knew how to fight?" said Clodia,

in the same tone that she might employ to complain about someone using an unfashionably scented oil at an orgy.

"They do, they do," said Tertius. "Unfortunately, so, it seems, do the British." Spring felt a flush of pride. "But don't worry, this is only the beginning. Look."

By the time the shouted orders reached their vantage point the Romans were already reforming, spreading out, each man now alone with his sword and shield and no longer vulnerable to the British hook-rams.

Trumpet blasts rang out from the wall of Saran Fort. The British reformed, too. Shields went up along the front line. More shields were unloaded from the chariots and passed forward rapidly to the second and third lines. Together, the three lines positioned their shields into a British tortoise.

"Well, I'll be a Greek," said Ferrandus.

The Roman charge hit shields and stopped. Spears lashed out and sliced into legionaries, and now it was the Britons' shield wall that was advancing, rolling over the spaced-out Romans.

"Fuck!" said Tertius.

"What are those carts?" asked Clodia.

Four huge ox-drawn carts were rolling up to the far flank of the Roman army. Shouts went up and a few legionaries charged the new threat, but the high-mounted chariot archers cut them down. The carts pulled round so that they were parallel to the Roman flank furthest from Spring and the spectators. Large doors dropped open in the side of each and dozens of giant war dogs sprang out. Spring was too far away to see it, but she imagined the huge amount of slobber coming from each animal's mouth. As legionaries turned to face the war dogs, chariot archers unleashed volley after volley into their exposed sides.

A knot of Roman cavalry galloped in to attack the dogs, but the archers let fly again and within moments most of the horses were riderless.

Spring was so intent on watching the dogs leap at the Romans, and so upset to see so many disembowelled by Roman swords – she thought, with a pang, of Sadie and Pigsy – that she didn't hear the new trumpeting, a blaring much louder than any previous fanfare, until Clodia said, "What's that?"

"With any luck," said Tertius, "that is what we call a battle-changer."

Chapter 5

Atlas stayed down and watched Nan hobble up the hill. He wasn't sure if he could have got to his feet and the threat of another kick from Ula kept him from trying.

And still Nan came, struggling now. He hadn't realised how difficult she found walking. Yet she'd spent hour after hour in the forest foraging for the ingredients to cure him. His initial ingratitude shamed him, and he vowed never to judge so hastily again. He had thought ill of her when she had saved him at great effort to herself. But what could she do against the druid from Eroo?

A look of cheery disdain on her face, Manfreena shouted:

"Who's this now? Are you a friend of Atlas? What do you hope to achieve? You look like a sweet old crone, but I am not known for my sympathy."

Nan held up a hand, supporting herself on her cane with the other. "Wait, wait," she said, just loud enough for them all to hear. "I'll get there soon. Don't kill the Kushite yet. It's in your interest to keep him alive. I'll explain why when I get there. Please have some patience for an old woman's poor knees." She hobbled on.

A while later, and Manfreena shouted: "I'm not known for my patience either!"

"Well, you're obviously not Kildare the Healer then," said Nan.

"What are you talking about? I've had enough. Ula . . . Ula? Where's Ula?"

"I'm here."

"But I can't see you . . . I can't see anything. What's happening? What's happ—"

Atlas heard a thump that sounded a lot like an Eroo druid collapsing. Nan tossed away her cane, snatched a bag from her back, jogged up to Atlas, squatted next to him and pulled out a water skin. "Danu's tits," she said, "I thought she was never going to die. The poison on your dart is the best there is, but you were meant to get closer and hit her in the face, you silly man. Here now, drink this."

As Atlas drank a hubbub swelled all around. It was the sound, he reckoned, that you'd expect from a crowd of people who'd been asleep for a couple of years, had just woken up somewhere strange, and were asking each other what the Bel was going on.

Standing on Saran's outer wall, Lowa nodded. This was what all the gruelling training had been for. She almost smiled when the British tortoise formed and drove the Romans back. It was too early for smugness – they outnumbered the Romans here but there were many more of the invader not far to the north – but so far everything was going to plan.

The war dog carts rolled into place and unleashed their canine broadside. The dogs had been trained for years to attack only men dressed as legionaries. She'd considered holding them back, since they were a devastating assault but also likely to be killed so she could use them only once. However, she wanted to crush this advance legion quickly and decisively so that she could get her army back in the fort before the main body of Romans returned.

As the dogs hit the Romans on the left, she gave the command for the chariot archers to switch their fire to the right for two salvos, then retreat, so that the dogs might run amok amidst the legionaries without being hit by their own side's arrows, and so that the rest of her infantry could advance and fresh soldiers could finish off the legionaries.

The chariots melted away to both flanks then halted, ready to harry any Roman flanking manoeuvres. The infantry behind them filled the gap and filtered forward into the shield line, where they swapped places with tired or injured soldiers. Lowa had seen the sections of her army shuffle and slot like this again and again on the practice field, but she'd never before noticed just how beautiful it was.

The Romans reformed tortoises on their front line, but the dogs ran about below their shields. Lowa couldn't see them ripping into the Romans' exposed legs as they'd been trained to do, but she could see the effects. From left to right in waves, sections of the Roman formation lost integrity as the dogs obeyed their training and fanned out, knocking men down with their bulk, ripping chunks from thighs and running on. The dogs had been yet another of Dug's ideas, inspired by training his own dogs Sadist and Pig Fucker – many, in fact, were Dug's dogs' offspring. How many more good schemes might the man have come up with had he lived? The fact that ghost Dug was markedly less helpful made Lowa think that he wasn't a ghost, and really was a creation of her exhausted mind and the constant stress of repelling an invasion.

The British line capitalised on the destruction wrought by the dogs and advanced steadily. Lowa reckoned more than half the legion were down. Given the distance of the rest of the Roman divisions, as reported by the shouters, she was confident that she could finish them before reinforcements came. By leaving a single legion within range of her fort, Caesar had seriously underestimated her. It was exactly the false confidence that she'd hope to instil by her retreat from Big Bugger Hill. For the first time in seven years of preparation, she began to believe that they might really beat the Romans.

Her coalescing confidence was ripped apart moments later by the trumpeting of an elephant, then another and another. She looked to the east and saw a herd of armoured elephants charging from behind a hill, heading for the infantry's left flank. The size of them stunned her. They were like whales that had sprouted legs and run ashore.

More shocking than their appearance, though, was the fact that they shouldn't have been there.

She'd received three shouts that morning telling her that all the elephants were on the east coast, three days' hard riding away. So it wasn't the appearance of the elephants that made it feel like her stomach was falling out of her arse, it was what it implied. She'd had shouts that the demons were just as far away, and that Caesar's five other legions were several hours' march to the north. It hadn't crossed her mind for a moment to question any of them. It did now.

"Legion to the south!" someone yelled from across the fort, confirming her fears. A breathless man arrived moments later. "There's another legion coming from the south!" he panted.

"Two legions coming fast from the west!" came a shout from the west wall.

"Shit," said Lowa.

The elephants were beyond the range of the fort's scorpions and catapults. The chariot archers on the right galloped at them and rained arrows on to the thundering beasts, but the archers on the elephants were protected in their mini mounted forts, and arrows pinged off the animals' armour. Those few arrows that did strike flesh had no effect. The beasts charged on. A few of the chariots had fire arrows, but the elephants hadn't heard that they were meant to be afraid of fire and these had no more impact than the standard arrows.

Lowa gave the command for Chamanca's cavalry, held in reserve behind the chariots, to loop round and attack the elephants from the rear, and then she gave the signal for the infantry to retreat. She needed to get the bulk of her army back into the lee of the fort's scorpions before too many of them were trampled and before two legions struck their left flank.

The cavalry swarmed out in fifty squads of six, modelled on Lowa's own cavalry company from Zadar's army. Each team of six had a leader, the role that Lowa had taken almost a decade before, and they trained and trained until they could move like flocks of birds in their sixes, and in synchronisation with the other teams. With wonderful unity they swept towards the mighty enemy.

Half the squads shot arrows to suppress the elephant archers, while the others galloped in holding aloft spears with long, serrated blades. The elephant commander saw the threat, but rather than swing to meet it, he waved his arms for the elephants to gallop on, deep into the press of infantry.

One of the trumpeters touched her arm and pointed to the west, to the far side of the battlefield from the elephants' charge where a multitude of legionaries was sprinting towards the gap between her fort and her infantry. There were thousands of them, on course to block her infantry – almost her entire army – from returning to safety. More and more appeared, running into the field between her and her army, well clear of the fort's scorpions' and catapults' range. Lowa saw two eagle standards, which meant almost ten thousand men.

Ten thousand men who were meant to be half a day's march to the north.

False shouts. She now knew that Caesar had captured her shouters and forced them to shout what he wanted. The previous year's mindless landing, the utter failure of the first invasion, the simple charge and attack at Big Bugger Hill, all of Caesar's actions so far had convinced Lowa that he wasn't the military genius he was reported to be. Had it all been a ruse, leading to this moment? She'd believed that she was the only general using vaguely advanced tactics, the superior commander, because she'd wanted to believe it.

What was it they said about pride?

She gave the order for the chariots on the left flank to retreat, out of the path of the Roman infantry, but it was too late. The elephants hit the right flank of her foot soldiers at the same moment as the legionaries hit the archer chariots on the left. They had similar, devastating effects. Chariot archers shot at the charging legionaries, but shields caught most of the arrows, then the legionaries were at them, hacking and stabbing at horses and charioteers. On the right, elephants were swinging their great tusks, goring and scything down crowds of soldiers – some Romans as well as British – and trampling them with iron boots.

Lowa ordered the infantry on the left to form a shield wall and push westwards, to save the archer chariots and meet the coming legionaries. She looked to the right. Her army was standing its ground, but all cohesion had been ripped to shit by the bladed tusks of the elephants. They'd felled one of the animals, but many more – at least thirty – were raging through the ranks. Chamanca's cavalry took down two more of the beasts, but the horses were struggling to push through the press of bodies, living and dead. Trampling through the infantry as if it were grass, the elephants ran clear of the cavalry archers' accurate range. Dark-skinned men popped up in the turrets and shot arrows into the surrounding Maidunites.

To the left the Romans had obliterated a good many of Lowa's chariots. Some legionaries were pursuing the surviving vehicles back to the fort, but most charged on, heading for the body of her army.

The enemy were still outside the range of her large fort-based projectile weapons, but some of the legionaries chasing the chariots came within range of her bow. She strung it and aimed.

Chamanca spat. The infantry was blocking her horses. Most of the soldiers, to be fair, were dead or dying and it was perhaps a bit much to expect them to crawl out of the way, but still, they were impeding her troops' progress and there were elephants' tendons to sever.

"Follow me! And do as I do!" she shouted to the cavalry near her, then leapt from her horse, grabbed a shield off a dead legionary and ran towards the nearest elephant. She sprang from gap to gap between the casualties like a particularly nimble deer crossing a tussocky marsh, arrows from elephant turrets missing her and zipping into the flesh of the downed. Some of the arrows punched shouts from the not quite dead and a couple more thwocked into her shield.

It was the messiest battlefield Chamanca had seen, and she'd seen some messy ones. Being sliced apart by tusk-blades and trampled by iron-shod elephants was not a tidy way to go. There were guts everywhere and so much blood that it collect in pools on the blood-saturated earth. So much blood. Blood . . . She stopped and crouched behind her shield next to a dying legionary, arrow-shot rather than crushed and split open like so many of the others. She stabbed her teeth into his neck and drank deep while arrows whacked into her shield.

Satisfied, for now at least, she glanced back. The cavalry were following, not as fast as her, but protected by shields and carrying their newly made leg-severing spears. She didn't need a special spear, she was good enough with her blade and ball-mace. She didn't need the shield either, she'd picked it up only to show the others what to do. She tossed it aside and leapt on, much faster now she was blood-fuelled, and more than able to dodge the elephanteers' arrows. She reached the first great grey animal and chopped into its leg.

Jagganoch shot arrows into spear-carriers as Bandonda trampled puny humans and butchered them with his tusks. There was nothing finer. Riding an armoured Yonkari war elephant through crowds of infantry was better than all sex, all food, all drink – everything. Bandonda was eviscerating and crushing a good number of fool Romans as well as dozens of Britons, but Jagganoch was not concerned. They should have learnt from the battle at the coast. If you want to live, do not block the path of Bandonda and his herd.

He saw that two legions of Romans were attacking from the west, directly towards him, so he commanded his squad to turn north. Killing allies when they were in the way was fine, but charging them directly when they weren't mixed up with enemy troops was not good form. As Bandonda responded to the reins, Jagganoch looked over the rest of his elephants. He could see only one killed, but two more went down as he watched, bucking, rolling and crushing some crew who didn't have the wherewithal to leap clear. What was this new threat?

It was the Iberian woman! Gripping an elephant's ear with one hand, she swung up to the turret and over its wall. She was wearing almost nothing and she moved like a cheetah. The crew were all dead in the blink of an eye. She grabbed the elephant's reins and pulled. It must have been luck, but somehow she got the succession of yanks and tweaks exactly right to make the elephant turn, bow its head and then ram its tusks up into the belly of the beast next to it.

He wanted that woman.

Behind her, in line with the speared elephant, a few dozen Maidunites advanced with bladed spears. He gave the order for the elephants to swing round to meet the challenge, at the same time as steering Bandonda directly for the Iberian's new mount.

Chamanca's beast thrashed around, destroying its herd-mate's stomach and ribs, but its tusks became trapped and it could not pull free. The crew of the tusk-speared, bucking elephant balanced like acrobats in their little fort, shooting arrow after arrow at her. From that short range, with her own animal tossing its head and lurching like a burning bear in a desperate attempt to free itself, the missiles were impossible to dodge. One sliced the side of her neck, another lodged in her arm. She somersaulted backwards off her mount and landed neatly, but something whacked the back of her head and she fell.

The world swam back into focus. She was on her back and Jagganoch was standing over her, reaching down for his long club. He must have thrown it at her, she realised. She rolled away but the arrow in her arm stuck in the soil. It didn't hold her for long, but it was long enough for Jagganoch to swing his club into the side of her head. She felt her skull smash, then everything went black.

Jagganoch had intended to keep the Iberian and mate with her. He'd never seen a better fighter, apart from himself, of course, so breeding with her was likely to create children at least nearly as capable as they were. So he was annoyed that, in his anger, he'd hit her too hard. He felt the wound, then her neck – yes, the bone was crushed and she had no pulse. No matter, he told himself. He had defeated her easily, so she was clearly not such a great fighter. There was a truism that even the best fighter could be unlucky. But Jagganoch believed that you made your own luck.

Back up on Bandonda, he took stock. He could not see any of the long-speared attackers still standing; his elephants had dealt with the new assault in moments, without further loss. It had surprised him at first when people attacked his elephants, rather than surrendering immediately or fleeing, but he'd learnt the reason for their foolishness. Previously the pink people had encountered only the forest elephants of the Carthaginians from north Africa and the even smaller eastern war elephants of the Persians. Jagganoch's elephants, bred and improved for centuries by his ancestors in the heart of Africa, were completely different animals – larger, braver and much stronger. Bandonda and the others were to the eastern and northern elephants what war dogs were to the pet pups of the pampered women of Rome.

Thinking of war dogs, he'd seen some running about, but could see no more. That was a shame. People expected his elephants to be afraid of dogs because all other types of elephants were, but Yonkari elephants trampled all animals as happily as they trampled people.

So the British dogs were defeated, and to the west and south the Romans had formed lines between the enemy and their hillfort, blocking their route to temporary safety. To the north, the half-destroyed Roman legion had rallied and, further to the north, he could see Caesar and his retinue of praetorians marching southwards followed by two more legions. The Romans were winning, but only because they had greater numbers and because Jagganoch's troop had killed so many. The British were better fighters than Jagganoch had expected, better than the Romans. Even now, the Roman lines pressing on three sides of the British infantry were static where the Romans' superior numbers should have allowed them to advance.

He was about to give the order for his elephants to turn back to the main battle and finish off the British infantry, when he heard a new horn note, ringing out from beyond the fort to the south.

Chapter 6

They rode north as fast as the aurochs could go. Atlas was nauseous from the lumpy downing of a lumpenly pulped version of Nan's invigorating stew, and the rhythmic lurching of the giant armoured bull beneath him was not helping.

The two hundred other riders from the forest of Branwin showed no signs of discomfort. Armoured in ringmail shirts and armed with stout-handled blades that were halfway between spears and swords, they looked grimly determined. They knew that they had much to atone for. Ula, riding along next to him, was still in her simple blue dress and armed with a long, elegant sword. Atlas had told her not to come, since she'd never ridden an aurochs and was no fighter as far as he knew, but she pointed out that she'd kicked his arse twice, wanted to make up for that, and besides, what did he know about her skills? And indeed she was riding the aurochs much more confidently than he was, so perhaps she might be useful in the battle to come.

His own aurochs snorted and he worried again that it might collapse under the weight of plate iron strapped to its flanks and head, the long iron blades attached to its forward-pointing horns, plus his own unusual bulk, but, no, it ran on, showing no more signs of fatigue than its herd-mates.

They crested a rise and he saw the fort, the legions and, dead ahead, the elephants. Immediately he knew where the beasts had come from. When Atlas had been no more than four years old, raiders on huge elephants from the Yonkari tribe to the south-west had invaded his tribe's land and rampaged northwards, killing all who didn't flee. His father and mother had been joint rulers of their village. Understanding that they could not defeat the elephants, they had surrendered, hoping that the rest of the village would be spared. That day was Atlas' earliest memory. He remembered them telling him to stay put and walking away, his mother steely-faced, his father unable to hold his tears as they bade farewell.

The Yonkari elephant captain tied up his parents and all the adults in the village. He explained that, as thanks for surrendering and making their task easier, all children would be spared. The rest would be killed. They forced the children to watch as the adults were murdered in a variety of ways, each more horrible that the last. His father had been one of the first, simply whacked on the head with a club, then his flesh stripped from his bones by the elephants. He could remember that his mother had been the last, but he couldn't remember what they'd done to her. He assumed his mind had obliterated the memory to preserve his sanity. He was both ashamed and glad that it had.

Atlas spent the next few years as a Yonkari slave, working in their fields and becoming stronger. When he was about eight years old, he escaped and killed the three men sent to hunt him down. He had not seen a central African elephant since, nor laid eyes on any Yonkari. Yet here they were. He was looking forward to killing a few more of them.

He nodded to Ula. She raised her horn to her lips and blew. The Aurochs tribe yelled, the giant cattle bellowed and they charged.

The remaining archer chariots reached the shelter of the fort's projectile weaponry. A cohort of legionaries followed, but scorpion bolts from the fort cut swathes through their ranks and they retreated. Lowa ordered the charioteers to spike their vehicles and bring their horses into the fort. It was the same command she'd given when surrounded on Frogshold by the Murkan, Dumnonian and Eroo armies. This situation here was not as bad, she told herself.

It wasn't great, though. The cavalry was gone, Chamanca nowhere to be seen. They'd had some effect on the elephants, killing maybe a quarter of the beasts, but the rest were still rampaging through the infantry.

The infantry, however, was holding out against the Romans on three sides, moving back steadily towards Saran Fort. It might take all day, but at this rate the majority of them would make it back to shelter.

The elephants were ripping into the infantry and still killing a great many, but their charge had been brought almost to a halt by men and women fighting back fiercely with long spears, and every now and then an elephant fell. It was hard to guess, but she reckoned out of the fifteen thousand men and women who'd taken to the field, only a few hundred at most had been killed, and almost of all of those by the elephants. The way things were going, Lowa reckoned that the elephants might kill two thousand of hers before they were stopped. It was a lot, it was a horrible thought, but if she were to beat Caesar there were going to be losses and she couldn't dwell on them. He'd lost twice that number in his first attack on Big Bugger Hill and hadn't faltered. Still, she wished that she was with her army, fighting, without time to think like this. She'd enjoyed potting a few legionaries earlier but there were no enemies in range now, and she had to stay where she was to co-ordinate her forces.

She was distracted by little Dug screaming angrily down in the fort, no doubt because a new plaything – a sandal or a stick or similar– had been taken from him. Her son was another problem. It had been a simple decision to keep him in the fort, because she didn't want to risk herself running off and deserting the army again to save him. However, now they were surrounded and he was stuck there, whereas just the day before she could have sent him and Keelin off west to Dumnonia or Kimruk or even over the sea.

Then she heard the aurochs horn.

Moments later the great cattle appeared around a hill to the east, Atlas riding the lead beast. They tore towards the elephants.

She felt a rush of elation. This should change things.

If the aurochs could take out the elephants, then it was possible her infantry might be able to force its way back to the fort relatively intact. Once she had them back in the fort, she was confident of holding out for a long while, while raiding the besieging Romans every night and thinning their finite ranks. It had been a mistake to believe the false shouts and commit her entire infantry, but it wasn't the end by any means.

The one thing, she thought, that could still ruin everything, was Felix's legion of demons. She scanned the land but could see no sign of them. The last shout had said that they were still at their base to the east, but with her shouter network compromised, that meant nothing.

As if to mock her, another shout rang out: "Demons remain at Corner Bay." The shout came from the west, the wrong direction – Corner Bay was to the east. Lowa guessed it was really meant as a taunt, and what it really said was "Demons nearby and about to attack." She hoped that it didn't.

Felix grinned as he pictured Lowa hearing that last shout. His operation to take over her messenger network had been a success. His Celermen had captured and gagged all of them swiftly and silently, without any raising the alarm. Then, after some light but painful torture and a three-pronged iron fork rammed into their spines, they'd shouted whatever he'd told them to. Amazing how compliant people were when you held the handle of a tool that could paralyse them with a twist. He'd made one of the shouters tell him how it felt, having that alien metal buried in his back, scraping bone and tugging at such vital cords. "Very bad" was the unsurprising gist of his reply.

Felix's Celermen and Maximen had killed a few captives and run to a wooded hollow to the west of the fort the night before. He guessed that the declivity was a pond in the winter, but it had been a sunny summer so it was dry, cool in the shade of the leaves, and hidden from both Romans and Britons. Since the first invasion of Britain he'd lost twenty-eight Celermen and nine Maximen, so he still had twelve of the former and eleven of the latter. The losses sounded heavy and indeed they were greater than he would have liked, but almost all of them had been killed by factors he hadn't anticipated; those wicked arrows from the new British bows, for example, or the raid that had caught them off guard. He'd learnt from his errors, become more controlled and more cautious, and from here on he would not lose his troops so carelessly. He was also confident that once Caesar had defeated the British, it would be no effort to capture Caesar himself and take over the Roman army. This far from Rome, it would be years before Pompey or Crassus or any of those fools sent anyone against him, and by then it would be far, far too late.

According to the Celerman watching the battle from the branch of a tree above, the Romans had the upper hand. Lowa had fallen for the false shouts and committed her entire force attacking one legion. She'd been surprised by the arrival of ten thousand men from the west. The elephants ripping into the east flank of her army had increased her woes.

"New British squad arrived!" called the Celerman. "Looks like aurochs in armour, couple of hundred of them, coming from the south-west."

Interesting, thought Felix. Surely they'd be no match for the Yonkari elephants? And if they were, and the British somehow turned the tide of the battle? Then Felix would defy Caesar's orders and his demons would leave their hiding place. The Romans were going to win this one.

Lowa held her breath as the African animals swung round to meet Britain's giant war cattle. The aurochs were a magnificent sight – thundering bovine muscle with swept-forward, iron-capped horns as long as chariot draught-poles. Each was so huge that the riders perched atop them, even Atlas, looked like midgets. Massive and formidable as the aurochs were though, the elephants were a great deal larger. But the aurochs were faster.

One elephant reared on its back legs to stamp down on an attacking aurochs, but the giant bull accelerated like a whipped horse, drove its long horns into the elephant's underside and ripped out a shiny cascade of intestines. The African beast crashed down onto aurochs and rider.

Most of the leading aurochs were stamped or gored, but not before they'd brought down several elephants. Unseated aurochs riders in ringmail finished off injured beasts with heavy blades and easily overcame the lightly armed Yonkari crews. The second rank of aurochs charged between the foreign animals, bellowing rage, ripping through armour with their horns, spilling great washes of blood and viscera.

Atlas' aurochs was impaled on a tusk, but he ran along its neck while pulling his axe from his back holster, and leapt onto the elephant's head. He dispatched the crew with a few powerful swings of his double-bladed weapon, but a heartbeat later an aurochs, smacked aside by one elephant's long snout, drove its horns into the back leg of Atlas' elephant. The African monster reared, trumpeting, and collapsed. The Kushite jumped and landed, leapt again to avoid being crushed by the falling elephant, then dodged out of the path of a galloping aurochs.

Lowa lost sight of him. Others battled on. Half the elephants were down but the rest were fighting like the trained, enraged monsters that they were. None was fleeing. A large section of legionaries swung to help the elephants, hurling pilums at the aurochs riders. Ringmail proved no defence against a javelin thrown full strength from a couple of paces.

The bronze-helmeted leader of the elephants rallied his remaining riders and charged the thickest press of aurochs. His elephant, the largest animal in the field, tossed three aurochs with its tusks then grabbed a passing rider with its long snout and threw her twenty paces into the air. This one was wearing a blue dress rather than ringmail. Lowa couldn't be sure at that distance, but it looked a lot like Ula. As she fell, the elephant swatted her with his snout, breaking her back.

The elephant counter combined with the legionaries' missile attack was effective. Soon there were only a few aurochs standing. But there were fewer elephants. Two aurochs charged the great lead elephant from either side and skewered it. The lead elephanteer jumped on to one rider, brained man and aurochs with his club, jumped back over his own beast, somersaulting as Chamanca might have done, and killed the other rider and his mount. Attackers dispatched, he leapt back onto his dying elephant, beat his chest and wailed.

The elephants were defeated. A few thrashed about, but the aurochs tribe finished them. Only a dozen aurochs were left standing from the two hundred that had attacked, but many of the riders had survived to make short work of the elephant archers and hold their own against the legionaries.

Several Africans fled but their bronze-helmeted leader fought on. He was doing well, running around and killing Britons with fearsome efficiency. Meanwhile, more and more legionaries were joining the battle, pressing towards the remaining Aurochs tribespeople.

Atlas reappeared, shouting at the Branwin foresters to rally to him and hewing down any legionaries who came within reach. He looked like he was searching the corpses and carcasses for something or someone – Chamanca, Lowa guessed. She looked about for the Iberian, but something else caught her eye, off to the north. Cantering into view with his praetorians around him was the unmistakeable red-and gold-clad figure of Julius Caesar. Running behind him were his remaining two legions, led by dozens of pairs of horses pulling scorpions and catapults.

Trapped between legions, her infantry were perfectly placed and contained for the Roman missiles to tear them to shreds. She told the trumpeter to blare out the command to speed the retreat to the fort. It was going to be tough; they still had two legions of Romans to fight through, plus a third if the legion in reserve to the south joined the battle.

"Big badgers' balls," she said.

Chapter 7

"Here comes the end." Ferrandus pointed at Caesar's advancing legions.

"They're beating the legionaries," said Spring.

"They're holding the legionaries, but once those scorpions start shooting – and look, he's got catapults, too – they're fuc— They're dead. The bolts and missiles will arc up nicely over the legionaries' heads, then come down and mince your British friends."

"Nicely put." Spring glared at him.

"My tact-free friend is right," said Tertius. "Surrender or death. Those are the options for the Britons. That's assuming Caesar lets them surrender."

Spring looked about desperately. Most of the charioteers had retreated back to the heavily armed hillfort, but they were few compared to the Roman forces. The cavalry were gone, the aurochs were gone and there were two legions between the infantry and the fort. The British men and women were doing amazingly well, surrounded but holding; more than holding – constantly refreshing their front lines from the centre, they were eating into the lines of attacking Romans. Moments before she had hoped and believed that the British might have been able to fight their way back to the fort. But now she saw that Ferrandus was right. As soon as the Roman projectile weapons rolled into range, things would get very messy for the remaining infantry. But it didn't mean that they were beaten! It simply *couldn't* mean that.

She strained her brain and clenched her fists and tried to pull magic from somewhere. She felt nothing. She hadn't felt a flicker since Dug had died. And anyway, even if she could kill Dug all over again, what could it possibly achieve? Last time she'd wanted all the enemy armies dead and the wave had come. Now with the Romans and British so close, even if she could set the land on fire or make it rain spears, she'd kill the Maidunites, too. Even if she'd had magic, there was nothing she could do.

She looked at the small figure of the blonde woman, pacing the north wall of the hillfort. Spring could feel her frustration and anxiety even at this distance.

"Can I go, please?" she asked the praetorians.

Ferrandus looked at Tertius. Tertius turned to Spring.

"It's possible that we could get away with letting you go, assuming Clodia went along with it. In a battle this size you can get away with pretty much anything by blaming it on the battle."

"Clodia?" asked Spring. Clodia looked back at her. She'd never seen such a serious expression on the Roman woman's face.

"But," continued Tertius, "even if we were certain to never be discovered, we wouldn't let you go."

"We've come to like you, you see, even if you are a barbarian." Ferrandus cocked his head. "And we'd rather you were alive."

"And of course we *might* be found out and crucified, and we'd rather that we were alive, too," added Tertius.

"There is that." Ferrandus nodded.

"Let her go," said Clodia.

"With all respect, your worship," said Ferrandus, "it's not your—"

Clodia nodded at her guards. They raised their bows and drew, arrows pointed at the praetorians. "If it were my people I'd want to be with them. I understand what Spring has to do and I know you do as well. Even if you don't, your alternative is an arrow or two in the chest." Clodia smiled.

"Well, if you put it like that," said Tertius.

"I will tell Caesar that I forced you to free her," said Clodia. "Would you like my guards to make it more convincing? Arrows in your legs perhaps?"

"I'm sure your word is good enough for Caesar," said Tertius.

Ferrandus nodded and untied Spring. She gathered her reins.

"Before you go," Tertius unwrapped a long leather bundle from their pack pony. "I've been keeping this for you. I was going to give it to you when they made you queen, but you might as well have it now."

He peeled off the remaining leather and revealed Dug's hammer.

Spring felt tears well in her eyes.

"I don't know what to say!" she said.

"Don't say anything, just bugger off and for Jupiter's sake *don't get killed*."

Atlas found Chamanca propped against a dead elephant, blinking.

"All right?" he asked.

"Yes, of course. I was simply surveying the scene before—" She choked, heaved and coughed up a gush of blood.

Atlas had never seen anybody vomit that much blood and live much longer. He dropped into a crouch and put a hand on her shoulder.

"Cham—"

He was interrupted by a voice behind him. "Another African – a Kushite, I think?" said the voice in Latin. "Kushite is my elephant's favourite food. He ate many in his youth."

Atlas stood and turned. The leader of the Yonkari was

walking towards him, swinging a club – the same sort of club that had killed his father. He looked exactly like the murderer from Atlas' memories. It couldn't be the same man, he was too young, but he could be the son of the man who'd killed his parents. Atlas decided that it definitely was. It would help him in the fight to come.

"Your dead elephant has no more need of sustenance," said Atlas.

"It speaks Latin? What a clever Kushite it is."

"It gets cleverer," said Atlas, tossing his giant axe lightly from hand to hand.

Spring rode down through the woods on the flank of the hill. She could hear the clash of iron and the shouts of the fighters, but block that out and, in the cool of the trees, with butterflies flitting between shafts of sunlight, she might have been a million miles from the fighting. She might have been walking through woods with Dug on that first day they'd met.

He was sitting on a branch of a dead tree where the track turned a corner.

"Are you sure that'll take your weight?" she asked.

"Aye, I don't think I weigh anything."

"Well, it's good to see you. I'll be seeing you more permanently soon."

"I don't think so."

"I'm going to join Lowa and fight to the end."

"I see you've got my hammer back. That's good and I'm sure you'd fight like an angry weasel, but I've a better plan than charging at the Romans and dying and losing my hammer again."

"Which is?"

"Rescue wee Dug. He's in the fort with Keelin. Fort's surrounded on all sides but this one, for now. You can ride in, grab the bairn and ride out."

"But—"

"I understand why you want to be at Lowa's side, but save him, and you save all that's left of me and Lowa. We can continue, through him."

"I suppose…" She was half convinced, but then she realised.

"Hang on, I've created you in my head, yes?"

". . . Aye."

"So my coward mind must have made you appear now to get me out of doing what's right."

"Rescuing wee Dug is the right thing to do."

"It's not."

"What would Lowa want you to do? What would I want you to do? And what's the right thing to do? Is dying more noble than rescuing a wee child?"

Had Spring not been on a horse, she would have stamped her foot.

Chamanca was amused by the concern in Atlas' eyes when she'd vomited blood. Had it been her own blood, he might have had cause to worry.

She tried to push herself up on her arms, but didn't have the strength. Her legs she couldn't feel at all. Maybe Atlas *had* been right to look so worried.

And now, as he squared up to the other African, she was worried. Atlas was a great fighter, but he didn't have magical speed at the best of times and now he looked slower than normal. By the sallowness of his skin, he was unwell. Jagganoch did have magical speed and his skin shone like a healthy fox's coat. She'd have to help her man, but that would require standing up at the very least, and she couldn't quite run to that yet. She could feel the dreadful wound to her head healing, but not fast enough.

The two men circled, club poised, axe flicking from hand to hand. Atlas was huge and hulking in his tartan trousers, sleeveless leather jerkin and iron armbands. Jagganoch, in his lion skin and legionary's skirt, was lithe, bouncy and terrifying.

Jagganoch darted in, his club blurring as he probed for a gap. Atlas parried with his axe handle, effectively but clumsily in comparison with the Yonkari. Jagganoch pressed. Atlas retreated and stumbled. A smile flashed onto the elephanteer's face as he swung his club for the killing blow. Chamanca tried to leap to Atlas' defence but could not.

Atlas' stumble had been a feint. He tossed his axe to his left hand, grabbed the club as it whizzed down, pulled it to one side and darted in with a head butt which pulverised Jagganoch's nose. Atlas threw the club aside, dropped his axe and stepped after the reeling Jagganoch, raising his fists. He jabbed his pulped nose once, twice. Jagganoch's head lolled. The Kushite dropped his fists and set to punching the Yonkari man's guts and ribs again and again, hammering hard as a horse trying to kick its way out of a burning stable. As Jagganoch began to falter and collapse, Atlas swung his fist down, around and up into the elephanteer's chin, shattering his jaw and lifting him off his feet. Jagganoch flew four paces and landed hard, out cold.

Chamanca felt bad for underestimating Atlas. He'd had it under control from the start. He was a much better fighter than she'd ever given him credit for. Better than Jagganoch certainly and − maybe − even a little better than she was.

The Kushite strode up to the unconscious elephanteer, ripped off his bronze helmet and tossed it away, grabbed his wrist and pulled him over to Chamanca. Holding him by his hair and his lion skin, Atlas lifted Jagganoch's head so that his neck was nicely in range of the Iberian's teeth.

"Thought you might want a drink," he said.

Unable to see the battle, Ragnall was frustrated. His section of cavalry had been ordered to ride around to the south of the fort to catch any Britons making a run for it. None of them had. They'd seen the aurochs charge past to the east and thankfully the aurochs hadn't seen them, or at least had had bigger fish to charge at. That had been the only interesting thing all day and now a whole legion had joined them guarding the southern escape route, so his section of the cavalry's role was redundant. However, orders were to stay there, so stay there they did. They could hear the battle. Ragnall was sure he could taste the adrenaline and battle lust thick in the air, but he didn't know what was happening. He had to go and see.

He rode up to the captain. "I want to check the east of the fort."

"Sure thing, whatever, go." The cavalry, comprised of men from conquered tribes, was more relaxed than the legions.

Ragnall galloped to the east. He could see people watching from the walls of Saran Fort. He wondered if any of them recognised him. Then, riding from the woods to the east, heading for the fort, was someone he recognised.

Spring stopped when she saw him. "Still a Roman then?" she said.

"You've escaped" was all he could think to say. She looked good, in her leather shorts, white shirt and riding boots – exact copies of Lowa's clothes, just like she was an exact copy of Lowa. They were evil female twins, twisted tools of the gods who existed only to bring him low.

"And you're still observant," she smirked.

Ragnall felt heat rise up his neck. Still she mocked him. He had started a new phase in his life. Hitting Spring had been a low. He was noble now. But she was *such an insolent little bitch*! She had no respect for him, not a scrap. Not as a man, not as her husband . . . He would have to teach her some. It had been a fair fight last time. He wouldn't let that happen again. She had the Northman's hammer at her side, he was surprised to see, but there was no way she was strong enough to wield it, so effectively she was unarmed. He pulled his sword from its scabbard.

"You're recaptured," he said. "Get off your horse."

"Sure thing. When I get to the fort!" Spring kicked her horse and galloped away.

Ragnall followed. His horse was faster. She turned and it was a joy to see her expression slide from cocky to concerned when she realised that he was going to catch her. She jinked the reins to dodge and weave, but it was easy to cover her evasions. He caught up well outside the range of the British archers on the fort and cracked her on the back of her head with the flat of his blade. She fell off, bounced and rolled to a crumpled stop. He circled around and jumped down next to her prone body.

He was worried that he'd killed her, but she was breathing regularly. He'd take her to Caesar, so that the new king and queen could be in the thick of things when the old queen was defeated. He wouldn't kill her, not yet, he decided. He'd keep her as a captive wife and teach her how to respect him.

He had nothing to tie her with. If she woke . . . he was stronger now from the exercise of riding all day and he was armed, but the idea of being bested by her again in a fight . . . There was a bulge in the pocket of her leather shorts. It was a bowstring. What a stroke of luck and a joyful irony! Praise Jupiter, said Ragnall to himself. It seemed like the gods were with him today. It was certainly his turn for it.

He turned the girl on to her front, laid Dug's hammer on her back and tied her hands to its shaft.

Chapter 8

Chamanca stood and shook herself. Jagganoch's blood was the best she'd ever tasted, and she felt fully restored. More than restored. Pressing her fingers to where he'd whacked her with his club, she could feel the bone swiftly reknitting.

Just as she was thinking what an amazing person she was, dozens of legionaries ran up, filing between dead aurochs and elephants, surrounding her and Atlas, pilums poised. Atlas raised his axe, Chamanca crouched, ready to leap into action.

"Surrender, we have you surrounded," said their leader, in a voice Chamanca recognised. He was wearing a plumed helmet, but she'd have known him anywhere.

"It's the masturbating centurion I told you about," she said to Atlas, in Latin so that all his men might hear. "He's the one who came into the tent where I was chained and beat his little bit of meat while the other Romans were all fighting Ariovistus."

"Silence! You cannot escape!" the wanker shouted, reddening as more legionaries piled in, some climbing onto dead elephants and aiming their spears at the British pair. There were dozens of them.

"He's right," said Atlas.

"I will not surrender."

"I'm going to. I've died quite enough times recently. We get captured, we live to fight another day."

"Maybe not, they might kill us."

"I know," said the mighty African Warrior. "But I also know I cannot win this fight and I don't want to see you die." He placed his axe on the blood-soaked ground and raised his hands.

Chamanca looked at her lover. His skin had a grey tinge and the spark had gone from his eyes. He was spent. She looked around. Maybe seventy legionaries looked back, all ready to hurl their spears. She still might have made it out of there, she'd faced tougher odds . . . Actually that probably wasn't true, but she had faced horrible odds and come through. Then again she'd been captured by the Romans before and come through. The thought of being captured again by the pervert centurion didn't appeal, but it was better than seeing Atlas die.

"Oh, for Fenn's sake," she said, and tossed her mace and sword down next to Atlas' axe.

"Keep those pilums on them!" the centurion cried excitedly. "Gather their weapons and tie them up."

Felix climbed the tree with the help of two Celermen. He did not like what he saw. The aurochs were finished, but so were the elephants. The British infantry were surrounded, and Caesar's newly arrived scorpions and catapults were ripping great holes into them, but the barbarians were fighting strongly, maintaining discipline, refreshing their front rank regularly and pushing back towards the fort. Soon the Romans to their south would be driven into range of the fort's scorpion bows and archers. Already he could see Lowa and her cursed longbow potting legionaries as if she were a wanton boy swatting flies.

He knew what would happen. Caesar would pull his legionaries away before they came in range of the fearsome firepower of the fort, the Britons would get back their redoubt and there would be a siege. That could last months.

It might even force the Romans to return to Gaul. He could not have that.

There was only one thing to do.

Lowa shot legionary after legionary, spreading panic through the back rows of the two legions between her infantry and the fort. All their Roman training, and they hadn't learnt how to put up an effective shield wall at the rear. The speed her men and women were pushing them, they'd be in range of the other archers and the scorpions soon. Many Britons were being taken out by the Romans' scorpions and catapults to the north, but not too many. That's what she had to tell herself. She could not think of the individual men and women dying. She was losing an acceptable proportion of her force to the Roman heavy weapons, and she was remedying the situation by bringing them back to the fort. Similarly, she told herself, she wasn't shooting retreating men who might have lovers and children, she was reducing the strength of the enemy.

"Lowa!" By the way the trumpeter shouted, she guessed he'd been trying to get her attention for a while, but she'd been fixed on plugging legionaries. She shook her head, feeling like she'd woken from a dream. The man was pointing. She looked, and did not like what she saw.

To the west, the Roman ranks were parting at the command of a small, balding man. Hulking behind him were the Ironmen. Tripping along in their wake came the Leathermen. There were a good deal fewer than Mal had reported from the attack at Big Bugger Hill, so his raid had been some success, but there were still quite enough.

They reached the front line and Felix held back while his troops passed. The Britons saw the Ironmen towering behind the legionaries and readied their shields. The Iron giants pushed the Roman soldiers aside and swung their swords.

They waded through the Britons, chopping, kicking and smiting. Behind them the Leathermen finished off any that the Ironmen missed. Men and women wielding every manner of weapon hurled themselves at the giants but none had any effect. Arrows and slingstones pinged off them. As they killed more and more, rather than tiring, their sword strokes and blade-legged kicks came faster and harder. The Britons tried to get round behind them, but were thwarted by the Leathermen, who were now moving so fast that it was hard to keep track of any individual.

Legionaries pressed behind the demons, exploiting the tear in the British ranks. The entire western flank of her army crumbled. She watched, praying to the gods to give her men and women strength, aching to see just one demon fall. None did. They pressed on, unstoppable.

Far, far too many were dying, far too quickly. With the attack of the demons the rest were doomed, too. They'd be destroyed before they reached the safety of the fort and the covering fire of the scorpions.

She was beaten. She briefly considered joining the defence against the demons, maybe she could take one down before she was killed. If she rode closer with her bow, then perhaps . . .

But no. She might kill one or two with her bow, but hundreds would die while she was trying. She'd tried to be objective about people dying since the Romans had landed, persuade herself that some losses were acceptable. By that same standpoint, these losses were not. It this continued, she'd be beaten and her entire infantry would be slaughtered.

She looked around. What else did she have? What else could she use?

There was nothing. Nothing. All her preparation, all that planning, all the training, all those lives! Everyone who'd died to get to this point . . . It was all for nothing now.

Fucked up the arse by Felix's demons. She was beaten. Now it was time to save as many of her men and women as she could.

She told her trumpeter what to signal and ran back to the body of the fort, shouting for her horse and for the gate to be opened. While a groom was fetching her mount, Lowa found Keelin. Little Dug was still asleep, but this time Lowa took him from the girl's arms. He moaned and raised a fat little pink hand as Lowa squeezed him to her chest, but he didn't wake up, even when a tear dripped from her cheek on to his golden hair.

Queen Lowa Flynn gave her son back to Keelin and swung up onto her horse. The groom handed her bow to her and she galloped from the hillfort.

Chapter 9

Praetorians forced Chamanca and Atlas to kneel to Caesar. Bound tightly as they were, the Iberian could only comply. She couldn't see past the people milling around, but very soon after they'd arrived she heard that Felix's demons were attacking. She saw anger flash on Caesar's face, saw him smother it, and then bark out orders for the legions as if Felix's intervention had been part of his plans. From the reports, the demons had turned the tide of the battle wholly in the Romans' favour. Chamanca regretted surrendering for the thousandth time. She'd have dealt with the demons. On the brighter side, Atlas seemed to be recovering. His skin was almost back to dark brown, and he was straining at his bonds. He was having no effect on them and it didn't look like he was going to, but at least he was trying.

"Lone horsewoman, sir," said a praetorian, pointing down the rise. Chamanca guessed what was coming and sighed.

Lowa rode into sight, slipped off her horse and strode up to Caesar. A couple of praetorians rushed to intercept her but Caesar called them back.

She knelt and placed her longbow staff and quiver on the ground in front of him.

"I surrender. Call off your monsters. My signaller is ready. My army will cease fighting the moment they step back."

Atlas translated, substituting the word "forces" for "monsters".

Caesar nodded and gave the orders. Trumpets sounded first from the Roman lines, then in reply from Saran Fort.

Lowa, Atlas and Chamanca knelt at Caesar's feet in silence as the noises of battle dwindled, to be replaced by the screams and cries of the wounded. Chamanca watched Caesar. He was looking over to the west, to where Felix's monsters had attacked. A hint of worry creased his brow. He wasn't sure if the magic-powered legion would obey his command, she guessed. After some tense heartbeats, half his mouth pulsed in a quick smile. It looked like Felix and his brood had complied.

That was lucky, thought Chamanca; it would be annoying to surrender and have your army massacred anyway.

The general looked down at his beaten opponent. "Queen Lowa Flynn of the British. Caesar accepts your surrender and salutes your bravery."

Atlas translated for her.

"Thanks," said Lowa. "Tell him that my army will return home. They will never be slaves."

"She salutes the skill of the Romans and requests the famous mercy of Julius Caesar. She would like her men and women to be allowed to return to their fields," said Atlas.

"Caesar will spare your army's lives, taking only a small number as slaves. However, he has no alternative but to execute you and your two generals."

Fenn's pissflaps, thought Chamanca.

Atlas translated Caesar's words.

Lowa nodded. "I am the only leader."

Atlas translated.

Caesar gestured at Chamanca and Atlas "These two are known. They have impeded the general's laudable aims too many times. They will also die. Praetorians! Three crosses facing south, now."

"Thank you for trying, Lowa," said Atlas, "but we too have fought our last battle."

"Tell him I have a son," said Lowa, "eighteen moons old. He is in the fort with his nanny, Keelin Orton. I'd like Caesar to spare him and to allow Keelin to remain with him."

Atlas explained her wish to Caesar.

"The leader of the Romans is not without mercy. So impressed has Caesar been with the British fighting and your command that I will raise your son as my own. He will want for nothing and he will be king of Britain when I deem him ready."

Atlas translated.

Lowa nodded. She looked as strong and heroic as if her army had defeated Caesar's. Chamanca expected nothing less. Lowa had had to try, she'd tried her best, and now it was time to die. Chamanca was proud to die alongside her, although the Iberian knew that most normal people took a day and a night to die on a cross. How long was it going to take someone as tough as her?

The praetorians returned and nailed crossbeams to uprights. Lowa had heard plenty of fearful descriptions of crucifixion. It was meant to be the worst possible death, but she'd always wondered how it could be worse than having your guts wound round a stick or any of Zadar's other many execution favourites. And now she was going find out. Whoopee, she told herself, every situation has a bright side.

Praetorians hauled Atlas and Chamanca to their feet. Lowa stood and walked over to the crosses. She didn't want to be presumptuous, but she guessed that the central one was hers. She indicated it and lifted her upturned palms in a "This one?" gesture. The praetorians nodded and she lay down on it, spreading her arms along the beams.

Strong men gripped her limbs and one pressed the tip of a large, square-cut iron nail into her palm, then whacked it with a mallet.

A bolt of agony jerked up her arm and spasmed through her head, her whole body. She tried to channel the pain, to focus her mind on something else, but it was hard to deny the all-consuming torture of having a fat nail driven through her hand. She could feel small bones shifting aside and snapping.

The second nail was worse, and the one through her ankles more painful still. She wasn't going to let these cunts see her scream though. Instead, she bucked with pain until she passed out.

She came to as the cross was being lifted.

She'd heard a joke once:

"What's the best thing about crucifixion?"

"The view."

It was a shit joke, but she saw that it contained some truth. Once she'd managed to supress the torment from her wrists and ankles at least enough to see, she saw for miles. Nearby the legions had surrounded her infantry, many of whom were already in irons. The rest were sitting on the battle-churned ground, looking dejected. Carts, full of slave irons Lowa guessed, were trundling towards them. So Caesar was going to enslave the lot of them. It wasn't a surprise, but still it was better than being dead. As slaves they'd have the chance to rise up, to escape or simply to be happy in servitude.

Behind them towered Saran Fort, defenders still peering from its walls. The Romans hadn't got to them yet, they were still free, but at the rate the Romans were going it wouldn't be long before they reached the fort.

Backdropping it all, the sky was white at the horizon, morphing into the darkest blue as it arched overhead. What a lot that sky had seen, thought Lowa.

Chapter 10

By the time Ragnall had obtained permission from his cavalry commander to take Spring to Caesar, the battle was over.

He rode along its eerily quiet flank. Eerily quiet, that was, apart from the skin-curdling screams of the wounded. After every other battle that Ragnall had seen, the chief sound from the Romans had been chattering, as they explained to each other just how awesome they'd been in the field. This one was different. Everything was subdued. Looking at the faces of the Romans and the Britons it was impossible to tell who'd won — it had been a tougher battle than the legionaries were used to. Other things marked the victors, though. Almost all of the Britons were already in chains and being led away. Already they were learning about Roman efficiency.

In a battle as hard-fought as this one, are there really any winners? Ragnall thought. It was thinking like that, he told himself, that marked him out as a man who should be king.

He arrived at the command hillock, dismounted, pulled Spring off the horse, slung her over his shoulder and headed for Caesar. He stopped to stare up at the three on the crosses. They all glanced at him, then looked away without a flicker of acknowledgement. It was worse than if they'd stared hatred at him. He felt heat spread up his neck and sweat trickle from his armpits.

It didn't matter, he told himself, they'd all be dead soon. He looked at Caesar, on the far side of the crosses, some fifty paces distant. The general nodded back. There you go, thought Ragnall. I have the respect of the greatest military leader in the world. Who cares if a dying queen and her freakish lackeys don't like me?

The girl was heavier than he'd expected, so it was something of a relief when she came round and said:

"You can put me down now."

Her hands were still tied to the hammer at her back, so he thought it was safe to do as she'd asked. It looked for a moment like she was going to come out with some cocky comment, but, to Ragnall's joy, her face crumbled in misery when she saw her heroes high on their crosses. He tried to stop himself gloating. Good kings didn't gloat. But he couldn't help it, and anyway he wasn't king just yet.

"Not so smart now, are you?" he said, poking her in the chest.

Before he'd seen she was moving, she leapt and smashed her shoulder into his chin. He stumbled back, tasting blood in his mouth, blinking. He saw the girl jump and tried to duck away, but her iron-heeled boot caught him in the side of the head and sent him crashing to the ground. His urge was to stay down, or to run, but Caesar was watching. As were the praetorians, Lowa, Chamanca, Atlas, a good portion of both armies . . .

He stood. The girl was bouncing from foot to foot, her hands still bound behind her. "Come on!" she shouted at him.

Two praetorians approached her from behind but Caesar said: "Hold."

So he was their sport now. They were all watching. She was younger, a woman – little more than a girl – and her hands were tied behind her back. He could not afford to lose. He slipped his sword from his scabbard.

"Boo!" shouted some legionaries, and Ragnall realised that winning with his sword would be almost as bad as losing,

and losing with it would be much worse. There was no gain
in using the sword. He tossed it away and held out his hands
towards Spring, fingers splayed and palms down. He danced
from foot to foot. He'd seen a brilliant bare-handed gladiator
start like this once, and defeat a man armed with a trident
and a net. Ragnall knew the girl was powerful, but he was
heavier, so he if could use his weight . . . He lunged. Spring
melted to the side, his hands grasped air and his balls
exploded. He fell and lay, shaking and crying with pain.
She had kneed him in the bollocks and he couldn't move.
The pain was astonishing and almost all-encompassing but,
even over his sobs, but he could still hear the laughter
ringing out all around him. He opened an eye and saw the
toe of Spring's boot speeding towards his face.

"Bring the girl to Caesar!" called Caesar.

A praetorian marched her at arm's length across the hillock.
Blood was dripping from Lowa's hands and ankles, but she
was smiling at Spring, not madly but warmly. When she
winked, Spring had to blink back tears.

The praetorian stopped her two paces from Caesar and
kept his fingers gripped around her biceps. She struggled
in his grip, but he was a strong man and she was held.

"Undo her bonds," said Caesar.

Spring heard a snick then her arms were free and Dug's
hammer fell to the ground behind her. Meanwhile, Ragnall
limped towards them, blood running from his broken nose,
supported by two praetorians who were doing their best to
remain grim-faced.

"Spring, you are a remarkable young woman. Caesar has
never seen anyone laugh on a cross before, yet you made
all three forget their pain for a moment when you bested
that boy. Even Caesar laughed at your antics. However, it
is clear that you will never be tamed, so you can never be
queen of Britain. Neither can you remain here because rebel-

lion is in your blood. However, partly because you have amused and mostly because you charmed Caesar at your wedding in Rome, he will free you, both from your bonds and your marriage. You will leave Britain and never set foot here again, or in any other of Rome's provinces, on pain of death."

Spring looked up at Chamanca, Atlas and Lowa. She could see the torment on their faces. Should she just accept Caesar's words and leave? She could take little Dug and go to Eroo. Or should she try to save her friends? If the latter, then how? It was impossible anyway, but standing here directly under Caesar's gaze, it was doubly so.

"And you." Caesar's gaze settled on Ragnall. "A king needs respect. You have lost the small amount that you had and you will not be king. However, you have worked hard for Caesar, so you will remain a Roman. You will stay in the cavalry, with the same prospect of advancement or failure that is every Roman citizen's right. Translate all this for your wife."

Ragnall looked at Spring, his eyes narrow. "He says blah, blah, stuff about being noble, some things about me making a fine king and that he will free you. He's asking you where you want to go."

"Oh, that's nice," said Spring. "Tell him please to give me one of the horses and I'll make my own way. If I could have four horses in case three of them tire, that would be great."

Ragnall looked at Caesar. "She curses you, spits on your generosity and demands to be crucified alongside her queen."

Caesar looked surprised, then serious: "Very well. Tell her to wait by the others. You, bring up a cross." He nodded at two praetorians, who jogged away.

Ragnall turned back to Spring: "He said all these nearby horses are taken. He's sent them to get four of his best, and asks you to wait over there." Ragnall pointed to the crosses.

"Sure thing!" said Spring. She looked up at Atlas, Lowa

and Chamanca as she walked towards them. They were trying to look heroic, but each was twisted by the pain of the metal spikes piercing their limbs. She had to do something, but what? If only Caesar really was sending four of his best horses. But even then . . .

She could have jumped and reached their ankles, but she'd never be able to pull those nails out. Even if she could have got them down somehow, they were surrounded by Caesar's special guard and his entire army. If she didn't do something very soon, she was going to be on a cross herself. On the plus side, Ragnall's vindictive shittiness had got her away from Caesar and everyone else's immediate attention.

She heard the general call to his praetorians to ride to the fort, demand that they open the gates, clear out the Britons and retrieve Lowa's son.

"And Keelin!" shouted Chamanca from her cross.

"Indeed, do not harm the nanny called Keelin and allow her to keep hold of the child."

Spring was glad to see that Lowa had arranged this as part of the deal, and also that Caesar was sticking to it. He'd done terrible things and no doubt he would do more, but he did appear to have some sort of moral code. It was a hypocritical, self-serving, disingenuous moral code, but at least he had one.

"Hold there!" shouted a voice that Spring knew and hated. Everyone turned and she took the opportunity to drop on to her chest, behind the pile of soil that had been dug out to plant the crucifixion uprights. She peered over it to see Felix walking up the hummock, his Leathermen following, Ironmen crashing along behind them.

"Felix!" cried Caesar. "Dare you command Caesar's praetorians?"

"Felix dares," said Felix. "Caesar will do what Felix tells him from this moment forth."

"He will not. Praetorians, kill Titus Pontius Felix," said Caesar.

Before the praetorians had done much more than move, the Leathermen were among them, diving, darting and slicing. Spring gasped. They were so fast! So much faster than before, and they'd been far too fast then. Within moments, most of the praetorians were dead. Nearby legionaries rushed in, but the Ironmen, almost as quick as the Leathermen, darted forward and slaughtered them so easily and so messily that no more legionaries dared attack. They took several steps back to encircle the hillock and look on warily from behind their shields.

"Get away now, Spring," whispered Lowa from above her. "Run. Stay low."

"Not without you!" said Spring, pressing herself into the grass.

She peeked up and saw the six head centurions, one from each legion, standing between Caesar and the demons. Ragnall stood next to them all like a passer-by who had wandered unwittingly onto a bard's stage and was now standing mouth agape, trying to work out what the Bel was going on while the audience laughed at him. Then he seemed to wake up, and he bent to pick up Spring's hammer. *Get off that!* Spring thought.

"Where is the girl Spring?" asked Felix, striding up. She pressed herself into the ground behind her pile of soil.

"Spring?" Caesar replied.

Felix turned to Ragnall. "Do you know, boy?"

Ragnall watched mesmerised as Felix's monsters killed the praetorians and legionaries like foxes among stupefied chickens. The heavily armoured ones were moving too fast for his eye to follow. The leather-clad ones were faster. The geysers of blood spouting from slashed-open men reminded him of the fountains in Pompey's theatre. He realised that he was watching with his mouth open and closed it quickly. He spotted Spring's hammer where it had fallen and picked it up. He doubted he'd be able to do much with it, but he'd dropped his sword fighting Spring and this seemed like the sort of time to be armed.

Felix shouted for his creatures to fall back and form a perimeter around himself, Caesar and the command group. Several hundred legionaries crowded round, but none dared attack. Behind them, other legionaries were leading the British prisoners away. If they'd seen the disturbance on the command hill, they were getting on with their work rather than running over to find out what was going on, as British soldiers would have done. That, thought Ragnall, shows why Roman culture will always be better than British.

"Where is the girl Spring?" said Felix

"Spring?" said Caesar.

"Do you know, boy?"

"Yes, she's . . ." He looked over to the crosses where he'd last seen her. Lowa, Atlas and Chamanca all shook their heads at him, each looking more threatening than the next. Ordering him what to do. People were always ordering him about. "She was over there last time I saw her, but she must have run."

"The boy lies. She is in the British fort," said Caesar. "I freed her and sent her there." Ragnall opened his mouth to say no, she wasn't, but he could feel Caesar telling him not to even though the general wasn't looking at him. For some reason, he obeyed.

"Hmm. Then command your legions to attack Saran Fort. I want the girl."

"I will not. The Britons have surrendered."

"Yet the fort's gates remain shut and the girl might be escaping as we speak. You will give the command to attack it."

"No."

"You," said Felix, pointing at one of his Celermen. "Kill the centurions, then press your blade one finger's breadth into Caesar's neck."

"Wait!" cried Caesar, as the Celerman leapt forward, sword flashing.

"Hold!" said Felix. His minion stood back. It was too late for one centurion, who was already down, hands clamped to his neck and blood squirting between his fingers. The remaining centurions stood between Caesar and Felix.

"You will all be dead in moments, including you, Caesar, if you do not command your troops to attack the fort."

"Give the order," sighed Caesar.

One of the centurions walked away down the low hill towards the armies, followed, on Felix's orders, by a Celerman. A moment later a trumpet rang out. The two legions nearest the fort turned and jogged towards it, shields coming up over their heads as they neared. As soon as they were in range, scorpion arrows flew from the fort in graceful arcs, followed by catapult-hurled incendiary buckets. The defenders might have surrendered, but they'd stayed prepared.

Great holes were blasted in the legionaries' tortoises, promptly filled as the legions ran on towards the fort. Behind them, the carts full of wall-mounting debris rumbled into place.

"I thought we agreed that you would rescue the wee boy." Dug sat atop the pile of soil sheltering her from Felix's gaze.

"Well things got a little in my way, didn't they?" she whispered.

Dug looked up at Chamanca, Lowa and Atlas on their crosses, then at the legions attacking Saran Fort, then back at Lowa. Her eyes were closed and she was breathing raggedly through gritted teeth, clearly in great pain and struggling for breath. Dug's eyes narrowed. "Spring, you have to save him. Now."

"How?"

"Here comes a horse. Why don't you jump on that?"

A riderless horse was walking towards her. One of its flanks was coated in blood but the animal seemed unharmed, nosing through the grass as if there wasn't a crowd of monsters a dozen paces away.

Spring jumped up and ran for it.

"There she is!" she heard Ragnall shout.

"Stop her!" Felix cried. Leather-clad arms were round her waist before she was halfway to the horse. She was being carried, struggling, towards Felix. She hated being carried, she decided. Nobody ever carried her anywhere for her benefit.

"So!" said Felix when the Leatherman plonked her down, keeping hold of her shoulders. "Finally I have you and your magic!"

Spring laughed. "I don't have any magic, you idiot."

Felix's default sneer twisted into a bulge-eyed stare. "Yes, you do."

"I really, really don't. Do I look like I'm lying?" He peered at her, she smiled back. His eyes bulged and his mouth opened a little.

"You do," he managed eventually. "I saw you at Maidun."

"You saw Dug Sealskinner at Maidun, and he died two years ago. His magic was linked to me, and I could use it, but I killed him to create a giant wave that drowned three armies and the magic died with him."

"You made the great wave?"

"Dug made that wave. It was his final act. And now, without him, there is no magic. I haven't felt a glimmer of it since. Really! I could have used it loads of times. Now would be great moment, for example, to explode your ugly bald head, but I can't. If I was some powerful druid, don't you think I would have used my magic to escape? To halt this invading army? Look into my eyes, you know I'm not lying."

Felix did, then shook his head. "Oh no, that simply cannot be right. There is great magic on this island. And it is nearby. I know it."

"Maybe, I wouldn't know, but it's not in me and you're a fool."

"I was wrong all this time . . ." Felix continued, looking disappointed. "Oh well," he said, perking up. "I'll find the source of magic, it shouldn't be hard with the whole island under my boot. And you, Spring? You can be the first casualty of my search."

He reached for his sword.

Chapter 11

Lowa watched as thousands of legionaries attacked Saran Fort. The defenders had seen the new Roman attack as a signal to resume hostilities, but, with almost all of her army in chains, the fort didn't have nearly as many defenders as it needed. It would not last long.

Meanwhile, the agony in her wrists and ankles was a little less intense. The pain from her wounds still pulsed through her like blades bisecting her limbs, and she had a strong urge to hang her head and weep, but she would not give in to it. Her sacrifice, she told herself, was to save her son. Then she told herself, no, her sacrifice was a result of her being an idiot taken in by false shouts.

Her thoughts were interrupted by Spring running out from below her, towards a riderless horse. Lowa felt a flash of hope for the girl, but Ragnall spotted her and shouted, a Leatherman flew in like a bolt from a scorpion and caught her. Lowa sighed so hard that it ripped at the nails in her hand. No more heavy sighing, she told herself.

The demon carried the girl to Felix. Lowa couldn't hear what they were saying, but Spring looked remarkably chipper. Caesar and his praetorians and the rest of the Leathermen were behind Felix. Ragnall stood off to one side. Lowa thought back to that night in the woods seven years before when she'd shagged him. Why had she done that? Had it really been Spring's magical wish? Surely not? Looking at him now, though, she couldn't work out why *else* she would have had her way with him. For all her killing under

Zadar's orders, betraying Dug and sleeping with Ragnall was one of her greatest regrets. But perhaps it had been the girl's magic all along and she should meet Dug in the Otherworld with a clear conscience?

Spring was laughing at Felix now. Was that a good thing? And was there an Otherworld? Lowa had always thought not; humans were simply conceited animals who'd deluded themselves that they were more special than slugs and squirrels. But then she'd seen magic, she'd felt it in her and she'd seen the Spring Tide . . . So maybe humans were special, maybe there were gods, and maybe when this cross torture finally killed her, she'd find herself in some idyllic field with her sister, Dug, her mother . . .

There was a flash of movement to the east. Seven cavalry were galloping across the only part of the landscape that wasn't full of legionaries, towards Felix. He was so intent on questioning Spring that he hadn't spotted them. Caesar had, though. He reached out to subtly tap his centurions and they all took a few paces back.

A woman led the seven cavalry, followed by two black-clad praetorians and four gaily dressed archers. As they closed, Lowa saw that the woman was in a white dress that was little more than a shirt, with a jewelled dagger on each hip. With her shining hair and spotless outfit, she looked like a parody of a Warrior. However, the praetorians brandishing swords and the other four, riding with their legs and raising bows with arrows strung, looked like they knew what they were doing.

But they were too late. Felix raised his blade to kill Spring.

The horsewoman shouted a command in Latin. Felix paused and turned as the arrows flew. One zipped into his arm and he dropped his sword, then the horses were on them. The Leathermen danced to avoid flashing hooves. The woman galloped straight at Felix, whooping some kind of hunting cry. The Leatherman holding Spring threw the girl to one side and leapt to bundle Felix clear. Ragnall saw the danger at the last moment and dived away, still clutching the hammer.

Seizing the moment, Spring ran from the confusion, towards the fort. Ragnall ran, too, in panicked flight towards the crosses. He looked over his shoulder and saw Spring. Hefting the hammer, he sprinted after her.

Felix, recovering his wits, also spotted Spring, grabbed a Leatherman, pointed at her and shouted.

The Leatherman flipped his sword in the air, caught it by the tip, drew his arm back and hurled it like a throwing knife, straight at Spring.

Ragnall reached Spring and leapt, hammer aloft.

The Leatherman's sword hit Ragnall square in the back and sliced through him. Ragnall fell and his hammerblow missed Spring by a finger's breadth. Spring turned, stopped, snatched the hammer from Ragnall's fingers and ran on.

Ragnall raised a hand after her, as if imploring her to stop, then collapsed.

Ha! Come on, Spring, Lowa thought, pain replaced by hope. She didn't know what she was hoping for, but by Danu she wanted the girl to get away.

Felix screamed orders and his Leathermen gave chase, the sword thrower out in front. Meanwhile, Caesar and his centurions were beating a hasty retreat, but Felix shouted another order and within moments they were surrounded by Ironmen.

Spring's mounted rescuers rallied and charged in among the Leathermen. The archers were killed almost immediately, but the praetorians fought well, delaying all but the lead demon. The female rescuer chased after him. Lowa wondered who she was. She might not look like a soldier, but her horse was the fastest the queen had ever seen and the woman knew how to ride it.

The two praetorians went down, one hamstrung and the

other to a mighty punch, and the crowd of demons ran after Spring. They were a long way back, but the lead demon was right on her, the horsewoman almost on him.

The Leatherman leapt for Spring. At the same moment the mystery woman threw herself from her horse, a dagger in each hand.

The dagger blades sank to the hilt into the demon's back to the hilt. Woman and monster tumbled in a ball of waving limbs. When they came to a stop, the demon had somehow taken a blade from his back and was straddling the woman, dagger held aloft. But Spring had stopped, too. She whirled the hammer in an arc and whacked it into the side of the demon's head.

The Leatherman fell, the woman leapt up, grabbed the dagger from the demon's hand, slammed it into his neck and shouted something at Spring.

Spring turned and ran on towards the fort. Or at least towards the backs of the several thousand legionaries attacking it.

Come on, Spring! thought Lowa. She didn't know what the girl could achieve, or how she could possibly escape by running into the massed ranks of the enemy, but, even as pain twisted in every part of her and each breath was a tortured trial, she willed her on and implored whatever gods were watching to help her.

Spring reached the back of the tortoise. As far as she could see from left to right were legionaries, all facing away from her with their shields overhead. Nearby was a whizz then a bang followed by screams, as an incendiary bucket landed on the Romans' shield roof and burning oil seared through the skin of the men below.

She glanced over her shoulder. Leathermen were coming.

There was only one way to go. She leapt like a salmon and vaulted on to one of the back-markers' raised shield.

It tilted horribly, but Spring jumped to the next one and she was away, leaping from shield to shield towards the fort. She could think of nothing but getting to little Dug. It was the same feeling of unshakeable purpose as when she'd killed his father. She had to reach the boy.

A scorpion bolt smashed down in front of her. She dodged a flying head and diverted around the hole left in the shield roof by the mighty barb. An incendiary bucket landed paces away and the shield below her fell away. She crashed down into legionaries. Before any of them had recovered from the surprise of a barbarian woman landing among them, she had scrambled back up onto their shields and was off.

She glanced behind her and saw Leathermen trying to follow across the shields. They were a good way back, and two fell between gaps in the tiny amount of time she was watching. They were much heavier than her. The top of a man-made tortoise, she thought, was one of the few surfaces in the world over which she might be quicker than the Leathermen.

As she approached the fort, arrows rained down around her in a deathly torrent. She reached the base of the Roman ramp. It was nearly completed and legionaries were marching up it, shields aloft. As she began the final sprint up it, an arrow slapped into her left shoulder.

Badgers' bollocks, she thought, running on. Her arm fizzed with pain and weirdness and she couldn't lift it. She sprinted up the slanted shield roof, injured arm flapping at her side. The legionaries at the front were carrying a bizarrely long and narrow wooden screen; Spring thought it must be for protection from arrows but they dropped it as she arrived and she saw that it was a bridge, spanning both of Saran's walls.

She leapt off the front rank of legionaries' shields.

Straight into a salvo of British arrows.

They weren't meant for her, she knew that, but they did

the damage all the same. At least two pierced her left arm to add to the one in her shoulder. One was in her right leg, one in her stomach, one through her cheek. Then another one in her stomach. And one in her chest.

She staggered on, across the bridge.

"I'm Spring!" she managed. Defenders grabbed her and pulled her through their ranks, but then they immediately turned to face the foe. Left alone, she was pirouetting, then falling off the other side of the wall. She dropped ten paces and crumpled onto the hard earth of the hillfort floor.

Chapter 12

Ragnall pawed at the sword tip protruding from his chest. You didn't come back from an injury like this, he thought. After all he'd survived – burial in Rome and all Harry the Fister's tortures, he thought he'd live for ever, but no, here was the sword, stuck in him, killing him. Whose sword was it and how had it got there? Maybe it was a dream? Surely he could not really be . . . *dying*?

Lying on his side, he could see Felix shouting at a Celerman as the creature pulled an arrow through the druid's arm. Caesar stood nearby, looking about himself as if seeking an opening. He wasn't going to find one, guarded by all those Maximen. The general didn't look as relaxed as normal, but he didn't look nearly as perturbed as he should have done. He appeared slightly frustrated, like an impatient man scanning a busy street for a friend who's late.

Behind the general were Lowa, Chamanca and Atlas on their crosses. Well, that was one consolation, thought Ragnall. He remembered what Felix had said about crucifixion, how it was a horrible death that could last for days. He tried to wish that Lowa's agony would last for an entire moon, but then he found he didn't really want it to.

And then he heard his mother calling. It was time to go home.

The arrows rained down on Spring. "Stop shooting," Lowa tried to shout at the fort's defenders, but it came out only as a croak. She tried to pull at the enormous iron nails pinning her hands, but she could hardly move her fingers, let alone shift the bolts.

On the fort wall, Spring was hit. She carried on, one arm lolling, running up the tortoise to the top of the fort wall. The bridge went down, Spring leapt and Lowa couldn't see her any more.

The five Leathermen who'd followed her across the shields reached the ramp but ignored it and leapt straight up the walls. Three of them were taken down by Maidunite arrows, but two landed successfully and sliced their way through defenders.

Chapter 13

"Come on, it's not that bad, up you get," said Dug.

Not that bad? thought Spring, *I've got a hundred arrows in me. You wouldn't get up.*

"Possibly not, but I always was lazy and you're not me. You have to get up."

Oh badgers' *bellends*, thought Spring as she pushed herself up agonisingly onto all fours, was today never going to end?

She stood. Colour had gone. The world was a slow-churning whirl of shadowy shapes melding together and drifting apart. Clarity returned for an instant and she saw a hut. Well, a hut wasn't much use. What was Dug's point? Where was she meant to go? The hut dissolved, the swirl returned and she staggered.

"Hurry up, they're coming!" said Dug.

You hurry up.

She tried to walk, but her arrow-stuck leg buckled and she fell, face whumping on the hard earth, arrows driving deeper and twisting into her ruined body. No, no, no. She was done, she wasn't going anywhere.

She heard a toddler's shout. She'd forgotten the name of the woman who looked after the child. It was one of her dad's old girlfriends. She remembered.

"Keelin!" she called weakly. She pushed herself up on one arm and saw a Leatherman run through the fort, looking about himself, not seeing her.

Idiot, she thought.

Then he spotted her.

Ah. She looked about for Dug, but he'd gone.

The Leatherman sprinted at her, shouting and beckoning to somebody else — another Leatherman, Spring guessed.

"Spring!" It was Keelin, holding little Dug.

"Put Dug down," Spring managed. Keelin raised an eyebrow and clutched the boy closer. Spring couldn't blame her. She probably wouldn't have handed a toddler to a dying, blood-soaked woman with loads of potentially hazardous arrows sticking out of her either. "*Do it!*" she shouted.

Dug screamed angrily, holding one arm out to Spring and scrabbling with the other arm and both feet to free himself from his nanny's grasp. "Well, if that's what you want—" said Keelin, plonking Dug on to the ground. Keelin was yanked aside by a Leatherman as Spring took the boy in her arms.

Time stopped.

Little Dug smiled. Big Dug looked out of his eyes. The child glowed, Spring's arrows dissolved and her flesh healed as she floated up from the ground, Dug smiling in her arms. A Leatherman leapt up at her. So. Slowly.

Clasping Dug in one arm she pointed a hand at the demon. The creature dissolved into a cloud of dust and fell to the ground like beautiful rain.

The fort all around — the huts, blacksmiths, food stores and the walls themselves — was aglow with great golden light. Spring realised it was coming from her and the child. A second Leatherman was running across the fort as if he were hip deep in the thickest mud. She pointed at him. His head spun round and popped off in a geyser of blood. She rose on up. The Maidunite defenders turned to look at her, shielding their eyes. The legionaries under their shields pressed on up the ramp, oblivious. Spring pointed her finger and they tumbled backwards.

She saw the crosses on the hill. She could see them in
detail, as if she were only ten paces away. Atlas, Chamanca,
Felix and everyone else were staring open-mouthed as she
rose. Unflappable Caesar was looking mildly confused, as if
she were nothing more than a much larger pigeon than you'd
usually expect to see. Ragnall was dead.

And Lowa?

Lowa was smiling.

Chamanca was not enjoying her crucifixion – it was tiresomely painful – so she was pleased with the diversion of
watching Spring run across the Roman army. She didn't see
the point of it, but it was amusing. Then a light rose from
the fort, brighter than the sun but somehow recognisably
Spring, holding baby Dug. Lowa was smiling. Did she understand what was happening? Atlas didn't, his mouth was
uncharacteristically agape, but Chamanca bet if they got out
of this he'd swear he'd been fully aware at every moment.

Spring pointed at Lowa. A beam of light burst from above
the fort and shot into the queen's chest. Her head bucked
then slumped forward, as if she were dead.

The iron nails holding her wrists and ankles melted, folded
back in on themselves and flowed along Lowa's limbs, torso
and head. Soon Lowa was coated in iron. Lowa *was* iron.

The iron queen fell from the cross and landed squarely.
Everybody stood back and watched as she walked over and
picked up her bow and quiver from where she'd placed
them in front of Caesar. The metal flowed from her skin and
coated the weapons.

Chamanca looked back to Spring as a bolt of light hit
her, square in the chest. She was blinded for an instant,
then she could see more clearly than ever before. The pain
disappeared immediately. She felt the nails melt and flow
out to cover her and seep into her, with a power a thousand
times more powerful than blood.

She heard Felix scream, "Get them!" as she dropped to the ground. Atlas landed at the same time, also iron-coated.

Oh yes, she thought. *Come and get us.*

Atlas ran for his axe. He saw an Ironman almost on Lowa, now glacially slow compared to the queen's magical speed. Lowa strung her iron bow in a trice, calmly nocked an iron arrow on the iron string, drew and shot. The missile hit the Ironman square in the sternum and went through him, drawing his armour with it. His chest collapsed inwards and exploded out of his back, showering the surrounding land and legionaries with guts, chunks of bone and shards of iron.

Atlas picked up his axe as an Ironman swung a sword at him. Iron raced along the wooden shaft of the axe as it became part of his metal being. He dodged the sword blow easily and swung his axe back-handed. The blade struck the thick metal on the Ironman's hip, sliced on upwards as if the demon were made of rotten wood, and out of the armoured shoulder. The monster fell away, stomach and chest opened and gore flopping out.

A second iron giant was coming at him but an iron arrow from Lowa blew him apart. Atlas looked for another to kill.

Chamanca screamed with joy as she picked up her ball-mace and short sword. Iron filled her weapons. It was more power than she'd felt before, more than she'd imagined possible. This was the strength of the very land – of the rock that lay beneath it all – flowing through her veins.

She looked around. Lowa and Atlas were slaughtering the Ironmen. The seven remaining Leathermen, however, were guarding Felix. She smiled and sashayed towards them. By Fenn, she thought, she must look amazing.

The Leathermen came at her.

She slipped clear of the first demon's sword lunge and

swung her ball-mace so fast and hard into the back of his neck that it came out of the front, exploding vertebrae, voice box, trachea, veins and arteries from his throat.

Two more advanced, blades flashing. She could see their moves. She *knew* their moves as if they'd been discussing them for weeks and were now running through the steps in slow motion for the fiftieth time. She jinked to avoid their stabs, tossed her weapons into the air, grabbed the demons by their sword hands, snapped their wrists and pushed their own blades up, through their stomachs and into their hearts. She pushed them away, stepped back and caught her falling mace and sword.

"Ha!" she shouted.

Three down, four more to go. Oh yes, she thought, running, leaping and spinning into them.

Lowa levelled her bow at the last Ironman, but saw Atlas running at him and held back. The Kushite leapt and brought his axe down two-handed into the base of the giant's neck, slicing through metal and man to his waist. The monster's chest and stomach sprang open, blood and guts sloshed out and he fell.

Chamanca was finishing off the last Leatherman. She'd dropped her weapons and was punching him repeatedly in the chest as he staggered back. The leather body armour was holding under the Iberian's iron-fisted onslaught, but Lowa could hear the ribs crunching and heart and lungs squelching as her punches destroyed them.

The Iberian took a step back, leapt, and two-foot-kicked her foe in the chest. The final Leatherman collapsed like a sackful of dead eels.

Well, there you go, thought Lowa.

She looked about for Felix and saw him running towards the legionaries, who'd been watching agog. Chamanca had told her what had happened on the wall at Wesont where she'd been captured by Caesar, when Felix had sliced the praetorian's throat to give himself power, so she guessed he was about to try the same here. She wasn't worried. She felt more than strong enough to deal with a thousand magic-powered Felixes.

"Chamanca, Atlas, make sure Caesar doesn't go anywhere," she said, and strolled after Felix, ready to face his magic.

But she wouldn't have to. The legionaries knocked him back with their shields and sent him sprawling. She walked up, put her iron foot on his neck and he was trapped.

Felix's gaze moved up the iron leg and torso to the iron face looking down at him. His Celermen and Maximen had all been destroyed and Lowa was about to crush his neck under her boot. He closed his eyes and waited.

And opened them again. Lowa was regarding him calmly and inquisitively, like a child looking into a rock pool. From one corner of his vision he could see the legionaries staring. From the other corner he saw a familiar figure approach, hips swinging.

"Lowa. I would like him, please." The iron Iberian's voice echoed strangely.

Lowa lifted her foot off his neck. Chamanca grabbed him by the hair and pulled him to his feet. She switched her grip to his neck, her iron fingers so tight that he could only just breathe.

"Do you remember all those children you killed when you were Zadar's druid?"

What a hypocrite she was. "You're worse that me." He struggled to speak. "You're a blood drinker. Are you going to drink mine?"

Chamanca shook her head. "I don't want your blood in me. This is for the children of Britain."

Holding his neck with one hand, she took his elbow in the other and squeezed. It popped and blood sprayed between her fingers. He screamed. He couldn't do anything else. The pain was incredible.

"And this," she said, "is for a girl called Autumn." Felix remembered her. The limping blacksmith's daughter. He did deserve punishment for what he'd done to that girl. And he got it. Chamanca dropped to a crouch, took his knees in her hands and crushed them both. He fell, then screamed and screamed and screamed, vaguely aware that he was being dragged along by his one good limb. He wondered where to.

Chapter 14

Lowa hadn't known that Chamanca was so inventive, but she was glad of it. The punishment she'd worked out for Felix herself didn't come to close to what Chamanca did to him. It took a long time and it was nasty. Even though it made Lowa feel so queasy that she turned away, and some of the legionaries who continued watching vomited, she was sure that anybody who knew the man would agree that he deserved every bit of it and more.

When Chamanca had finished and was wiping the blood, bone chips and brain from her hands on the grass, Lowa looked towards iron Atlas, standing next to Julius Caesar. The general was staring at something behind her in the sky.

It was Spring, floating through the air towards them like a goddess, carrying little Dug. The boy was grinning. Spring alighted gently on the hill. Lowa felt the iron flood from her body, through the soil and back into the rock below.

The girl walked over, holding little Dug by the hand as he toddled next to her. The little boy lifted his arms to Lowa. She took him up and hugged him tightly. He clasped her, burying his face in her neck. She breathed in deeply and he smelled of warmth and love – he smelled like big Dug.

She put the boy down and spoke to Spring. "Would you mind looking after him a moment more? I have something to do."

She walked over to where Atlas was standing next to Julius Caesar. Chamanca and Spring followed. On the way she passed the woman and the two black-clad Romans who'd helped to rescue Spring. All three were bruised and bloodied but smiling. She was glad that they'd survived their tussle with the demons. She smiled back at them and gave them a nod that she hoped conveyed welcome and gratitude.

Caesar coolly watched her approach.

"I retract my surrender," she said.

Atlas translated, Caesar said something and Atlas said: "He's querying whether a surrender can be retracted."

"Tell him it's my island and I make the rules here. And besides, it was the Romans who restarted the battle. I retract my surrender and I demand that he surrenders."

Atlas did, Caesar nodded then spoke at some length.

"He apologises for the behaviour of his druid," said Atlas. "But he sees no reason to surrender. He has most of your army in chains, and even if they were free he still outnumbers you."

"He's seen what my druid can do. Does he want me to kill every legionary now or would he rather take them home? He does not have to formally surrender, but he must promise to leave Britain this moon with all his legions." Lowa turned to Spring. "Spring, who are these three who saved you from Felix?"

"Tertius, Ferrandus and Clodia Metelli. They're two of Caesar's elite guard and. . . Clodia."

"All right. All his legions will go but one. We will keep that legion here for two years to tidy up the mess that he's caused. If the three of them agree to it, this legion will be commanded by Clodia Metelli, with Tertius and Ferrandus as her deputies. And here's the important part. No other Roman legionary will set foot again on British soil for a hundred years. If they do, British druids will kill every one of Caesar's family."

"Why not kill Caesar?" ask Chamanca. "He's done terrible things and he will do more if you let him go."

"Evil shit he may be," said Lowa, "but I trust him. I think we can count on him to remove his men, and not to come back."

"Why only a hundred years?"

"Because forever doesn't mean anything. A hundred years, they might actually stick to. If Britain hasn't learnt its lessons and made itself ready to repel invaders by then, it deserves to be conquered.

"Atlas, translate my demands, please, although not that last part."

"Can I?" asked Spring.

"I don't know, can you?"

"Yup."

"Then go for it."

Spring spoke in what sounded to Lowa like confident, flowing Latin. Caesar looked surprised initially, then listened, then spoke, at one point questioning Clodia, Ferrandus and Tertius, who looked like they all replied positively.

"He agrees to everything with two conditions," said Spring. "First one is easiest. He'll write the story of the invasion – I've heard him write his journals, he makes it up as he goes along – and he wants you to agree that neither you nor any of your agents will go to Rome and deny what he writes."

"Fine. Next?"

"He will leave a legion behind, on the condition that it's made up of volunteers from his legions as far as possible, that the men are treated well, and, most importantly, that after two years are up, they should be given land in Britain and remain here. I guess he doesn't want them flooding back to Rome and spoiling his story."

Lowa nodded, pleased to see that Spring's year with the Romans didn't seem to have caused any harm, in fact the opposite. She seemed more assured, and, most importantly, she didn't seem to hate Lowa any more.

Caesar's first condition she couldn't have given the smallest of craps about. He could tell whatever stories he liked as long as he buggered off. The second rather suited her. The Spring Tide had depopulated Dumnonian and Murkan land, and more men had been killed than women, so it would be no hardship to accept five thousand immigrants. She would have Spring, Atlas, Clodia and the two praetorians vet the legionaries and she'd send any they didn't like to Eroo, but Caesar didn't need to know that.

"Tell him I agree to his conditions."

Spring translated. Caesar nodded and wordlessly held out his hand. Lowa held out hers. He gripped her elbow, she gripped his and they shook.

Lowa looked around. Chamanca was holding Atlas' arm; the African was looking at her, a rare half-smile on his scarred face. It seemed Lowa hadn't stopped running since the day she'd given him that scar. Maybe now, finally, she could just sit down for a while, watch her son grow up and teach him to avoid people like Zadar – and herself, she supposed.

As if to confirm her resolve, little Dug stamped up to her, arms in the air, demanding to be picked up. She complied and he squealed with joy. Behind him, Spring was beaming.

"What will you do now, Spring?" Lowa asked.

"Thought I might come back to Maidun for a while and help you out? If you'll have me?"

"You'll be very welcome. But only for a while?"

"I've seen Rome, I've seen Gaul and I liked them, but both were too full of Romans. I want to see what's in the other direction."

Epilogue

Caesar left with all but one legion, within the moon as Lowa had demanded. He wrote that he'd crossed to Britain with five legions, won every battle and returned to Gaul with hostages and tribute promised. However, in reality, no hostage crossed the Channel and no tribute was ever paid. Nevertheless, to celebrate Caesar's marvellous adventure in Britain, twenty more days holiday was proclaimed on his return to Rome that winter.

After 54 BC no Roman legionary set foot on British soil for ninety-seven years. They couldn't quite manage the full hundred.

Historical note

Assuming you haven't just turned to this page because you're one of those people who reads the back of a book first in case they die before they finish it, congratulations for reaching the end of the Age of Iron trilogy. I hope you liked it. If you didn't and you got this far, then you're some kind of masochist and have only yourself to blame.

Right now, as I sit at my desk writing this, it's 2 April 2015. *Clash of Iron* will be released two weeks from today and *Reign of Iron*, which I'm finishing *right now*, will come out in six months (probably. You can be even less certain about the future than you can about the past). I don't know what I'm going to write next. I have some vague ideas, some of which include characters from Age of Iron. If you want to know what's coming, you can sign up to my newsletter at www.guswatson.com. If you want to tell me what should come next, I'm on Twitter as @GusWatson.

Anyway, since this is officially a historical note, let's get on with the history. I've covered the main points in the historical notes at the back of the first two books, and probably banged on enough about how I think that Caesar's diary is fabrication, and how it's unlikely that he crossed the Channel twice with two massive armies with the intention of returning to Gaul after a couple of months. There's a bibliography in *Clash of Iron* if you'd like to read more about the period. Here, I'll focus on how this third book does and doesn't tally with official history.

British people and their stuff

We don't know much about Iron Age Brits, but I've stuck largely to what we do. Throughout the trilogy, their huts, hillforts, clothes and so on mostly agree with the archaeologists. Those weapons and devices that I've invented – Lowa's bow, the T-shaped anti-tortoise poles, multistorey huts, giant carts full of war dogs – would all have been feasible. However, all the British characters and tribes are my own creation (almost – you'll find Dumnonia in the official list of tribes around at the time but that's it). There were almost certainly plenty of druids in Britain, but we don't know what they did.

Aurochs

The aurochs is an extinct species of giant cow, the last of which died in Poland in 1627. Officially aurochs died out in Britain about a thousand years before *Age of Iron* is set, but they really could have lived on as late as 54 BC. Just because we have no evidence for something doesn't mean it didn't happen (see "Numbers" section).

Numbers

According to Caesar, he brought two legions (ten thousand men) across the Channel in 55 BC and five legions (twenty-five thousand men) in 54 BC. To put that in perspective, William the Conqueror's successful invasion in 1066 was between five and seven thousand strong. I've used the same number of ships that Caesar describes for both invasions, but have added one legion to the second invasion, which is left behind in Britain on Lowa's demands (and therefore, in my reckoning, was left out of Caesar's diary).

"Do we have any other evidence?" you might ask. "For example, what does archaeology tell us about the size of his armies? Perhaps from the remains of his camps we can work out how many—"

Let me stop you there. Quite interestingly, I think, archaeologists have found no physical evidence whatsoever that Caesar's massive invasions of Britain in 55 and 54 BC took place at all. Not a shield, not any part of a boat, not a pilum point, not a Roman sausage. The invasions are mentioned by a couple of other Roman writers, but pretty much all our facts come from Caesar's diary of the invasion.

Roman people

The Romans I've mentioned mostly did exist. Cicero's younger brother, for example, actually was a renowned twat who hated his wife Pomponia and threw someone into a river in a bag of snakes. Cornelia Metella was married to Publius Licinius Crassus, and she was beautiful and good with a lyre. We don't see Publius Licinius Crassus after Ragnall and Spring's wedding for a good and (I think) interesting reason – google his name to find out why. Clodia Metelli was a glamorous socialite, but there's no evidence that she came along on the invasion of Britain. The only Romans I've totally made up are Felix, a few minor characters like the legionary who enjoyed giving directions to Spring, and the two main praetorians. Ferrandus the praetorian is the only character in any of the three books based on a modern person. He is Luc Ferrand, my friend who died in January 2014. He's in the book as a tribute, not because dead people can't sue.

Elephants

Caesar does not mention elephants. A later Roman historian says that he took one.

Demons

As I've said before, a few years after the events of *Age of Iron*, many people accept that a chap came along who could raise people from the dead, turn water into wine and so on, so many would say that there was definitely magic around at the time. I think if an evil druid did use magic to create all-powerful Warriors to aid the invasions, then it's exactly the sort of thing that Caesar would have stayed quiet about.

Acknowledgements

It's all about my wife Nicola. We had a son, Charlie, a year and a half ago and since then have been hermits, only prised from our house on weekdays by compulsory social events and at weekends by trips to the zoo, aquarium, toddler-orientated theme parks, soft play centres, etc. So she has borne the whole brunt of my "Oh isn't writing difficult" rants, without ever reminding me that she's one of the top women in British finance and all my spouting is just irrelevant, childish nonsense compared to the serious things she does during the day. Massive thanks to her for indefatigable support. Thanks also to Charlie for being such a joy to be with and for teaching both Nicola and me the effects of sleep deprivation. I'd also like to thank Joyce, Nicola's mother, who looks after Charlie during the day, which allows me to sit upstairs writing while he's downstairs with her, waddling about and shouting at his Lego.

Thanks to Angharad Kowal, my agent at Writers House, who got me the book deal and without whom these books would never have existed; Jenni Hill, my editor at Orbit whose ideas and edits have made the books massively better; Joanna Kramer, Gemma Conley-Smith, Clara Diaz and Felice Howden all at Orbit for helping in their various ways; Richard Collins for another great copy-edit.

I'd like to thank my family — David, Penny, Tim, Camilla and Christo — who all had their parts shaping me into the sort of character who reckons he can write novels.

Finally, I'd like to thank the person who looked after me

and my brother Tim for the first twelve years of my life and first fourteen of Tim's, and is most responsible for who we both are today (Tim is a vet). When I was three my father ran off with our cleaner, then he went and died in a plane crash three years later. My mother, who'd already had a bout with cancer, devoted her life to Tim and me, working crazy hours to send us to good schools and teaching us about the world in all her spare time. My interests in history, geography and zoology are all entirely down to her. She also tried to teach us about botany and show-jumping, but my developing brain couldn't accept those subjects (and still can't).

When I was twelve, cancer had its evil way and my mother died, before either of us boys had achieved anything, or thanked her for all she'd done (we went to live with my uncle and aunt and their two children, in case you were wondering who David, Penny, Camilla and Christo — the people this book is dedicated to — are).

Keen readers may have discerned that I'm an atheist. After my childhood it would be nuts to believe in any god, and if there is one, he or she has been such a dick to me, my bro and my mum that I'm not going to believe in him or her out of spite. However, I guess I'm really an agnostic, because there is a grain of me that believes it's possible that the dead live on, and can see what we're up to. If that is the case, I'd like to say thank you very much to my mother, that I hope she is well and that I wish she was here.

extras

about the author

Angus Watson is an author and journalist living in London. He's written hundreds of features for many newspapers including *The Times*, *Financial Times* and the *Telegraph*, and the latter even sent him to look for Bigfoot. As a fan of both historical fiction and epic fantasy, Angus came up with the idea of writing a fantasy set in the Iron Age when exploring British hillforts for the *Telegraph*, and developed the story while walking Britain's ancient paths for further articles. You can find him on Twitter at @GusWatson or find his website at www.guswatson.com.

Find out more about Angus Watson and other Orbit authors by registering for the free monthly newsletter at www.orbitbooks.net.

if you enjoyed

REIGN OF IRON

look out for

BLOOD SONG

Raven's Shadow: Book One

by

Anthony Ryan

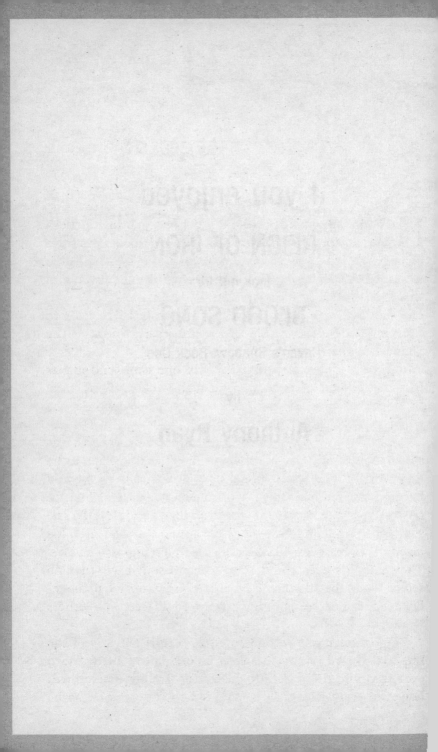

Verniers' Account

He had many names. Although yet to reach his thirtieth year, history had seen fit to bestow upon him titles aplenty: Sword of the Realm to the mad king who sent him to plague us, the Young Hawk to the men who followed him through the trials of war, Darkblade to his Cumbraelin enemies and, as I was to learn much later, Beral Shak Ur to the enigmatic tribes of the Great Northern Forest – the Shadow of the Raven.

But my people knew him by only one name and it was this that sang in my head continually the morning they brought him to the docks: *Hope Killer. Soon you will die and I will see it. Hope Killer.*

Although he was certainly taller than most men, I was surprised to find that, contrary to the tales I had heard, he was no giant, and whilst his features were strong they could hardly be called handsome. His frame was muscular but not possessed of the massive thews described so vividly by the storytellers. The only aspect of his appearance to match his legend was his eyes: black as jet and piercing as a hawk's. They said his eyes could strip a man's soul bare, that no secret could be hidden if he met your gaze. I had never believed it but seeing him now, I could see why others would.

The prisoner was accompanied by a full company of the Imperial Guard, riding in close escort, lances ready, hard eyes scanning the watching crowd for trouble. The crowd, however, were silent. They stopped to stare at him as he rode through, but there were no shouts, no insults or missiles hurled. I recalled that they knew this man, for a brief time he had ruled their city and commanded a foreign army within its walls, yet I saw no hate in their faces, no desire for vengeance. Mostly they seemed curious. Why was he here? Why was he alive at all?

The company reined in on the wharf, the prisoner dismounting to be led to the waiting vessel. I put my notes away and rose from my resting place atop a spice barrel, nodding at the captain. "Honour to you, sir."

The captain, a veteran Guards officer with a pale scar running along his jawline and the ebony skin of the southern Empire, returned the nod with practised formality. "Lord Verniers."

"I trust you had an untroubled journey?"

The captain shrugged. "A few threats here and there. Had to crack a few heads in Jesseria, the locals wanted to hang the Hope Killer's carcass from their temple spire."

I bridled at the disloyalty. The Emperor's Edict had been read in all towns through which the prisoner would travel, its meaning plain: no harm will come to the Hope Killer. "The Emperor will hear of it," I said.

"As you wish, but it was a small matter." He turned to the prisoner. "Lord Verniers, I present the Imperial prisoner Vaelin Al Sorna."

I nodded formally to the tall man, the name a steady refrain in my head. *Hope Killer, Hope Killer* . . . "Honour to you, sir," I forced the greeting out.

His black eyes met mine for a second, piercing, enquiring. For a moment I wondered if the more outlandish stories were true, if there was magic in the gaze of this savage. Could he truly strip the truth from a man's soul? Since the war, stories had abounded of the Hope Killer's mysterious powers. He could talk to animals, command the Nameless and shape the weather to his will. His steel was tempered with the blood of fallen enemies and would never break in battle. And worst of all, he and his people worshipped the dead, communing with the shades of their forebears to conjure forth all manner of foulness. I gave little credence to such folly, reasoning that if the Northmen's magics were so powerful, how had they contrived to suffer such a crushing defeat at our hands?

"My lord." Vaelin Al Sorna's voice was harsh and thickly accented, his Alpiran had been learned in a dungeon and his tones were no doubt coarsened by years of shouting above the clash of weapons and screams of the fallen to win victory in a hundred battles, one of which had cost me my closest friend and the future of this Empire.

I turned to the captain. "Why is he shackled? The Emperor ordered he be treated with respect."

"The people didn't like seeing him riding unfettered," the captain explained. "The prisoner suggested we shackle him to avoid trouble." He moved to Al Sorna and unlocked the restraints. The big man massaged his wrists with scarred hands.

"My lord!" A shout from the crowd. I turned to see a portly man in a white robe hurrying towards us, face wet with unaccustomed exertion. "A moment, please!"

The captain's hand inched closer to his sabre but Al Sorna was unconcerned, smiling as the portly man approached. "Governor Aruan."

The portly man halted, wiping sweat from his face with a lace scarf. In his left hand he carried a long bundle wrapped in cloth. He nodded at the captain and myself but addressed himself to the prisoner. "My lord. I never thought to see you again. Are you well?"

"I am, Governor. And you?"

The portly man spread his right hand, lace scarf dangling from his thumb, jewelled rings on every finger. "Governor no longer. Merely a poor merchant these days. Trade is not what it was, but we make our way."

"Lord Verniers." Vaelin Al Sorna gestured at me. "This is Holus Nester Aruan, former Governor of the City of Linesh."

"Honoured Sir." Aruan greeted me with a short bow.

"Honoured Sir," I replied formally. So this was the man from whom the Hope Killer had seized the city. Aruan's failure to take his own life in dishonour had been widely remarked upon in the aftermath of the war but the Emperor (Gods preserve him in his wisdom and mercy) had granted clemency in light of the extraordinary circumstances of the Hope Killer's occupation. Clemency, however, had not extended to a continuance of his Governorship.

Aruan turned back to Al Sorna. "It pleases me to find you well. I wrote to the Emperor begging mercy."

"I know, your letter was read at my trial."

I knew from the trial records that Aruan's letter, written at no small risk to his life, had formed part of the evidence describing curiously uncharacteristic acts of generosity and mercy by the Hope Killer during the war. The Emperor had listened patiently to it all before ruling that the prisoner was on trial for his crimes, not his virtues.

"Your daughter is well?" the prisoner asked Aruan.

"Very, she weds this summer. A feckless son of a ship-builder, but what can a poor father do? Thanks to you, at least she is alive to break my heart."

"I am glad. About the wedding, not your broken heart. I can offer no gift except my best wishes."

"Actually, my lord, I come with a gift of my own."

Aruan lifted the long, cloth-covered bundle in both hands, presenting it to the Hope Killer with a strangely grave expression. "I hear you will have need of this again soon."

There was a definite hesitation in the Northman's demeanour before he reached out to take the bundle, undoing the ties with his scarred hands. The cloth came away to reveal a sword of unfamiliar design, the scabbard-clad blade was a yard or so in the length and straight, unlike the curved sabres favoured by Alpiran soldiery. A single tine arched around the hilt to form a guard and the only ornamentation to the weapon was a plain steel pommel. The hilt and the scabbard bore many small nicks and scratches that spoke of years of hard use. This was no ceremonial weapon and I realised with a sickening rush that it was his sword. The sword he had carried to our shores. The sword that made him the Hope Killer.

"You kept that?" I sputtered at Aruan, appalled.

The portly man's expression grew cold as he turned to me. "My honour demanded no less, my lord."

"My thanks," Al Sorna said, before any further outrage could spill from my lips. He hefted the sword and I saw the Guard Captain stiffen as Al Sorna drew the blade an inch or so from the scabbard, testing the edge with his thumb. "Still sharp."

"It's been well cared for. Oiled and sharpened regularly. I also have another small token." Aruan extended his hand. In his palm sat a single ruby, a well-cut stone of medium weight, no doubt one of the more valued gems in the family collection. I knew the story behind Aruan's gratitude, but his evident regard for this savage and the sickening presence of the sword still irked me greatly.

Al Sorna seemed at a loss, shaking his head. "Governor, I cannot . . ."

I moved closer, speaking softly. "He does you a greater honour than you deserve, Northman. Refusing will insult him and dishonour you."

He flicked his black eyes over me briefly before smiling at Aruan, "I cannot refuse such generosity." He took the gem. "I'll keep it always."

"I hope not," Aruan responded with a laugh. "A man only keeps a jewel when he has no need to sell it."

"You there!" A voice came from the vessel moored a short

distance along the quay, a sizeable Meldenean galley, the number of oars and the width of the hull showing it to be a freighter rather than one of their fabled warships. A stocky man with an extensive black beard, marked as the captain by the red scarf on his head, was waving from the bow. "Bring the Hope Killer aboard, you Alpiran dogs!" he shouted with customary Meldenean civility. "Any more dithering and we'll miss the tide."

"Our passage to the Islands awaits," I told the prisoner, gathering my possessions. "We'd best avoid the ire of our captain."

"So it's true then," Aruan said. "You go to the Islands to fight for the lady?" I found myself disliking the tone in his voice, it sounded uncomfortably like awe.

"It's true." He clasped hands briefly with Aruan and nodded at the captain of his guard before turning to me. "My lord. Shall we?"

"You may be one of the first in line to lick your Emperor's feet, scribbler" – the ship's captain stabbed a finger into my chest – "but this ship is my kingdom. You berth here or you can spend the voyage roped to the mainmast."

He had shown us to our quarters, a curtained-off section of the hold near the prow of the ship. The hold stank of brine, bilge water and the intermingled odour of the cargo, a sickly, cloying mélange of fruit, dried fish and the myriad spices for which the Empire was famous. It was all I could do to keep from gagging.

"I am Lord Verniers Alishe Someren, Imperial Chronicler, First of the Learned and honoured servant of the Emperor," I responded, the handkerchief over my mouth muffling my words somewhat. "I am emissary to the Ship Lords and official escort to the Imperial prisoner. You will treat me with respect, pirate, or I'll have twenty guardsmen aboard in a trice to flog you in front of your crew."

The captain leaned closer; incredibly his breath smelt worse than the hold. "Then I'll have twenty-one bodies to feed to the orcas when we leave the harbour, scribbler."

Al Sorna prodded one of the bedrolls on the deck with his foot and glanced around briefly. "This'll do. We'll need food and water."

I bristled. "You seriously suggest we sleep in this rat-hole? It's disgusting."

"You should try a dungeon. Plenty of rats there too." He turned to the captain. "The water barrel is on the foredeck?"

The captain ran a stubby finger through the mass of his beard, contemplating the tall man, no doubt wondering if he was being mocked and calculating if he could kill him if he had to. They have a saying on the northern Alpiran coast: turn your back on a cobra but never a Meldenean. "So you're the one who's going to cross swords with the Shield? They're offering twenty to one against you in Ildera. Think I should risk a copper on you? The Shield is the keenest blade in the Islands, can slice a fly in half with a sabre."

"Such renown does him credit." Vaelin Al Sorna smiled. "The water barrel?"

"It's there. You can have one gourd a day each, no more. My crew won't go short for the likes of you two. You can get food from the galley, if you don't mind eating with scum like us."

"No doubt I've eaten with worse. If you need an extra man at the oars, I am at your disposal."

"Rowed before, have you?"

"Once."

The captain grunted, "We'll manage." He turned to go, muttering over his shoulder, "We sail within the hour, stay out of the way until we clear the harbour."

"Island savage!" I fumed, unpacking my belongings, laying out my quills and ink. I checked there were no rats lurking under my bedroll before sitting down to compose a letter to the Emperor. I intended to let him know the full extent of this insult. "He'll find no berth in an Alpiran harbour again, mark you."

Vaelin Al Sorna sat down, resting his back against the hull. "You speak my language?" he asked, slipping into the Northern tongue.

"I study languages," I replied in kind. "I can speak the seven major tongues of the Empire fluently and communicate in five more."

"Impressive. Do you know the Seordah language?"

I looked up from my parchment. "Seordah?"

"The Seordah Sil of the Great Northern Forest. You've heard of them?"

"My knowledge of northern savages is far from comprehensive. As yet I see little reason to complete it."

"For a learned man you seem happy with your ignorance."

"I feel I speak for my entire nation when I say I wish we had all remained in ignorance of you."

He tilted his head, studying me. "That's hate in your voice."

I ignored him, my quill moving rapidly over the parchment, setting out the formal opening for Imperial correspondence.

"You knew him, didn't you?" Vaelin Al Sorna went on.

My quill stopped. I refused to meet his eye.

"You knew the Hope."

I put my quill aside and rose. Suddenly the stench of the hold and the proximity of this savage were unbearable. "Yes, I knew him," I grated. "I knew him to be the best of us. I knew he would be the greatest Emperor this land has ever seen. But that's not the reason for my hate, Northman. I hate you because I knew the Hope as my friend, and you killed him."

I stalked away, climbing the steps to the main deck,

wishing for the first time in my life that I could be a warrior, that my arms were thick with muscle and my heart hard as stone, that I could wield a sword and take bloody vengeance. But such things were beyond me. My body was trim but not strong, my wits quick but not ruthless. I was no warrior. So there would be no vengeance for me. All I could do for my friend was witness the death of his killer and write the formal end to his story for the pleasure of my Emperor and the eternal truth of our archive.

I stayed on the deck for hours, leaning on the rail, watching the green-tinged waters of the north Alpiran coast deepen into the blue of the inner Erinean Sea as the ship's bosun beat the drum for the oarsmen and our journey began. Once clear of the coast the captain ordered the mainsail unfurled and our speed increased, the sharp prow of the vessel cutting through the gentle swell, the figurehead, a traditional Meldenean carving of the winged serpent, one of their innumerable sea gods, dipping its many-toothed head amidst a haze of spume. The oarsmen rowed for two hours before the bosun called a rest and they shipped oars, trooping off to their meal. The day watch stayed on deck, running the rigging and undertaking the never-ending chores of ship life. A few favoured me with a customary glare or two, but none attempted to converse, a mercy for which I was grateful.

We were several leagues from the harbour when they came into view, black fins knifing through the swell, heralded by a cheerful shout from the crow's nest. "Orcas!"

I couldn't tell how many there were, they moved too fast and too fluidly through the sea, occasionally breaking the surface to spout a cloud of steam before diving below. It was only when they came closer that I fully realised their size, over twenty feet from nose to tail. I had seen dolphins before in the southern seas, silvery, playful creatures that could be taught simple tricks. These were different, their size and the dark, flickering shadows they traced through the water seemed ominous to me, threatening shades of nature's indifferent cruelty. My shipmates clearly felt differently, yelling greetings from the rigging as if hailing old friends. Even the captain's habitual scowl seemed to have softened somewhat.

One of the orcas broke the surface in a spectacular display of foam, twisting in midair before crashing into the sea with a boom that shook the ship. The Meldeneans roared their appreciation. *Oh Seliesen*, I thought. *The poem you would have written to honour such a sight.*

"They think of them as sacred." I turned to find that the Hope Killer had joined me at the rail. "They say when a Meldenean dies at sea the orcas will carry his spirit to the endless ocean beyond the edge of the world."

"Superstition," I sniffed.

"Your people have their gods, do they not?"

"My people do, I do not. Gods are a myth, a comforting story for children."

"Such words would make you welcome in my homeland."

"We are not in your homeland, Northman. Nor would I ever wish to be."

Another orca rose from the sea, rising fully ten feet into the air before plunging back down. "It's strange," Al Sorna mused. "When our ships came across this sea the orcas ignored them and made only for the Meldeneans. Perhaps they share the same belief."

"Perhaps," I said. "Or perhaps they appreciate a free meal." I nodded at the prow, where the captain was throwing salmon into the sea, the orcas swooping on them faster than I could follow.

"Why are you here, Lord Verniers?" Al Sorna asked. "Why did the Emperor send you? You're no gaoler."

"The Emperor graciously consented to my request to

witness your upcoming duel. And to accompany the Lady Emeren home of course."

"You came to see me die."

"I came to write an account of this event for the Imperial Archive. I am the Imperial Chronicler after all."

"So they told me. Gerish, my gaoler, was a great admirer of your history of the war with my people, considered it the finest work in Alpiran literature. He knew a lot for a man who spends his life in a dungeon. He would sit outside my cell for hours reading out page after page, especially the battles, he liked those."

"Accurate research is the key to the historian's art."

"Then it's a pity you got it so wrong."

Once again I found myself wishing for a warrior's strength. "Wrong?"

"Very."

"I see. Perhaps if you work your savage's brain, you could tell me which sections were so very wrong."

"Oh, you got the small things right, mostly. Except you said my command was the Legion of the Wolf. In fact it was the Thirty-fifth Regiment of Foot, known amongst the Realm Guard as the Wolfrunners."

"I'll be sure to rush out a revised edition on my return to the capital," I said dryly.

He closed his eyes, remembering. "'King Janus's invasion of the northern coast was but the first step in pursuance of his greater ambition, the annexation of the entire Empire.'"

It was a verbatim recitation. I was impressed by his memory, but was damned if I'd say so. "A simple statement of fact. You came here to steal the Empire. Janus was a madman to think such a scheme could succeed."

Al Sorna shook his head. "We came for the northern coastal ports. Janus wanted the trade routes through the Erinean. And he was no madman. He was old and desperate, but not mad."

I was surprised at the sympathy evident in his voice; Janus was the great betrayer after all, it was part of the Hope Killer's legend. "And how do you know the man's mind so well?"

"He told me."

"Told you?" I laughed. "I wrote a thousand letters of enquiry to every ambassador and Realm official I could think of. The few who bothered to reply all agreed on one thing: Janus never confided his plans to anyone, not even his family."

"And yet you claim he wanted to conquer your whole Empire."

"A reasonable deduction based on the available evidence."

"Reasonable, maybe, but wrong. Janus had a king's heart, hard and cold when he needed it to be. But he wasn't greedy and he was no dreamer. He knew the Realm could never muster the men and treasure needed to conquer your Empire. We came for the ports. He said it was the only way we could secure our future."

"Why would he confide such intelligence to you?"

"We had . . . an arrangement. He told me many things he would tell no other. Some of his commands required an explanation before I would obey them. But sometimes I think he just needed to talk to someone. Even kings get lonely."

I felt a curious sense of seduction; the Northman knew I hungered for the information he could give me. My respect for him grew, as did my dislike. He was using me, he wanted me to write the story he had to tell. Quite why I had no idea. I knew it was something to do with Janus and the duel he would fight in the Islands. Perhaps he needed to unburden himself before his end, leave a legacy of truth so he would be known to history as more than just the Hope Killer. A final attempt to redeem both his spirit and that of his dead king.

I let the silence string out, watching the orcas until they had eaten their fill of free fish and departed to the east. Finally, as the sun began to dip towards the horizon and the shadows grew long, I said, "So tell me."